The Dreamer lying asleep on the flowery mound

(See p. x)

PEARL

Edited by

E. V. GORDON

OXFORD

AT THE CLARENDON PRESS

Oxford University Press, Amen House, London E.C.4

GLASGOW NEW YORK TORONTO MELBOURNE WELLINGTON
BOMBAY CALCUTTA MADRAS KARACHI LAHORE DACCA
CAPE TOWN SALISBURY NAIROBI IBADAN ACCRA
KUALA LUMPUR HONG KONG

FIRST PUBLISHED 1953

REPRINTED LITHOGRAPHICALLY IN GREAT BRITAIN
AT THE UNIVERSITY PRESS, OXFORD
FROM SHEETS OF THE FIRST EDITION
1958, 1963

PREFACE

AFTER the publication of their edition of *Sir Gawain and the Green Knight* in 1925 Professor J. R. R. Tolkien and my husband, Professor E. V. Gordon, started work on a similar edition of *Pearl*. Later, when he found himself unable to give sufficient time to it, Professor Tolkien suggested that my husband should continue the work alone. This he did, and at the time of his death in 1938 the edition was complete—complete, that is, in that no part was missing and all had been put into form, if not final form. Many factors combined to delay publication, and when at last I started the work of final revision in 1950 it was found necessary to reduce the size of the edition. A wish to do this in a way that would sacrifice as little as possible of the original material has made it necessary to make extensive alterations in the form. I wish to make it clear that there has been this considerable re-writing, and that if, in the process, errors or obscurities have crept in, the blame must be the reviser's. Some sacrifice of the original material there has been, especially in the Introduction.

My warmest thanks must go to Professor Tolkien, who had the original typescript for some time and added valuable notes and corrections; he has also responded generously to queries. I wish to thank, too, my colleague, Miss F. E. Harmer, for her encouragement and help, especially with the proofs. Other thanks there should be to those from whom my husband received help, but to avoid the risk of omitting some it seems safer to mention none, except, perhaps, Dr. C. T. Onions, whose collaboration on difficult problems must have yielded many a helpful suggestion, and Dr. Kenneth Sisam, who has always shown a warm interest in the edition. Finally, I wish to thank the Delegates of the Clarendon Press for undertaking the work of publication after so long a lapse of time.

IDA L. GORDON

Manchester, 1952

CONTENTS

The Dreamer lying asleep on the flowery mound.
British Museum, MS. Cotton Nero A. x, f. 37. *Frontispiece*
Photograph by courtesy of the Trustees of the British Museum.

ABBREVIATIONS

AFr.	Anglo-French.
cf.	in etymologies indicates indirect or uncertain relation.
Birch CS.	*Cartularium Saxonicum*, ed. by W. De Gray Birch.
B.T. Supp.	Supplement to Bosworth-Toller, *Anglo-Saxon Dictionary*.
EDD.	*The English Dialect Dictionary*.
EFris.	modern East Frisian dialects.
Falk and Torp	*Norwegisch-Dänisches Etymologisches Wörterbuch.*
from	is prefixed to etymologies when the word illustrated has an additional suffix or prefix not present in the etymon.
Icel.	modern Icelandic.
intens.	intensative.
KCD.	*Codex Diplomaticus Ævi Saxonici.*
K-group	The 'Katherine' group of West Midland texts.
Lat.	Latin.
MDu.	Middle Dutch.
ME.	Middle English.
Med. Lat.	Medieval Latin.
MLG.	Middle Low German.
NED.	*The Oxford (New) English Dictionary*.
North.	Northumbrian dialect of Old English.
Norw.	modern Norwegian.
OE.	Old English.
ODan.	Old Danish.
OFr., ONFr.	Old French, northern dialects of Old French.
ON., OEN., OWN.	Old Norse, especially Old Icelandic; Old East Norse; Old West Norse.
OSwed.	Old Swedish.

poet.	in poetic use only.
prec.	preceding word.
str.	strong.
Swed.	modern Swedish.
V.P.	Vespasian Psalter.
wk.	weak.
WFlem.	modern west Flemish dialects.
WS.	West Saxon.
*	is prefixed to forms theoretically reconstructed, and to references to emendations.
+	between elements shows that a compound or derivative is first recorded in Middle English.

PERIODICALS

CFMA.	*Classiques français du moyen âge.*
E.E.T.S.	Early English Text Society.
JEGPh.	*Journal of English and Germanic Philology.*
MÆ.	*Medium Ævum.*
MLN.	*Modern Language Notes.*
MLR.	*Modern Language Review.*
PMLA.	*Publications of the Modern Language Association of America.*

For details of articles and editions referred to see Bibliography.

INTRODUCTION

THE MANUSCRIPT

Pearl is one of four poems preserved in a small manuscript (the pages measuring about 7×5 in.) in the Cotton collection in the British Museum—MS. Cotton Nero A. x. *Pearl* stands first in the manuscript, and is followed by *Purity* (or *Cleanness*, as it is also called), *Patience*, and *Sir Gawain and the Green Knight*. They are all written in the same small handwriting, which has been dated in the end of the fourteenth century or the very beginning of the fifteenth. The manuscript has been reproduced in facsimile by the Early English Text Society under the care of Sir Israel Gollancz.

The earliest record of the manuscript is an entry in the catalogue, now MS. Harley 1879 in the British Museum, of the library of Henry Savile, of Bank in Yorkshire (1568–1617); it is there described as 'an owld boke in English verse beginning *Perle pleasants to princes pay* in 4° limned'. Of its earlier history, or how it came into the Cotton library, nothing is known. It is now bound between two Latin texts which are distinct manuscripts and have no connexion with the four poems. These folios are included in the folio numbering; the folios of the poems are numbered from 37 to 126, and of these *Pearl* with its illustrations occupies 37ª to 55ᵇ.

No titles are given to the poems in the manuscript. The well-known titles now used have been devised by modern editors. The beginning of each poem is marked by a large ornamented initial letter in blue and red, and the divisions of the poems are similarly marked by smaller initial letters in blue, with ornament in red.[1] The text of *Pearl* is divided

[1] It is noteworthy that the large þ is avoided; in the coloured letters *th* is always substituted.

in this way into sections of five stanzas, and these sections
correspond to those formed by the use of the refrains (see
Appendix I, p. 88). Only one such section contains six
stanzas (the one numbered XV), and this abnormality
seems temporarily to have confused the scribe, as he has
placed a coloured initial at the beginning of stanza 81, and
another in its proper place, at the beginning of 82.

The four poems are illustrated in colours, each painting
occupying a complete side of a folio. These pictures are
crude and inartistic, nor do they represent accurately the
details described in the poems. They were drawn before
they were painted, and the paint was not applied until
after the manuscript was sewn and perhaps bound.[1] It is
possible that the drawing was originally done only as a
rough guide to the illuminator for subject and treatment
and that a later painter has filled it in.

The four pictures illustrating *Pearl* stand at the beginning of the manuscript on folios 37-39. The first—reproduced as frontispiece—shows the dreamer lying asleep on
a flowery mound, as described in stanzas four and five; he
is wearing a long red gown with falling sleeves turned up
with white, and a blue hood laid back on his shoulders. A
scallop-shaped column extends upwards from his head.
This may perhaps represent the departure of his spirit in
the heavenly vision. In the second picture the dreamer is
standing by a stream, evidently that which separated him
in his dream from Heaven. He is wearing a long gown, but
no hood is visible. The third picture shows him conversing
across the stream with the maiden, who by her gestures
seems to be expressing disapproval of his words. She is
dressed in white, in the fashion of the end of the fourteenth,
or beginning of the fifteenth, century, high at the neck,
with long hanging sleeves. Her hair is plaited on each side

[1] See W. W. Greg, *MLR*. xix. 226-7.

and she wears a crown. The fourth picture depicts the dreamer's vision of the Heavenly City, and in the picture it is even more like a feudal manor than its description in the poem (see note to line 917). There is a hall with beams showing on the outside, and this is surrounded by an embattled wall, and just inside the wall is a tower. Not a single feature of this illustration corresponds with the description in the poem. The Pearl appears on the battlements, and on the other side of the stream the dreamer is kneeling with uplifted hands.

FORM AND PURPOSE

When *Pearl* was first read in modern times[1] it was accepted as what it purports to be, an elegy on the death of a child, the poet's daughter. The personal interpretation was first questioned in 1904 by W. H. Schofield, who argued that the maiden of the poem was an allegorical figure of a kind usual in medieval vision-literature, an abstraction representing 'clean maidenhood'. His view was not generally accepted, but it proved the starting-point of a long debate between the defenders of the older view and the exponents of other theories: that the whole poem is an allegory, though each interpreter has given it a different meaning; or that it is no more than a theological treatise in verse. Much space would be required to rehearse this debate, even in brief summary, and the labour would be unprofitable; but it has not been entirely wasted, for much learning has gone into it, and study has deepened the appreciation of the poem and brought out more clearly the allegorical and symbolic elements that it certainly includes.

A clear distinction between 'allegory' and 'symbolism' may be difficult to maintain, but it is proper, or at least

---

[1] The first printed edition, by Richard Morris (E.E.T.S.), appeared in 1864.

useful, to limit allegory to narrative, to an account (how-ever short) of events; and symbolism to the use of visible signs or things to represent other things or ideas. Pearls were a symbol of purity that especially appealed to the imagination of the Middle Ages (and notably of the four-teenth century); but this does not make a person who wears pearls, or even one who is called Pearl, or Margaret, into an allegorical figure. To be an 'allegory' a poem must *as a whole*, and with fair consistency, describe in other terms some event or process: its entire narrative and all its significant details should cohere and work together to this end. There are minor allegories within *Pearl*: the parable of the workers in the vineyard (lines 501–88) is a self-contained allegory; and the opening stanzas of the poem, where the pearl slips from the poet's hand through the grass to the ground, is an allegory in little of the child's death and burial. But an allegorical description of an event does not make that event itself allegorical. And this initial use is only one of the many applications of the pearl symbol, intelligible if the reference of the poem is personal, incoherent if one seeks for total allegory. For there are a number of precise details in *Pearl* that cannot be sub-ordinated to any general allegorical interpretation, and these details are of special importance since they relate to the central figure, the maiden of the vision, in whom, if anywhere, the allegory should be concentrated and with-out disturbance.

The basis of criticism, then, must be the references to the child or maiden, and to her relations with the dreamer; and no good reason has ever been found for regarding these as anything but statements of 'fact': the real experiences that lie at the foundation of the poem.

When the dreamer first sees the maiden in the paradisal garden, he says (242–5):

Art þou my perle þat I haf playned,
Regretted by myn one on ny3te?
Much longeyng haf I for þe layned,
Syþen into gresse þou me agly3te.

This explains for us the minor allegory of the opening
stanzas and reveals that the pearl he lost was a maid-child
who died. For the maiden of the vision accepts the identification, and herself refers to her death in line 761. In lines
411–12 she says she was at that time very young, and the
dreamer himself in lines 483–5 tells us that she was not yet
two years old and had not yet learned her creed or prayers.
The whole theological argument that follows assumes the
infancy of the child when she left this world.

The actual relationship of the child in the world to the
dreamer is referred to in line 233: when he first espied her
in his vision he recognized her; he knew her well, he had
seen her before (line 164); and so now beholding her visible
on the farther bank of the stream he was the happiest man
'from here to Greece', for

Ho wat3 me nerre þen aunte or nece.

'She was more near akin to me than aunt or niece.' *Nerre*
can in the language of the time only mean here 'nearer in
blood-relationship'. In this sense it was normal and very
frequent. And although it is true that 'nearer than aunt
or niece' might, even so, refer to a sister, the disparity in
age makes the assumption of this relationship far less
probable. The depth of sorrow portrayed for a child so
young belongs rather to parenthood. And there seems to
be a special significance in the situation where the doctrinal
lesson given by the celestial maiden comes from one of no
earthly wisdom to her proper teacher and instructor in the
natural order.

A modern reader may be ready to accept the personal

basis of the poem, and yet may feel that there is no need
to assume any immediate or particular foundation in auto-
biography. It is admittedly not necessary for the vision,
which is plainly presented in literary or scriptural terms;
the bereavement and the sorrow may also be imaginative
fictions, adopted precisely because they heighten the interest of the theological discussion between the maiden and
the dreamer.

This raises a difficult and important question for general
literary history: whether the purely fictitious 'I' had yet
appeared in the fourteenth century, a first person feigned
as narrator who had no existence outside the imagination
of the real author. Probably not; at least not in the kind
of literature that we are here dealing with: visions related
by a dreamer. The fictitious traveller had already appeared
in 'Sir John Mandeville', the writer of whose 'voyages'
seems not to have borne that name, nor indeed, according
to modern critics, ever to have journeyed far beyond his
study; and it is difficult to decide whether this is a case
of fraud intended to deceive (as it certainly did), or an
example of prose fiction (in the literary sense) still wearing
the guise of truth according to contemporary convention.

This convention was strong, and not so 'conventional'
as it may appear to modern readers. Although by those of
literary experience it might, of course, be used as nothing
more than a device to secure literary credibility (as often
by Chaucer), it represented a deep-rooted habit of mind,
and was strongly associated with the moral and didactic
spirit of the times. Tales of the past required their grave
authorities, and tales of new things at least an eyewitness,
the author. This was one of the reasons for the popularity
of visions: they allowed marvels to be placed within the
real world, linking them with a person, a place, a time,
while providing them with an explanation in the phantasies

of sleep, and a defence against critics in the notorious
deception of dreams. So even explicit allegory was usually
presented as a thing seen in sleep. How far any such
narrated vision, of the more serious kind, was supposed to
resemble an actual dream experience is another question.
A modern poet would indeed be very unlikely to put forward for factual acceptance a dream that in any way
resembled the vision of *Pearl*, even when all allowance is
made for the arrangement and formalizing of conscious
art. But we are dealing with a period when men, aware of
the vagaries of dreams, still thought that amid their japes
came visions of truth. And their waking imagination was
strongly moved by symbols and the figures of allegory, and
filled vividly with the pictures evoked by the scriptures,
directly or through the wealth of medieval art. And they
thought that on occasion, as God willed, to some that slept
blessed faces appeared and prophetic voices spoke. To
them it might not seem so incredible that the dream of a
poet, one wounded with a great bereavement and troubled
in spirit, might resemble the vision in *Pearl*.[1] However that
may be, the narrated vision in the more serious medieval
writing represented, if not an actual dream, at least a real
process of thought culminating in some resolution or
turning-point of the interior life—as with Dante, and in
Pearl. And in all forms, lighter or more grave, the 'I' of
the dreamer remained the eyewitness, the author, and
facts that he referred to outside the dream (especially
those concerning himself) were on a different plane, meant
to be taken as literally true, and even by modern critics
still so taken. In the *Divina Commedia* the *Nel mezzo del*

---

[1] Ek oother seyn that thorugh impressiouns,
  As if a wight hath faste a thyng in mynde,
  That therof comen swiche avysiouns.
        (*Troilus and Criseyde*, v. 372–4.)

cammin di nostra vita of the opening line, or *la decenne sete* of *Purgatorio xxxii*, are held to refer to real dates and events, the thirty-fifth year of Dante's life in 1300, and the death of Beatrice Portinari in 1290. Similarly the references to Malvern in the Prologue and Passus VII of *Piers Plowman*, and the numerous allusions to London, are taken as facts in someone's life, whoever the critic may favour as the author (or authors) of the poem.

It is true that the 'dreamer' may become a shadowy figure of small biographical substance. There is little left of the actual Chaucer in the 'I' who is the narrator in *The Boke of the Duchesse*. Few will debate how much auto-biography there is in the bout of insomnia that is made the occasion of the poem. Yet this fictitious and conventional vision is founded on a real event: the death of Blanche, the wife of John of Gaunt, in 1369. That was her real name, White (as she is called in the poem). However heightened the picture may be that is drawn of her loveliness and goodness, her sudden death was a lamentable event. Certainly it can have touched Chaucer far less deeply than the death of one 'nearer than aunt or niece'; but even so, it is this living drop of reality, this echo of sudden death and loss in the world, that gives to Chaucer's early poem a tone and feeling that raises it above the literary devices out of which he made it. So with the much greater poem *Pearl*, it is overwhelmingly more probable that it too was founded on a real sorrow, and drew its sweetness from a real bitterness.

And yet to the particular criticism of the poem decision on this point is not of the first importance. A feigned elegy remains an elegy; and feigned or unfeigned, it must stand or fall by its art. The reality of the bereavement will not save the poetry if it is bad, nor lend it any interest save to those who are in fact interested, not in poetry, but in documents, whose hunger is for history or biography or even for mere names. It is on general grounds, and considering its period in particular, that a 'real' or directly autobiographical basis for *Pearl* seems likely, since that is the most probable explanation of its form and its poetic quality. And for this argument the discovery of biographical details would have little importance. Of all that has been done in this line the only suggestion of value was made by Sir Israel Gollancz:[1] that the child may have been actually called a pearl by baptismal name, *Margarita* in Latin, *Margery* in English. It was a common name at the time, because of the love of pearls and their symbolism, and it had already been borne by several saints. If the child was really baptized a pearl, then the many pearls threaded on the strands of the poem in multiple significance receive yet another lustre. It is on such accidents of life that poetry crystallizes:

> And goode faire White she het;
> That was my lady name ryght.
> She was bothe fair and bryght;
> She hadde not hir name wrong.
>
> (*Boke of the Duchesse*, 948–51.)

'O perle', quod I, 'in perleȝ pyȝt,
Art þou my perle þat I haf playned?'

It has been objected that the child as seen in Heaven is not like an infant of two in appearance, speech, or manners: she addresses her father formally as *sir*, and shows no filial affection for him. But this is an apparition of a spirit, a soul not yet reunited with its body after the resurrection, so that theories relevant to the form and age of the glorified and risen body do not concern us. And as an immortal

---

[1] Edition of *Pearl*, p. xliii: 'He perhaps named the child "Margery" or "Marguerite".' The form Marguerite would not have been used; it is a modern French form.

spirit, the maiden's relations to the earthly man, the father of her body, are altered. She does not deny his fatherhood, and when she addresses him as *sir* she only uses the form of address that was customary for medieval children. Her part is in fact truly imagined. The sympathy of readers may now go out more readily to the bereaved father than to the daughter, and they may feel that he is treated with some hardness. But it is the hardness of truth. In the manner of the maiden is portrayed the effect upon a clear intelligence of the persistent earthliness of the father's mind: all is revealed to him, and he has eyes, yet he cannot see. The maiden is now filled with the spirit of celestial charity, desiring only his eternal good and the cure of his blindness. It is not her part to soften him with pity, or to indulge in childish joy at their reunion. The final consolation of the father was not to be found in the recovery of a beloved daughter, as if death had not after all occurred or had no significance, but in the knowledge that she was redeemed and saved and had become a queen in Heaven. Only by resignation to the will of God, and through death, could he rejoin her.

And this is the main *purpose* of the poem as distinct from its genesis or literary form: the doctrinal theme, in the form of an argument on salvation, by which the father is at last convinced that his Pearl, as a baptized infant and innocent, is undoubtedly saved, and, even more, admitted to the blessed company of the 144,000 that follow the Lamb. But the doctrinal theme is, in fact, inseparable from the literary form of the poem and its occasion; for it arises directly from the grief, which imparts deep feeling and urgency to the whole discussion. Without the elegiac basis and the sense of great personal loss which pervades it, *Pearl* would indeed be the mere theological treatise on a special point, which some critics have called it. But without the theological debate the grief would never have risen above the ground. Dramatically the debate represents a long process of thought and mental struggle, an experience as real as the first blind grief of bereavement. In his first mood, even if he had been granted a vision of the blessed in Heaven, the dreamer would have received it incredulously or rebelliously. And he would have awakened by the mound again, not in the gentle and serene resignation of the last stanza, but still as he is first seen, looking only backward, his mind filled with the horror of decay, wringing his hands, while his *wreched wylle in wo ay wraȝte*.

DOCTRINAL THEME

The doctrinal teaching of the maiden is an authoritative answer to the questions raised by the father, and it can be understood without a particular knowledge of theology if we are content to concern ourselves with his doubts and fears and misunderstandings, and to accept as he did the Pearl's answers. But because the doctrines discussed are themselves so profound, readers of *Pearl* are often tempted into a study of the theological problems for their own sake. And such study can be rewarding, especially when it concentrates on the medieval aspect: an acquaintance with the medieval views can often help to make the poet's attitude to his subject clearer and explain the proportions and emphasis of the poem.

The tone of the debate is struck at once when, in reply to the father's joy on recovering, as he thinks, his lost pearl, the maiden replies 'soberly', *Sir, ȝe haf your tale mysetente* (257). Here is to be no 'argument', but rather enlightenment of ignorance. For now that the maiden is glorified in Heaven, all is clear to her: she is one of those that *purȝoutly hauen cnawyng* in accordance with the promise of St. Paul (I Cor. xiii. 12). She tells her father that he is grieving for too 'brief a reason', for what he lost was but a rose, which bloomed and faded as roses do, but through the nature of the casket which encloses it, it has now become a pearl of price (268–72). And when the father thinks to join her across the sundering stream, she replies severely that he speaks as men of this world do, thoughtlessly, not knowing what he says. Does he suppose he can cross the stream without first suffering death and the judgement of God? Even his words of anguish and reproach, that he must then live his life out in the bitterness of grief, produce no pitying answer. He must learn to suffer God's will (360).

In more chastened mood the father then begs her at least to tell him of herself, for great though his own loss has been, much greater have been his fears for her. The Pearl then tells him that the Lamb has taken her as His bride,[1] and crowned her queen in Heaven. She explains that it is the nature of the kingdom of God that each one who comes there is crowned king or queen,[2] but that the Virgin Mary herself rules over them all:

> For ho is Quen of cortaysye. (444)

This *cortaysye*, of which Mary is Queen, is a quality possessed by all the members of that royal society, but it is more than earthly courtesy transferred to Heaven. It is the spirit uniting all Christians in one body:

> Of courtaysye, as sayt3 Saynt Poule,
> Al arn we membre3 of Jesu Kryst. (457–8)

---

[1] Cf. *Hali Meidenhad*, pp. 6–7 and 54–5 in the E.E.T.S. edition of 1922.

[2] This was a favourite image in the Middle Ages to express the exaltation of heavenly life. The ME. translation of King Philip's Lapidary (*English Medieval Lapidaries*, p. 19) speaks of the *angeles þat lyuen in þat joye . . . þat is þe life corouned, in þe which shal noon entre but he be kyng corouned or quene. Hali Meidenhad*, pp. 30–31, promises a crown to all and a *garlaunde* or *auriole* to maidens.

The words of St. Paul she has in mind are 1 Corinthians xii. 12–13, and she uses the term *cortaysye* to express the manifestations of this spirit of divine grace in Christian love and charity.

The father accepts the *cortaysye* of heavenly society, but he cannot believe that the child who did not live two years on earth, and could *neuer God nauþer plese ne pray* (484) would straightway be made queen in Heaven, when those that had *endured in worlde stronge*, and lived in penance all their lives, could receive no greater reward. The *cortaysye* which bestows so high an honour on one so unworthy is *to fre of dede*, 'too generous in its operation'.

The Pearl again rebukes him for his presumption. And to make clearer to him the operation of God's grace she tells him the parable from Matthew xx. 1–16: the labourers were brought to the vineyard at various hours of the day, and yet they all received a penny for their labour, little or much; and the last to come were the first to be paid. The parable is then explained: the *peny agrete*, 'a penny to all in common', is the blessedness of eternal life, which is granted equally to all the elect (*For mony ben called, paȝ fewe be mykeȝ*, 572), not as their right, but as the free gift of God's grace. Thus, the Pearl explains, she herself, who came *in euentyde into þe vyne*, as an infant dying young, one who has done little work in the vineyard, is paid straightway and lives in greater happiness and honour than any man could win by claiming judgement according to his due.

The father is not satisfied by this answer: then *Holy Wryt is bot a fable* when it says *þou quyteȝ vchon as hys desserte*; for it would seem, the more work done the less the reward. Again the Pearl rebukes him: there is no question of more or less in the kingdom of God; the bliss of Heaven is granted equally to all, 'whether little or much be due

to him as recognition of merit' (603–4).[1] For *þe gentyl
Cheuentayn is no chyche*[2] and never withholds this happiness from those who submit themselves to His mercy
through Christ. And she explains the apparent injustice of
her own high reward by defining the distinction between
the innocent and the righteous. Where, she asks, lives the
man, 'ever so holy in his prayer':

> Þat he ne forfeted by sumkyn gate
> Þe mede sumtyme of heueneʒ clere? (619–20)

No man can be so steadfast in virtue that he can win the
reward of Heaven thereby:

> Mercy and grace moste hem þen stere. (623)

But an infant who by baptism becomes an innocent, and
who dies without having committed any sin, receives
straightway the reward of Heaven. He who sins again after
being washed clean from sin by baptism, if he repents may
be granted God's grace through penance and prayer. But
the innocent, who *to gyle neuer glente*, is saved *by ryʒt*; for
God never decreed that the guiltless should suffer (668).

The Pearl supports her argument of the special position
of innocents by three further passages from scripture (in
lines 673–708), and by the words of Jesus:

> Do way, let chylder vnto me tyʒt.
> To suche is heuenryche arayed. (718–19)

And:

> hys ryche no wyʒ myʒt wynne
> Bot he com þyder ryʒt as a chylde. (722–3)

---

[1] For discussion of the meaning of these lines see note.

[2] Cf. the northern fourteenth-century *De Gracia: God is na chynche
of his grace, for he haues ynogh þerofe; for þofe he dele it neuer so ferre ne
to so mony he haues neuer þe lesse. For him wantes bot clene vessels til do
his grace inne.* (*Works of Richard Rolle*, ed. C. Horstman, i. 133.) The
parallel with *Pearl* was first pointed out by Carleton F. Brown.

She seems now to have succeeded in convincing and re-assuring her father that his child is undoubtedly saved, and is not suffering in the life to come because it died without knowledge of Christian teaching. He is now filled only with wonder at the radiant beauty of his Pearl, as she tells him how she came to that state when the Lamb called her to be His bride. The brides of the Lamb, she explains, are the company of the 144,000, of those untainted by spot or blemish, seen by John in the Apocalyptic vision of the New Jerusalem. And the dialogue ends with the father's own vision of the Heavenly City.

The Pearl's argument accords well, in general, with the teachings of the Church, though it is not always closely in accordance with the theologians in precision of expression or detail. St. Augustine and the Fathers generally declared that baptism washes away the sin which is our heritage from the guilt of Adam, and confers grace; and though some differences of opinion arose in the early medieval Church on this question of baptized children who died in infancy, the decisions of Popes in the fourteenth century confirmed the earlier opinion that they were undoubtedly saved.[1] It is possible, however, that the effect of these doubts was still felt in England at the time when *Pearl* was written. It is known, for instance, that Bradwardine, who lived in the poet's own time and country (and was read by Chaucer), believed that the baptized child, though saved, ranked lower in the hierarchy of Heaven than an adult with the merit of good works.[2] A knowledge of these divergent views may well have affected the emphasis on this point in the poem.

---

[1] See R. Wellek, *Studies in English*, iv, Charles University, Prague, 1933, pp. 20–22.

[2] See the passages cited by C. F. Brown, *PMLA*. xix. 134–5, and R. Wellek, op. cit., p. 20.

But the Pearl has been challenged, somewhat unfairly, on other points of doctrine. It is in accord with the personal basis of the poem that she should expound the doctrine of salvation by grace as an answer to the father's doubts and fears, and not attempt to give a general exposition of the doctrine as a whole or reflect on its implications. This incompleteness, so natural to the theme of the poem, has caused some misunderstanding, and the Pearl has even been accused of heresy because she asserts that the heavenly reward is the same for all. The accusation has been answered,[1] and the answer lies in a better understanding both of the Pearl's words and of orthodox doctrine. As St. Augustine says,[2] the penny, *quod omnes communiter habebunt*, is (as the Pearl herself explains) eternal life itself; it is given equally, necessarily, since all the elect are in the presence of God, and eternal life can be nothing but eternal; but this does not make the recipients equal. There are many mansions with the Father in Heaven, and some of the elect are in their natures more glorious than others. As the quality of their appreciation of the heavenly state differs, so is their reward greater or less. The Pearl does not explain how the doctrines of equal reward and unequal rank are to be reconciled; it is enough for the father to be assured that God does not withhold His grace from those who, like the infant, have no merit. But the poet cannot have meant to imply equality of rank in the equality of the reward; for he recognizes the grades in the hierarchy of Heaven when he places Mary above the other queens in Heaven; and the elders of Revelation, *þe aldermen so sadde of chere, Ryȝt byfore Godeȝ chayere* (885). The procession of

---

[1] See especially J. B. Fletcher, *JEGPh.* xx. 1 f., and R. Wellek, op. cit., pp. 15 and 22 f.

[2] *De Sancta Virginitate*, xxvi, Migne *Patrologia Latina*, vol. 40, col. 410, and elsewhere.

the 144,000 that follow the Lamb similarly implies a distinction of rank.

It has also been objected that an infant would not be admitted to this company: these are the *virgines* of the Apocalypse, and virginity is not yet a virtue in a child too young to have known temptation; such a child is an 'innocent' rather than a 'virgin'. But both for the place of high honour among the blessed of *innocentes*, and for the association with the *virgines* of the Apocalypse, the poet had authority, traditional or theological. The *innocentes* were often assigned a high place in the lists or litanies of the saints, and that they could with orthodoxy be included in the company of the Lamb is shown by the use of Apocalypse xiv. 1–5 as the lesson for the mass of the Holy Innocents,[1] 28 December. This does not necessarily imply that the Holy Innocents composed the whole of that company, and our poet obviously cannot have held this. But the complete identification was sometimes made,[2] and for this reason the Holy Innocents were often said to number 144,000.

There seems to have been a further tradition, which our poet is following, by which any child who resembled the Holy Innocents in youthful martyrdom or in dying innocent before the age of two (*a bimatu et infra*, Matt. ii. 16) might be assigned to that blessed company.[3] In the *Prioresses Tale*, 127 ff., the martyred boy, seven years old, is placed in the throng that follow *the whyte lamb celestial*. And it is significant in *Pearl* that though the maiden takes her place in the procession of the 144,000 *of such vergyneȝ in þe same gyse* (1099), she defines that

[1] The children slain by Herod (Matt. ii. 16).

[2] For English examples see the Towneley Play of Herod, and the carol *In die Sanctorum Innocentium*, no. 36 in the E.E.T.S. edition of Audelay.

[3] See further R. Wellek, op. cit., p. 25.

company in terms which include both 'virgins' and 'innocents':

> Forþy vche saule þat hade neuer teche
> Is to þat Lombe a worthyly wyf. (845–6)

A third point on which the theology of *Pearl* has been questioned is its application of the parable from Matthew to a child dying in infancy. Traditionally the workers in the vineyard are usually taken to be good Christians generally (as in *Pearl* 627–8:

> In þe water of babtem þay dyssente;
> Þen arne þay boroȝt into þe vyne.)

And the hours at which they were brought to the vineyard are taken to represent the different ages of life (infancy, youth, manhood, old age) at which they are converted. The fact that the Pearl, who died in infancy, says that she went 'at eventide' to the vineyard has seemed at variance with this interpretation. But the medieval mind was accustomed to seek for fresh significance, and encouraged by academic training to find new meaning, in familiar stories; and Bruno Astensis,[1] writing in the twelfth century, makes the eleventh hour (eventide) an hour which can apply to persons of any age who enter the vineyard shortly before death, i.e. at the eleventh hour in modern idiom. This does not contradict the traditional version in any essential: it does not affect the *sentence* of the parable, its illustration of the working of God's grace, since one who dies in infancy has done just as little work in the vineyard of the Church as one who is converted at the end of his life. It may be uncertain how far this new application of the parable was generally known in the fourteenth century, but it is easy to see that it would have a special appeal to the poet of *Pearl* as providing authority from

[1] See D. W. Robertson, *MLN*. lxv. 152.

scripture to prove the salvation and exaltation of his
innocent child.

SYMBOLISM OF THE PEARL

Comparison of ladies to pearls and other precious stones
was fairly common in courtly literature,[1] where it was often
suggested by the virtues of the gems given in the lapidaries,
which in their turn were founded on the precious stones
of scripture. But the symbolism of the pearl in this poem
is, of course, much more than a courtly compliment, and
it has its roots much deeper than courtly tradition. The
pearl as a symbol of the pure and precious was familiar in
medieval tradition generally, though not so familiar in
English writings as in Latin and French, and it derives
mainly from the parable of the pearl of price, from
Matthew xiii. 45–46. And as a symbol of purity it is not
surprising that it comes to be used especially of maidens
and maidenhood. Aldhelm describes holy maidens as
Christi margaritae, paradisi gemmae.[2]

But the symbolic use of gems is older than Christian
tradition, and in St. Margaret of Antioch in Pisidia we find
Margarita 'pearl' already used as a woman's name in the
third century, though according to her legend she was not
born a Christian. Her name and cult played a part in the
Christian association of the pearl and virginity, but her
cult itself was greatly reinforced by the medieval love of
pearls and their symbolism; it reached its height in the
west in the Middle Ages.[3] Several of the saints (among
countless other Margarets and Margerys) of whom she is
the name-ancestress belong to the period from the eleventh

---

[1] As in *Annot and John*, The Harley Lyrics, ed. G. L. Brook, p. 31.
[2] *De Virginitate*, Monumenta Germaniae Historica, Auct. Antiq. xv.
323.
[3] See *Seinte Marherete*, ed. F. M. Mack, E.E.T.S. 193 (1934), p. x.

to the fourteenth century, but not all of them are virgins.
In the *Legenda Aurea* is found the well-known preface to
the legend of the first St. Margaret: *Margarita dicitur a
quadam pretiosa gemma, quae margarita vocatur; quae gemma
est candida, parva, et virtuosa. Sic beata Margareta fuit
candida per virginitatem, parva per humilitatem, virtuosa
per miraculorum operationem. Virtus autem hujus lapidis
dicitur esse contra cordis passionem, et ad spiritus conforta-
tionem.*[1]

The poet of *Pearl* uses the pearl symbol variously, but
always with traditional significations,[2] and to express the
attributes of purity and preciousness. The poem begins
with praise of the poet's *precios perle wythouten spotte*,
which as the symbolism of the poem unfolds is the pure and
spotless maiden who has died, his precious child. When she
is found again in Heaven, the pearl becomes more definitely
a symbol of her immaculate spirit and the blessedness of
her heavenly state. And these significations are extended
to the other pearls in the poem. The maiden's raiment is
sewn with them in token of her innocence; her pinnacled
crown of pure white pearl is the privilege of her heavenly
blessedness;[3] the large and lustrous pearl she wears on
her breast, we are told, is none other than the pearl of
price that the merchant of Christ's parable gave all his
goods to buy: it is like the realm of Heaven, spotless, clean,
and clear, a symbol of the blessedness enjoyed by the
redeemed. Each gate of the Heavenly City is made of one
single unfading pearl.[4] The dreamer is counselled to forsake

---

[1] *Vitae Sanctorum*, Coloniae Agrippinae, 1618, tom. 3, p. 242.

[2] See W. H. Schofield, *PMLA*. xxiv. 635 for a list of significations.

[3] See below, p. xxxi (note). Such a celestial crown of pearl is identified
with the pearl of price of the parable by a thirteenth-century writer
William of Lanicia, Diæta Salutis, tit. 10, cap. 2, cited by Osgood, note
to line 1186, but wrongly ascribed by him to St. Bonaventure.

[4] Rev. xxi. 21. Hugo of Fouilly says that each gate consists of a single

this mad world and purchase for himself his own matchless pearl; those who gain it become themselves precious pearls for the Prince's delight. The symbolism of the pearl dominates the poem, and fills it with light and gives it deeper significance.

In Middle English, apart from *Pearl*, the most elaborate pearl symbolism is in Thomas Usk's *Testament of Love*, written in 1387–8. Here three values are given to the pearl, which is figured as a woman named Margaret, who 'betokeneth Grace, learning or wisdom of God, or else Holy Church'.[1] But the manipulation of the symbolism is awkward and mechanical compared with the harmony and simplicity of *Pearl*. So far as is known, there is no direct connexion between the two works.

SOURCES, ANALOGUES, AND TRADITIONS

The principal source from which the material of *Pearl* is drawn is the Vulgate Bible, of which three passages are especially important: the parable of the workers in the vineyard, Matthew xx. 1–16, the vision of the Heavenly City from Revelation xxi and xxii, and the procession of the 144,000 from Revelation xiv. In addition to these, a considerable number of short unconnected scriptural passages are quoted or echoed.[2] Usually the scriptural sources are followed closely, and they are skilfully adapted to their purpose in the poem. It was clearly the poet's intention to use scriptural authority as fully as he could, but in applying it to the theme of the poem he tends sometimes to colour it with the conceptions of his own time. Thus the maiden he sees in Heaven is wearing the white bridal

pearl because the justified enter Heaven through purity and unity of faith, an interpretation which brings to mind the pearl symbolism at the end of *Pearl*.

[1] Chap. 17, line 102.   [2] A list of these is given on pp. 165–7.

garment of fine linen, but her costume, nevertheless, is in the fashion of the poet's own day. The Heavenly City has all the details of that in Revelation, yet it is imagined in medieval form as a *bayle* or *manayre* (see notes to lines 917 and 992). The book which the Lamb reads is not a roll, but has square leaves. Occasionally the poet has taken minor liberties with the scriptural passages: in line 825 he adds words from Isaiah to the prophetic utterance of John the Baptist, and ascribes the whole to John. And he transfers the raiment of the symbolic bride of Revelation xix (representing the Church) to the Pearl. There are also a few actual inaccuracies: in giving the measurements of the Heavenly City the number twelve is changed to twelve thousand (see note to line 1029); in the list of stones in the foundation, the ruby as sixth stone is unscriptural.[1]

Almost all the scriptural passages used by the Pearl to support her exposition of the doctrine of grace are those used for the same purpose by the theologians: most of them are found, for example, in the anti-Pelagian writings of Augustine. It seems unlikely that the poet would be so well informed of all these passages in their doctrinal applications unless he had read some theological writings in which they were quoted. There is no evidence to show just which theologians he may have read, but beyond the common teaching of the Church at that time he need not have gone farther than Augustine. He has more scriptural texts in common with him than with any other writer on grace and salvation: he shares, or reflects, especially Augustine's predilection for the Psalms and the Epistles of St. Paul.

It would seem that the poet had read theological writ-

---

[1] The number of the Lamb's company is given as 140,000 in line 786, but here the error is probably the copyist's, since the right number is given in 869–70.

ings (as Chaucer did) without being himself a systematic
theologian. He avoids technical language, and he uses his
information as a poet and a layman seeking comfort rather
than as one interested in the problems for their own sake.
His interest may well have been particular to the occasion.

The allegorical interpretation of the Song of Songs,
which was general in the Middle Ages, is apparent in the
attribution to Christ of the bridegroom's words, when He
calls the Pearl to Him to be His bride (763–4), and possibly
the conception of the bride of Christ as a crowned queen
comes in part from the Song of Songs, iv. 8, Vulgate version.[1] In Revelation the elders before the throne wear
crowns, but not the 144,000 virgins. But the crown as a
heavenly reward is mentioned elsewhere in scripture, and
it is in accordance with the conception of heavenly life
general in the Middle Ages that the Pearl has her crown as
a queen in Heaven. That the crown represents also the
ornament of virginity is possibly implied in its description.[2] But the term *garlande* in 1186, which might seem
to support this suggestion, more probably refers to the
circle of the blessed in Heaven; (see note).

The passages from Revelation used in the poem are
treated for the most part in a different way from the other
scriptural passages. The poet makes little attempt at symbolical interpretations of these passages, such as were so
often given in commentaries or treatises on Revelation.

---

[1] Gollancz, *Pearl*, p. xxi. The same conception in the Office for Virgin
Saints still in use is based on this passage from the Song of Songs.

[2] The *coroune* closely resembles the special ornament of virginity
described in *Hali Meidenhad* (MS. B, E.E.T.S. edition, p. 30): *Alle ha
beoð icrunet, þe blissið in heouene, wið kempene crune. Ah þe meidnes
habbeð upo þeo, þe is to alle iliche imeane, a gerlonde [sche] schenre þen þe
sunne, an urle* [MS. T. *Auriole*] *ihaten o latines ledene. Þe flurs þe beoð
idrahe þron, ne þe ȝimmes þrin, te tellen of hare euene nis na monnes speche.*
Cf. *Pearl,* 207–8: *Hiȝe pynakled of cler quyt perle, Wyth flurted flowreȝ
perfet vpon.*

Instead, he uses the scriptural details pictorially to illustrate a scene which is to captivate the dreamer with its splendours. In this later part of the poem the poet does not need authority for doctrine: he has established all that he wished to establish about his child's destiny, and he is able to use the scriptural material more directly; although even here certain details suggest that he may have been using a commentary also,[1] most of the echoes of Revelation in the poem may well have come direct from scripture.

The framework of the poem as a whole—a vision seen in a dream—is the form popularized by the *Roman de la Rose*. And the influence of that poem, or the school of poetry derived from it, is clear in the general conception of the heavenly region in which the dreamer finds himself, the flowery garden, bright, clear, and serene. The most definite echo of detail and wording from the *Roman de la Rose* is in lines 749–53. But the direct influence of the *Roman* is neither so clear nor so extensive as has sometimes been claimed.[2]

To the same literary tradition belongs, too, the evident reliance in the poem on courtly manners as an unquestionable ideal of behaviour, and the influence of courtly love on the terms of thought; though here there is little sign of the direct influence of the *Roman de la Rose* itself. The poet must have been a man of polite education, probably of gentle birth, who knew his *cortaysye* at first hand: the courteous tone of the conversation, the manners, the details of dress and architecture, the jewels, belong to the aristocratic world of the time. But *cortaysye* to the poet was more than a sophistication of behaviour in polite

[1] See notes to lines 1007 and 1041.

[2] Schofield and Gollancz even identify allegorical personages from the *Roman*, though in each case (*gladneȝ* in 136, *myrþeȝ* in 140, and *resoun* in 52) the identification is contextually difficult, apart from the fact that allegorical abstractions are out of place in Heaven.

society: he sees it as a gentleness and sensitiveness of spirit pervading personal relationship. This is seen in his application of its terms to devotional and theological concepts. This application in itself was no new practice: there had been for some time a strong reciprocal influence between the ideas of *cortaysye* and those of religious thought, and a tendency towards interchange of terms; and *Pearl* affords an admirable illustration of the basic conception of *cortaysye* which made such interchange natural. Thus the Christian charity of the kings and queens of Heaven is *cortaysye*, not only because of the symbolism of royalty, but because *cortaysye* expresses the ideal of gentle behaviour which is the manifestation of divine charity. And so the dreamer who has not faith enough to accept Christ's word without visible proof is *vncortayse*, lacking in spiritual sensitivity, though he is as conscious of his manners as Sir Gawain himself. The Virgin Mary is *Quen of cortaysye*, not only because she reigns over the noble society of Heaven, but because she represents the ideal itself of Christian behaviour.

The idea of Mary as *Quen of cortaysye* is itself in the courtly tradition. Whether the greater emphasis on the worship of the Virgin in the Middle Ages was itself a cause or a result of the *courtois* attitude to women, the *courtois* attitude certainly affected the nature of that worship, and *Pearl* is in the medieval courtly trend in making Mary the ideal of graciousness.

In the courtly tradition, too, is the general effect of this use of courtly terms to describe devotional and theological aspects, the richness which they add to the spiritual and esthetic effect. Just as the heavenly scene, in addition to the visionary elements, has all the splendour of an earthly court, so the devotional element gains fervour from the emotional associations of these terms of courtly love. Even the grief of the father for his child—*fordolked of luf-daungere*, as if he were a lover separated from his mistress—gains in intensity from the courtly terms in which it is expressed.

The pearl symbol, too, plays its part in the blending of courtly fashion and Christian significance: the richness it adds to the poem is again the richness of the world of fashion. For this was the 'pearl age'. In western Europe generally during the thirteenth and fourteenth centuries pearls were fashionable as personal adornment, and they were worn in enormous quantities;[1] the dresses of men, as well as of women, were decorated with them, and they are noted in the descriptions of almost every festive occasion.[2] Arcyte in the *Knight's Tale* (A 2161) wore a coat-armour *couched with perles white and rounde and grete*; the lady seen by King James from his prison window in *Kingis Quair* wore pearls in her hair-fret, as did Achilles in *Confessio Amantis* when he was disguised as a girl; the company of trumpeters in *The Flower and the Leaf* (214) wore large collars set with pearls, and *many a perled garnement embroudred was* at the tournament in *Confessio Amantis* (i. 2510).

The poet's interest in pearls and other precious stones, and his knowledge of them, suggest that he may have read lapidaries. The terms in which he describes the stones and comments on their qualities are often reminiscent of the extant medieval lapidaries in Latin, French, and English,[3] and it is perhaps likely that he would be acquainted with so fashionable a form of literature. But there are no decisive parallels. The list of precious stones in the foundation of the New Jerusalem (lines 997–1020, Rev. xxi. 19–20)

---

[1] See J. J. Jusserand, *Literary History of the English People*, i. 264.

[2] See Kunz and Stevenson, *The Book of the Pearl*, 245.

[3] As was first pointed out by W. H. Schofield. See notes to lines 1007, 1012, 1015, 1041.

forms the basis of several of the earlier lapidaries, and several of them (including King Philip's Lapidary) connect this list in Revelation with the list of precious stones on Aaron's breast-plate, as *Pearl* does.[1] But the lapidaries derive this connexion from biblical commentaries, and the poet of *Pearl* may possibly have taken this detail, and others, direct from the commentaries themselves.

The striking resemblance of the general theme of *Pearl* to Boccaccio's *Olympia* is probably only one of the strange coincidences of literary history. Boccaccio, living roughly about the same time as the poet of *Pearl*, also wrote an elegy on the death of a little daughter, whom he sees in a vision, glorified in eternal life. But Boccaccio's treatment of the theme is quite different. His poem is cast in the more artificial form of an eclogue, serene and graceful: there is no rebellious grief, no fever of doubt, no theological argument. No one now claims to see any direct relation between the two poems. Yet the parallel is not without significance as an illustration of medieval conventions: Olympia is known to have lived on earth, and to have died as an infant, and, like the Pearl, in her glorified state she speaks as an adult and as one having authoritative knowledge.

The poet of *Pearl*, like most English poets of the fourteenth century, seems to have drawn on his foreign reading for his material. There is little trace of debt to any known English writing. But in the style and technique of the poem the influence of English poetic tradition is very clear. And it was a branch of that tradition least influenced by French practice, the alliterative tradition of the West Midlands and the North. This was a venerable poetic technique,

---

[1] See notes to lines 1007 and 1041. But the lapidaries do not account for the transference of the order of names of the children of Israel from the breast-plate to the Heavenly City. This indicates the use of a scriptural commentary by the poet.

reaching back to the Old English period, and with another root in the poetry of the Norse settlers, but modified considerably by material and forms of style accumulated during the Middle English period. The metre of *Pearl* comes from the alliterative line, only slightly modified by the use of rhyme,[1] and the poet uses the alliteration of the tradition, though not systematically. This obliges him to adopt also the diction peculiar to alliterative poetry, though again not so generally as in the unrhymed alliterative poems where alliteration was systematic. This use of the conventions of the native alliterative technique plays an important part in determining the general style of the poem.

The theological interests of *Pearl*, too, seem to be in the stream of English tradition. The doctrine of salvation by grace and the efficacy of baptism were subjects in which many were interested in fourteenth-century England. In the South Bishop Bradwardine (died 1349) produced his large work *De Causa Dei contra Pelagium*, in which he restated and developed the doctrines of Augustine on grace and predestination. The *Testament of Love*[2] combines discussion of grace, free will, and predestination with a symbolic pearl. The West Midland group of early thirteenth-century texts shows a special interest in holy maidenhood. And in the North Richard Rolle and his school produced the treatise *De Gracia* and other works describing the nature and effects of grace in man.

VERSE AND STYLE

In his choice of verse-form the poet of *Pearl* subjected himself to a double discipline, that of alliterative verse itself, and that of an elaborate rhyme-scheme combined with stanza-linking by echo and refrain. Either of these mediums is exacting in itself: together they provide a

---

[1] See Appendix I, p. 89.   [2] See p. xxix above.

highly 'artificial' metre, which, in the words of Dr. Osgood, 'involves the necessity of artificial dialect and occasionally distorted meanings and syntax'. And this, he adds, 'is in opposition to full facility of expression or spontaneity of feeling'.[1] While acknowledging the truth of this statement, few now would regard it as valid criticism of poetry. It has long been recognized that facility, or even 'naturalness', of expression in poetry is usually itself the result of art, which may sometimes choose to express itself in forms less facile or less natural without loss of poetic 'feeling'. The poetry of *Pearl* ranks with that of Dante or Donne as proof that an 'artificial' poetic form is itself no barrier to the expression of deep emotion.

But the discipline of an elaborate verse-form is severe; and here we have the danger: not in the 'artificiality', but in the difficulty. Artificiality, if we use the word in a derogatory sense, may come in when poets of inferior skill, who try to follow a fashion, find the struggle for authentic expression in an exacting medium too much for their art and fall back on the technique itself as a substitute for the effort and search for precision. It takes a very good poet to resist the temptation, especially in the Middle Ages, when the tradition of verbal art had been debased, and poets were often too easily satisfied; and notably in the alliterative tradition, where the conventions themselves often provided a stock of phrases and formulas ready-made for the taking. In the lesser poets, and in the greater ones too, at times when inspiration was not equal to the effort, the result is, all too often, loss of vitality, tastelessness, and lack of precision.

But failure of execution is no evidence of inherent defect in the art-form itself. The poet of *Pearl* is rarely guilty of using his technique in mechanical or slovenly fashion, and

[1] *Pearl*, p. lv.

in his poetry can be seen the great virtues of the alliterative tradition. The freedom of rhythm permits a more frequent use of homely idiom than does the more measured verse of the French tradition; and this can strike a note of simplicity (*I knew hyr wel, I hade sen hyr ere*), or racy vigour (*ne glauereʒ her nieʒbor wyth no gyle*). The alliteration can encourage concentration of meaning (*To penke hir color so clad in clot*), or rich elaboration, as in countless passages. Richness of description is, in fact, one of the outstanding features of this school of poetry. Even alliteration, cumbrous as it may sometimes be, can, when used with discretion as it is in *Pearl*, give an impression of metrical strength, without seeming over-emphatic or affected, as it so often does in non-alliterative poetry. And, as the alliteration in *Pearl* is not systematic, the poet has greater freedom in its use. When he wishes to be simple and direct, as he often does in the non-descriptive passages, the alliteration is rarely obtrusive. Time and time again throughout the poem comes expression of feeling as simple as in any non-alliterative poem:

> Art þou my perle þat I haf playned,
> Regretted by myn one on nyʒte?

> Ofte haf I wayted, wyschande þat wele.

> For I haf founden hym, boþe day and naʒte,
> A God, a Lorde, a frende ful fyin.

And in the exposition of the argument there is a forthright directness, as, for example, in the immediate and clear definition of the distinction between the innocent and the righteous in lines 661–72.

It is not so much the alliterative conventions which constitute the poetic restrictions in *Pearl* as the difficult rhyme-scheme the poet has chosen, and the larger pattern of the poem, the stanza-linking by echo and refrain. And it is here that the verse-form sometimes defeats him. There are some imperfect rhymes,[1] and most of the obscurities of meaning have their basis in a rhyme-word, probably distorted in meaning, or even possibly, on occasion, invented by the poet.[2] But even here we must beware of confusing the obscurities due to lack of precision with those of our own (inevitable) lack of knowledge. We sometimes have insufficient evidence for an understanding of the form or meaning of the poet's words; and the manuscript is so far from being careful that we are sometimes left in doubt whether the version before us is really what the poet wrote.[3] Of no other medieval poem is it more true to say, as Dr. Sisam said of medieval poetry generally, 'Every blur is a challenge'. Other distortions of meaning were perhaps less unnatural when they were written than we think them now: from its earliest days the art of alliterative poetry seems to have had as one of its elements a form of verbal ingenuity: the alliterative conventions themselves encouraged the use of oblique expression (developed to its highest degree in Icelandic poetry), and to listeners or readers bred in that tradition the use of words in unusual meanings may well have been both less puzzling and more effective than it is to us. When the poet in stanza-group IX uses *date* as a link-word with widely varying (and to us often strained) meanings, the distortions may well have seemed to contemporaries a form of verbal wit.

But this raises one of the basic problems of literary criticism as it concerns poetry so remote in language and tradition from our own. The scholar who steeps himself in

---

[1] See below, p. xlviii.
[2] See notes to lines 77, 107, 609, 616 for example.
[3] e.g. *offys* (?) 755, *blose* 911, *reget* 1064.

the tradition tends to try to judge it by the standards of its time, while the less learned tend to measure it by more modern values and often find it wanting. To avoid both dangers, by becoming familiar enough with the tradition to read the poetry with open ears and an open mind, without losing sight of absolute values, is not easy. To the unprejudiced student, willing to take the trouble to acquaint himself with its language and tradition, the poetry of *Pearl* should need no special pleading. He will probably find in the artificial form a setting admirably suited to the richness of the jewel it encloses. And beyond its decorative value he will feel the force which the verse pattern lends to the argument: the refrain in each stanza-group underlines the particular stage of thought with which that group is primarily concerned, and this is especially effective in a poem in which there is so much discourse. But, above all, he will feel the emotional effect, as moving as music itself, which the verse pattern adds to the feeling.

This special stanza form was probably chosen because it was felt to be a fitting vehicle for a poem of sorrow and reflection: extant examples of it are all moral laments, and deal mostly with death.[1] And written as it is here, with lines packed with significant words, and often heavily alliterated, it gathers as it is repeated over and over again a great weight of feeling. Yet it is not, as used in this poem, an actually mournful verse-form. It has, significantly, a swifter movement and a greater elaboration of refrain and echo than in the contemporary examples of it. And just as the richness of the vision, while not removing the dreamer's grief, overlays it with wonder and beauty, so the elaboration of the verse-form, though it gives full expression to that grief, at the same time lends an emotional

[1] See Appendix I, p. 87. Note especially that the stanza is used for the lament of Mary for her Child, *Filius regis mortuus est.*

excitement which lifts it above the level of mournful sadness. It is difficult, of course, to separate the musical effects of poetry from the significance of the words, but it is probably true to say that the verse-form plays no small part in conveying both the poignancy of the dreamer's grief and the transmutation of it which comes with his relief from doubt and assurance of hope. The repetition and variation on the verbal theme, of the separate stanza-groups, drive home to us with an emotional insistence the different stages of thought and feeling through which he passes until he reaches the peace which accepts immediate loss with faith and hope. So moving is the verse that, if its difficulties sometimes strain the poet's powers too far, the occasional lapses of precision or taste seem trivial in the light of the general achievement.

THE AUTHOR

Nothing is known of the author of *Pearl* beyond what can be inferred from internal evidence, and attempts to identify him have been unconvincing. Whether he was also the author of the other three poems in the manuscript, *Sir Gawain*, *Purity*, and *Patience*, is a question which must probably be left ultimately to personal impression: most of those who have studied the poems in detail have come to the opinion that they are by the same author. All four poems are written in the same dialect, and are localized, by vocabulary and other linguistic indications, in the same region (see below). They are linked also in varying degrees by verbal parallels and a similarity of descriptive talent; and they share an interest in certain problems of life: the value of purity, explained and illustrated in the three biblical stories in *Purity*, is at the heart of the theme of *Pearl*, and, applied to courtly behaviour, forms the motive of the story in *Sir Gawain*; the virtue of patience and acceptance of God's will, illustrated in the story of Jonah in *Patience*, is the lesson the dreamer has to learn in *Pearl*. And in all four poems there is evidence of religious zeal and devotion combined with knowledge and admiration of courtly life and ideals.

A comparison might be made with the 'Katherine' group of texts, where the works of the group are similarly unified in dialect, interest, and subject-matter, but where, as has been fairly shown,[1] the similarity derives from one specially active centre or 'school', rather than from one author. But the Katherine group is much less individual and distinctive in style, and the community of thought and interest has nothing like the same pressure. And the Katherine group does not show the same high level of poetic genius which in this group of poems would make separate authorship, for poems so closely localized, a remarkable phenomenon.

From internal evidence it is clear that the poet of *Pearl* was a man of education, though there is less emphasis on scholarship in his poem than in the work of Chaucer, Gower, or Langland. He shows, for instance, less interest in philosophy, and gives more attention to the arts and the aristocratic activities of his day. He may well have had a monastic education, but it is unlikely that he was himself a monk. As Osgood has pointed out, the Pearl would hardly have said to him: *I rede þe forsake þe worlde wode*, if he had already forsaken it at that time. He may have been a chaplain in an aristocratic household: that he once had a daughter is no decisive argument against this, for he may, for instance, have been ordained later in life. But his interest in theology might just as naturally be the interest of a pious layman who has found ecclesiastical guidance.

[1] S. T. R. O. d'Ardenne, *An Edition of þe Liflade ant te Passiun of Seinte Iuliene*, Paris and Liège, 1936, p. xliii.

The language of the poem shows little trace of the priest, as Osgood also argues, when he contrasts the reference at the end of the poem to the host which *þe preste vus schewe3 vch a daye* with Robert Mannyng of Brunne's interpolated line in his translation of Bonaventure's *Meditations*: *He þat þou seest in forme of brede.*

Though the dialect of the poem indicates that the southern Pennine region was the poet's place of upbringing, it is not necessary to assume that he was actually living there when he wrote.[1] If he was a member of a noble household he might have been living in any of the greater residential castles of the north-west.

DATE

Pearl cannot be dated with any precision. The downward limit is fixed by the date of the manuscript, which is not later than *c.* 1400; the details of costume belong to the second half of the fourteenth century (see note to line 228). More precise dating can only be comparative, on the assumption of common authorship for all four poems of the manuscript.

Purity shows some influence of Mandeville's Travels, written about 1356.[2] On the ground that *Patience* was imitated in poems not earlier than 1390, Dr. Mabel Day takes that date as the downward limit for *Patience*.[3]

[1] The choice of Clitheroe Castle, based partly on this assumption and partly on the identification (difficult to maintain) of the Pearl with Margaret Hastings, niece of John of Gaunt, owner of Clitheroe, (J. P. Oakden, *Alliterative Poetry in Middle English*, i. 258) is unsuitable, since Clitheroe was more a fortress than a residential castle.

[2] C. F. Brown, *PMLA*. xix (1904), 149. Gollancz (*Cleanness*, p. xiv) also saw in this poem some influence of *Le Livre du Chevalier de la Tour Landry*, written in 1371–2, but his evidence is thin and dubious.

[3] *Siege of Jerusalem*, pp. xxix–xxx. Literary borrowing in alliterative poems, all drawing on a common stream of tradition, is always doubtful, but this seems a probable instance.

Details of costume, armour, and architecture in *Sir Gawain* point to some time in the last quarter of the century as the date of that poem. There are indications, though nothing approaching proof, that *Patience* and *Purity* are earlier than *Sir Gawain*;[1] but there is nothing to show the chronological position of *Pearl* in the series. If all four poems are by the same author, the maturity of workmanship in *Pearl* would put it probably later than *Purity* or *Patience*. On the same assumption, too, one can discern a development in method of approach: in *Purity* and *Patience* the author seems to be working out with great care the moral values of these virtues in human life, and in *Pearl* and *Sir Gawain* he seems to be putting his conclusions to the test. This is a process of development discernible to some extent also in Chaucer's work.

We should probably be justified in setting the limits for the whole group of poems as *c.* 1360–95, and the maturity of *Pearl* would put it late rather than early in this period.

DIALECT

The dialect of *Pearl* and its three companion poems is now generally agreed, with few dissentients, to belong to the North-West Midlands.[2] There can be little doubt, at least, that the language of the extant text belongs to that area, and the evidence of those linguistic elements— rhymes, alliteration, and vocabulary—which are least subject to scribal alteration indicates that that was the area

---

[1] See, for example, R. J. Menner, *Purity*, pp. xxxiii f.

[2] So R. Morris, F. Knigge, K. Luick, K. Sisam, R. Jordan, R. J. Menner, and others. J. R. Hulbert considers there is insufficient evidence. C. O. Chapman assigns the poem to Yorkshire. Within the North-West Midland area, south Lancashire is the usual choice, with Cheshire as a possibility. But H. C. Wyld and M. S. Serjeantson considered north Derbyshire a more likely locality.

of its original composition. This evidence is to be judged by comparison, not only with contemporary writings (though these naturally supply the most important criteria of dialect in the period), but also with the usage of later dialects as they are known in more modern records and in living speech at the present day. Place-names of the North-Western counties also have some value as corroborative evidence.

RHYMES

The following rhymes point to a region where Midland dialects are influenced by, and to some extent blended with, Northern:

(i) In words containing the descendant of OE. *ā*. This usually appears as open *ǭ*, rhyming with *o* which has been lengthened in an open syllable: *more* 168, 234, 600; *aros* 181; *ston* 206, 380, 822, &c. But it sometimes appears as *ā*, rhyming with *a* lengthened in an open syllable: *brade* 138; *mare* 145; *wate* 502, *abate* 617. *Mare* in 145, rhyming with *fare*, is distinguished in the rhyme-scheme from *more* 156 in the same stanza; this seems clear proof that the variation was the poet's own (probably for rhyming convenience). The same variation is found in the rhymes of other North Midland poets, in the west as far south as Shropshire in the works of Myrc and Audelay, but the *a* forms are less frequent in the Shropshire poets. (On the form *totȝ* 513, see note.)

(ii) In words containing close *ō* from lengthening and lowering of *u* in an open syllable: *sum* 584, rhyming with *come, dome*, &c.; *gome* 697 and the pp. *-nome* 703, rhyming with *dome, com*; *won* 918, rhyming with *done, bone*. This development is chiefly Northern, but is found in some North Midland texts; it occurs only sporadically elsewhere.

(iii) In verbal inflexions. These show a predominance of Midland, with a smaller proportion of Northern types. The Midland pres. indic. pl. appears in *stryuen* 1199, *we bene* 785; the Northern type in *þay gotჳ* 510. In the first person sg. the ending *eჳ* is found when the verb is separated from its subject in *byswykeჳ* 568 (see note, and cf. *I leue* 469, *I lede* 409). This usage was Northern and extreme North Midland, as in modern dialect. *Wasse* 1108, 1112, for past pl. 'were', is distinctly Northern; cf. *were* 6, 87, *wore* 154, *ware* 151. *Todraweჳ* 280, pres. 2 sg., is Northern and North Midland. On the ending *-ande* of the pres. partic. see Appendix IV, p. 99 (note).

The following rhymes indicate a region in the west, rather than in the east or centre, of the North Midlands:

(i) In words containing *p*, *t*, *k* from unvoicing of *b*, *d*, *g* at the end of a word. This took place (*a*) in unstressed syllables: *justyfyet* 700; (*b*) in stressed syllables following a liquid or nasal consonant (still found in Lancashire and north Derbyshire in some words): *rert* 591, *dyssente* 627, *bitalt* 1161, *bycalt* 1163; *among* 905 (rhyming with *þonc*, *wlonc*, *bonc*), *flonc* 1165. In *fonte* (OE. *funden*) 170 the *d* has been unvoiced after becoming final by loss of final *e* in pronunciation. (This development is already evidenced in the West Midlands; cf. the 'Katherine' group some 150 years earlier); and (*c*) in stressed syllables following a vowel: *abate* 617. The unvoiced consonant has been extended analogically to a position where it is not final in *fateჳ* 1038. There are no examples in rhyme of the unvoicing of final *b*, but see Appendix II, p. 93 (2).

(ii) In words containing the *i*-mutation of Anglian *al*. In some areas this became *el* (before the front *l*). In the West it became in ME. *al*, as in *Pearl* in *malte* 1154, *walte* 1156, but cf. *welle* 365. Actually no Western texts have only the *al* development.

(iii) In words containing long *ē*. The rhymes of *Pearl* distinguish between open *ē* and close *ē*. In the North-East Midlands (e.g. in *Havelock* and Robert of Brunne) older close *ē* and open *ē* have become identical; as also in Northern dialects, including part at least of the West Riding (as in Laurence Minot). In *Pearl* etymological open *ē* rhymes with open *ē* in twenty-one groups of rhymes,[1] nine of which contain four or six rhyme-words each; etymological close *ē* rhymes with close *ē* in thirty-five groups,[2] of which twenty-four contain four or six rhymes each. In several rhyme-groups with *ē* there occur rhymes which are apparently not etymologically true: some can probably be explained;[3] some are probably due to textual corruption;[4]

---

[1] In stanza 2, rhyme b, 3a (though the quality of *e* in *fede* is not known), 8b, 9b, 14b, 25a, 27b, 35a, 47b, 54a, 61c, 62c, 63c, 64c, 65c, 68c, 69c, 70c, 78a, 80a, 80b.

[2] In 4b, 6b, 8a, 10a, 17b, 20a, 21c, 22c, 23b, 23c, 24c, 25b, 25c, 26c, 27c, 28a, 28c, 29c, 30c, 34b, 40a, 41a, 52b, 60a, 62a, 64a, 66a, 67b, 70a, 74b, 88a, 89a, 93a, 96a, 99a.

[3] In 9b (rhyme with open *ē*), in *reuerez* 105 the *ē* had been shortened in English use, and short *e* was normally open in quality. A short *e* lengthened under artificial stress usually retained its open quality, as in the last syllable of *Jerusalem* in stanzas 66–70.

In 10a (rhyme with close *ē*) *stepe* 113 etymologically should have open *ē*, but a variant with close *ē* is known in ME., e.g. in *King Alysaunder* 7041 *stepe* rhymes as here with *depe* 'deep'. Early modern English has frequent spellings with *i*, representing ME. close *ē*, and this type is represented in the modern spelling *steep*. The influence of the natural opposite *deep* may be the cause of this aberrant development.

In 14b (rhyme with open *ē*), *pere* 167 should by etymology have close *ē*, but open *ē* is found in other Midland texts, cf. *pær* in Orm, and *pear* in the K-group.

In 61c (rhyme with open *ē*) *pres* 730 has AFr. open *ē*.

[4] In 30c *leme* 358 is emended to *fleme*: see note. In 82b (rhyme with open *ē*) *preued* 983 is possibly a textual corruption for *breued*: see note. The *ē* in *breued* is often assumed to be close *ē* (after the quite independent late ON. *bréfa*), but was probably open *ē* from lengthening of short *e*.

In 97a (rhyme with open *ē*) *stere* 1159 is possibly a textual corruption for *scere* (see note).

others remain without explanation and must probably be regarded as inaccurate rhymes.[1]

(iv) *lone* 1066, rhyming with *mone*. In *lone* the rounded vowel (from Germanic short *a* before a nasal), lengthened in an open syllable, is distinctively Western. Although an inaccurate rhyme it is sufficient evidence for the rounded vowel, since the alternative *lane* would be too remote in sound to be tolerable as rhyme.

(v) *warpe* 879 as infin. and pres. is West Midland; it is perhaps a regional development from OE. *weorpan* (see *Seinte Iuliene*, ed. d'Ardenne, p. 169).

But one clear phonological type is found in *Pearl* which does not normally occur in the extreme West. This is in words with earlier *ē* standing before ȝ and a following vowel, or before final *h* (spelt in this MS. ȝ, *gh*). In the extreme West this *ē* remains; farther east it is raised to *ī*. With one apparent exception all the rhymes of this type in *Pearl* are with *ī*: *yȝe* 302, *lyȝe*, *dyȝe*, *syȝe*, rhyming with *sorquydryȝe*, *tryȝe*; *hyȝe* 454; *byȝe* 466; *syȝ (MS. *seȝ*) *hit* 698, rhyming with *justyfyet*, &c.; *dryȝe* 823; *syȝe* 1033. The apparent exception in 200 where *ene (MS. *yȝen*) rhymes with *wene*, *schene*, &c., cannot be regarded as a genuine variant in view of the strong evidence for the *ī* type in rhyme and spelling throughout: it must rather be looked upon as a form not natural to the poet's own speech and used here for the purpose of rhyme. The boundary between the *ī* and *ē* areas cannot be drawn with any precision, but the predominance of *ī* forms at least rules out western Lancashire or Cheshire. In the stanzaic *Life of Christ*, written at Chester, hardly any *ī* forms are found, and in the Hale MS. of romances the proportion of *ē* forms is fairly high.

---

[1] e.g. in 6b the rhyming of *sweuen* 62 and *cleuen* 66 with *meuen*, &c.; and in 40a *heue* 473 (if it is pres. tense, as seems contextually most natural) with *leue* and *greue*.

Rhymes pointing to a northerly part of the West Midland area are:

(i) *among, stronge, longe, fonge* rhyming with *ʒonge* 474; and *euensonge, stronge, longe* with *ʒonge* 535. This pronunciation [ung] can still be heard in south Lancashire and east Cheshire; and actual spellings in *ung* are found in some North-Western manuscripts, as in the Hale MS. of romances and the manuscript of Audelay's poems. This *ung* development is regular and frequently attested only in the North-West Midlands (including part of the West Riding).

(ii) in words containing *o* lengthened in an open syllable. This lengthened *o* had a quality distinct from close *ō* and open *ō* (from OE. *ā*), but when not self-rhymed could rhyme with either, more frequently with open *ō* (from *ā*), to which it was probably nearer. This distinction endures in modern North-West dialects, where ME. *ō* from lengthening has produced [ǫi] as in *coil* 'coal', but ME. *ō* from *ā* has given [uə] as in [uəl] 'whole'. Normally in Midland and Southern dialects *ō* from lengthening seems to have fallen together with *ō* from *ā*. In *Pearl* lengthened *ō* rhymes with *ō* from OE. *ā* in *clos* 183 (mod. dial. *clois*), *porpose* 185, rhyming with *aros, chos*; similarly *porpos* 508, *clos* 512; *schore* 166, rhyming with *more*, and similar rhymes in 231–39. But lengthened *ō* rhymes with close *ō* (OE. *ō*) in *trone* 920, rhyming with *mone* 'moon', &c.; *mote* 972, rhyming with *fote* 'foot'; *lone* 'lane' 1066 (mod. dial. *loin*), rhyming with *mone* 'moon'. In *vpone* 1054 the length given to the *o* may be artificial.

(iii) The Scottish and North-Western auxiliary verb *con*, frequently used in *Pearl*, occurs twice in rhyme, 381, 827.

Thus the phonological and grammatical characteristics proved by rhyme point to a locality certainly in the North-West Midlands, and within this area a region not in the extreme west, and one bordering on the Northern dialect area. The district which best satisfies these conditions is the southern Pennine country.

VOCABULARY

There are in *Pearl* and its companion poems many words apparently peculiar to the North-West, and some of them are still restricted to the dialects of that region. The evidence of such words can hardly be pressed to a definite conclusion in individual cases, since extant ME. texts are too few and often too uncertainly localized to provide complete information, and in modern times the currency of many dialect words has been restricted. Thus *As helde* 1193 is now known only in Lancashire, but the phrase is recorded in ME. texts also from Shropshire. But it is the close relationship between the vocabulary as a whole of the *Pearl* group and the vocabulary of modern dialects of the North-West that is significant. The following list contains a selection of the more distinctive dialect words which occur in *Pearl*. Similar lists can be compiled from the other three poems, and taken together they provide a considerable body of evidence of locality.

cagge 512, *Purity* 1254, 'bind'. Other ME. instances in *Dest. of Troy* 3703, *Wars of Alex.* 1521, which are probably North-Western but from north of the Ribble. Mod. dial. *cadge* in the same sense recorded from Lancs.

deuely 51. Now Yorks. and Ches., and best attested from Ches. See *MÆ.* i. 2. 127.

dryȝly 125, 'continuously'. *Dreely* is similarly used in modern Ches. dialect; applied to unremitting rainfall it is more widespread: Yorks., Lancs., Ches., north-west Derby.

flaȝt 57, 'turf'. Mod. dial. *flaught*, 'a turf dried and used for fuel', Yorks. and Lancs.

helde in the phrase *as helde* 1193, and also found in ME. Shrop.

texts (see note). Still current in south Lancs. and known in the same phrase *as held*.

huyle 41 (see note), *hyul* 1205. Mod. dial. *hile*, 'thick clump of plants' (Rochdale), and in the compounds *whimberry-hile, rush-hile, pisamoor-hile*, 'ant-hill'.

keue 320, 981, 'sink'. Mod. dial. *keave*, 'plunge', Cumb., Westm.

ledden 878, *laden* 874, 'sound (of many voices)'. Modern *ledden*, 'noise, din', south Ches.

schym 1077, 'bright'. Mod. *shim*, Ches., Shrop.

sulpe 726, *Purity* 15, &c., 'pollute, defile'. This may (as Gollancz suggests) be the same word as mod. *soup*, 'soak, drench', Cumb., Westm., Yorks., Lancs.

Still more striking is the local character of the topographical terms in this group of poems. Many of these were rare words, and their close correspondence, not only with the words used in modern dialects, but with the names of places and natural features, in the southern Pennine region gives strong corroboration to the evidence of the rhymes. Thus *greue* (*Pearl* 321, *Sir Gawain* 207, &c.) is the invariable form in the poems, never *groue*, and *greave* is still the usual, and very frequent, form in the place-names of the north-west counties; *bonk* (*Pearl* 102, &c.) similarly, though it is now usually altered to *bank* on maps. *Shore* (as in *Pearl* 166 and *Sir Gawain* 2161 applied to a steep rock-side) occurs as a place-name in south-east Lancashire, as does *Hile* (cf. *Pearl* 41, 1172, 1205). *Tor* (*Pearl* 875, *Purity* 951) is a Pennine name, occurring mostly in Derbyshire, though there are one or two examples in south-east Lancashire. The terms for 'stream' used in the poems are *borne, broke, strynde, gote*: the first two are still commonly used; *strynde* appears in the Derbyshire name Strines, and *gote* is now dialectal *goit* and the name of the river Goyt in north-west Derbyshire. The term *beck* is not used in the poems, and at the present day is rarely found in the Pennine country south of the most northerly parts of Lancashire; similarly, *bach* does not occur in the poems, though it is the usual term for a stream on the Cheshire plain.

Thus the evidence of the topographical terms, as of the rhymes and vocabulary, places the *Pearl* group in the southern Pennine region, the area stretching from the southern edge of the Peak district north-west along the Pennine chain as far as Clitheroe and upper Ribblesdale.

SELECT BIBLIOGRAPHY

This list is intended to include only the more essential and directly relevant publications on *Pearl*. For a fuller list see *A Manual of the Writings in Middle English*, by J. E. Wells, Yale Univ. Press, 1916; supplements 1919, 1923, 1926, 1929, 1932, 1935, 1938, 1941.

The abbreviations of the names of periodicals, &c., are those used by Wells; see his list on pp. 753 f.

EDITIONS

Early English Alliterative Poems, ed. R. Morris, E.E.T.S., 1864. Revised and reprinted 1869, 1885, 1896, 1901. Contains *Pearl, Cleanness (Purity)*, and *Patience*. [M]

Pearl, ed. with modern English rendering by I. Gollancz, London, 1891. [G¹]

—— Revised and privately printed, London, 1897. This text was not available.

The Pearl, ed. C. G. Osgood, Boston, 1906. [O]

Pearl, ed. with modern rendering, together with Boccaccio's *Olympia*, by Sir Israel Gollancz, London, 1921. [G²]

The Pearl, ed. S. P. Chase and students of Bowdoin College, Boston, 1932. [C]

Lines 361–612 in K. Sisam's *Fourteenth Century Verse and Prose*, Oxford, 1923. [S]

Editions of the other poems ascribed to the author of *Pearl*.

Sir Gawain, ed. Sir F. Madden for the Bannatyne Club, 1839.

—— ed. R. Morris, E.E.T.S., 1864. Text revised by Sir I. Gollancz 1897, 1912.

—— ed. J. R. R. Tolkien and E. V. Gordon, Oxford, 1925; corrected impressions 1930, 1936.

—— re-edited by Sir I. Gollancz, E.E.T.S., 1940. A new edition with notes, based on material left by Gollancz, revised by Dr. M. Day, with new introduction. Study of the dialect of the MS, Cotton Nero A. x., by Dr. M. S. Serjeantson.

Purity, ed. R. J. Menner, Yale Univ. Press, 1920.

—— ed. Sir I. Gollancz, as *Cleanness*, London, 1921. Part II (Glossary and illustrative texts) with the assistance of Dr. M. Day, 1933.

Patience, ed. H. Bateson, Manchester Univ. Press, 1912 ; 2nd ed. 1918.
—— ed. Sir I. Gollancz, London, 1913 ; 2nd ed. 1924.
Saint Erkenwald, ed. C. Horstmann, in *Altenglische Legenden (Neue Folge)*, Heilbronn, 1881. Text only.
—— ed. Sir I. Gollancz, London, 1922.
—— ed. L. Savage, Yale Univ. Press, 1926.

FACSIMILE

Pearl, Cleanness, Patience, and Sir Gawain, reproduced in facsimile from MS. Cotton Nero A. x. in the British Museum, with an introduction by Sir I. Gollancz, E.E.T.S., 1923. Useful information added in review by W. W. Greg, *MLR.* xix. 223.

LITERARY SOURCES AND ANALOGUES

Le Roman de la Rose, par Guillaume de Lorris et Jean de Meun, ed. by E. Langlois, 5 vols. Paris, 1914–24.
The Romaunt of the Rose (the Chaucerian translation of the *Roman de la Rose*), ed. by W. W. Skeat in vol. i of the Oxford Chaucer, or ed. by F. N. Robinson in his edition of Chaucer, pp. 663 f.
Olympia, ed. and translated by Sir Israel Gollancz in his 2nd ed. of *Pearl*, 1921.
Biblia Sacra Vulgatae Editionis, ed. by P. M. Hetzenauer, Innsbruck, 1906.
Novum Testamentum Latine secundum editionem Sancti Hieronymi, editio minor by H. J. White, Oxford, 1911. The handiest edition of the Vulgate New Testament.
Sancti Aurelii Augustini *Opera Omnia* in Migne's *Patrologia Latina*, vols. 32–44.

THE HISTORICAL BACKGROUND

Kunz and Stevenson, *The Book of the Pearl*, London, 1908.
L. Pannier, *Les Lapidaires français du moyen âge des xiiᵉ, xiiiᵉ, et xivᵉ siècles*, Paris, 1882.
P. Studer and J. Evans, *Anglo-Norman Lapidaries*, Paris, 1924.
J. Evans and M. S. Serjeantson, *English Medieval Lapidaries*, E.E.T.S., 1933.

THEME AND STRUCTURE

C. F. Brown, 'The Author of *The Pearl* considered in the Light of his Theological Opinions', *PMLA*. xix (1904), 115–53.

W. H. Schofield, 'The Nature and Fabric of *The Pearl*', *PMLA*. xix (1904), 154–215: maintains that *Pearl* is an allegory.

—— 'Symbolism, Allegory, and Autobiography in *The Pearl*', *PMLA*. xxiv (1909), 585–675: abandons systematic allegory, but still denies the personal reference of the poem.

G. G. Coulton, 'In Defence of *The Pearl*', *MLR*. ii (1906), 39–43: destructive analysis of Schofield's first article.

R. M. Garrett, '*The Pearl*: an Interpretation', Univ. of Washington, Seattle, 1918: the Pearl interpreted as a symbol of the Eucharist. (See review by C. F. Brown, *MLN*. xxxiv (1919), 42, and the comments by Sister Mary Madeleva.)

J. B. Fletcher, 'The Allegory of the Pearl', *JEGPh*. xx (1921), 1 ff.: that *Pearl* is at once an allegory and an elegy. The Pearl is taken to symbolize the Virgin Mary in spite of stanza 37.

W. K. Greene, '*The Pearl*: a New Interpretation', *PMLA*. xl (1925), 814–27: that the vision is a mere literary device, and the maiden herself a mere lay figure for the conduct of a theological discourse.

Sister Mary Madeleva, '*Pearl*: A Study in Spiritual Dryness', New York, 1925: the best known and most elaborate attempt to establish total allegory; breaks down signally on the references to the child. And why, if the Pearl is an allegory of the poet's loss of the sensible sweetness of God, should it be necessary to discuss at length the place in Heaven of innocent children?

E. Hart, *MLN*. xlii (1927), 113–16: answers fully the objection raised by Sister M. Madeleva that 'innocents' were not 'virgins'.

R. Wellek, '*The Pearl*: An Interpretation of the Middle English Poem', *Studies in English*, IV, Charles University, Prague, 1933. Excellent summary with useful contributions.

D. W. Robertson, Jr., 'The "Heresy" of *The Pearl*: The Pearl as a symbol', *MLN*. lxv (1950), 152–61.

LITERARY HISTORY

The Cambridge History of English Literature, vol. i, chap. xv (by I. Gollancz), Cambridge, 1907.

J. P. Oakden, *Alliterative Poetry in Middle English*, vol. ii. *A Survey of the Traditions*, Manchester, 1935, pp. 69 f.

THE AUTHOR

H. N. MacCracken, 'Concerning Huchown', *PMLA*. xxv (1910), 507–34.

O. Cargill and M. Schlauch, '*The Pearl* and its Jeweller', *PMLA*. xliii (1928), 105–23.

C. O. Chapman, 'The Musical Training of the *Pearl* Poet', *PMLA*. xlvi (1931), 177–181.

—— 'The Authorship of *The Pearl*', *PMLA*. xlvii (1932), 346–53.

METRE

C. S. Northup, 'The Metrical Structure of *Pearl*', *PMLA*. xii (1897), 326–40.

M. Medary and A. C. L. Brown, articles on the stanza-linking, in *The Romanic Review*, vii (1916), 243 ff. and 271 ff.

C. O. Chapman, 'Numerical Symbolism in Dante and *The Pearl*', *MLN*. liv (1939), 256 ff.

TEXTUAL AND INTERPRETATIVE

W. Fick, Prefatory notes to the work listed under Language, below. [F]

H. Bradley, *Academy* xxxviii. 201 and 249. On lines 689–92.

R. Morris, *Academy* xxxix. 602, and xl. 76.

F. Holthausen, Herrig's *Archiv* xc. 142–8. [H]

O. F. Emerson, *Modern Philology* xix (1921), 131 ff. [E¹]; *PMLA*. xxxvii (1922), 52 f. [E²]; *PMLA*. xlii (1927), 807 ff. [E³]

A. S. Cook, *Modern Philology* vi (1908), 197 ff.

E. Tuttle, *MLR*. xv (1920), 298 f.

E. V. Gordon and C. T. Onions, *Medium Ævum* i. 2 (1932), 126 ff., and ii. 3 (1933), 165 ff.

M. Day, *Medium Ævum* iii. 3 (1934), 241 f.

P. J. Thomas, 'Notes on *The Pearl*', *London Medieval Studies*, ed. Chambers, Norman, and Smith (1935), vol. i.

E. M. Wright, *JEGPh*. xxxviii (1939), 1 ff. ('Notes on *Pearl*', wrongly entitled 'Additional Notes on *Sir Gawain and the Green Knight*').

—— *JEGPh*. xxxix (1940), 315 ff.

J. Sledd, *MLN*. lv (1940), 381. *Inlyche* and *rewarde*.

Mary V. Hillman, *MLN.* lvi (1941), 457 (*Inlyche* and *rewarde*) ; *MLN.* lviii (1943), 42 ; *MLN.* lix (1944), 417 ; *MLN.* lx (1945), 241.

Marie P. Hamilton, *MLN.* lviii (1943), 370.

Dorothy Everett and Naomi D. Hurnard, 'Legal Phraseology in a passage in *Pearl*', *Medium Ævum* xvi (1947), 9 ff.

LANGUAGE

W. Fick, *Zum mittelenglischen Gedicht von der Perle. Eine Lautuntersuchung,* Kiel, 1885.

F. Knigge, *Die Sprache des Dichters von Sir Gawain and the Green Knight, der sogenannten Early English Alliterative Poems, und De Erkenwalde,* Marburg, 1885.

J. R. Hulbert, 'The "West Midland" of the Romances', *Modern Philology* xix (1921–2), 9 and 11.

M. S. Serjeantson, 'The Dialects of the West Midlands', *Review of English Studies* iii (1927), 54 f., 186 f., 319 ff. See especially p. 327.

J. P. Oakden, *Alliterative Poetry in Middle English,* vol. i, *The Dialectal and Metrical Survey,* Manchester, 1931.

DICTIONARIES

A New English Dictionary on Historical Principles, ed. Sir J. A. H. Murray, H. Bradley, Sir W. Craigie, C. T. Onions. 10 vols. Oxford, 1888–1928. [*NED*.].

The English Dialect Dictionary, ed. J. Wright. 6 vols. Oxford, 1898–1905. [*EDD*.].

NOTE ON THE EDITED TEXT

The spelling of the manuscript is reproduced except for corrections or scribal errors. Emendations are indicated by footnotes where the original forms of the manuscript are quoted. When the emendation was made by an earlier editor or commentator, his identity is indicated by the initial letter of his surname. A selection of variant readings proposed in earlier editions is also included in the footnotes, and these, too, are referred to their authors by an initial. The initials used and the names referred to are given below.[1] Spellings normalized by earlier editors are not treated as variants.

No emendations have been introduced into the text on metrical grounds, but rhymes have been restored in several places where the original form is clearly indicated by rhyme and general usage. Variant types of spelling in rhyme are left unchanged if it seems likely that they were current variants of identical sounds, as, for example, the final syllables of the rhyme-words *reprené* and *peny*.

The contractions of the manuscript forms have been expanded without notice. There can be no doubt about any of them except q̵ and wᵗ. q̵ was a normal abbreviation of Latin *quod*, but in vernacular manuscripts was used also for the past tense of the verb; the word is nowhere written in full in the manuscript, and q̵ may be taken as representing its usual *quod* (so Dr. Sisam and this text), or, since the form *cope* occurs in *Sir Gawain* 776, *quoþ* may be regarded as the expanded form (so Gollancz). Wᵗ is a form of the preposition 'with', which when written in full is sometimes spelled with *i* and sometimes with *y*. In the manuscript as a whole and in the text of *Pearl*, spellings with *y* are more numerous, and *wyth* has accordingly been adopted as the expansion in this text. Words which stand divided in the manuscript, such as *in noghe* for *innoghe* 366, have been joined without indication of the manuscript division. But when the second element begins with *v*, which indicates an initial letter, a hyphenated form has been used, as in *on-vunder*, &c. The long *i* of the manuscript is printed as *j*, except

[1] E = O. F. Emerson   G = Israel Gollancz   O = C. G. Osgood
     C = S. P. Chase   H = F. Holthausen   S = K. Sisam
     F = W. Fick   M = R. Morris

For details of editions and notes by these scholars, see the Bibliography.

in *iwysse*, *ichose*, and the pronoun *I*. Capital letters are used as in modern English, and the editor is responsible also for the punctuation. The only diacritic that has been added to manuscript forms is the acute accent, used to mark a final weakly stressed *e* when it stands for etymological *i* or Old French *é*, as in *cortaysé* 480.

The text is edited from a new transcription of the manuscript, from which a few new readings were obtained: *profered* 235 is legible; *niyʒt* 630 is possible for *myʒt* of earlier editions; *ʒys* 635 is legible; *hande* 802 for earlier *lande* is possible.

The treatment of the text is conservative, the manuscript forms being retained in numerous places where they had been altered by editors and commentators, but new emendations are made in lines 210, 358, 616, 935, 1012, 1064, and earlier tentative suggestions accepted and supported in 672 and 1086.

PEARL

I

Perle, plesaunte to prynces paye
 To clanly clos in golde so clere,
 Oute of oryent, I hardyly saye,
Ne proued I neuer her precios pere.
So rounde, so reken in vche araye,   5
So smal, so smoþe her sydeȝ were,
Quere-so-euer I jugged gemmeȝ gaye,
I sette hyr sengeley in synglere.
Allas! I leste hyr in on erbere;
Þurȝ gresse to grounde hit fro me yot.   10
I dewyne, fordolked of luf-daungere
Of þat pryuy perle wythouten spot.

Syþen in þat spote hit fro me sprange,
Ofte haf I wayted, wyschande þat wele,
Þat wont watȝ whyle deuoyde my wrange   15
And heuen my happe and al my hele.
Þat dotȝ bot þrych my hert þrange,
My breste in bale bot bolne and bele;
Ȝet þoȝt me neuer so swete a sange
As stylle stounde let to me stele.   20
For soþe þer fleten to me fele,
To þenke hir color so clad in clot.
O moul, þou marreȝ a myry iuele,
My priuy perle wythouten spotte.

---

8 synglere F, G¹, syngulere O, G², C: synglure MS. 11 fordolked
MS, C: fordokked G, Kölbing, M (Acad. xxxix. 602). 17 hert: herte
G, E¹, C. 23 iuele: mele M, G.

Þat spot of spyseȝ mot nedeȝ sprede,   25
Þer such rycheȝ to rot is runne;
Blomeȝ blayke and blwe and rede
Þer schyneȝ ful schyr agayn þe sunne.
Flor and fryte may not be fede
Þer hit doun drof in moldeȝ dunne;   30
For vch gresse mot grow of grayneȝ dede;
No whete were elleȝ to woneȝ wonne.
Of goud vche goude is ay bygonne;
So semly a sede moȝt fayly not,
Þat spryngande spyceȝ vp ne sponne   35
Of þat precios perle wythouten spotte.

To þat spot þat I in speche expoun   f. 39^b
I entred in þat erber grene,
In Augoste in a hyȝ seysoun,
Quen corne is coruen wyth crokeȝ kene.   40
On huyle þer perle hit trendeled doun
Schadowed þis worteȝ ful schyre and schene,
Gilofre, gyngure and gromylyoun,
And pyonys powdered ay bytwene.
Ȝif hit watȝ semly on to sene,   45
A fayr reflayr ȝet fro hit flot.
Þer wonys þat worþyly, I wot and wene,
My precious perle wythouten spot.

Bifore þat spot my honde I spenned
For care ful colde þat to me caȝt;   50
A deuely dele in my hert denned,
Þaȝ resoun sette myseluen saȝt.

25 mot *O*, myȝt *M*, *G*¹: *all but* t *blotted in MS.*   26 runne *G*: runnen *MS.*   35 spryngande *M*: sprygande *MS.*   46 fayr reflayr *MS*: fayrre flayr *G*¹.   49 spenned *M, O, G*²: spennd *MS, G*¹.   51 deuely *MS, G*², *C*: dencly *M, G*¹, deruely *O*.

I playned my perle þat þer watȝ spenned
Wyth fyrce skylleȝ þat faste faȝt;
Þaȝ kynde of Kryst me comfort kenned,   55
My wreched wylle in wo ay wraȝte.
I felle vpon þat floury flaȝt,
Suche odour to my herneȝ schot;
I slode vpon a slepyng-slaȝte
On þat precios perle wythouten spot.   60

II

Fro spot my spyryt þer sprang in space;
My body on balke þer bod in sweuen.
My goste is gon in Godeȝ grace
In auenture þer meruayleȝ meuen.
I ne wyste in þis worlde quere þat hjt wace,   65
Bot I knew me keste þer klyfeȝ cleuen;
Towarde a foreste I bere þe face,
Where rych rokkeȝ wer to dyscreuen.
Þe lyȝt of hem myȝt no mon leuen,
Þe glemande glory þat of hem glent;   70
For wern neuer webbeȝ þat wyȝeȝ weuen
Of half so dere adubbemente.

Dubbed wern alle þo downeȝ sydeȝ   f. 40ª
Wyth crystal klyffeȝ so cler of kynde.
Holtewodeȝ bryȝt aboute hem bydeȝ   75
Of bolleȝ as blwe as ble of Ynde;
As bornyst syluer þe lef on slydeȝ,
Þat þike con trylle on vch a tynde.

---

53 spenned *MS*: penned *H, G²*, *E²*, *C*.   54 fyrce *H, G²*: fyrte *MS*,
M, G¹, O, E³, C.   60 precios *M*: precos *MS*.   68 ryche *G, E¹, C*.
72 adubbemente *G*: adubmente *MS*.

Quen glem of glode3 agayn3 hem glyde3,
Wyth schymeryng schene ful schrylle þaý schynde.   80
Þe grauayl þat on grounde con grynde
Wern precious perle3 of oryente:
Þe sunnebeme3 bot blo and blynde
In respecte of þat adubbement.

The adubbemente of þo downe3 dere   85
Garten my goste al greffe for3ete.
So frech flauore3 of fryte3 were,
As fode hit con me fayre refete.
Fowle3 þer flowen in fryth in fere,
Of flaumbande hwe3, boþe smale and grete;   90
Bot sytole-stryng and gyternere
Her reken myrþe mo3t not retrete;
For quen þose brydde3 her wynge3 bete,
Þay songen wyth a swete asent.
So gracios gle couþe no mon gete   95
As here and se her adubbement.

So al wat3 dubbet on dere asyse
Þat fryth þer fortwne forth me fere3.
Þe derþe þerof for to deuyse
Nis no wy3 worþé þat tonge bere3.   100
I welke ay forth in wely wyse;
No bonk so byg þat did me dere3.
Þe fyrre in þe fryth, þe feier con ryse
Þe playn, þe plontte3, þe spyse, þe pere3;
And rawe3 and rande3 and rych reuere3,   105
As fyldor fyn her bonkes brent.
I wan to a water by schore þat schere3—
Lorde, dere wat3 hit adubbement!

81 þat [I] on *H, G²*.   89 flowen: w *altered from* 3 *in MS*.   95
gracios *M*: gracos *MS*.   103 feirer *G*.   106 bonkes, o *imperfect*
in MS.

The dubbemente of þo derworth depe   f. 40^b
Wern bonkeȝ bene of beryl bryȝt.   110
Swangeande swete þe water con swepe,
Wyth a rownande rourde raykande aryȝt.
In þe founce þer stonden stoneȝ stepe,
As glente þurȝ glas þat glowed and glyȝt,
As stremande sterneȝ, quen stroþe-men slepe,   115
Staren in welkyn in wynter nyȝt;
For vche a pobbel in pole þer pyȝt
Watȝ emerad, saffer, oþer gemme gente,
Þat alle þe loȝe lemed of lyȝt,
So dere watȝ hit adubbement.   120

III

The dubbement dere of doun and daleȝ,
Of wod and water and wlonk playneȝ,
Bylde in me blys, abated my baleȝ,
Fordidden my stresse, dystryed my payneȝ.
Doun after a strem þat dryȝly haleȝ   125
I bowed in blys, bredful my brayneȝ;
Þe fyrre I folȝed þose floty valeȝ,
Þe more strenghþe of ioye myn herte strayneȝ.
As fortune fares þer as ho frayneȝ,
Wheþer solace ho sende oþer elleȝ sore,   130
Þe wyȝ to wham her wylle ho wayneȝ
Hytteȝ to haue ay more and more.

More of wele watȝ in þat wyse
Þen I cowþe telle þaȝ I tom hade,
For vrþely herte myȝt not suffyse   135
To þe tenþe dole of þo gladneȝ glade;

111 Swangeande: s *altered from* w *in MS.* 115 As *M*: a *MS.*
122 wlonk: wlonke *G, E*[1], *C.* 134 þaȝ tom I hade *H, G*[2]. 136
gladneȝ: Gladneȝ *G,* gladeneȝ *E*[3].

Forþy I þo3t þat Paradyse
Wat3 þer ouer gayn þo bonke3 brade.
I hoped þe water were a deuyse
Bytwene myrþe3 by mere3 made;   140
By3onde þe broke, by slente oþer slade,
I hoped þat mote merked wore.
Bot þe water wat3 depe, I dorst not wade,
And euer me longed ay more and more.

More and more, and 3et wel mare,   f. 41ª 145
Me lyste to se þe broke by3onde;
For if hit wat3 fayr þer I con fare,
Wel loueloker wat3 þe fyrre londe.
Abowte me con I stote and stare;
To fynde a forþe faste con I fonde.   150
Bot woþe3 mo iwysse þer ware,
Þe fyrre I stalked by þe stronde.
And euer me þo3t I schulde not wonde
For wo þer wele3 so wynne wore.
Þenne nwe note me com on honde   155
Þat meued my mynde ay more and more.

More meruayle con my dom adaunt:
I se3 by3onde þat myry mere
A crystal clyffe ful relusaunt;
Mony ryal ray con fro hit rere.   160
At þe fote þerof þer sete a faunt,
A mayden of menske, ful debonere;
Blysnande whyt wat3 hyr bleaunt.
I knew hyr wel, I hade sen hyr ere.

138 ouer *G²*, over *O*: oþer *MS*.   140 myrþe3: myrche3 *M* (*Acad.*
xxxix. 603); Bytwene mere3 by Myrþe *G*.   142 hoped *M*, *G*, *C*:
hope *MS*, *O*.   144 ay *G*: a *MS*, *O*, *C*.   154 wo *MS*, *O*, *E³*, *C*:
woþe *G²*.

As glysnande golde þat man con schere,   165
So schon þat schene an-vnder shore.
On lenghe I loked to hyr þere;
Þe lenger, I knew hyr more and more.

The more I frayste hyr fayre face,
Her fygure fyn quen I had fonte,   170
Suche gladande glory con to me glace
As lyttel byfore þerto watȝ wonte.
To calle hyr lyste con me enchace,
Bot baysment gef myn hert a brunt.
I seȝ hyr in so strange a place,   175
Such a burre myȝt make myn herte blunt.
Þenne vereȝ ho vp her fayre frount,
Hyr vysayge whyt as playn yuore:
Þat stonge myn hert ful stray atount,
And euer þe lenger, þe more and more.   180

IV

More þen me lyste my drede aros.   f. 41^{b}
I stod ful stylle and dorste not calle;
Wyth yȝen open and mouth ful clos
I stod as hende as hawk in halle.
I hoped þat gostly watȝ þat porpose;   185
I dred onende quat schulde byfalle,
Lest ho me eschaped þat I þer chos,
Er I at steuen hir moȝt stalle.
Þat gracios gay wythouten galle,
So smoþe, so smal, so seme slyȝt,   190
Ryseȝ vp in hir araye ryalle,
A precios pyece in perleȝ pyȝt.

179 atount *MS, M, O*: astount *G, C*.   185 hoped *G, C*: hope *MS,
M, O*.   192 precios *M*: precos *MS*.

Perleȝ pyȝte of ryal prys
Þere moȝt mon by grace haf sene,
Quen þat frech as flor-de-lys   195
Doun þe bonke con boȝe bydene.
Al blysnande whyt watȝ hir beau biys,
Vpon at sydeȝ, and bounden bene
Wyth þe myryeste margarys, at my deuyse,
Þat euer I seȝ ȝet with myn ene;   200
Wyth lappeȝ large, I wot and I wene,
Dubbed with double perle and dyȝte;
Her cortel of self sute schene,
Wyth precios perleȝ al vmbepyȝte.

A pyȝt coroune ȝet wer þat gyrle   205
Of mariorys and non oþer ston,
Hiȝe pynakled of cler quyt perle,
Wyth flurted flowreȝ perfet vpon.
To hed hade ho non oþer werle;
Her here leke, al hyr vmbegon,   210
Her semblaunt sade for doc oþer erle,
Her ble more blaȝt þen whalleȝ bon.
As schorne golde schyr her fax þenne schon,
On schyldereȝ þat leghe vnlapped lyȝte.
Her depe colour ȝet wonted non   215
Of precios perle in porfyl pyȝte.

Pyȝt watȝ poyned and vche a hemme   f. 42ᵃ
At honde, at sydeȝ, at ouerture,
Wyth whyte perle and non oþer gemme,
And bornyste quyte watȝ hyr uesture.   220

197 beau biys: beauuiys *MS*, beau uiys *M*, beau mys *G*, *C*, bleaunt of
biys *O*.   200 ene *G*, *C*: yȝen *MS*, *M*, *O*.   209 werle *MS*, *M*, *G*, *C*:
herle *O*.   210 here leke: lere leke *MS*, here-leke *O*, *E*³, *C*, here heke
M, *G*.   217 Pyȝt watȝ poyned & *MS*, *Craigie*, *G*²: Pyȝt & poyned
watȝ, *G*¹, *O*, *C*.

Bot a wonder perle wythouten wemme
Inmydde3 hyr breste wat3 sette so sure;
A manne3 dom mo3t dry3ly demme,
Er mynde mo3t malte in hit mesure.
I hope no tong mo3t endure　　　　　　　225
No sauerly saghe say of þat sy3t,
So wat3 hit clene and cler and pure,
Þat precios perle þer hit wat3 py3t.

Py3t in perle, þat precios pyece
On wyþer half water com doun þe schore.　　230
No gladder gome heþen into Grece
Þen I, quen ho on brymme wore.
Ho wat3 me nerre þen aunte or nece;
My joy forþy wat3 much þe more.
Ho profered me speche, þat special spece,　　235
Enclynande lowe in wommon lore,
Ca3te of her coroun of grete tresore
And haylsed me wyth a lote ly3te.
Wel wat3 me þat euer I wat3 bore
To sware þat swete in perle3 py3te!　　　　240

V

'O perle', quod I, 'in perle3 py3t,
Art þou my perle þat I haf playned,
Regretted by myn one on ny3te?
Much longeyng haf I for þe layned,
Syþen into gresse þou me agly3te.　　　　245
Pensyf, payred, I am forpayned,
And þou in a lyf of lykyng ly3te,
In Paradys erde, of stryf vnstrayned.

225 tonge *G, E¹, C*.　　229 pece *F, E²*: pyse *MS*, pryse *M*, pyece *G,
O, C*.　　235 spece *G, O, C*: spyce *MS, M*.

What wyrde haþ3 hyder my iuel vayned,
And don me in þys del and gret daunger? 250
Fro we in twynne wern towen and twayned,
I haf ben a joyle3 iuelere.'

That iuel þenne in gemme3 gente   f. 42ᵇ
Vered vp her vyse wyth y3en graye,
Set on hyr coroun of perle orient, 255
And soberly after þenne con ho say:
'Sir, 3e haf your tale mysetente,
To say your perle is al awaye,
Þat is in cofer so comly clente
As in þis gardyn gracios gaye, 260
Hereinne to lenge for euer and play,
Þer mys nee mornyng com neuer nere.
Her were a forser for þe, in faye,
If þou were a gentyl iueler.

'Bot, iueler gente, if þou schal lose 265
Þy ioy for a gemme þat þe wat3 lef,
Me þynk þe put in a mad porpose,
And busye3 þe aboute a raysoun bref;
For þat þou leste3 wat3 bot a rose
Þat flowred and fayled as kynde hyt gef. 270
Now þur3 kynde of þe kyste þat hyt con close
To a perle of prys hit is put in pref.
And þou hat3 called þy wyrde a þef,
Þat o3t of no3t hat3 mad þe cler;
Þou blame3 þe bote of þy meschef, 275
Þou art no kynde iueler.'

A iuel to me þen wat3 þys geste,
And iuele3 wern hyr gentyl sawe3.

262 nere *O, G*, ner *E²*, *C*: here *MS, M, E³*.

'Iwyse', quod I, 'my blysfol beste,
My grete dystresse þou al todraweȝ.   280
To be excused I make requeste;
I trawed my perle don out of daweȝ.
Now haf I fonde hyt, I schal ma feste,
And wony wyth hyt in schyr wod-schaweȝ,
And loue my Lorde and al his laweȝ   285
Þat hatȝ me broȝt þys blys ner.
Now were I at yow byȝonde þise waweȝ,
I were a ioyful jueler.'

'Jueler', sayde þat gemme clene,   f. 43ᵃ
'Wy borde ȝe men? So madde ȝe be!   290
Þre wordeȝ hatȝ þou spoken at ene:
Vnavysed, for soþe, wern alle þre.
Þou ne woste in worlde quat on dotȝ mene;
Þy worde byfore þy wytte con fle.
Þou says þou traweȝ me in þis dene,   295
Bycawse þou may wyth yȝen me se;
Anoþer þou says, in þys countré
Þyself schal won wyth me ryȝt here;
Þe þrydde, to passe þys water fre—
Þat may no ioyfol jueler.   300

VI

'I halde þat iueler lyttel to prayse
Þat leueȝ wel þat he seȝ wyth yȝe,
And much to blame and vncortayse
Þat leueȝ oure Lorde wolde make a lyȝe,

286 broȝt *M* : broȝ *MS* ; blys : blysse *G, E¹, C.*   290 Wy, lordeȝemen *F* ;
men : mon *E³.*   302 leueȝ *G* : loueȝ *MS, M, O, C.*   303 vncortayse
G : vncortoyse *MS.*   304 leueȝ : lyueȝ *altered to* leueȝ *in MS.*

Þat lelly hyȝte your lyf to rayse,   305
Þaȝ fortune dyd your flesch to dyȝe.
Ȝe setten hys wordeȝ ful westernays
Þat leueȝ noþynk bot ȝe hit syȝe.
And þat is a poynt o sorquydryȝe,
Þat vche god mon may euel byseme,   310
To leue no tale be true to tryȝe
Bot þat hys one skyl may dem.

'Deme now þyself if þou con dayly
As man to God wordeȝ schulde heue.
Þou saytȝ þou schal won in þis bayly;   315
Me þynk þe burde fyrst aske leue,
And ȝet of graunt þou myȝteȝ fayle.
Þou wylneȝ ouer þys water to weue;
Er moste þou ceuer to oþer counsayle:
Þy corse in clot mot calder keue.   320
For hit watȝ forgarte at Paradys greue;
Oure ȝorefader hit con misseȝeme.
Þurȝ drwry deth boȝ vch man dreue,
Er ouer þys dam hym Dryȝtyn deme.'

'Demeȝ þou me', quod I, 'my swete,   f. 43ᵇ   325
To dol agayn, þenne I dowyne.
Now haf I fonte þat I forlete,
Schal I efte forgo hit er euer I fyne?
Why schal I hit boþe mysse and mete?
My precios perle dotȝ me gret pyne.   330
What serueȝ tresor, bot gareȝ men grete
When he hit schal efte wyth teneȝ tyne?

307 westernays *MS, M, Bradley, G*: besternays *O*, bestornays *E²*, *C*.
308 leueȝ *G, O, E², C*: loueȝ *MS*.   309 is *M*: ſs *MS*.   312 dem: deme
G, C.   319 counsayle *G, E³, C*: counsayl *MS*.   323 man *G¹*: ma
MS, M, O, G², C.   331 gareȝ *MS*: gare *G*.

Now rech I neuer for to declyne,
Ne how fer of folde þat man me fleme.
When I am partleȝ of perle myne, 335
Bot durande doel what may men deme?'

'Thow demeȝ noȝt bot doel-dystresse',
Þenne sayde þat wyȝt. 'Why dotȝ þou so?
For dyne of doel of lureȝ lesse
Ofte mony mon forgos þe mo. 340
Þe oȝte better þyseluen blesse,
And loue ay God, in wele and wo,
For anger gayneȝ þe not a cresse.
Who nedeȝ schal þole, be not so þro.
For þoȝ þou daunce as any do, 345
Braundysch and bray þy braþeȝ breme,
When þou no fyrre may, to ne fro,
Þou moste abyde þat he schal deme.

'Deme Dryȝtyn, euer hym adyte,
Of þe way a fote ne wyl he wryþe. 350
Þy mendeȝ mounteȝ not a myte,
Þaȝ þou for sorȝe be neuer blyþe.
Stynt of þy strot and fyne to flyte,
And sech hys blyþe ful swefte and swyþe.
Þy prayer may hys pyté byte, 355
Þat mercy schal hyr crafteȝ kyþe.
Hys comforte may þy langour lyþe
And þy lureȝ of lyȝtly fleme;
For, marre oþer madde, morne and myþe,
Al lys in hym to dyȝt and deme.' 360

335 perle *O, G², C*: perleȝ *MS, M, G¹*.   342 in *M*: & *MS, O*.   353
stynt *G, C*: stynst *MS, M, O*.   358 And: & *MS*, þat alle *G²*; fleme:
leme *MS, M, G, O*.   359 marre *MS, M*: marred *G, O, E³, C*; madde:
mende *H*.

VII

Thenne demed I to þat damyselle: f. 44ᵃ
'Ne worþe no wrathþe vnto my Lorde,
If rapely I raue, spornande in spelle.
My herte watȝ al wyth mysse remorde,
As wallande water gotȝ out of welle.   365
I do me ay in hys myserecorde.
Rebuke me neuer wyth wordeȝ felle,
Þaȝ I forloyne, my dere endorde,
Bot kyþeȝ me kyndely your coumforde,
Pytosly þenkande vpon þysse: 370
Of care and me ȝe made acorde,
Þat er watȝ grounde of alle my blysse.

'My blysse, my bale, ȝe han ben boþe,
Bot much þe bygger ȝet watȝ my mon;
Fro þou watȝ wroken fro vch a woþe,   375
I wyste neuer quere my perle watȝ gon.
Now I hit se, now leþeȝ my loþe.
And, quen we departed, we wern at on;
God forbede we be now wroþe,
We meten so selden by stok oþer ston.   380
Þaȝ cortaysly ȝe carp con,
I am bot mol and manereȝ mysse.
Bot Crystes mersy and Mary and Jon,
Þise arn þe grounde of alle my blisse.

'In blysse I se þe blyþely blent,   385
And I a man al mornyf mate;
Ȝe take þeron ful lyttel tente,
Þaȝ I hente ofte harmeȝ hate.

363 I *supplied by* G.   369 kyþeȝ H: lyþeȝ MS.   378 And: & MS,
If E³.   381 carpe G, C.   382 manereȝ H, G², C: marereȝ MS,
M, O, marreȝ G¹, mariereȝ *Schofield*.

Bot now I am here in your presente,
I wolde bysech, wythouten debate, 390
3e wolde me say in sobre asente
What lyf 3e lede erly and late.
For I am ful fayn þat your astate
Is worþen to worschyp and wele, iwysse;
Of alle my joy þe hy3e gate, 395
Hit is in grounde of alle my blysse.'

'Now blysse, burne, mot þe bytyde', f. 44^b
Þen sayde þat lufsoum of lyth and lere,
'And welcum here to walk and byde,
For now þy speche is to me dere. 400
Maysterful mod and hy3e pryde,
I hete þe, arn heterly hated here.
My Lorde ne loue3 not for to chyde,
For meke arn alle þat wone3 hym nere;
And when in hys place þou schal apere, 405
Be dep deuote in hol mekenesse.
My Lorde þe Lamb loue3 ay such chere,
Þat is þe grounde of alle my blysse.

'A blysful lyf þou says I lede;
Þou wolde3 knaw þerof þe stage. 410
Þow wost wel when þy perle con schede
I wat3 ful 3ong and tender of age;
Bot my Lorde þe Lombe þur3 hys godhede,
He toke myself to hys maryage,
Corounde me quene in blysse to brede 415
In lenghe of daye3 þat euer schal wage;
And sesed in alle hys herytage
Hys lef is. I am holy hysse:
Hys prese, hys prys, and hys parage
Is rote and grounde of alle my blysse.' 420

396 in MS: and S.   406 mekenysse E³, C.

VIII

'Blysful', quod I, 'may þys be trwe?
Dysplese3 not if I speke errour.
Art þou þe quene of heuene3 blwe,
Þat al þys worlde schal do honour?
We leuen on Marye þat grace of grewe,   425
Þat ber a barne of vyrgyn flour;
Þe croune fro hyr quo mo3t remwe
Bot ho hir passed in sum fauour?
Now, for synglerty o hyr dousour,
We calle hyr Fenyx of Arraby,   430
Þat freles fle3e of hyr fasor,
Lyk to þe Quen of cortaysye.'

'Cortayse Quen', þenne sayde þat gaye,   f. 45ᵃ
Knelande to grounde, folde vp hyr face,
'Makele3 Moder and myryest May,   435
Blessed bygynner of vch a grace!'
Þenne ros ho vp and con restay,
And speke me towarde in þat space:
'Sir, fele here porchase3 and fonge3 pray,
Bot supplantore3 none wythinne þys place.   440
Þat emperise al heuen3 hat3,
And vrþe and helle, in her bayly;
Of erytage 3et non wyl ho chace,
For ho is Quen of cortaysye.

'The court of þe kyndom of God alyue   445
Hat3 a property in hytself beyng:
Alle þat may þerinne aryue
Of alle þe reme is quen oþer kyng,

433 sayde *M*: syde *MS*.   436 bygynner *M*: bȳgyner *MS*.   441
heuen3 *MS*, *M*: heuene3 *O*, *C*.

And neuer oþer ȝet schal depryue,
Bot vchon fayn of oþereȝ hafyng,   450
And wolde her corouneȝ wern worþe þo fyue,
If possyble were her mendyng.
Bot my Lady of quom Jesu con spryng,
Ho haldeȝ þe empyre ouer vus ful hyȝe;
And þat dyspleseȝ non of oure gyng,   455
For ho is Quene of cortaysye.

'Of courtaysye, as saytȝ Saynt Poule,
Al arn we membreȝ of Jesu Kryst:
As heued and arme and legg and naule
Temen to hys body ful trwe and tryste,   460
Ryȝt so is vch a Krysten sawle
A longande lym to þe Mayster of myste.
Þenne loke what hate oþer any gawle
Is tached oþer tyȝed þy lymmeȝ bytwyste.
Þy heued hatȝ nauþer greme ne gryste,   465
On arme oþer fynger þaȝ þou ber byȝe.
So fare we alle wyth luf and lyste
To kyng and quene by cortaysye.'

'Cortaysé', quod I, 'I leue,   f. 45^b
And charyté grete, be yow among,   470
Bot my speche þat yow ne greue,

.   .   .   .

Þyself in heuen ouer hyȝ þou heue,
To make þe quen þat watȝ so ȝonge.
What more honour moȝte he acheue   475
Þat hade endured in worlde stronge,

457 Poule *MS*, *M*, *G*[1], *S*: Paule *O*, *G*[2], *C*.   460 tryste *M*, *G*, *E*[2],
C: tyste *MS*, *O*, *S*.   461 sawhe *MS*.   462 myste *MS*: lyste *H*.
469 Cortayse *MS*: Cortaysye *G*, *E*[2], *C*.   472 *A line missing in the*
MS; *G suggests*: Me þynk þou spekeȝ now ful wronge.

And lyued in penaunce hys lyueʒ longe
Wyth bodyly bale hym blysse to byye?
What more worschyp moʒt he fonge
Þen corounde be kyng by cortaysé?   480

IX

'That cortaysé is to fre of dede,
Ʒyf hyt be soth þat þou coneʒ saye.
Þou lyfed not two ʒer in oure þede;
Þou cowþeʒ neuer God nauþer plese ne pray,
Ne neuer nawþer Pater ne Crede;   485
And quen mad on þe fyrst day!
I may not traw, so God me spede,
Þat God wolde wryþe so wrange away.
Of countes, damysel, par ma fay,
Wer fayr in heuen to halde asstate,   490
Oþer elleʒ a lady of lasse aray;
Bot a quene! Hit is to dere a date.'

'Þer is no date of hys godnesse',
Þen sayde to me þat worþy wyʒte,
'For al is trawþe þat he con dresse,   495
And he may do noþynk bot ryʒt.
As Mathew meleʒ in your messe
In sothfol gospel of God almyʒt,
In sample he can ful grayþely gesse,
And lykneʒ hit to heuen lyʒte.   500
"My regne", he saytʒ, "is lyk on hyʒt
To a lorde þat hade a uyne, I wate.
Of tyme of ʒere þe terme watʒ tyʒt,
To labor vyne watʒ dere þe date.

479 he *O*, *G²*, *C*: ho *MS*, *M*, *G¹*.   480 cortayse *MS*: cortaysye *O*,
G², *C*.   481 cortayse *MS*: cortaysye *G²*, *C*.   486 fyrste *G*, *E²*, *C*.
488 away: a way *E³*.   499 In sample *O*, *S*: In-sample *G*, Insample *C*.

'"Þat date of ȝere wel knawe þys hyne.   f. 46ᵃ 505
Þe lorde ful erly vp he ros
To hyre werkmen to hys vyne,
And fyndeȝ þer summe to hys porpos.
Into acorde þay con declyne
For a pené on a day, and forth þay gotȝ,   510
Wryþen and worchen and don gret pyne,
Keruen and caggen and man hit closͅ.
Aboute vnder þe lorde to marked totȝ,
And ydel men stande he fyndeȝ þerate.
'Why stande ȝe ydel?' he sayde to þos.   515
'Ne knawe ȝe of þis day no date?'

'"'Er date of daye hider arn we wonne',
So watȝ al samen her answar soȝt.
'We haf standen her syn ros þe sunne,
And no mon byddeȝ vus do ryȝt noȝt.'   520
'Gos into my vyne, dotȝ þat ȝe conne',
So sayde þe lorde, and made hit toȝt.
'What resonabele hyre be naȝt be runne
I yow pay in dede and þoȝte.'
Þay wente into þe vyne and wroȝte,   525
And al day þe lorde þus ȝede his gate,
And nw men to hys vyne he broȝte
Welneȝ wyl day watȝ passed date.

'"At þe date of day of euensonge,
On oure byfore þe sonne go doun,   530
He seȝ þer ydel men ful stronge
And sade to hem wyth sobre soun,

505 þys *MS, O, S, E³*; hys *G.*   510 on: *omitted by G, E³.*   513
marked totȝ *MS*: market dotȝ *H.*   523 resnabele *G.*   524 pay *G*:
pray *MS, M.*   527 nwe *G, E², C.*   529 At þe date of day *O, G²*, of
the day *G¹*: At þe day of date *MS, M.*   532 sade *MS, M, G*: sayde
O, C; hem *M*: hen *MS.*

'Wy stonde ȝe ydel þise dayeȝ longe?'
Þay sayden her hyre watȝ nawhere boun.
'Gotȝ to my vyne, ȝemen ȝonge,   535
And wyrkeȝ and dotȝ þat at ȝe moun.'
Sone þe worlde bycom wel broun;
Þe sunne watȝ doun and hit wex late.
To take her hyre he mad sumoun;
Þe day watȝ al apassed date.   540

X

'"The date of þe daye þe lorde con knaw,   f. 46ᵇ
Called to þe reue: 'Lede, pay þe meyny.
Gyf hem þe hyre þat I hem owe,
And fyrre, þat non me may reprené,
Set hem alle vpon a rawe   545
And gyf vchon inlyche a peny.
Bygyn at þe laste þat standeȝ lowe,
Tyl to þe fyrste þat þou atteny.'
And þenne þe fyrst bygonne to pleny
And sayden þat þay hade trauayled sore: 550
'Þese bot on oure hem con streny;
Vus þynk vus oȝe to take more.

'"'More haf we serued, vus þynk so,
Þat suffred han þe dayeȝ hete,
Þenn þyse þat wroȝt not houreȝ two,   555
And þou dotȝ hem vus to counterfete.'
Þenne sayde þe lorde to on of þo:
'Frende, no waning I wyl þe ȝete;
Take þat is þyn owne, and go.
And I hyred þe for a peny agrete,   560

538 and: & & *MS*.   542 meyny *MS*, meny *G²*.   544 reprene
MS, S: repreue *M*, repreny *O, G*.   546 inlyche: ilyche *E²*, *S*.   557 on:
om *altered to* on in *MS*.   558 waning *G, O*, wrang *M*: wanig *MS*.

Quy bygynne3 þou now to þrete?
Wat3 not a pené þy couenaunt þore?
Fyrre þen couenaunde is no3t to plete.
Wy schalte þou þenne ask more?

'"'More, weþer louyly is me my gyfte,   565
To do wyth myn quat-so me lyke3?
Oþer elle3 þyn y3e to lyþer is lyfte
For I am goude and non byswyke3?'
Þus schal I'", quod Kryste, "hit skyfte:
Þe laste schal be þe fyrst þat stryke3,   570
And þe fyrst þe laste, be he neuer so swyft;
For mony ben called, þa3 fewe be myke3."
Þus pore men her part ay pyke3,
Þa3 þay com late and lyttel wore;
And þa3 her sweng wyth lyttel atslyke3,   575
Þe merci of God is much þe more.

'More haf I of joye and blysse hereinne,   f. 47ᵃ
Of ladyschyp gret and lyue3 blom,
Þen alle þe wy3e3 in þe worlde my3t wynne
By þe way of ry3t to aske dome.   580
Wheþer welnygh now I con bygynne—
In euentyde into þe vyne I come—
Fyrst of my hyre my Lorde con mynne:
I wat3 payed anon of al and sum.
3et oþer þer werne þat toke more tom,   585
Þat swange and swat for long 3ore,
Þat 3et of hyre noþynk þay nom,
Paraunter no3t schal to-3ere more.'

564 aske *G*, *E*², *C*.   565 louyly *MS*, *M*, *G*¹, *E*³: lawely *O*, *C*, leuyly *G*².
572 called *M*, *O*, *G*, *C*: calle *MS*.   581 wel nyght *M*, *G*¹.   586 longe
G, *E*¹, *C*.

Then more I meled and sayde apert:
'Me þynk þy tale vnresounable. 590
Goddeȝ ryȝt is redy and euermore rert,
Oþer Holy Wryt is bot a fable.
In Sauter is sayd a verce ouerte
Þat spekeȝ a poynt determynable:
"Þou quyteȝ vchon as hys desserte, 595
Þou hyȝe kyng ay pretermynable."
Now he þat stod þe long day stable,
And þou to payment com hym byfore,
Þenne þe lasse in werke to take more able,
And euer þe lenger þe lasse, þe more.' 600

XI

'Of more and lasse in Godeȝ ryche',
Þat gentyl sayde, 'lys no joparde,
For þer is vch mon payed inlyche,
Wheþer lyttel oþer much be hys rewarde;
For þe gentyl Cheuentayn is no chyche, 605
Queþer-so-euer he dele nesch oþer harde:
He laueȝ hys gyfteȝ as water of dyche,
Oþer goteȝ of golf þat neuer charde.
Hys fraunchyse is large þat euer dard
To Hym þat matȝ in synne rescoghe; 610
No blysse betȝ fro hem reparde,
For þe grace of God is gret inoghe.

'Bot now þou moteȝ, me for to mate, f. 47ᵇ
Þat I my peny haf wrang tan here;
Þou sayȝ þat I þat com to late 615
Am not worþy so gret fere.

596 pretermynable *M*: pᴇrtermynable *MS*. 609 dard: *O suggests*
fard. 611 hem *MS, O, G², S*: him *G¹*, hym *E²*. 613 now: inow
E³, C. 616 fere: lere *MS, M*, here *G, C*, bere *E³*.

Where wyste3 þou euer any bourne abate,
Euer so holy in hys prayere,
Þat he ne forfeted by sumkyn gate
Þe mede sumtyme of heuene3 clere?   620
And ay þe ofter, þe alder þay were,
Þay laften ry3t and wro3ten woghe.
Mercy and grace moste hem þen stere,
For þe grace of God is gret inno3e.

'Bot innoghe of grace hat3 innocent.   625
As sone as þay arn borne, by lyne
In þe water of babtem þay dyssente:
Þen arne þay boro3t into þe vyne.
Anon þe day, wyth derk endente,
Þe niy3t of deth dot3 to enclyne: 630
Þat wro3t neuer wrang er þenne þay wente,
Þe gentyle Lorde þenne paye3 hys hyne.
Þay dyden hys heste, þay wern þereine;
Why schulde he not her labour alow,
3ys, and pay hem at þe fyrst fyne?   635
For þe grace of God is gret innoghe.

'Ino3e is knawen þat mankyn grete
Fyrste wat3 wro3t to blysse parfyt;
Oure forme fader hit con forfete
Þur3 an apple þat he vpon con byte.   640
Al wer we dampned for þat mete
To dy3e in doel out of delyt
And syþen wende to helle hete,
Þerinne to won wythoute respyt.
Bot þeron com a bote astyt.   645
Ryche blod ran on rode so roghe,

---

630 niy3t *or* my3t *MS*: *Kölbing and E² suggest* ny3t, my3t *M, G, O, C.*
635 3ys: s *faint in MS*; hem *O, G², E²*: hym *MS*.

And wynne water þen at þat plyt:
Þe grace of God wex gret innoghe.

'Innoghe þer wax out of þat welle,   f. 48ᵃ
Blod and water of brode wounde.   650
Þe blod vus boȝt fro bale of helle
And delyuered vus of þe deth secounde;
Þe water is baptem, þe soþe to telle,
Þat folȝed þe glayue so grymly grounde,
Þat wascheȝ away þe gylteȝ felle   655
Þat Adam wyth inne deth vus drounde.
Now is þer noȝt in þe worlde rounde
Bytwene vus and blysse bot þat he wythdroȝ,
And þat is restored in sely stounde;
And þe grace of God is gret innogh.   660

XII

'Grace innogh þe mon may haue
Þat synneȝ þenne new, ȝif hym repente,
Bot wyth sorȝ and syt he mot hit craue,
And byde þe payne þerto is bent.
Bot resoun of ryȝt þat con not raue   665
Saueȝ euermore þe innossent;
Hit is a dom þat neuer God gaue,
Þat euer þe gyltleȝ schulde be schente.
Þe gyltyf may contryssyoun hente
And be þurȝ mercy to grace þryȝt;   670
Bot he to gyle þat neuer glente
And inoscente is saf and ryȝte.

649 out *M*: out out *MS*.   656 inne *MS, O*: in *G*.   672 And: As *H*:
At *MS, M, O, G, C*; inoscente *MS*: inoscence *G*; and (&) *MS, M, O*:
by *G*.

'Ry3t þus I knaw wel in þis cas
Two men to saue is god by skylle:
Þe ry3twys man schal se hys face, 675
Þe harmle3 haþel schal com hym tylle.
Þe Sauter hyt sat3 þus in a pace:
"Lorde, quo schal klymbe þy hy3 hylle,
Oþer rest wythinne þy holy place?"
Hymself to onsware he is not dylle: 680
"Hondelynge3 harme þat dyt not ille,
Þat is of hert boþe clene and ly3t,
Þer schal hys step stable stylle":
Þe innosent is ay saf by ry3t.

'The ry3twys man also sertayn f. 48ᵇ 685
Aproche he schal þat proper pyle,
Þat take3 not her lyf in vayne,
Ne glauere3 her nie3bor wyth no gyle.
Of þys ry3twys sa3 Salamon playn
How Koyntise onoure con aquyle; 690
By waye3 ful stre3t ho con hym strayn,
And scheued hym þe rengne of God awhyle,
As quo says, "Lo, 3on louely yle!
Þou may hit wynne if þou be wy3te."
Bot, hardyly, wythoute peryle, 695
Þe innosent is ay saue by ry3te.

'Anende ry3twys men 3et sayt3 a gome,
Dauid in Sauter, if euer 3e sy3 hit:
"Lorde, þy seruaunt dra3 neuer to dome,
For non lyuyande to þe is justyfyet." 700

673 þus *M*: þus þus *MS*.   675 face *M*: fate *MS*.   678 hy3e *G, E¹*,
C; hylle *G*: hylle3 *MS, M*.   683 step: steppe *G, E³*.   688 nie3bor
MS, M, G¹: ne3bor *O, G²*.   690 Koyntise onoure *Bradley*: kyntly oure
MS, kyntly oure kyng hym *G¹, O, C*, kyntly oure Koyntyse hym *G²*.
691 ho *Bradley*: he *MS, O, G², C*.   698 sy3 *G*: se3 *MS, M, O*.   700
For *M*: sor *MS*.

Forþy to corte quen þou schal com
Þer alle oure causeȝ schal be tryed,
Alegge þe ryȝt, þou may be innome,
By þys ilke spech I haue asspyed:
Bot he on rode þat blody dyed,   705
Delfully þurȝ hondeȝ þryȝt,
Gyue þe to passe, when þou arte tryed,
By innocens and not by ryȝte.

'Ryȝtwysly quo con rede,
He loke on bok and be awayed   710
How Jesus hym welke in areþede,
And burneȝ her barneȝ vnto hym brayde.
For happe and hele þat fro hym ȝede
To touch her chylder þay fayr hym prayed.
His dessypeleȝ wyth blame let be hem bede   715
And wyth her resouneȝ ful fele restayed.
Jesus þenne hem swetely sayde:
"Do way, let chylder vnto me tyȝt.
To suche is heuenryche arayed":
Þe innocent is ay saf by ryȝt.   720

XIII

'Iesus con calle to hym hys mylde,   f. 49ᵃ
And sayde hys ryche no wyȝ myȝt wynne
Bot he com þyder ryȝt as a chylde,
Oþer elleȝ neuermore com þerinne.
Harmleȝ, trwe, and vndefylde,   725
Wythouten mote oþer mascle of sulpande synne,

701 com *MS, M, O*: come *G, E³, C.*   709 quo [so] *H, G*; con: cone
E¹, C; rede: arede *Kölbing.*   711, 717, 721 Jesus: jhc̄ *MS.*   714
touch *M*: touth *MS.*   715 hem *O, G²*: hym *MS, M, G¹.*   721 Ryȝt
added at beginning of line by E³; hys mylde *MS*: þys mylde *Kölbing*,
he smylde *H.*

Quen such þer cnoken on þe bylde,
Tyt schal hem men þe ȝate vnpynne.
Þer is þe blys þat con not blynne
Þat þe jueler soȝte þurȝ perré pres,   730
And solde alle hys goud, boþe wolen and lynne,
To bye hym a perle watȝ mascelleȝ.

'This makelleȝ perle, þat boȝt is dere,
Þe joueler gef fore alle hys god,
Is lyke þe reme of heuenesse clere: 735
So sayde þe Fader of folde and flode;
For hit is wemleȝ, clene, and clere,
And endeleȝ rounde, and blyþe of mode,
And commune to alle þat ryȝtwys were.
Lo, euen inmyddeȝ my breste hit stode.   740
My Lorde þe Lombe, þat schede hys blode,
He pyȝt hit þere in token of pes.
I rede þe forsake þe worlde wode
And porchace þy perle maskelles.'

'O maskeleȝ perle in perleȝ pure,   745
Þat bereȝ', quod I, 'þe perle of prys,
Quo formed þe þy fayre fygure?
Þat wroȝt þy wede, he watȝ ful wys.
Þy beauté com neuer of nature;
Pymalyon paynted neuer þy vys,   750
Ne Arystotel nawþer by hys lettrure
Of carped þe kynde þese properteȝ.
Þy colour passeȝ þe flour-de-lys;
Þyn angel-hauyng so clene corteȝ.
Breue me, bryȝt, quat kyn offys   755
Bereȝ þe perle so maskelleȝ?'

733 makelleȝ *MS, M, E³, C*: maskelleȝ *G, O*.   735 heuenesse clere
MS: heuenes spere *G², C*.   739 ryȝtwys *M*: ryȝtywys *MS*.   752
carped *G*: carpe *MS, O*; properteȝ *MS*: propertyȝ *G, O, C*.   755 offys
O, C: oftriys *MS*, of triys *G*, of priys *M*, ostriys *Bradley*.

'My makeleȝ Lambe þat al may bete',   f. 49^b
Quod scho, 'my dere destyné,
Me ches to hys make, alþaȝ vnmete
Sumtyme semed þat assemblé.   760
When I wente fro yor worlde wete,
He calde me to hys bonerté:
"Cum hyder to me, my lemman swete,
For mote ne spot is non in þe."
He gef me myȝt and als bewté;   765
In hys blod he wesch my wede on dese,
And coronde clene in vergynté,
And pyȝt me in perleȝ maskelleȝ.'

'Why, maskelleȝ bryd þat bryȝt con flambe,
Þat reiateȝ hatȝ so ryche and ryf,   770
Quat kyn þyng may be þat Lambe
Þat þe wolde wedde vnto hys vyf?
Ouer alle oþer so hyȝ þou clambe
To lede wyth hym so ladyly lyf.
So mony a comly on-vunder cambe   775
For Kryst han lyued in much stryf;
And þou con alle þo dere out dryf
And fro þat maryag al oþer depres,
Al only þyself so stout and styf,
A makeleȝ may and maskelleȝ.'   780

XIV

'Maskelles', quod þat myry quene,
'Vnblemyst I am, wythouten blot,
And þat may I wyth mensk menteene;
Bot "makeleȝ quene" þenne sade I not.

757 makeleȝ *MS, M, E*³, *C*: maskeleȝ *O, G*.   768 And (&) *MS*: He *G*².   778 maryage *G*.   784 sayde *O, E*², *C*.

Þe Lambeʒ vyueʒ in blysse we bene,   785
A hondred and forty fowre þowsande flot,
As in þe Apocalyppeʒ hit is sene ;
Sant John hem syʒ al in a knot.
On þe hyl of Syon, þat semly clot,
Þe apostel hem segh in gostly drem   790
Arayed to þe weddyng in þat hyl-coppe,
Þe nwe cyté o Jerusalem.

'Of Jerusalem I in speche spelle.   f. 50ᵃ
If þou wyl knaw what kyn he be,
My Lombe, my Lorde, my dere juelle,   795
My ioy, my blys, my lemman fre,
Þe profete Ysaye of hym con melle
Pitously of hys debonerté :
"Þat gloryous gyltleʒ þat mon con quelle
Wythouten any sake of felonye,   800
As a schep to þe slaʒt þer lad watʒ he ;
And, as lombe þat clypper in hande nem,
So closed he hys mouth fro vch query,
Quen Jueʒ hym iugged in Jerusalem."

'In Jerusalem watʒ my lemman slayn   805
And rent on rode wyth boyeʒ bolde.
Al oure baleʒ to bere ful bayn,
He toke on hymself oure careʒ colde.
Wyth boffeteʒ watʒ hys face flayn
Þat watʒ so fayr on to byholde.   810

---

786 fowre *supplied by G, while O and E³ follow MS.*   788 John *M*:
Johñ *MS.*   792 o *G, O*: o *imperfect in MS,* u *M* ; Jerusalem *G, O*:
jlrm̃ *MS, and so in following stanzas (except in line 804), expanded as*
Jerusalem *by E², C.*   799 gyltleʒ: l *altered faintly from* s *in MS.*
800 felonye *MS*: felone *G², E³, C.*   802 in hande nem: in hande men
MS, in lande nem, (lande *taken as reading of MS*) *M, G, O, C*: in bonde
men *F*, in honde men *Kölbing*, in honde con nem *H.*   803 query
MS: quere *G, E³.*   804 jhrm̃ *MS.*

For synne he set hymself in vayn,
Þat neuer hade non hymself to wolde.
For vus he lette hym flyʒe and folde
And brede vpon a bostwys bem;
As meke as lomp þat no playnt tolde   815
For vus he swalt in Jerusalem.

'In Jerusalem, Jordan, and Galalye,
Þer as baptysed þe goude Saynt Jon,
His wordeʒ acorded to Ysaye.
When Jesus con to hym warde gon,   820
He sayde of hym þys professye:
"Lo, Godeʒ Lombe as trwe as ston,
Þat dotʒ away þe synneʒ dryʒe
Þat alle þys worlde hatʒ wroʒt vpon.
Hymself ne wroʒt neuer ʒet non;   825
Wheþer on hymself he con al clem.
Hys generacyoun quo recen con,
Þat dyʒed for vus in Jerusalem?"

'In Ierusalem þus my lemman swete   f. 50^b
Twyeʒ for lombe watʒ taken þare,   830
By trw recorde of ayþer prophete,
For mode so meke and al hys fare.
Þe þryde tyme is þerto ful mete,
In Apokalypeʒ wryten ful ʒare;
Inmydeʒ þe trone, þere say"nteʒ sete,   835
Þe apostel Iohn hym saʒ as bare,
Lesande þe boke with leueʒ sware
Þere seuen syngnetteʒ wern sette in seme;
And at þat syʒt vche douth con dare
In helle, in erþe, and Jerusalem.   840

815 lomp *MS*: lomb *M, G, O, C*.   817 In *supplied by G*.   825
wroʒte *G, E¹*.   829 swete *G*: swatte *MS, M*.   830 þare: *second letter
not clear in MS, probably* a *altered from* e.   836 John *M*: iohñ *MS*;
saʒ *G*: saytʒ *MS*, syʒ *O, C*.   838 in seme *M, E²*: inseme *O*, in-seme *G²*.

XV

'Thys Jerusalem Lombe hade neuer pechche
Of oþer huee bot quyt jolyf
Þat mot ne masklle moȝt on streche,
For wolle quyte so ronk and ryf.
Forþy vche saule þat hade neuer teche   845
Is to þat Lombe a worthyly wyf;
And þaȝ vch day a store he feche,
Among vus commeȝ nouþer strot ne stryf;
Bot vchon enlé we wolde were fyf—
Þe mo þe myryer, so God me blesse.   850
In compayny gret our luf con þryf
In honour more and neuer þe lesse.

'Lasse of blysse may non vus bryng
Þat beren þys perle vpon oure bereste,
For þay of mote couþe neuer mynge   855
Of spotleȝ perleȝ þat beren þe creste.
Alþaȝ oure corses in clotteȝ clynge,
And ȝe remen for rauþe wythouten reste,
We þurȝoutly hauen cnawyng;
Of on dethe ful oure hope is drest.   860
Þe Lombe vus gladeȝ, oure care is kest;
He myrþeȝ vus alle at vch a mes.
Vchoneȝ blysse is breme and beste,
And neuer oneȝ honour ȝet neuer þe les.

'Lest les þou leue my tale farande,   f. 51ᵃ   865
In Appocalyppece is wryten in wro:

843 maskle *G¹*, maskelle *G²*.   848 nouþer: non oþer *MS, O, C*:
noþer *G²*.   856 þat *O, G²*: þa *MS*, þay *M, G¹, E²*.   860 on: o *of* on
blotted and illegible.   861 lombe *M, O, C*: lonbe *MS*, loumbe *G*.
865 tale *from the catchwords*: talle *in the text. The whole line occurs as
catchwords on the preceding page, in the form*: leste les þow leue my tale
farā[de].

"I seghe", says John, "þe Loumbe hym stande
On þe mount of Syon ful þryuen and þro,
And wyth hym maydenneȝ an hundreþe þowsande,
And fowre and forty þowsande mo.   870
On alle her forhedeȝ wryten I fande
Þe Lombeȝ nome, hys Fadereȝ also.
A hue from heuen I herde þoo,
Lyk flodeȝ fele laden runnen on resse,
And as þunder þroweȝ in torreȝ blo,   875
Þat lote, I leue, watȝ neuer þe les.

'"Nauþeles, þaȝ hit schowted scharpe,
And ledden loude alþaȝ hit were,
A note ful nwe I herde hem warpe,
To lysten þat watȝ ful lufly dere.   880
As harporeȝ harpen in her harpe,
Þat nwe songe þay songen ful cler,
In sounande noteȝ a gentyl carpe;
Ful fayre þe modeȝ þay fonge in fere.
Ryȝt byfore Godeȝ chayere   885
And þe fowre besteȝ þat hym obes
And þe aldermen so sadde of chere,
Her songe þay songen neuer þe les.

'"Nowþelese non watȝ neuer so quoynt,
For alle þe crafteȝ þat euer þay knewe,   890
Þat of þat songe myȝt synge a poynt,
Bot þat meyny þe Lombe þat swe;
For þay arn boȝt fro þe vrþe aloynte
As newe fryt to God ful due,
And to þe gentyl Lombe hit arn anioynt,   895
As lyk to hymself of lote and hwe;

874 laden *MS, O*: leden *G²*, *C*.   884 fonge: feng *H*, fonged *E³*.
892 þat swe *Kölbing, O, G²*: þay swe *MS, M, G¹, E²*.

For neuer lesyng ne tale vntrwe
Ne towched her tonge for no dysstresse.
Þat moteles meyny may neuer remwe
Fro þat maskeleȝ mayster, neuer þe les."'   900

'Neuer þe les let be my þonc',   f. 51ᵇ
Quod I, 'My perle, þaȝ I appose ;
I schulde not tempte þy wyt so wlonc,
To Krysteȝ chambre þat art ichose.
I am bot mokke and mul among,   905
And þou so ryche a reken rose,
And bydeȝ here by þys blysful bonc
Þer lyueȝ lyste may neuer lose.
Now, hynde, þat sympelnesse coneȝ enclose,
I wolde þe aske a þynge expresse,   910
And þaȝ I be bustwys as a blose,
Let my bone vayl neuerþelese.

XVI

'Neuerþelese cler I yow bycalle,
If ȝe con se hyt be to done ;
As þou art gloryous wythouten galle,   915
Wythnay þou neuer my ruful bone.
Haf ȝe no woneȝ in castel-walle,
Ne maner þer ȝe may mete and won ?
Þou telleȝ me of Jerusalem þe ryche ryalle,
Þer Dauid dere watȝ dyȝt on trone,   920
Bot by þyse holteȝ hit con not hone,
Bot in Judee hit is, þat noble note.
As ȝe ar maskeleȝ vnder mone,
Your woneȝ schulde be wythouten mote.

904 ichose: jchose *MS*.   905 among *MS*: amonc *G*, *E²*.   911
blose *MS*, *M*, *O*: wose *G²*.   912 vayle *G*, *E³*, *C*.   918 won *MS*,
M, *O*, *C*: wone *G*, *E³*.

'Þys moteleȝ meyny þou coneȝ of mele,   925
Of þousandeȝ þryȝt so gret a route,
A gret ceté, for ȝe arn fele,
Yow byhod haue, wythouten doute.
So cumly a pakke of joly juele
Wer euel don schulde lyȝ þeroute,   930
And by þyse bonkeȝ þer I con gele
I se no bygyng nawhere aboute.
I trowe alone ȝe lenge and loute
To loke on þe glory of þys gracious gote.
If þou hatȝ oþer bygyngeȝ stoute,   935
Now tech me to þat myry mote.'

'That mote þou meneȝ in Judy londe',   f. 52ª
Þat specyal spyce þen to me spakk,
'Þat is þe cyté þat þe Lombe con fonde
To soffer inne sor for maneȝ sake,   940
Þe olde Jerusalem to vnderstonde;
For þere þe olde gulte watȝ don to slake.
Bot þe nwe, þat lyȝt of Godeȝ sonde,
Þe apostel in Apocalyppce in theme con take.
Þe Lompe þer wythouten spotteȝ blake   945
Hatȝ feryed þyder hys fayre flote;
And as hys flok is wythouten flake,
So is hys mote wythouten moote.

'Of motes two to carpe clene,
And Jerusalem hyȝt boþe nawþeles—   950
Þat nys to yow no more to mene
Bot "ceté of God", oþer "syȝt of pes":
In þat on oure pes watȝ mad at ene;
Wyth payne to suffer þe Lombe hit chese;

932 and *before* I *deleted by* G, E³, C.   934 gracious *M*: *gracous
MS*.   935 lygyngeȝ *MS, eds*.   938 spakk *MS, O, G*: spake *E², C*.
944 in theme: *E³ omits* in.   945 lompe *MS*: Lombe *eds*.

In þat oþer is noȝt bot pes to glene   955
Þat ay schal laste wythouten reles.
Þat is þe borȝ þat we to pres
Fro þat oure flesch be layd to rote,
Þer glory and blysse schal euer encres
To þe meyny þat is wythouten mote.'   960

'Moteleȝ may so meke and mylde',
Þen sayde I to þat lufly flor,
'Bryng me to þat bygly bylde
And let me se þy blysful bor.'
Þat schene sayde: 'Þat·God wyl schylde;   965
Þou may not enter wythinne hys tor,
Bot of þe Lombe I haue þe aquylde
For a syȝt þerof þurȝ gret fauor.
Vtwyth to se þat clene cloystor
Þou may, bot inwyth not a fote;   970
To strech in þe strete þou hatȝ no vygour,
Bot þou wer clene wythouten mote.

XVII

'If I þis mote þe schal vnhyde,   f. 52b
Bow vp towarde þys borneȝ heued,
And I anendeȝ þe on þis syde   975
Schal sve, tyl þou to a hil be veued.'
Þen wolde I no lenger byde,
Bot lurked by launceȝ so lufly leued,
Tyl on a hyl þat I asspyed
And blusched on þe burghe, as I forth dreued,   980
Byȝonde þe brok fro me warde keued,
Þat schyrrer þen sunne wyth schafteȝ schon.

958 flesch *M*: fresth *MS*.   977 I *supplied by M, O.*   981 keued
MS, M, G, C: breued *O*.

In þe Apokalypce is þe fasoun preued,
As deuyseȝ hit þe apostel Jhon.

As John þe apostel hit syȝ wyth syȝt,   985
I syȝe þat cyty of gret renoun,
Jerusalem so nwe and ryally dyȝt,
As hit was lyȝt fro þe heuen adoun.
Þe borȝ watȝ al of brende golde bryȝt
As glemande glas burnist broun,   990
Wyth gentyl gemmeȝ an-vnder pyȝt
Wyth banteleȝ twelue on basyng boun,
Þe foundementeȝ twelue of riche tenoun;
Vch tabelment watȝ a serlypeȝ ston;
As derely deuyseȝ þis ilk toun   995
In Apocalyppeȝ þe apostel John.

As John þise stoneȝ in writ con nemme,
I knew þe name after his tale:
Jasper hyȝt þe fyrst gemme
Þat I on þe fyrst basse con wale: 1000
He glente grene in þe lowest hemme;
Saffer helde þe secounde stale;
Þe calsydoyne þenne wythouten wemme
In þe þryd table con purly pale;
Þe emerade þe furþe so grene of scale;   1005
Þe sardonyse þe fyfþe ston;
Þe sexte þe rybé he con hit wale
In þe Apocalyppce, þe apostel John.

Ȝet joyned John þe crysolyt   f. 53ᵃ
Þe seuenþe gemme in fundament;   1010

984 Jhon: Jhōn *MS.*   985 John: Jhñ *MS.*   996 John: Johñ
MS, and so also in 1008, 1009, 1021, 1032, 1033, 1053.   997 John
supplied by G.   998 name *MS, M, O, C*: names *G*¹, nameȝ *G*².   999,
1000 fyrste *G, E*¹*, C.*   1004 þrydde *G*²*, E*¹*, C.*   1007 rybe *MS,*
sarde *G*².

Þe a3tþe þe beryl cler and quyt;
Þe topasye twynne-hew þe nente endent;
Þe crysopase þe tenþe is ty3t;
Þe jacynght þe enleuenþe gent;
Þe twelfþe, þe gentyleste in vch a plyt,   1015
Þe amatyst purpre wyth ynde blente;
Þe wal abof þe bantels bent
O jasporye, as glas þat glysnande schon;
I knew hit by his deuysement
In þe Apocalyppe3, þe apostel John.   1020

As John deuysed 3et sa3 I þare:
Þise twelue degres wern brode and stayre;
Þe cyté stod abof ful sware,
As longe as brode as hy3e ful fayre;
Þe strete3 of golde as glasse al bare,   1025
Þe wal of jasper þat glent as glayre;
Þe wone3 wythinne enurned ware
Wyth alle kynne3 perré þat mo3t repayre.
Þenne helde vch sware of þis manayre
Twelue forlonge space, er euer hit fon,   1030
Of he3t, of brede, of lenþe to cayre,
For meten hit sy3 þe apostel John.

XVIII

As John hym wryte3 3et more I sy3e:
Vch pane of þat place had þre 3ate3;
So twelue in poursent I con asspye,   1035
Þe portale3 pyked of rych plate3,

1012 twynne-hew: how *MS, eds.*   1014 jacynght *G*: jacyngh *MS.*
1015 gentyleste *MS*: tryeste *G²*.   1017 bent *MS*: brent *G*.   1018 O:
a later hand has added f *in the MS.*   1020 John: Jhñ *MS.*   1030
Twelue þowsande forlonge er euer hit fon *G².*   1035 poursent *M, G²*:
pourseut *G¹, Bradley, O, C.*   1036 ryche *G, E¹.*

And vch ȝate of a margyrye,
A parfyt perle þat neuer fateȝ.
Vchon in scrypture a name con plye
Of Israel barneȝ, folewande her dateȝ,　　　　　1040
Þat is to say, as her byrþ-whateȝ:
Þe aldest ay fyrst þeron watȝ done.
Such lyȝt þer lemed in alle þe strateȝ
Hem nedde nawþer sunne ne mone.

Of sunne ne mone had þay no nede;　　f. 53ᵇ　1045
Þe self God watȝ her lombe-lyȝt,
Þe Lombe her lantyrne, wythouten drede;
Þurȝ hym blysned þe borȝ al bryȝt.
Þurȝ woȝe and won my lokyng ȝede,
For sotyle cler noȝt lette no lyȝt.　　　　　1050
Þe hyȝe trone þer moȝt ȝe hede
Wyth alle þe apparaylmente vmbepyȝte,
As John þe appostel in termeȝ tyȝte;
Þe hyȝe Godeȝ self hit set vpone.
A reuer of þe trone þer ran outryȝte　　　　1055
Watȝ bryȝter þen boþe þe sunne and mone.

Sunne ne mone schon neuer so swete
As þat foysoun flode out of þat flet;
Swyþe hit swange þurȝ vch a strete
Wythouten fylþe oþer galle oþer glet.　　　　1060
Kyrk þerinne watȝ non ȝete,
Chapel ne temple þat euer watȝ set;
Þe Almyȝty watȝ her mynster mete,
Þe Lombe þe sakerfyse þer to refet.

1041 byrþ whateȝ *G*¹, *O*, *C*: byrþe-whateȝ *G*². 　　1046 selfe *G*, *E*¹,
C; lombe-lyȝt *MS*: lompe *eds*. 　1050 lyȝt *MS*: syȝt *G*². 　1058 As
G: A *MS*. 　1063 mynster: mynyster *MS*. 　1064 refet: reget *MS*, *eds*.

Þe ȝateȝ stoken watȝ neuer ȝet,   1065
Bot euermore vpen at vche a lone;
Þer entreȝ non to take reset
Þat bereȝ any spot an-vnder mone.

The mone may þerof acroche no myȝte;
To spotty ho is, of body to grym,   1070
And also þer ne is neuer nyȝt.
What schulde þe mone þer compas clym
And to euen wyth þat worþly lyȝt
Þat schyneȝ vpon þe brokeȝ brym?
Þe planeteȝ arn in to pouer a plyȝt,   1075
And þe self sunne ful fer to dym.
Aboute þat water arn tres ful schym,
Þat twelue fryteȝ of lyf con bere ful sone;
Twelue syþeȝ on ȝer þay beren ful frym,
And renowleȝ nwe in vche a mone.   1080

An-vnder mone so great merwayle   f. 54ᵃ
No fleschly hert ne myȝt endeure,
As quen I blusched vpon þat bayle,
So ferly þerof watȝ þe fasure.
I stod as stylle as dased quayle   1085
For ferly of þat frelich fygure,
Þat felde I nawþer reste ne trauayle,
So watȝ I rauyste wyth glymme pure.
For I dar say wyth conciens sure,
Hade bodyly burne abiden þat bone,   1090
Þaȝ alle clerkeȝ hym hade in cure,
His lyf were loste an-vnder mone.

1068 anvnder *M*: an vndeȝ *MS*.   1076 selfe *G, E¹, C*.   1083
bayle *G²*: baly *MS, M, G¹*, bayly *O*.   1086 frelich *suggested by M*:
freuch *MS, G, O, C*, french *M*.

XIX

Ry3t as þe maynful mone con rys
Er þenne þe day-glem dryue al doun,
So sodanly on a wonder wyse   1095
I wat3 war of a prosessyoun.
Þis noble cité of ryche enpryse
Wat3 sodanly ful wythouten sommoun
Of such vergyne3 in þe same gyse
Þat wat3 my blysful an-vnder croun: 1100
And coronde wern alle of þe same fasoun,
Depaynt in perle3 and wede3 qwyte;
In vchone3 breste wat3 bounden boun
Þe blysful perle wyth gret delyt.

Wyth gret delyt þay glod in fere   1105
On golden gate3 þat glent as glasse;
Hundreth þowsande3 I wot þer were,
And alle in sute her liuré3 wasse;
Tor to knaw þe gladdest chere.
Þe Lombe byfore con proudly passe   1110
Wyth horne3 seuen of red golde cler;
As praysed perle3 his wede3 wasse.
Towarde þe throne þay trone a tras.
Þa3 þay wern fele, no pres in plyt,
Bot mylde as maydene3 seme at mas,   1115
So dro3 þay forth wyth gret delyt.

Delyt þat hys come encroched   f. 54^b
To much hit were of for to melle.
Þise aldermen, quen he aproched,
Grouelyng to his fete þay felle.   1120

Legyounes of aungeleȝ togeder uoched
Þer kesten ensens of swete smelle.
Þen glory and gle watȝ nwe abroched;
Al songe to loue þat gay juelle.
Þe steuen moȝt stryke þurȝ þe vrþe to helle   1125
Þat þe Vertues of heuen of joye endyte.
To loue þe Lombe his meyny in melle
Iwysse I laȝt a gret delyt.

Delit þe Lombe for to deuise
Wyth much meruayle in mynde went.   1130
Best watȝ he, blyþest, and moste to pryse,
Þat euer I herde of speche spent;
So worþly whyt wern wedeȝ hys,
His lokeȝ symple, hymself so gent.
Bot a wounde ful wyde and weete con wyse   1135
Anende hys hert, þurȝ hyde torente.
Of his quyte syde his blod outsprent.
Alas, þoȝt I, who did þat spyt?
Ani breste for bale aȝt haf forbrent
Er he þerto hade had delyt.   1140

The Lombe delyt non lyste to wene.
Þaȝ he were hurt and wounde hade,
In his sembelaunt watȝ neuer sene,
So wern his glenteȝ gloryous glade.
I loked among his meyny schene   1145
How þay wyth lyf wern laste and lade;
Þen saȝ I þer my lyttel quene
Þat I wende had standen by me in sclade.
Lorde, much of mirþe watȝ þat ho made
Among her fereȝ þat watȝ so quyt!   1150
Þat syȝt me gart to þenk to wade
For luf-longyng in gret delyt.

1133 hyse *G, C*.

XX

Delyt me drof in yȝe and ere,   f. 55ᵃ
My maneȝ mynde to maddyng malte;
Quen I seȝ my frely, I wolde be þere,   1155
Byȝonde þe water þaȝ ho were walte.
I þoȝt þat noþyng myȝt me dere
To fech me bur and take me halte,
And to start in þe strem schulde non me stere,
To swymme þe remnaunt, þaȝ I þer swalte.   1160
Bot of þat munt I watȝ bitalt;
When I schulde start in þe strem astraye,
Out of þat caste I watȝ bycalt:
Hit watȝ not at my Prynceȝ paye.

Hit payed hym not þat I so flonc   1165
Ouer meruelous mereȝ, so mad arayde.
Of raas þaȝ I were rasch and ronk,
Ȝet rapely þerinne I watȝ restayed.
For, ryȝt as I sparred vnto þe bonc,
Þat brathþe out of my drem me brayde.   1170
Þen wakned I in þat erber wlonk;
My hede vpon þat hylle watȝ layde
Þer as my perle to grounde strayd.
I raxled, and fel in gret affray,
And, sykyng, to myself I sayd,   1175
'Now al be to þat Prynceȝ paye'.

Me payed ful ille to be outfleme
So sodenly of þat fayre regioun,
Fro alle þo syȝteȝ so quyke and queme.
A longeyng heuy me strok in swone,   1180

1158 bur *MS*, *eds*: bar *NED s.v. Take, sense 7 d*.   1168 restayed
MS, *M*, *G*: restayd *O*.   1170 brathþe *O*: brathe *M*, *G*, *C*: bratþe *MS*,
with þ *superimposed on an* h.   1179 quyke *G*, *O*: quykeȝ *MS*, *M*.

And rewfully þenne I con to reme:
'O perle', quod I, 'of rych renoun,
So watȝ hit me dere þat þou con deme
In þys veray avysyoun!
If hit be ueray and soth sermoun   1185
Þat þou so stykeȝ in garlande gay,
So wel is me in þys doel-doungoun
Þat þou art to þat Prynseȝ paye.'

To þat Prynceȝ paye hade I ay bente,   f. 55ᵇ
And ȝerned no more þen watȝ me gyuen,   1190
And halden me þer in trwe entent,
As þe perle me prayed þat watȝ so þryuen,
As helde, drawen to Goddeȝ present,
To mo of his mysterys I hade ben dryuen;
Bot ay wolde man of happe more hente   1195
Þen moȝte by ryȝt vpon hem clyuen.
Þerfore my ioye watȝ sone toriuen,
And I kaste of kytheȝ þat lasteȝ aye.
Lorde, mad hit arn þat agayn þe stryuen,
Oþer proferen þe oȝt agayn þy paye.   1200

To pay þe Prince oþer sete saȝte
Hit is ful eþe to þe god Krystyin;
For I haf founden hym, boþe day and naȝte,
A God, a Lorde, a frende ful fyin.
Ouer þis hyul þis lote I laȝte,   1205
For pyty of my perle enclyin,
And syþen to God I hit bytaȝte
In Krysteȝ dere blessyng and myn,

1185 if *M*: if *MS*.   1186 stykeȝ *MS*, *M*: strykeȝ *G, O, C*.   1190 gyuen *G²*, *C*: geuen *MS, M, G¹, O*.   1193 helde *MS, M, G*: helder *O*: holde *E²*, *E³*.   1196 moȝte *G²*: moȝten *MS, M, O, C*.   1201 *O supplies* hym *after* sete.   1205 hyul (*or* hyiil) *MS*, hyul *G²*: hyiil *O*: hyl *M, G¹*.

Þat in þe forme of bred and wyn
Þe preste vus scheweȝ vch a daye. 1210
He gef vus to be his homly hyne
Ande precious perleȝ vnto his pay.

Amen.   Amen.

NOTES

1–4 'Pearl, pleasing to a prince's delight to set fairly in gold so bright, I say firmly that I never found her precious equal among those of the orient.' The first two lines are probably not an apostrophe; the construction, reduced to its simplest form, is: 'As for the Pearl, I never found her equal.' (Cf. 105–6 and 597 for similar syntax.) *To clanly clos* is taken as a 'split infinitive', a usage not uncommon at the time (see *Sir Gawain* 88, 1540, 1863). The alternative, to take *clos* as the adjective 'enclosed', and *to* as the adverb 'too', gives a less natural meaning, whether it is applied to the jewel or to the maiden. To say that the pearl gives pleasure to a prince to set in gold is both natural and symbolically satisfactory: compare the similar statement made about the pearl symbolizing Saint Margaret in the Scottish *Legend of Saint Margaret* 23 f.:

> Þarfor oft men wil it ta
> And set it in bruchis and in ryngis;
> Þare-in delyt has mychtty kyngis.

For the symbolism of the pearl in this poem see Introduction, p. xxvii. In most of this stanza the symbolism is clear. At the end of the poem, where the last stanza group has as its refrain the phrase used here in the opening line, *Prynce3 paye* is used to refer to Christ. This seems a good reason for taking *prynces* here as singular, meaning literally a prince of this world and symbolically Christ.

3 *oryent*: the orient is specified because pearls of the east were finer and more valuable than those of the west. *Oute of oryent* would suggest lustrous beauty as well as value to the medieval reader (see *NED*. s. *Orient*, senses A. 2 b, and B. 2).

4 *her*: it is not necessarily because the pearl symbolizes the maiden that the feminine pronoun is used; in *Purity* 1119 f. the pearl is similarly referred to by the feminine pronoun, where there is no personal symbolism. See further the note on 10.

6 *So smal, so smoþe her syde3 were*: the poet must have had the image of the little girl in his mind; compare line 190. ME. poetry frequently uses *smal* of fair women (cf. *The Owl and the Nightingale* 204), and the lady's sides are often mentioned. Chaucer's Cryseyde had *sydes longe, flesshly, smothe, and whyte* (*Troilus* III, 1248), and

Osgood compares *The Erl of Tolous* 352: *Hur syde longe, her myddyll small*, *The Parliament of Love* 54 (similar), and Chaucer's *Miller's Tale* 48.

10 *hit*: the pearl. The slipping of the pearl through the grass onto the ground symbolizes the death of the little girl. In the preceding lines the pearl is referred to by feminine pronouns (cf. the note on 4). The poet's use of feminine or neuter for the pearl seems to be governed partly by his poetic purpose and partly by general ME. usage, in which there was a distinction between the nominative and the other cases, the nominative being much more definite in its indication of sex or gender. Thus in Myrc's *Instructions for Parish Priests*, 1875–6:

> Loke þat þy candel of wax *hyt* be,
> And set *hyre* so þat þow *hyre* se.

The poet of *Pearl* uses *he* of the jasper in 1001, but for the pearl, while he tends to use the feminine form in the genitive or accusative, he always uses the neuter in the nominative, where the feminine *ho* would suggest a female figure and over-emphasize the personal symbolism. Later, in 283–4, where he has to maintain the pearl-symbolism in the presence of the actual maiden symbolized, he uses the neuter even in the accusative.

yot: an unusual form, probably of *ȝode* 'went', for which the poems in this MS. have also the variants *ȝed(e)*, *ȝod(e)*, *ȝe(u)de* (rhyming with *leude* in *Sir Gawain* 1124). This is similar to the series found in *Sir Ferumbras: ȝede, ȝeode, ȝude, ȝot* (the only other known example of *yot*, but there rhyming with an original long vowel). For the short vowel compare *yad*, *yadden* quoted in *NED.* s. *Yode*; (cf. also *yodd*, *yedd* in *Cursor Mundi*, but rhyming with a long vowel). See Appendix VI, under Weak Verbs, p. 116, and *MÆ.* i. 2. 126–7.

11–12 'I am pining away, grievously wounded, through the power of my love for my own pearl, that had no flaw.' The wounding power of love was a familiar idea: compare *Lyrics of the Thirteenth Century* (ed. C. Brown, 86/3):

> loue is to myn herte gon wiþ one spere so kene,
> nyht ant day my blod hit drynkes, myn herte deþ me tene.

16 *heuen*: there is nothing to show that this is not simply the infinitive form of *heue* 'lift'. But the form *heuened* in *Sir Gawain*

349 makes it probable that the verb is *heuen* 'exalt, increase': see Glossary, HEUE and ḤEUEN.

17 *Þat* refers to the action of 14, the watching by the grave and longing for the pearl.

19–22 'Yet it seemed to me that there was never any song so sweet as the still hour would bring me in its peace. In truth many (such songs) came to me, thinking of her fresh hue wrapped round so by clods.' Lines 19–20 are adversative to the preceding two lines: though the poet felt grief, the sweetest of verse would come into his mind. He is evidently describing the genesis of the poem from verses that came to him by the grave, as he pondered his sorrow and the dispensations of God's providence.

23 *iuele* 'jewel', wrongly read by Morris as *mele*, which Gollancz adopted as an emendation. *Mele* would give natural sense: *myry mele* was a current phrase for 'joyous thing' (see *NED*. s. *Meal*, sb.², sense 2 f). The rhyme, however, which requires a long open *e*, supports *iuele*, since *mele* (Anglian *mēl*) has close *e*; and 'jewel' gives satisfactory sense.

29 *fede*: presumably the same word as *fede* in *Sir Tristram* 2474, where *forest fede* is probably equivalent to *hor wode* 'grey wood', the kind of forest described in *Sir Gawain* 741–9. The sense agrees with that of the adjective *fade* (OFr. *fade*) 'faded', 'having lost colour', but the vowel *e* is obscure. Gollancz suggests derivation from ON. *feyja* 'decay', but the form is then equally difficult, and the sense less satisfactory.

31–32 These lines are closely paralleled in *Piers Plowman*, C-text, xiii. 179–81. No direct relationship with *Pearl* is likely; both poets are paraphrasing the same verses in John (xii. 24–25).

37–38 The precise use of the prepositions should be observed: the poet goes *into* the herb-garden *to* the spot in that garden where the grave is.

39 The emphasis on the cutting of the corn suggests that the *hyȝ seysoun* is Lammas, as Gollancz understood it to be, rather than the feast of the Assumption of the Virgin, as Osgood assumed. There may be an intention to suggest the gathering of the Lord's harvest, with the pearl as one of the 'first-fruits'; cf. 894.

41 *huyle*: the grave-mound, which in 1205 is called *hyul*. If these

forms are correct, they represent a word distinct from *hyl, hylle,* the usual forms of 'hill' in this MS. It is suggested (see Gollancz, p. 119) that *huyle, hyul* may represent the modern dialect *hile,* current in south-east Lancashire (Rochdale). *Hile* normally means 'a thick cluster of plants', as in *whimberry-hile, rush-hile,* &c.; but the word is also used of a mound in *pisamoor-hile* 'ant-hill'. The grave-mound overgrown with flowers might therefore be described naturally as a 'hile'. In line 1172, where the mound is referred to as a *hylle,* the word has probably been confused (possibly by the copyist) with 'hill'; so also in the glossary *Catholicum Anglicum* compiled in 1483 *hylle* appears for *hile* in *A Rysche hylle: cirpetum.* The origin of *hile* is unknown.

43-44 The *worteȝ* here named were all spices. Peonies were then regarded primarily as spice-bearing plants, and were quite different from the flamboyant peonies of modern gardens, with flowers doubled and redoubled by the horticulturist's science. The passage is perhaps a reminiscence of the spices growing in Mirth's garden in the *Roman de la Rose* (ed. Langlois 1341-6), as Gollancz suggested. But the correspondence is not very close; cf. the Chaucerian translation of the lines (1367-72):

> Ther was eke wexyng many a spice,
> As clow-gelofre, and lycorice,
> Gyngevre, and greyn de parys,
> Canell, and setewale of prys,
> And many a spice delitable
> To eten whan men rise fro table.

Spices were the most precious of plants, and it was not unusual to plant them in the *erbere*; cf. *The Pistill of Susan* 103, *Spices speden to spryng in erbers enhaled.* But in the romances spices were commonly found in any landscape or garden intended to be surpassingly charming or luxuriant: so in *King Alysaunder* 6792 f.; *Sir Thopas* 49-54; *Maundeville's Travels,* chap. 59. The use of plants for spice brought no utilitarian associations to the medieval mind; spices were then costly, and the flowers of spice-plants were believed to have the richest scents. The comparison of the lady Joan to a series of spices in the lyric *Annot and Johon* (*Lyrics of the Thirteenth Century,* p. 136) further illustrates the medieval feeling for spices.

46 *fayr reflayr*: Gollancz in his first edition read *fayrre flayr,* a tempting reading, since it makes the construction of the sentence

more pointed; and, though *fayrer* is the usual form of the comparative in this MS., *fayrre* might be compared with *feier* in 103. The sense is satisfactory, however, as the text stands: 'If it was fair to look upon, fair also was the odour that floated from it.'

51 'A desolating grief lay deep in my heart.' *Deuely* is identical with modern dialect *deavely, davely*, used in the North and North-West in the senses 'lonely' and 'desolate'. The word is used most in Yorkshire and Cheshire: see *Deavely* in *NED.* and *EDD.* The word is probably a naturalized form (descended from late OE. **deaflic*) of ON. *daufligr*, which appears in Middle English and modern dialects as *dowly*. See *MÆ.* i. 2. 127.

52 It is not necessary to assume an echo of the *Roman de la Rose* (2997 f.) here: *resoun* is not a personification in this passage, and the idea of reason stilling the passions is a commonplace.

54 'With vehement thoughts that contended obstinately.' The nature of Christ gave him grounds for comfort, but his self-will made him suffer in the pain of his sorrow.

59 *slepyng-slaȝte*: 'sudden onset of sleep' (such as falls on those who have wept). *NED.* has the meaning 'a spell of sleep' here, but only from this passage and *Patience* 192. The usual meaning of *slaȝt* is 'a violent or sudden blow'.

60 *precios: precos* MS. A similar omission of *i* in the same terminal group of letters occurs in *prec[i]os* 192 and *grac[i]os* 95, *grac[i]ous* 934. The copyist's exemplar probably had *precōs, gracōs*, with an abbreviating stroke above the line to express the *i*. This stroke was by some accident omitted by the copyist. The form *gracōs* with this abbreviation is actually found in the text of *Sir Gawain* 216.

61 *in space*: not 'into space' (meaning 'into spatial distance'), which is a recent use, but 'after a time'; cf. the unambiguous use of the phrase in *The Destruction of Troy* 2811.

65 'I had no idea at all where it was' is probably the meaning, rather than 'I had no idea where in this world it was'. Cf. 293.

66 *cleuen* is probably past tense. The past plural of this verb otherwise occurs only once in this group of poems, as *clouen* in *Purity* 965. But *cleuen* is also a recognized type of past plural in the second strong conjugation; cf. *fleten* 21 and *flete* in *Sir Gawain*

1566. Variant forms of the past tense are found in most conjugations: see Appendix VI, under Strong Conjugations, p. 113.

77 *on slyde3*: this has usually been taken (so Osgood, Gollancz, and *NED.*) as *onslyde3* with the sense 'slip open, unfold' or 'sway'. The former meaning would suit the context, but requires the taking of *on-* as verbal *un-* (OE. *on-*, *un-*), which elsewhere is always *vn-* in this MS., as generally in Middle English. Probably *on* is adverbial 'on them'. Rhyme may have dictated the use of *slyde3*, but the poet had a vivid pictorial imagination, and having regard to the usual senses of *slide*, it seems most likely that he saw the polished silver foliage sliding, with no rustle, one leaf over another, while the leaves at the branch ends quivered.

86 *Garten*: plural, attracted from agreement with the singular subject by *downe3*.

100 *worpé*: the accent is editorial. The sense is clearly 'worthy', and although *worpe* 'worthy' is found in Middle English, it was usual to distinguish 'worthy' as *worpy* from 'worth', *worpe*. The use in *Pearl* is not entirely clear, owing to ambiguous spellings, but it is probable that the poet made this distinction. For the spelling *worpé* for *worpy* see Appendix II, p. 94, and Sisam, *Fourteenth Century Verse and Prose*, p. 226. By recognition that -*e* in ME. texts may represent the final sound developed from OE. *ig* and French *ie*, as well as from French *é*, Dr. Sisam was able, by the use of the editorial accent, to remove a number of unnecessary emendations from the text of *Pearl*. Cf. *cortaysé* 469, *pené* 510, *reprené* 544, &c.

103 *feier*: the MS. reading has been retained as a possible form of *feierre*, comparative of *feier*. Cf. note to 46.

105 *rawe3 and rande3 and rych reuere3*: the *rawe3* were either hedgerows or rows of trees, and *rande3* strips of land, especially strips lying beside a stream or body of water (see *NED.* s. *Rond*, and *EDD.* s. *Rand*; and cf. *strothe rande* in *Sir Gawain* 1710). The *rych reuere3* may be streams; that is the reference of this fairly frequent alliterative phrase in other ME. poems, e.g. *Morte Arthure* 62, 2279; *Golagros and Gawain* 248. But here it seems that the dreamer passes over the *rych reuere3* before he reaches the stream in 107; *reuere3* therefore probably has the alternative sense 'meadows along the bank of a stream', a meaning frequent in Old French and not uncommon in Middle English.

106 *her bonkes*: the banks of the *randeȝ* and *reuereȝ* where they meet the stream. In Middle English the term 'banks' was less frequently associated with the watercourse than now, and even when the stream lay at the foot of the slope the *bonke* was regarded as a feature of the ground, rather than as the border of the stream.

107 *a water*: as is revealed later, this is the river of the water of life, proceeding out of the throne of God. See Rev. xxii. 1–2, and lines 974, 1055–60.

schereȝ: the identity and sense of this word are uncertain, and the context is indecisive. *NED.* takes it to be a derivative of the adjective *schere* 'bright', and glosses it '? of water: To run bright and clear', a sense not known elsewhere and of doubtful authenticity. Gollancz identified it with OE. *sceran* (the water cuts into the bank). But as the verb is intransitive it may more readily be identified with *Sheer* v.² in *NED.* 'to swerve, alter course.' According to *NED.* this verb is of obscure origin and development, and is not recorded in English before the seventeenth century, and then only with nautical reference. But there is a clear example in *The Man in the Moon* (*Lyrics of the Thirteenth Century*, 89/4), *for doute leste he valle, he shoddreþ ant shereþ* (i.e. shrinks away); and if the suggestion (*MLN.* lix. 43, *Sheer off*) is correct, that this verb is an aphetic form ultimately from Latin *exerrare*, then the restriction to nautical use is a later specialized development. Translate: 'meanders along by the shore'.

113 *stepe*: commonly used in Middle English of eyes, in the sense 'staring, glaring', or of jewels (or eyes or stars) in the sense 'brilliant'. See *NED.* s. *Steep*, sense 2 a and b. The rhyme of *e* from OE. *ēa* with *e* from OE. *ē* (*swepe*, *slepe*) is apparently defective, but see Introduction, Dialect, p. xlvii, note 3.

115 *strope-men*: of uncertain meaning and derivation. *Strothe* in *Sir Gawain* 1710 appears to be derived from ON. *storð* 'stalks of herbage', but the North-West place-names containing Stroth, Strother (Lancashire, Lake counties, Northumberland) point to a native OE. *strōð, *strōðor, an old neuter word, cf. *sæl*, *salor*, &c. (see Mawer, *Place-names of Northumberland and Durham*, pp. 191 and 240, and Tolkien, *Chaucer as a Philologist*, Philological Society Transactions, 1934, pp. 56 f.). *Strōð appears to have had the meaning 'marshy land (overgrown with brushwood)', and probably

influenced the development of the imported ON. *storð*. Here *strope-men* is probably used in a generalized poetic sense to mean 'men of this world' (see *MÆ*. i. 2. 128), but *strope* would probably carry with it also, pictorially, a suggestion of the dark, low earth onto which the high stars look down.

116 *Staren*: this use of *stare* is not exactly equivalent to 'shine', but seems bound up with its application to stars, though these are not always explicitly mentioned. Cf. *Wars of Alexander* 3796: *as ai stremand sternes stared all paire wedis; Destruction of Troy* 7349: *The sternes full stithly starond o lofte*.

124 *Fordidden*: plural, attracted from the singular subject by the intervening nouns in 121 and 122; cf. 86 and note.

129–32 'Even as fortune acts wherever she makes trial, whether she allot delight or sorrow, the man to whom she sends her will chances (in result) to have ever more and more'; fortune visits whatever man she wishes to test, sending him continuous good or bad luck for the time being. The idea of fortune as a fickle goddess testing the hearts of men was common in medieval literature; cf., for example, the *Roman de la Rose*, especially 4837 f. In *Sir Gawain* 489, 1549, *frayne* is used in the sense 'make trial of'; and *hitte* is used in the sense 'meet with, attain as a result' in *Purity* 479; see *NED*. s. *Hit*, v., sense 11.

139–40 The following interpretation is suggested: 'I thought the stream was a division made by pools, separating the delights.' The general conception of the landscape and its stream flowing from pool to pool was probably suggested by the garden of Deduit in the *Roman de la Rose*, and is clear enough; but there are several ambiguities of detail: (i) *deuyse* (used in the sense 'division' in Wyntoun's *Chronicle* vi. 1041, *c*. 1420) might alternatively be 'device', referring to an artificial conduit such as was cut between the fountains in the garden of Deduit. (ii) *by* in this group of poems is usually used to express position rather than means or agency: *by mereȝ made* therefore may mean 'made by the side of pools' (i.e. made so as to join them); but *by* is sometimes used of agency (cf. *Sir Gawain* 20), and so the phrase may mean 'made by means of pools'. (iii) *myrþeȝ* may mean precisely 'pleasure gardens' (so Osgood), but more probably the sense here is more general, and *myrþeȝ* = *weleȝ* in 154.

142 *hoped: hope* MS. The final *d* or *t* of the weak past tense or

past participle has been omitted five times in *Pearl*; cf. *hope*[*d*] 185, *calle*[*d*] 572, *carpe*[*d*] 752, *bro3*[*t*] 286; and *jacyngh*[*t*] 1014 is probably similar. In all these cases the next word begins with *þ*, which by the normal process of assimilation in Northern and Western dialects of this period would become *t* when the preceding word ended in a dental consonant. A combination like *hoped þat* would be pronounced *hopet tat*, and later reduced to *hope tat*. Thus the copyist was here writing *hope* for the past tense as it was actually pronounced, though he retained the conventional spelling *þat* for *tat*, as he did throughout the MS. Forms like *hope* and *bro3* are such severe phonetic spellings, however, that they seem grammatically incomplete, and are normalized in the text. See further *MÆ.* i. 2. 132 ff.

145 *mare* as a variant of *more* when required by rhyme is not unusual in the North-West Midlands, and is not in itself evidence of origin near the Northern dialect area. *Mare* and similar forms preserving OE. *ā* unrounded occur as far south as Shropshire, as in the poems of Audelay (ed. E. K. Whiting, p. 2, l. 39), *mare* rhyming with *ware* 'aware'; and in Myrc, *Instructions for Parish Priests* 264, *mare: fare*. See Introduction, under Dialect, p. xlv.

154 *wo*: referring to the difficulty and pain that might result from attempting to reach the delights visible on the other side of the stream. But there is much to be said for Gollancz's emendation to *woþe*; the poet has already spoken of the *woþe3* 'perils' of the passage across the stream, and the phrase produced by the emendation, *wonde for woþe*, occurs in *Sir Gawain* 488. The assumed omission of *þe* would be a familiar type of error, since the next word begins with *þe*. But the MS. reading *for wo* gives satisfactory sense, and *wo* provides a good contrast with *wele3*.

165 *schere*: glossed 'to make bright or pure' by *NED.*, while *schorne golde* in 213 is regarded as gold that has been cut. The verb *schere* 'to make bright or pure' is doubtful, since the only evidence for its use in a non-figurative sense is here and in 107. Gollancz claimed *schorne* in 213 as part of the same verb, but if *schere* 'to make bright' existed, it would be a causative weak verb with pp. *schered*. Probably here as in 213 the verb is *schere* 'to cut', and the poet is thinking of gold cut into thin strips to make *fyldor*; in 213 it is the girl's *fax* 'hair' that is like *schorne golde*; cf. *The Fair Maid of Ribblesdale* (*Harley Lyrics* 7/12), *a fyldor fax to folde*.

172 'As had hitherto been wont (to come) thither (i.e. to me) but little (i.e. not at all)'; cf. line 301. Alternatively: 'As used (to come) to me a little time before,' i.e. when the Pearl was living.

178 *whyt as playn yuore: playn* might be taken in the context to mean 'absolute, sheer', but the simile is conventional, and in its use elsewhere polished ivory is meant; as, for example, in the *Roman d'Alexandre* (ed. Michelant, Stuttgart, 1846, p. 342), where maidens *ont les dens plus blans que yuores planés. Playn* has this same sense in *Purity* 1068.

179 'Which threw my heart into astounded confusion.' *Stonge* is used to denote the driving into a specified condition by affecting with keen emotion: see *NED.* s. *Sting,* v.[1], sense 5. *Atount* has usually been regarded, perhaps rightly, as an error for *astount*; but *atount* possibly represents an Anglo-French form of OFr. *atoner,* a nearly related synonym of *estoner. Atoner* is descended from Latin *attonare,* while the more usual *estoner* represents an unrecorded **extonare.*

197 *biys: uiys* MS. Apoc. xix. 8 states that it was allowed to the bride of the Lamb to array herself in shining white bysse: *Et datum est illi ut cooperiat se byssinum splendens, candidum.* The line as emended follows the scriptural source exactly. *Beau* is found in other western alliterative poems as a conventional epithet, as in *Richard the Redeless* iii. 1, and *Siege of Jerusalem* 587.

199 *at my deuyse*: usually rendered 'in my opinion' (Osgood, Gollancz, and *NED.* s. *Device,* sense 4, where this line is the earliest example). Another common meaning of *deuyse* in Middle English is 'desire, will' (*NED.* sense 3). In this context, and in similar ones referring to number or quality of exceptional order, *at* (*my*) *deuyse* seems to have had a meaning something between the two: 'As many (or as fine) as one (I) could (wish to) think of.' Cf. *Sir Gawain* 617, and *Audelay's Poems* 45/37:

> Of al þe flours at my deuyse,
> 3et Floure of Iesse 3et bers þe prys.

209 *werle* is probably a form of ME. *wherl, whirl* 'whorl'. This sense has not been found elsewhere as early as the Middle English period (see *NED.* s.v.), but it is an easy development from the basic etymological sense; cf. OE. *hwirfling* 'something round, orb'; *hwirflede* 'rounded'; *sin-hwyrfel* '(completely) round'. Bradley

glossed *werle* as ' ? garland' in the additions to the ME. dictionary, but the etymological associations of the word, and the qualification *oþer* here, imply a more general sense of 'circlet': besides the *pyȝt coroune* she wore no other circlet to confine her hair. An alternative suggestion is that *werle* is derived from the stem of the verb 'wear' with the suffix *-el*: (so *NED.*; and Holthausen similarly suggests OE. *werels cognate with ON. *vesl* 'attire'.)

210 *here*: MS. *lere* is unintelligible. The text as emended may be rendered (lines 210–12): 'Her hair, lying all about her, enclosed her countenance, grave enough for (i.e. to befit) a duke or an earl, her complexion whiter than ivory.' *Semblaunt* and *ble* are both objects of *leke*, past tense of *louke* 'to enclose'. In *al hyr vmbegon*, literally 'having enclosed her all around', *hyr* is historically a dative, as can be seen in the less ambiguous impersonal sentences like *Me is wo begon*; see *NED.* s. *Bego*, sense 8, and *Woe-begone*. A similar picture of luxuriant hair enclosing the face is found in *Sir Gawain* 181 f., where the Green Knight's long hair, together with his beard, covers his neck and shoulders like a *kyngeȝ capados*.

215–6 'The deep white of her complexion lacked nothing of the colour of the precious pearls set in the embroidery.' *Colour* in reference to the complexion implies whiteness, just as in 753: *Þy colour passeȝ þe flour-de-lys.* For the idiomatic use of *non* = 'no amount (of a quality)', cf. *Cursor Mundi* 9916: *Of suete grennes þai wantes nan*; while the omission of *colour* following the verb is natural since *non* is a pronoun. The alternative interpretation: 'Her intense white complexion had no lack of pearls set round it in embroidery' is less effective. A. S. Cook in *Modern Philology* vi. 197 suggested that *colour* is for 'collar', but, while it is true that large collars were worn at the time, *depe* is a less natural adjective with 'collar' than with 'colour'; cf. Chaucer's *Squire's Tale* 511: *So depe in greyn he dyed his coloures*, meaning 'he made the colouring (of his pretence) so vivid'; whereas a large collar of the period is described as *brode*, cf. *The Flower and the Leaf* 215. The spelling of the MS. form, moreover, makes it likely that 'colour' is intended.

225–6 'I believe no tongue could suffice to say any adequate word of that sight'. *Endure* in this sense of 'have power to perform an action' occurs in Trevisa (Sisam's *Fourteenth Century Verse and Prose*, p. 147, l. 42), and *sauerly* in the sense of 'to one's liking' in *Sir Gawain* 2048.

228 A very definite picture of the maiden's appearance has been given. Her costume is a simple form of the aristocratic dress of the second half of the fourteenth century. She wore a *bleaunt* (163): this was a loose flowing surcoat, made of *biys* (197), that is, of fine white linen (or possibly silk), with openings at the side (198), extending from the lowest hem up towards the waist. These openings in the *bleaunt* are found in the second half of the fourteenth century and in the fifteenth. The *bleaunt* had short sleeves reaching to the elbow, and from the back of the sleeves hung long *lappeȝ* (201); these usually tapered to a sharp point and often reached nearly to the ground. Sleeves of this kind were typical of aristocratic costume all through the fourteenth century. Here they were trimmed with a double row of pearls, and other hems of the *bleaunt* also were decked with pearls (198–200, 202). The *bleaunt* probably reached to the maiden's feet, but through the openings and at the sleeves her *cortel of self sute* (203) could be seen. This was the under-dress, a closer-fitting garment than the *bleaunt*; it reached from neck to feet, and had close-fitting sleeves to the wrists. The wrist-bands (*poyned* 217) were trimmed with pearls, as were the portions of the *cortel* visible through the side-openings of the *bleaunt* (218) and the opening of the *bleaunt* at the neck (*ouerture* 218), while on her bosom was fastened a single large pearl (221–2). On her head she wore a lofty crown set with pearls (205), of elaborate design, such as a queen might wear. Her golden hair flowed loose over her neck and shoulders, as befitted a maiden and a bride; the matrons of the time were more elaborately coifed, and the hair was held in place usually by a fret. The abundance of pearls in the whole costume has special symbolical significance, but it reflects contemporary fashion also: see Introduction, p. xxxiv. The picture of the maiden in the MS. does not agree in details of costume with the description in the poem. The girl is depicted in a *bleaunt*, but no openings are visible in it, and consequently the *cortel* cannot be seen. No pearls are shown, and the hair is coifed, not hanging loose.

231 'No gladder man from here to Greece.' Cf. *Sir Gawain* 2023: *Þe gayest into Grece*. This form of expression is probably of French origin; cf. the *Roman de la Rose* 542–3:

> N'avoit jusqu'en Jerusalen
> Fame qui plus bel col portast.

Osgood cites other passages from French poetry where Constantinople is mentioned in the same manner. Greece does not seem to have been used elsewhere in such phrases, and may have been chosen by this poet for convenience of alliteration and rhyme.

233 See Introduction, p. xiii.

254 *y3en graye*: the child's eyes may really have been *graye*, but that is the conventional colour for beautiful eyes in ME. poetry. Cf. *Sir Gawain* 82, Prologue to the *Canterbury Tales* 152; and in a note on the latter passage Skeat quotes many more parallels. *Graye* applied to eyes often renders *vair* in French romances (as in the Chaucerian *Romaunt of the Rose*), and *vair* (ultimately from Latin *varius*) is often of uncertain meaning in its application to eyes. Possibly gray-blue or blue is meant.

257 On the use of *Sir* see Introduction, p. xvii f.; and of *3e* plural for polite singular see Appendix V, pp. 105–6.

259 *clente*: the usual sense of this word is 'riveted', and if that is its meaning here, it qualifies *cofer*. *As* in the next line then equates *in þis garden* with *in cofer*: 'which is in a coffer, so fairly riveted, being in this garden so charmingly gay'. But neater syntax is obtained by taking *as* as correlative with *so*; *clente* then refers to the *perle* and may be rendered 'fastened, enclosed': 'your pearl ... which is enclosed in coffer so fairly as to be in this garden. ...'

274 *þe* is dative: 'that has clearly made for you something out of nothing', i.e. has made an eternal pearl out of a short-lived rose.

307 *westernays*: this otherwise unknown word Osgood emended to *besternays* 'turned round, reversed' (OFr. *bestorneis*): in many medieval hands *b* closely resembled the first part of *w*, and the *w* of *worde3* preceding might have led the copyist to expect another *w* alliterating. Bradley, and later Gollancz, was of the opinion that *westernays* was an altered form of *besternays* in actual use, the alteration being due to the influence of *west*, since the word was applied to a church which faced west instead of east as was then usual. Sister Mary V. Hillman (*MLN*. lviii. 42) suggests the reading *west ernays* 'empty pledge' (from OE. *wēste*, and *ernays = erneis*, see *NED*. s. *Earnest*, sb.²). The meaning of lines 307–8 would then be: 'You account His words a quite empty pledge who (= when you) believe nothing unless you see it.' Cf. *Destruction of Troy* 5002: *Þou set noght our saghe.*

313–15 *bayly, dayly* rhyme here with *fayle, counsayle,* and it is uncertain whether they represent OFr. *baillie* 'dominion, domain', OFr. *dalier* 'trifle', or OFr. *baille* 'castle wall, castle', ON. *deila* 'contend, dispute'. There appears to be confusion, in the MS. spellings, of *bayly* from *baillie* and *bayle* from *baille*, but where the words appear in unambiguous contexts the rhymes are distinct: in 442 where *bayly* must represent *baillie* it rhymes with *cortaysye*, whereas in 1083 MS. *baly* (probably a scribal error) must mean 'castle wall' and rhymes with *quayle, trauayle*. It seems probable that the *-ly* spelling in such words represents palatal *l*, and is not equivalent to *-ly* from OFr. *-li*; see Appendix V, p. 104. Moreover, for *dayly* the meaning 'contend, dispute' from ON. *deila* is probably more satisfactory here than 'trifle' from OFr. *dalier*.

331 *gareʒ*: the finite verb after *bot* is good Middle English idiom, and editors were wrong in emending to *gare*. Cf. *The Owl and the Nightingale* 1452: *luue ne deþ noʒt bute rest*, where the rhyme with *ilest* shows that *rest* is the present tense, not the infinitive; also *Towneley Plays* 18/318: *Ther myne did bot smoked*.

333 *declyne*: according to *NED*. 'turn away, depart', but in the *Wars of Alexander*, which is very close to *Pearl* in diction, *declyne* is used in the sense 'fall from prosperity': *He þat enhansis hym to heʒe, the heldire he declynes* (2714).

335–6 'When I am deprived of my pearl, what can one judge (of such a situation) but lasting grief.' The emendation to *perle* (MS. *perleʒ*) is required by the context; the MS. form may be due to the proximity of *partleʒ*. *Myne* is probably dissyllabic, with *-e* either retained in emphatic use from the older forms of the oblique cases, or added on the analogy of such adjectives as *hire* and *oure* which normally kept their *-e* in emphatic positions.

344 'You who must of necessity endure, be not so impatient.' The admonition to patience and obedience to the will of God is similar to that in *Patience*; cf. especially: *And quo for þro may noʒt þole, þe þikker he sufferes* (6).

346 *Braundysch* and *bray* are intransitive; *brapeʒ* is a 'cognate' accusative. Translate: 'Struggle and bray in your anguish.' The metaphor is that of a doe stricken in the chase; a fuller description of what the image implies occurs in *Sir Gawain* 1159–63.

349 *adyte* is the French *aditer* 'accuse', rather than from OE.

adihtan or *adihtian* 'arrange, dispose', influenced by the French word, as Osgood and Gollancz held. Translate: 'Judge the Lord, ever arraign Him (i.e. though you may judge, &c.), He will not turn aside from the path one foot.' The sense of the stanza as a whole is similar to that of Psalm l. 6 (·Vulgate text): *Tibi soli peccavi et malum coram te feci, ut justificeris in sermonibus tuis et vincas cum judicaris.*

358 *fleme*: MS. *leme* is not known in any sense which fits the context. Gollancz identified it with OE. *lēman* 'to gleam', ascribing to it here the dubious sense 'glance'; but the context requires a transitive verb, parallel with *lype* in the preceding line. Derivation from ON. *lemja* 'beat' has also been suggested, but *lemja* appears in English dialects as *lam*, with the vowel of the past stem, and a form *leme* from *lemja* would have an open *e*, whereas a close *e* is required for rhyme with *deme*; *lemja* (and *lam*), moreover, have the sense 'thrash (so as to cause lameness)', not 'beat (off)', which is required here. Mrs. Wright (*JEGPh.* xxxviii. 10) cites Northern and Midland dialect *Leam* 'to separate nuts from the husk', for the derivation of which *EDD.* suggests 'Norwegian dialect *lema*, (*lima*, *lemma*) "to dismember", cf. OE. *lim* (pl. *leomu*)'. But the rhyme is doubtful.

359 *marre oper madde*: in altering *marre* to *marred*, and rendering the phrase 'marred or made', editors have missed the sense and construction of this phrase. *Marre* is OFr. *marrir* 'lament', and *madde* is the same verb as *madde* in *Sir Gawain* 2414, meaning 'act madly'. It is similarly said of the ghost in *The Aunters of Arthur* 110 that *Hit menet, hit muset, hyt marret for madde*, where the final phrase means that it raised lamentations like one demented. The verbs *marre oper madde* are both concessive subjunctives, and are thus parallel in use to *Deme* and *adyte* in 349. Translate 359-60: 'For, though you may lament or rave, or mourn and conceal it, (yet) all lies in God's power to dispose and judge.' Alternatively, *mype* may be an earlier form of modern dialect *mither* 'to fret, worry', common in south Lancashire and Cheshire (Yorks. *moither*). The origin of *mither* is unknown, but it may have developed from *mithe* by analogy with such verbs as *bother*, *natter* and is possibly related ultimately to ON. *mœðask* (*móðr*) of similar meaning.

362 'Let my Lord not be offended.'

365 As there is no analogy between the actions denoted by *gotȝ*

out and *remorde* in the preceding line, it seems likely that *gotȝ out of welle* is a 'contact-clause' = *þat gotȝ*, &c. Translate: 'My heart was all afflicted with a sense of loss, like gushing water that runs from a fountain.' The basis of the simile is probably Psalm xxi. 15 (Vulgate), where the Psalmist says of his sorrow: *Sicut aqua effusus sum*.

383 'But the mercy of Christ, and Mary and John.' The *mersy* is Christ's, and not Mary's and John's. The poet is thinking of the three figures in the Crucifixion scene. Lines 383-4 are a way of saying that Christ's mercy of redemption, shown in the Crucifixion where Mary and John stood close at hand, is the sole source of the poet's happiness.

388 *harmeȝ hate*: sorrows were traditionally hot, like those of the Seafarer in the OE. poem which *seofedun hat' ymb heortan*; cf. also *Christ* 500, 539; *Guthlac* 933, &c.; and the ME. phrase *kele of care* 'comfort (lit. cool) one's sorrow' (*NED*. s. *Keel*, v.).

396 *in grounde*: Sisam's emendation of *in* to *and* removes all dubious idiom, and assumes a not uncommon type of error, the misreading of the sign for *and* as *in* (the reverse mistake has been assumed in 342). But, though no precise parallel can be adduced, the MS. phrase seems natural enough, in the sense 'at the foundation (of)', to be retained.

417 *herytage*: cf. Rom. viii. 16-17: 'We are the children of God (*filii Dei*). And if children, then heirs, heirs of God, and joint heirs (*coheredes*) with Christ.' This 'heritage' is often referred to by writers on salvation by grace. *Erytage* in 443 is similarly the share of eternal life received as a *filius Dei*. We become *filii Dei* when our original sin is remitted in baptism.

430 *Fenyx of Arraby*: the phoenix is here made the symbol of Mary because it was unique (and see next). Chaucer similarly asserts that the Duchess Blanche was:

> The soleyn fenix of Arabye;
> For ther livyth never but oon. (*Boke of the Duchesse*, 982-3)

This parallel is pointed out by Osgood, who observes that in medieval literature the phoenix was commonly used as a symbol of Christ, and only rarely of Mary. Fletcher points out other parallels in Albertus Magnus, *De Laudibus Beatae Mariae Virginis*, where Mary is described as *singularis* in beauty and virtue (v. i. 1), and compared with the phoenix *quae est unica avis sine patre* (VII. iii. 1).

431 *þat freles fleʒe of hyr fasor*: 'Which flawless flew from its Creator.' The previous interpretations of this line have identified *fasor* with *fasure* 1084 meaning 'fashion, form', thus missing the special significance of the analogy, namely, that Mary was immaculate from the moment of her creation. Sister Mary V. Hillman points this out in a note (*MLN*. lviii. 43) where she quotes passages from the Phoenix Homily and the OE. poem of the Phoenix, which stress the fact of the creation of the marvellous bird by God. On the phonological relation of *freles* to ON. *frýjulaust*, see Appendix IV, p. 100.

432 *Quen of cortaysye*: on the meaning of *cortaysye* see Introduction, p. xxxii. In 457 Saint Paul is named as an authority on heavenly *cortaysye*, and in the passage referred to (1 Cor. xii. 12–13) Paul is speaking of divine grace. *Quen of cortaysye* is therefore the equivalent of the theologians' *Regina gratiae*, and similarly in 425 *Marye þat grace of grewe* is the equivalent of *Mater (divinae) gratiae*.

435 *May*: the derivation of this word is complex, since OE. *mǣg* conceals more than one word in its non-west-Saxon form: (i) **mēg* 'maiden' = ON. *meyj-* (as *ēg = eyj-*), (ii) *mēge = māge*, feminine of *mǣg* 'kinsman', (iii) *mǣge* 'maiden', the old nominative of *mǣgeþ*, cf. *hæle/hæleþ*.

439 'Sir, many contest here and win the prize.' See *NED*. s. *Prey*, sense 1 b. Metaphors of the race (or other games) are frequent in Saint Paul: cf. especially 1 Cor. ix. 24–25.

459 *naule*: it is now generally agreed that Gollancz was right in taking this as 'navel'. *Naule* as 'nail' from ON. *nagl* would offer no phonological difficulty, since the rhyme with *Poule* indicates a monosyllable; but ON. *nagl* is not found elsewhere in English, whereas *naule, noule* is a not uncommon form of 'navel'. Contextually, too, 'navel' is more suitable: the list includes head, extremities and middle (*naule*), parts chosen to represent the whole extent of the body. The navel to the medieval writer or reader had none of the modern associations of indelicacy. As J. B. Fletcher has pointed out (*JEGPh*. xx. 2), Albertus Magnus in *De Laudibus Beatae Mariae Virginis* compared the navel of the Virgin to a wine-cup in the hand of the Holy Ghost.

460 *tryste*: MS. *tyste*. The MS. form might be interpreted as a variant spelling of *ty3te* 'tight, firm' (so Osgood and Sisam). But while *st* is used in many ME. texts for *3t* (where *3* is the palatal voiceless fricative = OE. *h*), there is no instance of such a spelling in this MS. unless *myste* in 462 stands for *my3te* (see next). Moreover, rhymes of forms containing *s* = *3* with words containing ordinary sibilant *s*, though found in ME., are rare, and both this type of spelling and this type of rhyme are especially rare in Northern and North Midland texts. It seems better, therefore, to emend to *tryste*, an emendation supported by the common currency of the alliterative phrase *true and tryste* and its variant *traist and true* in Middle English: for examples see *NED*. s. *Trist* and *Traist*.

462 *myste*: this word has been taken by all editors as a spelling of *my3te* 'might', but both spelling and rhyme offer difficulties: see note on 460 above. It seems more likely that *NED*. is right in recognizing the existence of a noun *myste* 'spiritual mysteries'. This would be contextually more suitable here. Saint Paul in the passage referred to in this stanza (1 Cor. xii) is speaking of spiritual gifts and the spiritual union of Christians; the whole passage is *de spiritalibus*. Compare the words of William of Shoreham (ed. Konrath, 23/629–30), when he refers to these same words of Paul:

> Cryst and hijs membrys, men,
> O body beþe ine mystyke.

See further *MÆ*. ii. 3. 171.

463 *gawle* is a remarkable form for so early a date if it is for 'gall', OE. *galla*. It rhymes here with words containing the ME. diphthong *aul*; whereas the ME. form is usually *galle* and normally rhymes with *al* (as *galle* 'impurity', also from OE. *galla*, in 189 and 915, rhymes with *calle*, *byfalle*, &c.). It has been suggested that *gawle* should be derived from OE. *gāgol* 'wanton'; but this is unsatisfactory. *Gāgol*, so far as is known, has not descended into Middle English, and the use of the adjective as an abstract noun would be unusual. Moreover, the sense 'wantonness' does not suit the context here: what Saint Paul says is that there is no schism between the members of the Christian body, nor is one member jealous of the honours bestowed on another (1 Cor. xii. 12–25). The sense 'rancour' gives a fair paraphrase of Paul's idea, and is a well-established meaning of ME. *galle* 'gall'. The spelling *gaule* for the parallel word meaning 'impurity' occurs in *Patience* 285 and

Purity 1525. It is strange that this should be the only word in these poems in which diphthongization of *a* before *l* is evidenced. This change is usually assigned to the fifteenth century (see Jordan, § 267), and if it is really as early as the end of the fourteenth, other words containing *al* might be expected to show signs of it.

476 'Who had endured (i.e. remained) steadfast in the world.' The reference is to the doctrine of perseverance in righteousness.

482 *coneʒ*: probably an auxiliary of the present tense. Though the context is indecisive here, this particular form as an auxiliary occurs elsewhere only as a present: see Glossary. Of the four poems in this MS. only *Pearl* shows this use of *con* as an auxiliary of the present as well as of the past tense, and this—one of the few differences in linguistic usage to be found within the group—may be due to the greater exigencies of metrical structure. Even as an auxiliary of the past tense *con* is much more frequent in *Pearl* than in *Sir Gawain*, which has fewer rhymes, and more frequent in *Sir Gawain* than in the unrhymed *Purity*. And it is significant that in every instance where *con* expresses the present tense the following infinitive is in rhyme, whereas the infinitive after *con* of the past tense may be in the middle of a line, as in 78.

483–5 On the significance of these lines see Introduction, p. xiii.

489 *damysel*. In the careful glossary to his edition of *Galeran* (*CFMA*. Paris, 1925) Foulet defines *damoiselle* as a term of respect addressed to an unmarried woman irrespective of rank. Unlike *dame*, *damysel* does not seem to have been a formalized term of address within the family. Nevertheless, its use here is no argument that the Pearl was not the dreamer's daughter: he is rebuking her (as he thinks) for presumption, and *damysel* would be something like modern 'miss' in a speech of reproof. Cf. the use of *ʒe* and *þou*; see Appendix V, pp. 105–6.

492 *date* here becomes the linking-word of the group of five stanzas which follow, and thus this word, which in its ordinary uses was not of frequent occurrence, has to be used ten times in the positions fixed by the metrical form. In working the word into these positions the poet sometimes strains its meaning a little, as when he makes *date of daye* mean 'dawn' in 517 and 'end of the day' in 541. Here in 492 it seems that the recognized sense 'limit' has been extended slightly: 'that is too exalted a point to reach'.

That the basic meaning here is 'limit' is implied by the Pearl's answer: 'There is no limit to his generosity.'

505 *þys hyne*: the labourers. *Þys(e)* 'these' is often used in Middle English with reference to persons or things not previously mentioned, but familiarly known, and especially with reference to the whole class of such things or persons. See *NED*. s.v. *These*, sense II. c.

513 *totȝ*: this is an interesting form, found nowhere else, so far as is known. It rhymes here with words containing older *ā* (*ros*, *gotȝ*, *þos*) and also with *o* in *porpos*, *clos*. Elsewhere in the poems of this group the contracted (Northern) forms of *take*: *ta*, *tas*, *tan(e)*, &c., are frequent. But since *ā* in these forms is a later product, not derived from OE. *ā*, it should remain as *ā* in any dialect that used or adopted these forms. So *ma*, *matȝ*, *made* from *make* (cf. modern *made*, not *mode*). The most probable explanation of *totȝ* is that it is an analogical form, due to the translation of *ā* into its variant *ǭ*. But this would only be likely to occur, whether in real speech or in artificial language, in an area on the border of the 'North' and the 'Midlands'; that is, an area where *ǭ* was normally used, but for many words containing this *ǭ* Northern variants with *ā* were familiar to the ear. An *o* form *tone* occurs in *Sir Gawain* 2159. This, however, rhymes with *grone* (OE. *grānian*), and may have been produced by scribal alteration, first of *grane* to *grone*, and then, consequentially to preserve the visible rhyme, of *tane* to *tone*. This *tone* illustrates, none the less, how such artificial or analogical forms could be produced in an area of competing *ā/ǭ* forms. See Tolkien, foreword to Haigh, *Dialect of Huddersfield District*, p. xiv.

524 *pay*: a survival of the old use of the present to express future tense. In this group of poems an auxiliary is much more frequently employed than this usage.

532 *sade*: all editors except Gollancz normalize this form as *sayde*. *Sade*, however, was probably a genuine form in the copyist's usage, and possibly in that of the original text. There are five other forms in this MS. with *ay* reduced to *a*; *sade* 784, *satȝ* 677, *saȝ* 689, and *sade* in *Purity* 210. Moreover in *Pearl* 836 *saȝ* 'saw' in the exemplar has been misinterpreted by the copyist as the form meaning 'says', and he has transcribed it as *saytȝ*. *Sad(e)* also occurs sporadically as the past tense or past participle in other North-Western texts, as in the *Stanzaic Life of Christ* 8976 and *Audelay's*

Poems (p. 20, l. 266). The writing of *a* for *ay* appears only in the verb 'say' in this group of poems, and is therefore not likely to be connected with the northern simplification of diphthongs, which took place in all positions. *Sade* and *sat3* more probably originated as unaccented forms, used together with *sayt3* and *sayde* as stressed forms.

536 *þat at 3e moun*: 'what you can'. *At* as a relative appears not uncommonly in Northern texts and appears to be derived from ON. *at*, but here, as Sisam has observed, *þat at* is more likely to be a development of *þat þat*, through the intermediate stage *þat tat* (cf. note on *hope* 142). *At* does not occur as a relative elsewhere in this group of poems, and *þat at* is also found in other texts where the relative *at* from ON. is not used, as in Myrc, *Instructions for Parish Priests* 658, and *Towneley Plays* 2/40, 105/149, 332/207.

565 'Moreover, is my act of giving lawful to me (have I the right), to do as I will with my own?' *Weþer* introduces the question and has no equivalent in modern use. This line and the three following are based on Matt. xx. 15. For the form *louyly* for *la3ely*, see Appendix II, p. 94 (6 and 7), and *MÆ*. ii. 3. 172.

568 *byswyke3* is not an artificial form introduced for the sake of rhyme, but the natural form of Northern and North Midland idiom. The syntactical convention of these dialects required that, whenever a pronoun was the subject of more than one verb, the first verb should end in -*e* or have no inflexion, and the second end in -(*e*)*s*, no matter what was the person of the pronoun. This is still the usage of most Northern and North Midland dialects (J. Wright, *English Dialect Grammar*, § 435). See *MÆ*. ii. 3. 173.

572 *myke3* is an aphetic form of *amike* 'friend', Latin *amīcus*. Here *myke3* must have the extended sense 'chosen companions of the Lord', since it renders *electi* in *multi sunt enim vocati, pauci autem electi* (Matt. xx. 16). See *MÆ*. ii. 3. 174.

580 'If they demand an award according to strict justice.' *To aske* is an absolute infinitive.

596 *pretermynable*: (*pertermynable* MS.) a word of uncertain meaning, since it occurs only here, and the *verce in Sauter* (Psalm lxi. 13) which the poet is paraphrasing gives little clue to the intended meaning. Apparently it is made up of *pre+termynable*, used in an active sense (see *NED*. s. -*able*, -*ble*); and it is usually

interpreted as 'pre-ordaining', and assumed to represent a scholas-
tic Latin **praeterminabilis*, rendering Greek προορίζειν, the usual
word in the New Testament for 'pre-ordain'. Osgood suggests that
the idea of 'pre-ordaining' is derived in this passage from Albertus
Magnus' comment on the passage from the Psalm: *Primo, divinae
voluntatis ordinatio aeterna et perfecta*, &c. Alternatively, the poet
may have coined the epithet, for convenience of rhyme, from the
ME. verb *termyne* 'determine', with *per* as an intensive prefix, to
express the idea 'power belongeth unto God', in the preceding
verse of the Psalm. In that case MS. *per-* need not be emended.

600 This line should be divided into the phrase-groups *euer þe
lenger þe lasse* and *þe more*, the first meaning 'continually the less
(work done)', and the second 'the more (able to earn)'. *Euer (þe)
lenger* is an idiomatic phrase used with comparatives in Middle
English to express a constant relation between the comparative
and some varying condition; for other examples see the *Canterbury
Tales* A 3872, E 687, F 404; and *MÆ*. ii. 3. 174. The meaning of
599–600 is then: 'Then the less work done, the greater the capacity
for earning, and so continually in a constant (inverse) ratio.'

602 *joparde*, rhyming with *rewarde, harde* (OFr. *reward*, OE.
heard) must represent *jopart*, a form attested elsewhere, and
probably due to ME. or AFr. misunderstanding of *jo parti* 'divided
game' as *jo part* 'lost game.' See *NED*. s. *Jeopard* and *Jeopardy*.

603–4 On the theological significance of these much discussed
lines see Introduction, p. xxi f. There the meaning 'what is due as
recognition of merit' (see *NED*. s. *Reward*, sense II. 4) is suggested
for *rewarde*. It is a sense of the word closely related to 'estimation,
worth'; see *NED*. (sense I, 3) and *MÆ* ii. 3. 175. J. Sledd (*MLN*.
lv. 381) and Mary V. Hillman (*MLN*. lvi. 457) maintain that the
ordinary meaning 'reward' is intended here, since line 606 and
other evidence in the poem proves that the poet regarded the elect
as having graded rewards, besides the common reward of heavenly
bliss. But in this particular passage it is not the graded rewards
that are being discussed: the whole point is that the workers are
paid alike (they all receive heavenly life) whatever the amount of
work done, i.e. whether little or much be due to them as recognition of merit. Line 606 refers not to the graded rewards of the elect,
but to its immediate context: God is no niggard, either in His
rewards or in His punishments. The suggestion of Marie P. Hamil-

ton (*MLN*. lviii. 370) that *payed inlyche* means 'fully contented' is similarly unsuitable to the argument, as well as unconvincing in itself.

605 See Introduction, p. xxii.

607–8 'He pours out his gifts (as copiously) as water from a drain, or streams from a deep source that has never ceased to flow.' There are still proverbial expressions current in Lancashire and the West Riding about the rapid dispersal of 'dike-watter', as 'It'll go like dike-watter', said of money in the hands of a reckless spender; or 'he (or it) goes as fast as dike-watter', said of a person or thing that wastes rapidly away. By 'dike-watter' is meant water that collects in rainy weather and is carried off rapidly in gutters or drains; and this is probably the basis of the metaphor in 607. Then, to make the point that the source is inexhaustible, the metaphor of the *gote3 of golf* is added. *Golf* may well be the same word as Northern dialect *goaf, goave*, now used chiefly to mean 'the space left in a coal-mine after the whole of the coal has been extracted' (*EDD*.). Here the *gote3 of golf* seem to be streams that spring from a deep source; there are several of these in the Pennine limestone country whose volume of water does not vary in either the wettest or dryest seasons. See *MÆ*. ii. 3. 176.

609–10 A notoriously difficult passage: the reference of the pronouns is uncertain; *fraunchyse* may mean either 'generosity' (of God) or 'privilege, liberation' (of the man *þat euer dard*); and there are two verbs which could give past tense *dard* in Middle English, OE. *durran* 'dare' and OE. *darian* 'lurk in dread'. Thus the passage has been interpreted variously, as, for example: 'That man's privilege is great who ever stood in awe of Him who rescues sinners', or: 'His (God's) generosity, which is always inscrutable (*lit*. lay hidden) is abundant to the man who rescues his soul from sin.' The former interpretation raised the objection (Morris, *Acad*. xxxix. 602, and Sisam, *Fourteenth Century Verse and Prose*, p. 227) that *dard to* is hardly possible as an expression for 'stood in awe of'. But the second interpretation offers still greater difficulties: *þat euer dard* is an unnatural phrase to use of the inscrutability of God's grace, since it is in the past tense, and ME. *dare*, though it may mean 'lie hidden', bears usually a connotation of fear; moreover, *Hym þat mat3 in synne rescoghe* 'him that makes rescue in sin' certainly seems more applicable to God than to a man who rescues his own soul, especially in a passage emphasizing the bounty of God's grace, not grace conferred according to merit. The first interpretation then would seem preferable, and, although no parallel to the use of *dare* with *to* can be adduced, it seems not unlikely that the poet, hard pressed for a rhyme-word (in a series of six), is using *dard to* in the sense 'cowered to, shrank in fear before', having in mind possibly such phrases as *bowed to, louted to*; cf. *felle to* 'prostrated themselves before' in 1120. *Dare* is used in a similar context in 839, and in *Pety Job* 475–6:

> Thys maketh me to drowpe and dare
> That I ame lyke a pore penaunte.

Fraunchyse would then imply the passive aspect of mercy and grace, the state of one who receives them.

611 *hem*: for the use of the plural pronoun after the indefinite singular (*Hys* 609 referring to anyone who *euer dard*, &c.), cf. 685–7 and note.

613 *now*: echoes *inoghe* of the preceding stanza, showing that the poet in linking his stanzas aimed primarily at an echo of sound, not necessarily a repetition of the same word. It is evident also that the syllable -*nogh*- was equivalent in sound to *now* (then pronounced [nuː]).

616 *fere*: MS. *lere* is not known in any sense that would fit the context. The emendation *here* of some editors is likewise unknown in a suitable sense: that *here* is a form for *hire* 'wages' is formally incredible in this text. ME. *fere* in the phrase (*with*) *grete fere* probably derives ultimately from OFr. *afe(i)re*, commonly used in the phrase *de grant afeire* 'of high rank' or 'with great pomp and circumstance'. The aphetic form may have arisen in this phrase, but occurs elsewhere by itself; cf. *Destruction of Troy* 18, and (probably) *Sir Gawain* 267. Rhymes with close *e* suggest that this word has become confused or blended with *fere* from ON. *fœri* 'power, ability'; cf. *Lyrics of the Thirteenth Century* 43/79, where *fere* rhymes with close *e*; yet bears a sense nearer to OFr. *afeire* than to ON. *fœri*. Alternatively (if the emendation is accepted) *fere* here may be derived from OE. *gefere* 'company', and refer to the company of Heavenly queens.

630 *niy3t*: previous editors read *my3t*. The form *niy3t* occurs also in *Sir Gawain* 929 and *Purity* 1779, and *niy3(t)* in *Purity* 359: see

Appendix II, p. 94. There is no distinguishing dot over the *i* in any of these three occurrences, and the distinction between *m* and *ni* must be made from the context. Here either *niy3t* or *my3t* would give good sense: *niy3t* has been chosen, following the suggestion of Kölbing (ES. xvi. 273), since it completes the metaphor of the day in the vineyard representing the life of man: death is, naturally, the night at the end of the day. Lines 629–32 may be rendered: 'Soon the day, into which darkness is creeping, does sink towards the night of death; those who never committed sin before they departed the noble Lord then pays as His workmen.' Mrs. Wright (*JEGPh*. xxxviii. 15) points out that the sense 'draw to an end' for *enclyne* (*MÆ*. ii. 3. 179) is unnatural, and compares 957 for the position of *to*. *þat* in 631 is the relative pronoun anticipating *hys hyne*.

635 *at þe fyrst fyne*: the meaning 'at the first end' (i.e. at the end of the first day), assumed by previous editors, seems unsatisfactory. There is no mention of a 'first' day in the parable or in the poem, and to assume one (implying a possibility of a 'second' day) makes nonsense of the *niy3t of deth*. Mrs. Wright's suggestion that *at þe fyrst* is an adverbial phrase, and *fyne* an adverb, 'Pay them first in full', seems preferable. Or *at þe fyrst* may mean 'at once': the innocent receive the full reward of Heaven immediately.

653 *þe water is baptem*: this was a familiar symbolic idea, as Osgood shows, citing Cyprian and Tertullian among the Fathers, and in Middle English Richard Rolle (ed. Horstmann ii. 361), and William of Nassington 26/277 f.:

> owt ran to oure saluacyone
> The precyous blode of oure raunsome
> With þe water of baptym clere and thyn.

656 'Through which Adam drowned us in death.' The form *inne* is probably due to misunderstanding of *wyth in* in the exemplar as the adverb *wythinne*; *inne* is, however, a possible form of the preposition, and has therefore been retained in the text.

657–9 'Now there is nothing in the round world between us and bliss but what He has withdrawn, and that (the bliss) is restored in a blessed hour.'

663 *sor3 and syt*: an alliterative phrase of Scandinavian origin; see Introduction, p. xxxvi, and Appendix IV, p. 98.

665-6 'Reason, which cannot deviate from what is just, requires that the innocent should be saved'; i.e. it is only reasonable that the innocent should be saved. *Resoun* was the proverbial companion of *ry3t* in Middle English. It was current idiom to say *it is resoun and ry3t* (cf. *The Prick of Conscience* 6891), perhaps in imitation of OFr. *c'est raison e droit*.

672 'And (he that is) innocent is redeemed and sanctified by divine grace' (taking *ry3te* as an adjective). Or MS. *At* may be emended to *As*: 'being innocent, &c.' See *MÆ*. ii. 3. 179.

685-7 'Whatsoever righteous man spends not his life in folly shall certainly approach that fair stronghold'—a curious indefinite use of *her* 'their', similar to modern colloquial 'their' after 'anyone'. The sense 'treat with contempt' for 'take in vain' is probably of later date, since the English version of the Latin *non accepit in vano animam suam* is 'who hath not lifted up his soul unto vanity'.

689 *sa3*: 'says' not 'saw'. 'Says how' is good idiom from OE. times (cf. *The Seafarer* 2), and Solomon did not claim to see the righteous man's reception by Wisdom. On the spelling *a* for *ay* see note to 532. The more normal spelling of this form is *sat3*, but final *3* was sometimes used in monosyllabic words instead of *t3*; cf. *say3* 615 (beside *sayt3* 315, &c.)

690 This line as it stands in the MS. is defective. Henry Bradley (*Acad*. xxxviii. 201) first perceived from the reference to Solomon in the preceding line and from the sense of the following lines that the source was Wisdom x. 10: *Haec* [sc. *Sapientia*] *profugum irae fratris iustum deduxit per vias rectas, et ostendit illi regnum Dei, et dedit illi scientiam sanctorum, honestavit illum in laboribus et complevit labores illius*. The righteous man of this passage was traditionally said to be Jacob, and the poet seems to have known this identification, and to have adapted 693 f. from Genesis xxviii. 12-15 where Jacob had his vision of Heaven. The source makes it clear that some word for Wisdom must come into 690 as the subject, and alliteration indicates the word *Koyntise*. The reconstructed *How* [*Koyntise on*]*oure con aquyle* 'How Wisdom obtained honour (for him)' is roughly equivalent to the statement that Wisdom *honestavit illum in laboribus*. The sense would be made still clearer, and the metre smoother, by the insertion of *hym* after *onoure* as indirect object. The reconstructions of the line suggested by Gol-

lancz: *How kyntly oure [Kyng hym] con aquyle* (first edition), and *How kyntly oure [Koyntise hym], &c.* (second edition), are based on the fact that medieval commentators identified Wisdom with Christ. It is perhaps unlikely that the idea was so generally familiar that the poet would refer to Him as 'our Wisdom'.

691 *ho*: *he* MS. The emendation is necessary, since *Koyntise* could only be 'she' (Vulgate *haec*): *e* and *o* were often confused in this MS. as in others of the period; cf. the emendations in 302, 308, 479, 1012.

703–4 Previous editors have disagreed about the meaning and derivation of *Alegge*, but have agreed in interpreting it as an imperative: 'Renounce your claim [and] you may be received' (Gollancz); 'Urge your privilege [and] you may, &c.' (Osgood). Miss Everett and Miss Hurnard in a note on the legal phraseology of this passage (*MÆ*. xvi. 9) suggest a rendering more suitable to the context, taking *Alegge* to be a conditional subjunctive: 'If you plead right (or righteousness) you may be trapped (or refuted in argument) by this same speech that I have seen', the 'speech' being the statement in 700, that no living man is justified before God. For this interpretation of *innome* they cite *The Owl and the Nightingale* 541, and for the spelling with double *n* they compare *innoghe* 625, 636, &c., and *inoghe* 612, &c., to show that where *i* was prefixed to a word beginning with *n* the spellings *in*, *inn* were, in this MS., regarded as equivalent. This interpretation renders more intelligible the *Bot* of line 705: If you claim salvation as a right (or by your righteousness), your plea may fail; *but* may Christ grant you to pass by innocence and not by right (or righteousness).

721 This group of stanzas is not linked with the preceding group; only here does the system of linking fail. See Appendix I, p. 88.

733 *makelleʒ*: editors have emended this, and *makeleʒ* in 757, to *maskelleʒ* in order to preserve regularity of the stanza link. But the poet may well have deliberately utilized the similarity in sound of the two epithets to make play on the two aspects of the pearl symbolism—the purity of innocence and the peerlessness of the heavenly state—without losing the sound echo which is the prime function of the stanza links (cf. 613 and note). The symmetry in the use of the two epithets, as they stand in the MS., and the final union of them both in the last line of the stanza group *A makeleʒ may and*

maskelle3 gives the impression of conscious stylistic purpose in the alternation. On the other hand, it might be argued that *maskelle3* in this line would be a more suitable antecedent to the clause *For hit is wemle3, clene, and clere* in 737; and that the spelling with double *l*, the only occurrence of that spelling for this word, is less natural in *makele3 = make-le3* than in *maskelle3 = maskel-le3*.

735 *heuenesse clere*: on the grounds that *heuenesse* is an abnormal form and that the rhyme-word *clere* is repeated in the same group, Gollancz emended to *heuenes spere*. If emendation is felt to be necessary, *heuenes skere* would be better (ON. *skærr* 'bright, clear', used most frequently of the heavens); *skere* 'pure' occurs in *Sir Gawain* 1261. The MS. reading can however be defended: the same phrase occurs as *heuene3 clere* in 620, and the addition of the otiose -*se* in *heuenesse* is paralleled in *hysse* 'his' 418, *wa'sse* 'was' 1108. For reiteration of rhyme-word see also 49/53, 702/707, 1046/1050, 1108/1112.

749–52 These lines are reminiscent of a passage in the *Roman de la Rose* (ed. Langlois 16013 f.) where it is argued that neither the 'philosopher' (the student of natural science)—Plato, Aristotle, or any other—nor the artist, not even Pygmalion, can imitate successfully the works of Nature. It was this passage that made it a poetic fashion to say that Pygmalion's work could not vie with Nature's as found in the lady whom the poet desires to praise. As is illustrated by Osgood in his note on these lines, there were many such references in Old French literature; but here the juxtaposition of Nature with both Aristotle as the typical philosopher and Pygmalion makes it highly probable that the poet is echoing the *Roman de la Rose* itself. Chaucer too was among the poets who echoed this passage from the *Rose*, in the Physician's description of Virginia (Oxford Chaucer, iv. 290 f. and note in v. 260–1).

753 In the *Roman de la Rose* 16239, a little beyond the passage echoed in the preceding four lines of *Pearl*, the face of Nature is described as fair as the fleur-de-lis. The comparison of ladies to this flower was fairly common in Old French poetry, and may have been known to the poet of *Pearl* as a general poetic convention (cf. 195), but the position of the comparison here suggests that he still had the passage from the *Rose* in mind.

755 *offys*: Morris and Gollancz read the MS. form as *of triys*; Osgood says '*offys* in MS. is sufficiently clear'. Further examination

shows that the form is either *oftriys* or *ostriys*. But Osgood's *offys*, though it cannot be given MS. authority, may be accepted as a happy emendation. Gollancz, taking *triys* as a form of 'truce', rendered lines 755–6: 'What kind of peace bears as its symbol the spotless pearl?' But *triys* as a form of 'truce' does not exist, and the use of *of* after *quat kyn* is not good ME. idiom (cf. *Quat kyn þing* in 771 and elsewhere). Henry Bradley, with characteristic ingenuity, suggested *ostriys* as 'oysters'. This was possibly not intended seriously, and even if the form and rhyme were normal, the plural 'oysters' would be absurd. The *perle* of this passage is not the emblematic jewel, but the maiden herself (745), and in the next stanza (the reply to the question) her office or place in the court of Heaven, Bride of the Lamb, is described. See *MÆ.* ii. 3. 180.

760 *semed*: *alþaȝ vnmete Sumtyme semed þat assemblé* means literally 'although at one time (earlier, while I was an earthly child) such an association befitted (or would have befitted) ill (unsuitably).' But 'befitted unsuitably' is equivalent to 'seemed unfitting', and here we have an interesting example of the sort of context from which the sense 'seem, appear' developed (with some influence of 'see', no doubt).

761 *yor worlde wete*: the Pearl has in mind the contrast between the rough and rainy climate of this world and the eternally bright and serene atmosphere of Heaven. This was traditional; see, for example, *The Orison of our Lady*, 38–39 and 58.

775 *comly on-vunder cambe*: 'fair beneath comb', a poetic periphrasis for 'fair lady'; cf. OE. *heard under helme* 'warrior'.

790 *þe apostel*: the John who gives his name as the author of Revelation was from the second century commonly believed to be John the apostle.

797 *melle*: this form is usually derived from OE. *meðlan* (so *NED.*), but the natural development of *ðl* in Middle English is *dl*. The change to *ll* might take place more easily in the past tense *maþlde*, but *melle* may be due to contact with OFr. *medler, meller* 'meddle'. Many of the senses of *melle* 'meddle' (in business dealings) are very close to those of OE. *meðlan*.

799–804 See Isaiah liii. 7.

800 *Wythouten any sake of felonye*: 'No criminal charge being proved against Him.'

802 *hande*: previous editors read the MS. here as *lande*. It appears, however, that the second stroke of the *h* has been joined to the first upright stroke of the *a*. The MS. should accordingly be read as *hande*, which gives more natural sense in the context than *lande*, and had already been suggested by some commentators as an emendation.

806 *boyeʒ* is here probably a term of opprobrium, 'wretches', 'ruffians', though etymologically the same word as modern 'boy'. It might less probably be identified with a different word meaning 'executioners': see *NED.* s. *Boie*, and *MÆ.* ix. 3. 121 ff.

815 *lomp* 'lamb', a Western form (cf. 945); see Appendix II, p. 93, and Appendix III, p. 95.

817 *In* at the beginning of the line has been lost in the MS. text, either through misunderstanding, or through haplography of abbreviated *j̄* immediately before the *j* of the following word.

817–18 There is no record of John the Baptist having baptized elsewhere than in Jordan. The statement here may be based on a vague impression formed from the scriptural accounts of John baptizing men from Jerusalem and Galilee; and doubtless the poet's ideas of the geography of Palestine were vague.

819 *Ysaye*: pronounced as four syllables, *Í-za-i-e*.

822 *as trwe as ston*: 'as steadfast as rock'. The same phrase is written above the picture of the lady visiting Sir Gawain (see frontispiece, *Sir Gawain*, ed. Tolkien and Gordon). It is not uncommon in Middle English; cf. the *Towneley Play of Noah* 38/315, where Noah says to the dove: *Þou art trew for to trist as ston in þe wall.*

824 '(The sins) that all mankind has been active in committing.' For this sense of *wroʒt vpon* see *NED. Upon*, sense 22 *b*.

831 *ayþer prophete*: Isaiah and John the Baptist.

837 *leueʒ sware*: see Introduction, p. xxx.

855 'For they could never think of quarrelling.' In spite of the temptation to take *mote* here as 'spot, blemish', in contrast with *spotleʒ* in the following line, *mote* 'dispute' gives a better meaning in the context. See *MÆ.* ii. 3. 183.

859 'We have complete understanding.' This complete know-

ledge is promised in 1 Cor. xiii. 11–12, and Augustine in *De Pecca-torum Meritis et Remissione* applies the promise specifically to the baptized infant.

860 'From One Death all our trust is drawn.' In so far as *hope* implies 'hope' it must mean of the resurrection of the body: we have died the ordinary death of corruption, but from Christ's death, which alone is incorrupt, our *full* hope proceeds.

865 'Lest you should be less inclined to believe my seemly discourse.' *Les* (a little strained to fit the repetitive scheme) is a shortened way of saying 'less than desirable' or 'less because the preceding statement seems incredible'. Or possibly the poet is (as often) playing upon words here, and *les* is the adjective 'false' (occuring also in *Purity* and *Patience*). *Farande*, as Mrs. Wright suggests (*JEGPh.* xxxviii. 18), may be an adjective which takes colouring from its noun, as 'nice' does in modern English; she would translate here 'wondrous'.

866 *Appocalyppece*: probably stressed *Áppocalýppece*.

869 *maydenneʒ*: renders *virgines* in Apoc. xiv. 4, where, how-ever, the 144,000 are specifically described as men. The word *mayden* in Middle English was used of either sex (see *NED.* s.v.), and the poet here clearly intends his *maydenneʒ* to include women, since the Pearl herself is one of them, and possibly he thought of them as all women, since in 785–6 he describes them as *þe Lambeʒ vyueʒ*. Many theologians understood the *virgines* to be celibates of the Church irrespective of their sex on earth; Bede, for example, in *Explanatio Apocalypsis* (Migne xciii. 173) quotes Augustine to that effect. And since this applied also to the maidens who were the wives of the Lamb in spiritual marriage, it is possible that the poet also held this view. On the inclusion of infants among these virgins, see Introduction, p. xxv.

875 *as þunder þroweʒ in torreʒ blo*: 'as thunder rolls among dark hills'. Cf. *Purity* 951–2:

> Clowdeʒ clustered bytwene, kesten vp torres,
> Þat þe þik þunder-þrast þirled hem ofte.

NED. suggests that in both these passages *torr* has the sense 'heavy mass of cloud', but as both contexts are indecisive, a depar-ture from the usual sense is hardly justified. The term *tor* is still used, in the south Pennine region, of high, sharply rising hills, a sense which fits the *Pearl* passage well, while in *Purity* the same sense is probably used figuratively, of tor-like masses of cloud.

884 *modeʒ*: C. O. Chapman (*PMLA*. xlvi. 177 f.) argues that *modeʒ* here is used in the technical sense of modes in ecclesiastical music. But the simple 'tune, melody, strain of music' had been a well-established sense of Latin *modus* from classical times onwards, and it is the more natural sense to take here. It is doubtful whether the technical sense existed in English before the sixteenth century. See *MÆ*. ii. 3. 184.

900 *neuer pe les*: 'notwithstanding' (any considerations implied).

901–2 'Let my thanks (for all you have told) by no means be (thought) less, though I (still) ask questions'—no more than a courteous form of apology. For consideration of the extra stanza in this group, see Appendix I, p. 88.

905 *I am bot mokke and mul among*: 'I am but filth and dust mingled', as being mortal flesh. Cf. 382, and *Purity* 735–6, in a similar apology (addressed to God):

> tatʒ to non ille,
> ʒif I mele a lyttel more þat mul am and askeʒ.

Among in the present passage is the adverb 'together'; cf. *Purity* 1414: *Tymbres and tabornes tukket among.*

909 'Now, gracious maiden, who are endued with simplicity . . .' —but the exact sense of *sympelnesse* is uncertain. Possibly it refers to lack of pride, but the description of the 144,000 in Rev. xiv. 5, 'And in their mouth was found no guile', indicates perhaps that lack of guile is meant here.

911 *blose*: a word unknown in Middle English. Mrs. Wright, following Gollancz in his 1891 edition and Emerson, suggests that it is the French adjective *blos* 'privé de bon sens', used here as a noun 'churl'. Gollancz emended to *wose* 'wild man' from OE. *-wāsa* in the compound *wuduwāsa*, but the word is not known in Middle English apart from its compound, and *wāsa* does not itself mean 'wild'. It may be an error for ME. *bose* (*bosse*) 'a leather bottle', applied to persons who are untaught, crude; cf. Lyndesay, *Monarche* 2579:

> Thocht sum of ʒow be gude of conditione . . .
> I speik to ʒow auld bosis.

In *Richard the Redeless* iii. 98, the word *bosse* is applied to a bear, and *boistous* in Middle English is often used of boars or bears. *Bustwys as a bose* would then be similar in sense to: *men þat were vnkonnynge and boistous as bestes* (Higden, Rolls Ser. II. 311).

917 *woneȝ in castel-walle*: the dreamer thinks of the Heavenly City as a feudal town, consisting of a castle with a cluster of buildings set within the castle wall. Later he actually sees the City as such a castle: he describes it as a *manayre* in 1029, meaning a castle and its precinct, and in 1083 as a *bayle*, meaning a walled castle. The illustration in the MS. medievalizes the City even more completely: see Introduction, p. xi.

932 *&* at the beginning of the line has been deleted, as in Gollancz's text. It would be possible to retain the *and* and construe *by þyse bonkeȝ* in 931 with *lenge and loute* in 933, as Osgood does: 'And by these slopes where I have tarried—and I see no building anywhere about—I suppose that you dwell alone in retirement, to look &c.' But the deletion of *&* gives a simpler and more natural construction, and *alone* is more probably the adverb 'only': 'And by these slopes where I linger I see no dwelling anywhere about. I believe you make your way (hither) and stay only to look on the beauty of this fair stream'.

935 *bygyngeȝ*: MS. *lygyngeȝ* is not recorded elsewhere, and would normally denote a mere lodge or temporary shelter (ON. *liggja* 'to lie'), hardly to be described as 'stout'; whereas *bigging* is a common ME. word (cf. 932 and *Sir Isumbras* 78). Confusion between the letters *l* and *b* is easy.

944 *in theme con take*: the idiom (which has been questioned: Emerson would delete *in*) is probably paralleled in *Patience* 37, *in teme layde*, which is more naturally interpreted as 'spoken of' or 'described' than as 'coupled together', as most authorities have rendered the phrase.

950–2 The name Jerusalem is interpreted as meaning etymologically and symbolically 'city of God' or 'vision of peace'. The former interpretation seemed to medieval etymologists to be supported by passages in scripture where Jerusalem is called 'city of God', as in Heb. xii. 22, and Rev. iii. 12. The other interpretation as 'vision of peace' was the more usual one in the Middle Ages, and there are many examples of it in Old and Middle English literature:

see A. S. Cook's note on line 50 of Cynewulf's *Christ*. A typical
sample of the use of this etymology for symbolical interpretation
of the scriptures may be found in Gregory's *Cura Pastoralis* ii. 10
(in Alfred's translation in Sweet's *Anglo-Saxon Reader*, p. 13, 161 f.).

969–70 'From without you can see that radiant precinct, but
from within not a foot.' Gollancz has no punctuation after *fote*,
and takes *not a fote* with *strech* in the following line: 'Thy vigour
availeth not to enter in its street one foot.' But in a sentence in
which a negative adverbial phrase begins the statement, subject
and verb are usually inverted; *hat3 þou* would be expected here
rather than *þou hat3*. *Inwyth* clearly goes closely with *Vtwyth*, and
both refer to the position of the dreamer.

981 'Sunk down (from Heaven) on the other side of the brook
from me.' Here the dreamer beholds the city from a hill, just as
John from a hill saw the New Jerusalem 'descending out of heaven'
(Rev. xxi. 10). *Keued* is to be connected with ON. *kefja* (Gollancz).

983 *preued*: may be a scribal error for *breued*, the usual word for
'set down in writing' (cf. *Sir Gawain* 2521 and *Destruction of Troy*
14, 65, &c.). But some senses of *preue* 'give proof, show' are close
to those of *breue* 'declare, announce', and it is difficult to be sure
that the MS. form is not original. For the rhyme see Introduction,
p. xlvii (note 4).

992 *bantele3*: the meaning is fixed by the description of the city
in Revelation, and by the equivalence of *bantele3* here with the
foundemente3 and *tabelment* in the next two lines. The *bantele3* were
the tiers or coursings (*tabelment*) which served as foundations
(*foundemente3*) of the city. They were arranged in the form of steps.
The word occurs also in *Purity* 1459, where the cups at Belshazzar's
feast were fashioned like castles *Enbaned vnder batelment wyth
bantelles quoynt*; here the *bantelles* are projecting horizontal coursings at the top of the wall. Cf. the description of the Green Knight's
castle in *Sir Gawain* 790 f., and see further *MÆ*. ii. 3. 184 f.

997 *As John þise stone3 in writ con nemme*: actually the sixth
stone is called *sardinus* in the Apocalypse, and the *sardinus* was
not a ruby: see note to 1007.

998 *name*: singular in anticipation of the following lines, in
which the name of each separate stone is given. The distributive

singular was a more frequent use in Old and Middle English than now.

999 *Jasper*: the name of 'any bright-coloured chalcedony except carnelian, the most esteemed being of a green colour' (*NED*.). Hence *He glente grene* 1001. In modern usage 'jasper' is the name of a stone that is red, yellow, or brown.

1003 *calsydoyne*: in the early Middle Ages this name was known mainly from the passage in Revelation which is the poet's source here, and it was only vaguely identified. By the thirteenth century, however, it was applied to a species of white quartz 'having the lustre nearly of wax, and being either transparent or translucent' (*NED*.). It is evident from 1004 that this is the stone intended here. Cf. also Trevisa's translation of Bartholomeus Anglicus, *De Proprietatibus Rerum* (xvi, xvii): *Calcidonius is a pale stone and sheweth dymme colour meane betwene Berell and Jacynct*. The name chalcedony is now given also to coloured varieties of stone of similar composition, including the sardonyx, sard, and chrysoprase, which here form distinct layers of the foundation.

1006 *sardonyse*: a variety of onyx, in which the white background was variegated by layers of red or brown sard (carnelian).

1007 *rybé*: the Vulgate text (Apoc. xxi. 20) has *sardinus* or, as a frequent variant, *sardius*, and the Greek σάρδιον, a name which was not usually given to the ruby, but to the carnelian. But *sardius* in the Vulgate also rendered the Hebrew *odem*, one of the gems on the high-priest's breast-plate (Exod. xxviii. 17), and there in some doubt as to whether the Hebrew word meant a ruby or some other red stone. Several of the early commentators and lapidaries took the stone on Aaron's ephod to be the ruby. The *Lapidaire en Vers* (Pannier 264/877–8) states specifically that the ruby was worn by Aaron, but just as definitely (907–9) that it was not one of the foundation stones of the Heavenly City; so also King Philip's Lapidary (Pannier, p. 295). The tradition that it was a ruby on the breast-plate is represented in the Authorized Version; the Revised Version more cautiously has *sardius* in the text and 'or, ruby' in the margin. In the present passage in *Pearl* Gollancz altered *rybé* to *sarde* on the grounds that *sarde* supplies alliteration and agrees with the Vulgate text; *rybé* he thought was due to a scribe's desire to differentiate *sarde* from *sardonyse* in the preceding line. The man who wrote *rybé*, however, must have made some investigation into the names of the gems, and the poet is more likely to have gone to this trouble than a copyist. Moreover, the phrase *as her byrþ-whateȝ* in 1041 (see note) shows that the poet had connected the description of the Heavenly City with the details of the high-priest's ephod and breast-plate, given in Exod. xxviii, the very passage which is the source of the tradition that the *sardius* was a ruby. Hence there can be little doubt that *rybé* was the poet's own word.

1009 *crysolyt*: a yellowish-green stone, here perhaps the chrysolite of modern times, or possibly a variety of beryl.

1011 *beryl cler and quyt*: the beryl is a clear transparent stone, and in the Middle Ages the name was given to crystal and fine glass as well; hence the poet thinks of the typical beryl as *cler and quyt*. Though the beryl proper is sometimes white, it is ordinarily a pale green.

1012 *twynne-hew*: the MS. has *how*, and *ow* does not occur elsewhere in this MS. as a spelling of the diphthong in this word. One of the normal forms is *hew*, which was evidently the original form here; *e* and *o* were easily confused (see note to 691). To establish the sense of the word Gollancz quotes Bede's commentary on Revelation (Migne, xciii. 200): *Topazius . . . duos habere fertur colores, unum auri purissimi, et alterum aetherea claritate relucentem.* This is said in the same words by Hrabanus Maurus *De Universo* xvii. 7 (cxi. 468 in Migne), whence the statement passed into the tradition of the lapidaries.

1013 *tyȝt*: the past participle of *tyȝe* 'tie', used in the extended sense 'connected, fastened', either anticipating the technical architectural use recorded rather later in *NED.*, or possibly in a figurative application parallel to that of *joyned* 1009. The form was pronounced [ti : t], and is thus a good rhyme with *quyt*, &c.; see Appendix II, p. 92 (note), and *MÆ.* ii. 3. 185 f.

1014 *jacynght*: MS. *jacyngh*. All known forms of this word in Middle English have a final *t*, which has accordingly been supplied here. Cf. the note to *hope* 142. The name jacinth is now given to a reddish-orange stone, but in the Middle Ages it was a blue or violet stone, perhaps a variety of sapphire.

1015 *þe gentyleste in vch a plyt*: the London Lapidary says of the amethyst that *hit is comfortable in all sorowes* (though the French original has *yvresse* 'drunkenness', not 'sorrows'), and this statement is adopted in the Peterborough Lapidary. In the Latin Lapidary in MS. Digby 13 the amethyst is said to have protecting power against a long list of dangers and misfortunes: see Studer and Evans, *Anglo-Norman Lapidaries*, p. 380. The last is probably the tradition on which the present line is based.

1017 *bent*: Gollancz's emendation to *brent* 'steep' is plausible, but not necessary; *bent* may mean 'bound, fastened', as in 664, and the sense is here extended to 'fixed', 'set'. This sense-extension is parallel to that of *ty3t* in 1013.

1025 'The streets of gold were lustrous as glass.' This is a rendering of *platea* (or *plateae* in some MSS.) *civitatis aurum mundum, tamquam vitrum perlucidum* in Apoc. xxi. 21, but *bare* can hardly be a translation of *perlucidum*. It seems rather to express the general idea of the simile in the original—not that the streets themselves were transparent, but that they shone like (transparent) glass. Thus *bare*, as in 836, means 'clear to the sight', here 'unobscured (by dust)'.

1029 *sware* does not mean 'dimension' (Gollancz) or 'side of a square' (Osgood), but has its normal meaning: since the city is cubic in form, each side is a square: 'Each square side thus contained twelve furlongs' space in height, width and length, ere it came to an end' (*fon . . . to cayre*, lit. 'ceased to proceed'). This measurement does not agree with Rev. xxi. 16, which has 'twelve *thousand* furlongs'. Gollancz assumes that *þowsande* stood in the original text, and it is true that a numeral m̄ could easily be missed or misunderstood by the copyist. If the omission of *þowsande* is not scribal, it may have arisen from the poet's use of a commentary in which the verse explained was given in an abbreviated form. Thus in Bede's *Explanatio Apocalypsis* (Migne xciii. 196) is written *Et mensus est civitatem per stadia duodecim*, and then the comment follows. If the comment concerned itself with the significance of the number twelve, as it well might do, the poet may have overlooked the fact that the actual text had twelve *thousand*.

1035 *poursent*: 'compass', 'enclosing wall'; as each side had three gates, twelve could be seen in the whole surrounding wall. Since *n* and *u* are indistinguishable in the MS., the word might be read as *pourseut* 'succession' (so Bradley in ME. dictionary, and

Osgood), which would fit the sense well here: the dreamer is concerned about the order of the gates (1040–2). But 'succession' as a meaning of *pursuit* is not known in Middle English, and is rare at any time in English. *Poursent* 'compass' is a known ME. word, and the unambiguous form *pursaunt* occurs in that sense in *Purity* 1385.

1038 *fate3*: 'fades'. This is a new formation made on the analogy of those parts of the verb in which the *d* had become final and in consequence unvoiced to *t*. See Introduction, p. xlvi.

1041 *as her byrþ-whate3*: 'according to the fortunes of their birth'; that is, in the order of their birth. The phrase is equivalent to *folewande her date3* in the preceding line. In Rev. xxi. 12 it is said that the names of the twelve tribes of the children of Israel were written on the gates of the Heavenly City; this was in imitation of the earthly Jerusalem, as described in Ezek. xlviii. 30–34. The names there are not given in order of birth; this detail comes from the description of the precious stones on the high-priest's ephod in Exod. xxviii. For brief accounts of the medieval writers and commentators who deal with the stones named there, see Evans and Studer, p. xvi, and Pannier, p. 210. On the shoulder-pieces of the ephod were two onyx stones engraved with the names of the children of Israel *iuxta ordinem nativitatis eorum*. These passages in Revelation and Exodus were traditionally associated because of their similar lists of precious stones; cf. the note on *rybé* 1007. The poet may have used a commentary which referred to the Exodus passage, or the lapidaries (which in this matter are based on the commentators) may have led him to it. See Introduction, p. xxxiv f., and *MÆ*. ii. 3. 186 f.

1043 *strate3*: the MS. form has been retained because forms with *a* occur elsewhere in Middle English, but it is a doubtful form for this poem. In *Poema Morale* (Trinity MS. 235) *strate* shows the South-Eastern change of *æ* to *ā*: in La3amon's *Brut* 16366 *straten* shows a fairly common spelling in that text of *a* for *ai*; in Minot's poem on Edward before Tournay (ed. Hall vi. 56) *strate* is probably a deliberate use of the Flemish form. Since *strete* is the usual form in this MS. (cf. 971, 1025, 1059; *Purity* 787) we may have here an example of a not uncommon scribal error: if the word in the exemplar were *gate3*, a scribe expecting *strete3* (after 1025) might write *strate3*.

1046 *lombe-ly3t* 'lamp'. Editors have normalized *lombe* to *lompe*, but *lombe* is a Western 'reverse spelling'; see Appendix II, p. 93.

1050 'For (all) being transparent and clear, nothing hindered any light;' *sotyle* and *cler* are probably adjectives virtually qualifying *no3t*, which here is the negative of 'all', attracted to the negative 'no'.

1063 *mynster*: *mynyster* MS. The meaning of the word is fixed by the poet's authority for this passage, Apoc. xxi. 22: *Dominus enim Deus omnipotens templum illius est, et Agnus*. It seems improbable that the poet meant 'minister'.

1064 *refet*: MS. *reget* is not known in Middle English, and the sense 'redeemed', assumed by deriving it from *re-+gete* (ON. *gæta*) is unsuitable in the context. In Heaven, in the presence of saved souls, it is not the redemptive aspects of the Sacrifice that are to be emphasized, but worship and soul's refreshment. Mrs. Wright's suggestion of *refet* 'refection, nourishment', therefore, fits the context well. According to *NED.* the noun *refet* appears to be applied only to fish, but the examples quoted are late Middle English, and earlier the word must almost certainly have had its more general, etymological, sense 'refreshment' (OFr. *refait*), since it is closely related to the ME. verb *refete* 'to refresh, nourish' (*Pearl* 88, *Patience* 20). The past participle of the verb is fairly common in Middle English and would be formally suitable here, since it appears to rhyme with either long or short *e*, but it would be difficult to construe '(was) refreshed' here with *Lombe*. Translate: 'the Lamb, the sacrifice, was there as refreshment'. Cf. 862 *He myrþe3 vus alle at vch a mes*.

1069 *The mone may þerof acroche no my3te*: 'The moon can draw to itself no might therefrom.' *Acroche* often has the sense 'lay hold of what is not one's own', and the poet probably has in mind the traditional idea of the moon as a thief of light: because she is 'too spotty' she has no place in the Heavenly City, and so cannot steal light from its radiance as she does from the sun in this world.

1073 *to euen*: this has sometimes been wrongly joined, but the syntax is correct and idiomatic: where an auxiliary verb (as *schulde*) was followed by two infinitives, the second was preceded by *to*. See *NED. To*, branch B. v. 19.

1079 *frym*: this is the first recorded occurrence of this word in

English, and as it rhymes with words from OE. *-imm, -imb*, the connexion with OE. *freme* (*NED.*) is uncertain.

1082 *No fleschly hert*: compare 61 and 63, where it is made clear
that it is the spirit of the dreamer which beholds the heavenly
vision. Cf. also 1090.

1083 *bayle*: *baly* MS. See note to 313–15.

1085 Osgood compares the *Clerkes Tale* 1206: *thou shalt make
hym couche as doth a quaille.*

1086 *frelich*: MS. *freuch* is unintelligible. The emendation to
frelich, suggested by R. Morris, gives excellent sense and is palaeo-
graphically explicable, since *li* with *l* written rather short (as often
in this MS.) could easily be misread as *u* or *n*. The word occurs as
frelych in *Purity* 162, where it is applied to the feast representing
the kingdom of Heaven, and in *Patience* 214, *frelych Dryȝtyn*.

1087 *nawþer reste ne trauayle*: implies 'no bodily sensations',
just as *in wele and wo* implies 'in all circumstances'.

1093–6 'Just as the mighty moon rises before the light of day
all sinks down, even thus suddenly in wondrous wise I became
aware of a procession.' When the moon has arisen in the day-time,
it becomes visible in the evening even before the day has gone,
appearing as it were miraculously without any warning of its
coming. So the procession in the Heavenly City appeared *wythouten
sommoun*. A subtle and unusually elaborate simile. The moon is
maynful by tradition; cf. the heathen Norse poem *Vǫluspá*: *máni
ne vissi hvat megins átti*, and the lyric *Annot and John* 31: *þourh
miht of þe mone*. It is possible that *maynful* implies a full moon; cf.
Ælfric (*Homilies*, ed. Thorpe i. 102): *Is . . . ælc licamlice gesceaft
ðe eorðe acenþ fulre and mægenfæstre on fullum monan þonne on
gewanedum.*

1126 *Vertues of heuen*: one of the nine orders of angels; *of heuen*
is often added to make the reference to heavenly powers clear.

1148 *sclade*: for normal *slade*. *Sl* frequently appears as *scl* from
OE. times onwards; see Sisam, *Herrig's Archiv* cxxxi. 305 f. After
s the *l* was unvoiced, and the breath on-glide which is characteristic of the voiceless *l* was strengthened and acquired stress until
it developed into the voiceless fricative [χ]: this then either

passed into *c* = [k], or was lost again. The [k] so produced can be heard in Scottish dialects, as in *sklate* 'slate'.

1157–8 The general meaning seems to be 'I thought nothing could hinder me', but the precise meaning is uncertain. Gollancz identified *To fech me bur* with the modern dialect phrase 'to take one's birr' (cf. 'to fetch one's feeze'), meaning 'to gather impetus for a leap by taking a short run', and he took the passage to mean 'that if no one prevented the birr or the "take-off", he would start on his swim. . . .' It is a tempting interpretation, but it entails difficulties: it necessitates rendering *dere to* as 'hinder from', and if that may be regarded as a fairly natural extension of the usual meaning of *dere* 'harm' there remains the greater difficulty of *take me halte*. Gollancz's 'take-off' (for 'take hold') is unconvincing; *take me halte* may mean either "strike me lame' (see *NED*. s. *Take*, sense 7 d) or 'take hold of me': in either case it must imply hindrance of some sort. It seems safer therefore to take *fech me bur* as 'fetch me a blow' (see *NED*. s. *Fetch*, sense 8). Translate: 'I thought nothing could hinder me, by striking me a blow or stopping my advance.'

1159 *stere*: 'restrain' (see *NED*. s. *Steer*, v.[1], sense 5). But *stere* does not give a good rhyme here, and the form may be an error for *skere* (*scere*) 'frighten off'; cf. *scere* in *The Wars of Alexander* 3865, and see Introduction, p. xlvii (note 4).

1186 *styke3*: emended by editors to *stryke3* on the assumption that the *garlande gay* refers to the maiden's crown described in 205–6. More probably the *garlande* is a metaphorical description of the Heavenly procession, the circle of the blessed, and *styke3* therefore may be retained with its usual meaning of 'set' (cf. *Purity* 157, 583): 'If it is true that you are thus set in a bright garland then it is well with me in this dungeon of sorrow that you are to that Prince's pleasure.' See Sister Mary V. Hillman, *MLN.* lx. 224, where she quotes passages from Dante's *Paradiso*, with *ghirlande* used in this same way to describe the circle of the blessed.

1193 *As helde*: Gollancz's suggestion that *helde* in this line is identical with the modern dialectal *helt* 'readily, likely' (still used in south Lancashire: see *EDD*.) receives strong support from the occurrence of *helt* in Shropshire texts of the early fifteenth century: Myrc, *Instructions to Parish Priests* 907; *Festial* 136/19, 186/34,

206/2. It is unlikely, however, that *helde, helt* is an English comparative form (OE. **held*) as Gollancz suggested, since the comparative sense does not appear at any time in English in this form of the word. It is, rather, a positive inferred from the comparative *helder*, adopted from ON. *heldr*. The senses 'assuredly, readily' are the natural positives of the senses of *helder* 'rather, more readily'; and 'likely' is an easy extension of 'readily'. In the present passage *as helde* may be interpreted (after Gollancz) with intensive *as* 'as likely as possible', 'very likely'; or, as in present-day Lancashire idiom, with correlative *as*: 'as likely as not', 'quite probably'.

1205 *lote*: probably 'lot, fortune, hap', though possibly it is a different word (from ON. *lát*) meaning 'utterance' or 'song'; if 'utterance' is meant the reference would be to the discourse of the Pearl to the dreamer; if 'song' is meant it would refer to the poem itself which had its origin in the vision. The meaning of *lote* can hardly be stretched to include the sense 'vision' (Gollancz): although ON. *lát* can mean 'appearance' it refers to personal appearance (often including behaviour).

1207 *hit*: the Pearl, which he now willingly commits to God.

1209-12 The punctuation of these lines is, perhaps, uncertain. *þat* in 1209 may refer to *Kryste3* in the preceding line, '(Christ) whom in the form of bread and wine . . .'. Or possibly the last four lines are the prayer introduced by *þat*: 'May He, in the form of bread and wine which the priest shows to us each day, grant us to be His own servants and precious pearls for His pleasure.' Cf. the lyric *Suete Iesu, King of Blysse* (*Harley Lyrics*, p. 52):

> Suete Iesu, al folkes rééd,
> graunte ous er we buen ded
> þe vnderfonge in fourme of bred,
> ant seþþe to heouene þou vs led.

APPENDIXES

I. METRE

THE STANZA

The stanza is of twelve lines, each of four stresses and often heavily, but not regularly, alliterated. There are three groups of rhymes in each stanza, in the scheme a b a b a b a b b c b c. Poems in this metrical pattern are fairly common in Middle English; at least seventeen other examples are extant.[1] All except *Pety Job* are in a more southerly dialect than *Pearl*, but most of them clearly belong to the West Midlands. None of them, however, can reasonably be regarded as the metrical model for *Pearl*, which has a swifter movement and a more elaborate system of stanza-linking than any of them. The nearest to *Pearl* is *Pety Job*, where there are actually several echoes or similarities of phrase or diction.[2] These similarities can be attributed partly to its subject and partly to the alliterative tradition, for there can be little doubt that it was from the West Midland tradition that these poets took this stanza form. Many structural features found in *Pearl* are also found in these poems, such as the use of heavy alliteration, a refrain, and con-catenation of a simple kind—indicating that the poet did not invent these, though he seems to have elaborated or modified their use. For instance, all the other poems in this stanza agree in having a repeated last line (Latin or English) which con-tinues throughout. None besides *Pearl* links the end of the stanza with the beginning, nor, even when long, are they broken into groups with a changed refrain. In many of them the stanza is marked into three quatrains, while in others there is a tendency, not amounting to a regular system, to divide the

[1] *Political, Religious and Love Poems*, ed. Furnivall, E.E.T.S. (2nd ed., 1903), pp. 191, 233, 238, 244. *Hymns to the Virgin and Christ*, ed. Furnivall, E.E.T.S. 1867, pp. 12, 18, 79. *Minor Poems of the Vernon MS.*, vol. i, ed. Horstmann, E.E.T.S. 1892, p. 134; vol. ii, ed. Kail, 1901, pp. 658, 672, 675, 683, 692, 704, 730, 740. *Audelay's Poems*, ed. Whiting, E.E.T.S. 1931, p. 155; *Pety Job*, ed. Horstmann, *Yorkshire Writers*, vol. ii, p. 380.

[2] e.g. *Lorde, ffor the loue off Mary and Iohne*, 323; *In thys woffull wepyng dale* (= world), 410; *lorde that art lykened to a lambe*, 515; *Lorde that arte curteyse and hende*, 659; and *faunt* = child.

stanza by principal pauses into quatrains. The same tendency is noticeable in *Pearl*, but here too the division is not systematic; it is fairly clear in about seventy of the hundred and one stanzas. In others only the final quatrain is clearly marked, and there are a few which show no trace at all of quatrain arrangement. In many stanzas the final quatrain plays a part similar to that of the sestet in a sonnet.

THE GROUPING AND LINKING OF THE STANZAS

The poem is divided into twenty groups of stanzas, five in each, except that in group XV there are six stanzas. There is no apparent reason for the introduction of an extra stanza, and Osgood suggests that 72[1] was a stanza intended to be cancelled that has been accidentally included. But the explanation in 72 that the heavenly pearls *purȝoutly hauen cnawyng* is important. 76 is more likely to be the otiose one, since all it says is 'Excuse me if after all I ask a question', and the question is asked in 77. Only the first two lines of 76 are really necessary, and it would seem that the form here has so far defeated the poet that he has had to expand them into a whole stanza.[2]

The division into groups is marked in the poem by the use of a refrain running through five stanzas, and replaced by a new refrain in the next five; and in the MS. the beginning of each group is indicated by a coloured capital. Each stanza is linked to the next by the repetition of its last word in the line following, a form of linking called *concatenatio*. The link-word naturally changes with the refrain, and as the new refrain does not appear until the end of the first stanza of the new group, the link-word of the last group is repeated at the beginning of the next: thus the stanza groups are linked by *concatenatio* as well as individual stanzas. The linking fails at line 721, possibly

---

[1] Stanza 72 begins on l. 852; stanza 76 on l. 901.

[2] C. O. Chapman, 'Numerical Symbolism in Dante and the Pearl', *MLN*. liv. 256, maintains that the extra stanza was inserted by the poet to bring the number to ninety-nine, the last two stanzas being, he claims, outside the main theme. While there seems no doubt that the numbers three, four (and their multiple twelve) have symbolic significance in the description of the Heavenly City (following Revelation), the evidence for any numerical symbolism in the poem as a whole seems unconvincing. We may ask why the poet chose five as the number of stanzas in a group if three was so significant that he found it necessary to insert an extra stanza to achieve the required multiple.

through textual corruption, since the keyword *ryȝt* is one easy to work with.[1]

Concatenation is a device commonly found in Old French and Provençal stanzaic poetry, and was adopted in Middle English from French sources. It was well known in English use, however, long before *Pearl* was composed, and was probably adopted together with the stanza from West Midland example. The earliest use of it is in the Harley lyrics,[2] and of the poems composed in the *Pearl* stanza four have systematic concatenation and four have incomplete linking. Concatenation is found in the North, too, in the *Aunters of Arthur*, and four of Minot's songs, but is much less commonly used there than in the West.

In the final group of stanzas the phrase *prynceȝ pay*, used in the first line of the poem, is brought into the refrain, and the final occurrence of the refrain echoes the first even more closely. This device of ending on the same note as the beginning is also found in *Patience* and *Sir Gawain*. Outside this group of poems it is not often found in Middle English.[3]

RHYTHM

The lines of the *Pearl* stanza are the four-stress lines found elsewhere in the same stanza, but more closely assimilated to the rhythms of alliterative poetry. Most rhymed Middle English verse (apart from Chaucer, Gower, and many of the lyrics) descends from the rhythms of the old alliterative line modified in varying degrees by adaptation to rhyme-schemes. *Pearl* is even nearer than most rhymed verse to the alliterative cadences, possibly because the author was accustomed to compose un-rhymed alliterative verse also. The chief effect of this close relationship is that the line is not measured, has not a fixed number of syllables, like the lines of French verse, nor is it systematically iambic[4] or anapaestic,[5] as the modern reader tends to make it. The essential basis of the line consists of four stresses ('lifts'), around which are arranged unstressed elements ('dips'), varying in number from three to five. The posi-

---

[1] MS. *Iesus* is the subject of the preceding sentence, and need not have been repeated. Possibly the repetition replaced *He ryȝt*.

[2] See G. L. Brook, *The Harley Lyrics*, p. 19.

[3] *Aunters of Arthur, Octavian* (southern version).

[4] Cf. Osgood, xliii: 'The line is in general iambic'.

[5] Cf. Gollancz, xxiv, note: 'the trisyllabic character of the metre'.

tion of the dips and the number of syllables in them is variable, the old rhythmic variety of the alliterative line being inherited and only slightly reduced by the addition of rhyme. Thus we find dips between the lifts consisting of one, two, or three syllables; or there may be no dip at all between the lifts, and we then have the 'clashing' of stresses familiar in OE. poetry. It is not always easy to be certain, however, whether some of these clashing stresses are original or whether they have come into the MS. through textual corruption by the dropping of final inflexional *e*; and some editors and commentators[1] try to avoid clashing of stress by alteration of the text wherever possible. The whole question of the pronunciation of final -*e* is difficult (see Grammar), and these doubtful cases of clashing stress must probably remain a matter of controversy. Among the fairly clear examples of clashing stress in *Pearl* are:

> 203 Her cortel of sélf súte schene
> 315 Þou saytȝ þou schal won in þís báyly
> 990 As glemande glás búrnist broun

The traditional freedom in the treatment of the dips allows the poet to begin the line with a stressed or unstressed syllable at will. The lines may be comparatively long, containing as many as thirteen (or possibly fourteen) syllables:

> 726 Wythouten motę oþer masclę of sulpande synne
> 909 Now, hynde, þat sympelnesse coneȝ enclose

Or they may be comparatively short, containing as few as seven syllables:

> 193 Perleȝ pyȝtę of ryal prys
> 564 Wy schaltę þou þennę ask more?
> 709 Ryȝtwysly quo con rede

The influence of the alliterative metre is seen also in the tendency to divide the line by a light caesura after the word bearing the second stress:

> 13 Syþen in þat spote ‖ hit fro me sprange
> Ofte haf I wayted ‖ wyschande þat wele

This division coincides, of course, with natural English phrasing and may therefore be felt to be metrically unremarkable,

---

[1] Notably Gollancz, Emerson, and S. P. Chase.

but it is notable that whereas the first two stresses, or the second two, may fall within a single word, as in 83, 91, 590, 594, 596, 866, &c., the middle two are never made inseparable by falling within one word. In fact the line in *Pearl* is probably more truly understood as a modification of the alliterative line than as a basically French line partly assimilated to the alliterative tradition.

The addition of rhyme and the balance of lines within a stanza has in several respects altered the ordinary practice of the alliterative poets. The lines are shorter and crisper than in *Purity*, *Patience*, and *Sir Gawain*, and never have more than four stresses, whereas certain types of the unrhymed alliterative line had five. As a result many syllables bear the lift which in a longer line would normally be too light, as, for example, *con* in 691.

ALLITERATION

The alliteration is not systematic, and it varies considerably. Sometimes all four stressed words in a line alliterate (as in 1, 18, 40, 55, &c.), sometimes three (as in 2, 4, 8, 11, 14, &c.), or two (as in 7, 10, &c.), and in many lines (roughly one in four) there is no alliteration at all. The alliteration tends to be heavier in the descriptive passages than in the theological discussion in the middle of the poem. As in the unrhymed alliterative poems of the group, in *Pearl* words beginning with *h* may alliterate with words beginning with a vowel, as in 3, *Oute of oryent, I hardyly saye.* (Similarly 39, 58, 209, &c.) Original *wh* (written *wh*, *w*, *qu*) probably alliterates with *w* in 15, 32, 65, 131, &c.

II. SPELLING

The most notable characteristics of spelling in *Pearl* are:

1. The manifold use of ȝ. This is in origin *two* letters, though their shapes are identical in the MS.: (A) the medieval ȝ, called Yogh;[1] and (B) the letter *z*.

A. This originally represented the two values of fricative *g* in Old and Early Middle English: front (palatal) or back (velar) [as in German *segen*, *sagen*]. These sounds had become weakened

[1] See *NED*. s.v. Yogh.

in the fourteenth century to the *y* and *w* of modern English, and *y* and *w* already frequently replaced ȝ in later fourteenth-century spelling.

(i) ȝ represented *y* [j, i̯] (*a*) always initially, as in ȝonge 'young'. Here *y* is in this MS. occasionally substituted, especially in the pronominal forms *yow*, *your*, &c.; (*b*) medially after *e*, *y* (*i*), as in *seȝe*, *yȝe*. In this position *yȝ* (*iȝ*) had become [ī] or [i̯i]. So *wyȝ* 100 = [wī]. This weakening is shown by the use of *yȝe* for *ie* in French words, such as *sorquydryȝe* 309, *tryȝe* 311, which rhyme with English *yȝe*, *lyȝe*, *dyȝe*, *syȝe*. Note also the rhymes *hyȝe* 454, *byȝe* 466, with *cortaysye*; and **syȝ hit* 698 with *justyfyet*.

(ii) ȝ represented the sound *w* [w, u̯] only medially after the vowels *a*, *o* and the consonants *l*, *r*, as in *boȝe*, *folȝed*, *sorȝe*. Here *w* was frequently substituted, as in *lowe* 236, *towen* 251, *saweȝ* 278, &c.

(iii) But before *t* the letter ȝ had been substituted in the fourteenth century for OE. and earlier ME. *h*. Here it had the *voiceless* fricative sound of German *ch*: (*a*) after *e*, *y* (*i*) the front (palatal) sound, as in German *ich*; (*b*) after *o*, *a* the back (velar) sound as in German *doch*. Examples of (*a*): *bryȝt* 110, *tyȝt* 503,[1] *syȝt* 226, *heȝt* 1031; of (*b*) *poȝt* 137, *broȝte* 527, *saȝt* 52. The same voiceless sounds occurred originally in words where OE. and early ME. had final *h*. Final ȝ has consequently these values in a few words, as in (*a*) *welneȝ* 528, *hyȝ* 'high' 39, (from OE. and early ME. *nēh*, *hēh*); and (*b*) *saȝ* 'saw' 836, *loȝe* 119, *poȝ* 345 (from OE. *sæh*, *luh*, and early ON. **poh*).

Note that the tendency of the MS. to omit an original final *e* or to add an unhistorical *e* makes the distinction of 'final' and 'medial' not always clear. Thus *wyȝ* 100 is for older *wyȝe*, OE. *wiga*; *segh* 790 and *seghe* 867 probably represent the same form.

In all these uses, except initially, *gh* could be used to represent ȝ (cf. the use of *th* to represent *þ*, as in *That* 253, &c.). So *gh*, ȝ, *w* were largely interchanged medially. In this MS. *gh* is chiefly used *finally* (where ȝ represents older *h*) or in *agh*, *ogh* (where ȝ = *w*). Thus *oghe* = *owe* = *oue* in *rescoghe* 'rescue' 610, rhyming with *inoghe* (also spelt *innoȝe* 624). Note also that *now* 'now' (OE. *nū*) is used at the beginning of stanza 52 (l. 613) to link with *inoghe*. See Phonology 13.

---

[1] *tyȝt* in 1013 = [tīt] as rhyme with *quyt* shows, and is a different word, reduced from *tyȝet* = *tyȝed* 'tied'.

B. ʒ = z. In OFr. z was used (both alone and in the combination *tz*) with the sound of [ts]. This [ts] in OFr. became simplified in pronunciation to [s], and ultimately (along with original *s*) voiced initially and medially. ME. spelling tradition (using the minuscule form ʒ) adopted this value in these positions (thus *ʒeferus* in *Sir Gawain* 517), while in final position ʒ probably represented both voiceless and voiced *s*. In this MS. *tʒ* (from influence of French) is used only for voiceless *s*, as in *watʒ, hatʒ, gotz, saytʒ*, &c., and is restricted to the end of stressed monosyllables, while simple ʒ occurs most frequently in unstressed syllables. This seems to indicate a distinction in sound, and it is likely that final -ʒ in the common unstressed ending -*eʒ* was pronounced as the voiced sound. Some words possibly had a double pronunciation according to stress; e.g. *maskelleʒ* in rhyme has the voiceless *s* in 744, 768, 780; when not stressed -*leʒ* may well have had the voiced sound as in modern North-Western dialects.

2. The voiced plosives *b, d, g*, when final were unvoiced in the West Midlands to *p, t, k*, respectively: see above, p. xlvi. The traditional spelling as *b, d, g* is often kept at the end of a word when the pronunciation is clearly *p, t, k*. Thus *þyng* and *þynk* are both found; *among* 905 rhymes with *wlonc*; traditional *lombe* occurs beside the more phonetic *lomp(e)* 815, 945. Examples of 'reverse' spellings with *d* for etymological *t* are *poyned* 217, *marked* 513, *coumforde* 369, and *lombe* 'lamp' 1046.

3. *qu* varies with *wh* and *w* as a spelling for the descendant of OE. *hw*. The use of *qu* is a convention adopted from Northern usage, though the sound represented is [w], not the [χw] found in the North. In this text *qu*, *wh*, and *w* are variants found in the same words, as in *queþer, wheþer, weþer* and *quy, why*, and *wy*.

qu representing [kw] from OE. *cw* and OFr. *qu* is invariable in *Pearl*, but *wh* = *qu* occurs in *Sir Gawain*.

4. *w* is sometimes written for *v*, and *v* or *u* for *w*: *vayned, veued, vyf, vyueʒ, scheued*; and, conversely, *merwayle, awayed*. This peculiarity is well known in Northern texts, but is found in North-Western MSS. also, as in *The Stanzaic Life of Christ*, and *Audelay's Poems*.

5. *w* is also used to represent a diphthong, probably [iu]. The sources of this sound are OE. *ēow, īw* (never *ēaw*), and OFr. *ü*: it is also spelt *ew* and *u(e)*: *swe* 892, *hwe* 896, rhyming with

knewe, due; *trwe* 421, *blwe* 423, *remwe* 427 rhyming with *grewe*; *fortwne* 98. In *drwry* 'cruel' 323, *w* is used to represent a rounded vowel derived from OE. *ēo* (or lengthened *eo*), which is usually spelt *u*, as in *vrþe, burne*, occasionally *ou*, as in *rourde, bourne*. But this is probably due to confusion with, or orthographic influence of, *drwry, drury* 'love-making', OFr. *druerie*, a word appearing frequently in *Sir Gawain* and *Purity*.

6. *aʒ, oʒ, au, aw, ou, ow* occur as variant spellings of one sound, the diphthong *au* of various origins (OFr. *au*, OE., ON. *ăg*, OE. *af* before a consonant, OE. *āw*), though *aʒ* only appears in *Pearl* in words containing OE. or ON. *ăg*, or OE. *æh*, as in *þaʒ* 'though'. Thus *Poule* 457 rhymes with *naule, sawle*; and *knaw* 541 with *owe, rawe, lowe*. *Owe* is identical with *oʒe* 552 (but has a different sound from *innoʒe* 624). *Louyly* 565 is for *lawely* 'lawful' (see next).

7. Etymological *i*(*y*) in an unaccented syllable often appears as *e*. The sound of final [ĭ] and of OFr. *é, ée, ie* was evidently already close or identical. Thus we find *e* used for *i*, as in *worþé* 100 (see note); *reprené* 544; for *ie* in *cortaysé* 469; *y* used for *é* in *city* beside *cité*. (The accent is editorial.) The use of *y* for obscured *e* is doubtful: *louyly* 565, *dayly* 313, *bayly* 315, *baly* 1083 are possibly miswritten (see notes); but cf. *vnsoundely* in *Purity* 201 and *vnsoundyly* in *Sir Gawain* 1438; *pryuely* in *Purity* 238 and *pryuyly* 1107.

8. A redundant *i* is sometimes inserted beside *y*, as in *niyʒt* 630 (see note), *Krystyin* 1202, *fyin*, 1204, *enclyin* 1206.

9. A final *e* unsounded is added not infrequently to a stressed monosyllable, as in *spotte* 24, 36 (the rhyme requires *spot*), *wace, wasse* (variant spellings of *watʒ*), &c.; and even after an unstressed syllable at times, as in *heuenesse* 735 (see note). It is often difficult to decide whether the *-e* was sounded or not; see below, pp. 106 ff.

III. PHONOLOGY

The phonology of the rhymes has been discussed above (Introduction, p. xlv) in so far as it provides evidence of dialect; and the conclusion is there reached that the original dialect was that of the southern Pennine region. The phonology of the extant copy as a whole does not differ materially from the indications of the rhymes, and it is likely that this copy was made somewhere in the North-West. Thus the text of *Pearl* apart from rhymes shows:

1. Western rounding of *a* to *o* before nasal consonants, as in *bonke, plonteȝ, londe,* &c. But the rounding is not consistently represented: *sprange, wan, lande,* &c.

2. Western *al* from OE. *æl* as mutation of *al*: *malte* 224; *el* also occurs in *welle*: cf. *walle-heued* in *Purity* 364.

3. Unrounding of the sound [ü], fronted *u* as in French, to [i]. This usually appeared as *i* or *y*. It is characteristic of the West that this unrounding occurred much later than in the East or South-East, and so affected several words of French origin: *fryte* 29, 87, *dystryed* 124 (both with AFr. (ü) from older [ui]); *rybé* 1007.[1] Other examples of this unrounding in French words appear in *Sir Gawain* in *nyȝe* 'harm', *anious, tryfle,* and in *Purity* in *kyryous* 1109, *nye* (beside *curious, nuyed*). On the double development of French [ü] see p. 104. In words of Norse or English origin the unrounding is normal; but the sound [ü] still survived probably in certain words where the spelling is with *u*. The only words of this kind in *Pearl* are *bur(r)e, burde, lureȝ, busyeȝ, gulte* (beside *gylteȝ*). A following *r* or *l* and a neighbouring labial consonant seem to have favoured the retention of rounding. In *vche, muche, suche,* and *blusched* it is probable that the [ü] had been retracted to [u], a development usual in Midland dialects before *ch, sh,* where *u* is frequent in modern English (as in *crutch, hutch, thrush, rush,* &c.). This has not, however, occurred in *prych* 17.

4. The late Western development of OE. *eo, éo.* This diphthong was simplified as [ö] and eventually unrounded, later than in other dialects, to *é.* But before *r* this [ö] often developed to [ü], usually spelt *u,* occasionally *ou,* as in *vrþe* (beside *erþe* 840), *vrþely, burne* and *bourne* 'man', *rourde* 112. On *drwry* see above under Spelling 5.

5. The Western unvoicing of the plosives *b, d, g,* when final: see above under Spelling 2, and add *dubbet* 97, *fonte* 327, *dyt* 681.

6. The Northern and North Midland unvoicing of *v* to *f* when it came to stand final by the loss of final *-e: luf, pryf* 851, &c.

[1] Unrounded [i] in *rybé* (OFr. *rubi*) seems peculiar to the North-West, and is found in the *Aunters of Arthur* (Douce MS.), and in early modern Lancashire documents (see *NED.*); the form *rebé, reby* occurs in the Hale MS. of the *Aunters* and in *The Sege of Jerusalem.*

This unvoicing was probably not always expressed in spelling, and final *-ue* was written for voiceless *f*; it is then extended as a 'reverse' spelling to original *f* in *saue* 'safe' 696.

7. (*a*) North Midland treatment of *ā*. OE. and ON. *ā* is usually rounded to *ō* [ǭ]; but not invariably, as rhymes show. In *Pearl* there is no certain case of the retention of *ā* except in rhyme: *raas* 1167 is from ON. *ras* with lengthening (originally in dissyllabic oblique cases); *halde* probably has short [a]: see Accidence, p. 115.

(*b*) In the combinations which yield *āw* in early ME., *ā* was not rounded to [ǭ]; *ăw* included *ā* from *ă* lengthened, as well as from OE. and ON. *ā*, and the *w* was from older *w* or *ȝ* (see Spelling, p. 92). In consequence of this merging of *ow*, *aw* the orthographic combinations *aw*, *aȝ*, *ow*, *oȝ* tended to become confused (see Spelling 6). The rhymes in *Sir Gawain* 1640 f. *lawe* 'law', *knowe* 'know', *drowe* for *drawe* 'draw' exemplify the change and the confusion; cf. *louyly* 'lawful' in *Pearl* (see Spelling 6 and 7). This change also affected *ow* developed from OE. *ēow* in one or two words: *Pearl*, *rauþe* 858, *trawþe* 495, *traw* 'believe' 487, where *au*, *aw* is from older *ou*, *ow*; cf. *trowe* 933. Cf. also *fawre*, *faure* in *Purity*.

8. The North Midland variation between *qu*, *wh*, and *w* as representing OE. *hw*; see Spelling 3.

9. The Northern and North Midland development of *squ* to *sw* in *sware* 1023.

10. The same variation between *ī* and *ē* before *ȝ* as in the rhymes (see p. xlviii), which tells against an extreme westerly origin. The proportion of forms with *ē* is slightly higher in the text as a whole than in the rhymes. Examples are: *heȝt* 1031 (beside *hyȝt* 501 in rhyme); *seȝ hit* 698 substituted (as the rhyme shows) for *syȝ hit* in the original text; *seȝ*, *seghe* 'saw' 158, 790, 867; *leghe*, pa. t. 214, *fleȝe*, pa. t. 431.

These characteristics, together with the grammatical forms, point to the North-West, but not to the extreme west of that area.

There remain some phonological developments which are not important as dialectal evidence, but must be understood for the ready interpretation of the poet's forms.

11. In the combinations *br* and *dw* a glide vowel appears between the plosive and the semi-vowel in *dewyne* 11, *dowyne* 326, *boroȝt* 628, *bereste* 854.

12. OE. *ēow* and *īw* have become a diphthong [iu], identical with the diphthong developed from OFr. *ü* and *eu*. This diphthong is spelt *w*, *ew*, or *u*: *nwe*, *huee* 842, *hwe* 896; and note the rhymes in lines 421 &c.: *trwe*, *blwe*, *grewe*, *remwe*.

13. OE. *ō* in combinations which yield *ōw* in early ME. was raised to *ū*, and the *w* either remains as a labial glide, or, if final, is absorbed in the *ū*. This combination is spelt *ow*, *oȝ* or *ogh*: *inoghe* 612, rhyming with *rescoghe* (OFr. *rescou-*) and echoed in the link-word *now* 613 (see note); *innoghe* 636: *alow*; *innoghe* 648: *roghe* (OE. *rūg-*); *innogh* 660: *wythdroȝ*. Probably *ō* in some other positions was beginning to pass into *ū*: this is suggested by the spelling *goud(e)* 'good' which is frequent throughout the whole manuscript.

14. *ir* (*yr*) and *er* before a consonant have become identical, as is shown by rhyme and the confusion of *er* and *yr* in spelling. Thus *gyrle* 205 and *werle* 209 (both with etymological *ir*, *yr*) rhyme with *perle*, *erle*; *yr* is written for etymological *er* in *lantyrne* 1047 and **fyrce* 54, and *er* for *ir* in *werle* 209. This is the beginning of the process by which *er*, *ir*, *or*, *ur* have all become [ör] in modern north-western dialects.

15. [ūr], normally spelt *our*, also appears as *or*, perhaps indicating a lowering of [ū] to [ō]: *yor* 'your'; *corte* beside *court*; *bor* 964, *flor*, *tor*, *fauor*, *cloystor*, rhyming with *vygour*; *fasor* rhyming with *dousour*; *nieȝbor*, &c.

IV. SCANDINAVIAN ELEMENT

The Scandinavian element in the vocabulary of *Pearl*, though considerable—there are about 130 words probably of Scandinavian origin—is not proportionately as large as in the other three poems of the group. This may be accounted for by the theme of the poem and its treatment, especially the long passages given to discourse on the Heavenly Mysteries and theological doctrine, roughly lines 241–972. The Scandinavian element in ME. vocabulary was rich in concrete words, such as abound in this poet's descriptive passages, but included comparatively few words useful to the theologian or the poet of spiritual experience. There was, however, a number of Scandinavian words in literary use which had been pressed into service for their usefulness in alliterative composition. In *Pearl* these Scandinavian words specially associated with alliterative diction are also fewer than in the other poems of the group. An example is *trone* 1113, pa. t. of *trine* chiefly found in alliterative verse; *þryuen and pro* 868 may be a formula coined by medieval poets, but some such phrases come ready made from Scandinavian tradition, as *set(t)e sa3t(e)* (ON. *setja sátta*), *brende golde* (ON. *brent gull*), *sor3 and syt* (ON. *sorg ok sút*). Of these the first was originally a legal rather than a poetic formula, and only the last had any currency in Scandinavian verse. *Tor to knaw* is a variant of the formula *tor for to telle*, which is an adaptation of such Scandinavian expressions as *tortalit* and *torvelt at telja* 'difficult to tell'. Two other phrases, *happe and hele* and *Fader of folde and flode*, are paralleled in ON. *happ ok heill* and *foldar faðir* (applied as in *Pearl* to God); but the similarity of the English phrases is possibly accidental. In *stroþemen* the first element may have the sense 'grass-grown earth' developed in Norse poetry; see, however, note to 115. Traces of Norse poetic tradition are rare in *Pearl* as in Middle English generally; the special literary uses of Scandinavian words usually developed afresh in Middle English. We find in *Pearl* some Scandinavian words used in senses clearly developed in alliterative use, as *carpe* 'discourse' (ON. *karp* 'boast'), *cayre* 'traverse' (ON. *keyra* 'drive'), *rayke* 'flow, roll on' (ON. *reyka* 'wander'). These are typical of the large stock of synonyms collected by the alliterative poets to express in various alliterations the notions of speaking and going. On the other hand, the slightly extended senses given to *keue, wro, hytte3* are a contextual development in *Pearl*, and were not usual in general alliterative use. The sense-development in *won* from 'expectation' to 'dwelling-place' was widespread, and though particularly frequent in alliterative verse or prose was not confined to it. Some of the Scandinavian words used in *Pearl* were rare words, probably taken from colloquial use rather than poetic diction, and used to meet needs of rhyme and alliteration: such are *freles, keue, fla3t, strope* in *stroþemen* (?). (It is noteworthy, also, that many of the words used in extended meanings occur in rhyme.)

Few of the words and particles of the grammatical machinery are of Scandinavian origin in this group of poems. Native English conjunctions, pronouns, auxiliary verbs, and forms of the verb 'to be' are used where Scandinavian forms are preferred or are normal in such texts as the *Ormulum, Havelock, The*

Wars of Alexander, or *Cursor Mundi*. The only Scandinavian pronoun in *Pearl* is *þay*; *at* is probably English (see note 536). Scandinavian *þoȝ* 'though' occurs once, but English *þaȝ* is the usual form. The ending of the present participle is *-ande*,[1] beside less usual English *-yng*. This indicates a less intimate blending of Scandinavian with English than in Yorkshire, Durham, and Lincolnshire, where the Scandinavian settlers were most numerous.

These settlers were both Danes and Norwegians, but at the time of the settlements (876–*c*. 950) they spoke dialects of Scandinavian that differed very little. It is often not possible to distinguish the Scandinavian words in English as specifically Norwegian or Danish. Of those in *Pearl* it is probable that *bayn, boun, bone, farande* are Norwegian; *bredful, drounde, gyue, in melle, trone* (pa. t.), *wyngeȝ* (though the phonological criterion here is not conclusive) are probably Danish.

A certain number of Scandinavian words were adopted in English in the OE. period; of those in *Pearl* OE. forms are recorded of *calle, dyȝe, ȝete, hytteȝ, laweȝ, louyly, saȝt(e), wrang(e)*. But these are not recorded in Northern OE. texts, and probably few of the Scandinavian words have descended to the dialect of *Pearl* from OE. usage; they are rather survivals of the Scandinavian tongue which was spoken in various Northern districts as late as 1200, and were adopted in English at various periods. In a few words, however, an OE. stage must be taken into account. *Dyȝe* 'die' and *keste* 'cast' were adopted in OE. and assimilated to native English word-types. Thus ON. *deyja* appears in very early ME. as *deȝen* (OE. **dēgan*), from which *dyȝe* is regularly descended. *Keste* and *deuely* represent older **cæstan* and **deaflic*, anglicizings of ON. *kasta* and *daufligr*. *Ȝete* is explained by *NED.* as formed on the model of ON. *játa*. *Laweȝ* is a new plural from OE. *lagu* (f. sg.) from ON. *lagu* (neut. pl.). But the greater number of Scandinavian words first came into English in the ME. period.

---

[1] It is doubtful whether *-ande* is entirely Sc. in origin. This ending is not infrequent in O.North., especially in the second class of weak verbs, while *-onde* is found sporadically in late WS. In the SE. (Essex), archaic OE. *-ændi* would naturally develop to *-ande*, and this is probably the source of *-ande* in such texts as *Sir Orfeo*. There was evidently a basis in native usage which was extended under Sc. influence. Note the regular use of *-ande* in the '*West Midland*' *Prose Psalter*, which otherwise shows very little Sc. influence.

Owing to the similarity of English and Norse the number of words in Northern dialects blended from the two sources must have been large; but when cognate Norse and English words had the same meaning and forms which would give the same result in ME., it is impossible to be sure of Scandinavian influence: such words are usually assumed in the Glossary to be of native etymology only. Clear examples of blending are found, however, as *drem*, with form from OE. *drēam* and meaning from ON. *draumr*, *erle* from OE. *eorl* (cf. *eorl* in *Orm.*) with meaning from ON. *jarl*. *Agayn* has its *g* from ON. *gegn*, but both meaning, and form of initial syllable, show blending with English *aȝayn*. Hybrid formations occur in *outsprent*, *serlypeȝ*; *kyrk* is the OE. word *cirice* adopted in Norse as *kirkja* and then readopted in English from Norse.

ON. forms are cited in the Glossary with the normalized spelling of OIcel., as in modern editions and grammars, wherever this corresponds sufficiently closely with the language of the Scandinavian settlers in England. In some instances forms older than those of OIcel. are required for the explanation of the ME. forms: these when given are marked *: thus *poȝ* 345 is from **þŏh* (OIcel. *þó*, with loss of final *h*); *bonke* 196 is from **banke* (OIcel. *bakki* with assimilation of *nk* to *kk* and change of *e* in unaccented syllable to *i*); *wrange* 15 and *wro* 866 are from **wrangr*, **wrá* (OIcel. *rangr*, *rá* with loss of *w* initially before *r*); *freles* 431 is from **frœja(laust)* (OIcel. *frýjulaust* with mutation of *œ* to *y* before a following *j*); *syt* 663 is from **sýt* (OIcel. *sút* which has the unmutated vowel generalized throughout the paradigm).

The sounds of ON. resembled those of OE., and those which were identical received the same treatment in ME. For example, ON. *á* was rounded to *ǫ* just as was OE. *ā*, as in *bope*. ON. *a* before a nasal consonant was equated with OE. *a/o* before a nasal consonant, and usually appears in *Pearl* rounded to *o*: *bonk*, *flonc*, *wonted*; but also *prange*, *wrange*.

ON. *æ* was a long vowel, the equivalent of OE. *ǣ* and having the same development in ME. to *ē* [ẹ̄]: so *prete* 561 from ON. *prǽta*. It may be noted, however, that ON. *æ* seldom corresponded etymologically with OE. *ǣ*. Its usual source was the mutation of *ā*, which normally corresponded with Anglian *ē* (mutation also *ē*). Thus *nere* in 404 has close e [ẹ̄] and thus the vowel of Anglian *nēh*, *nērra*, not of ON. *nær*. *Mele* which has [ẹ̄] in 925 is more difficult. It may be from, or influenced by, ON. *mæla*, a very common word in Norse; but derivation from OE. *mǣlan* cannot be ruled out. This has regularly *ǣ* not *ē* in OE.[1]

ON. initial *g*, medial *gg*, *ng*, and initial and medial *k* were always plosives (as in modern *get*, *king*), and did not show the palatal development of OE. *g*, *c*, *sc* seen in modern *yield*, *child*, *bridge*, *hinge*, *ditch*, *ship*. The presence of *g*, *k* is thus often a good test of Scandinavian origin. Thus *gyue*, *skyfte*, *kyste*, *kyrk*, *gete* are seen to be Norse, or influenced by Norse, compared with the corresponding native *yeue*, *schifte*, *cheste*, *chirche*, *ȝete*. But ON. medial *g* (not *gg*, *ng*) was an open (fricative) sound, identical with OE. *g* and treated like it (becoming *y*, *ȝ*), as in *agayn* (ON. *i gegn*), *laweȝ* (= *laȝes*; ON. **lagu*).

Very few Norse endings were preserved in ME.; (for -*ande* of the present participle see above). -*sk* of the Scandinavian middle (reflexive) voice was ordinarily dropped: see *pryf* and *keue* in the Glossary. The *r* of the nominative form of adjectives (m. sg.) and nouns (str. m.), as cited in the Glossary, was not adopted in ME. (In *anger* the *r* was part of the stem.) In weak verbs, where there was variation in vowel between the mutated form of the present and the unmutated form of the past, sometimes it was the present stem that was adopted, as in *keue* (ON. *kefja*, pa. t. *kafði*) and sometimes the past stem as in *wale* (ON. *velja*, pa. t. *valði*). A new positive *helde* has been coined for the comparative *helder* (recorded in *Sir Gawain*), from ON. *heldr*, for which there was no ON. positive.

V. FRENCH ELEMENT

The French element is large in the vocabulary of all four poems of the group, and it is proportionately as large in *Pearl* as in the others or slightly larger: there are more than 500 words of French origin in *Pearl*, about 800 in *Sir Gawain*, and about 650 in *Purity*. *Pearl* is closer to French poetic tradition than the others and less closely bound to the alliterative technique. There is about the same proportion of French words as in the

[1] It is related to *mæþel* (*maþelian*), and though the phonology of these forms is difficult, it is not clear that the *ǣ* was here developed sufficiently early to share in the change to *ē* in Anglian. The word *stǣlan*, *stǣlwyrðe*, showing a similar relation to *stapol*, also seems to have had *ǣ* not *ē*.

works of Chaucer and Gower, though native English culture dominates the composition of the poem much more obviously than, for example, *Troilus* or *Confessio Amantis*. Much of the vocabulary of Christian faith and doctrine is French: *bonerté, herytage, innocens, vergynté, Vertues*, &c.; and specially characteristic is the use of terms of French *courtoisie* in religious applications (see pp. xxxii ff.). *Pearl* has fewer of the French terms relating to the sciences and crafts than the other poems, though it contains a good number: the various precious stones named, the details of architecture (of the Heavenly City), the flowers in the *erbere*, the details of the Pearl's clothing—these are things that were the concern of high society, and they are described mainly in French terms.

The French words adopted are nearly all found to be Anglo-French (Anglo-Norman) in form, in so far as the Anglo-French types can be distinguished from Central French. The distinction is often difficult to draw, even when the forms are variable, since many of the familiar Anglo-French characteristics were shared with continental Norman and the neighbouring northern and western French dialects. Among these characteristics are the following:

1. *ei* did not become *oi* as in CFr., but remained in early ME., later becoming *ai*; it appears in *Pearl* as *ai, ay*: as in *faye, cortayse* (cf. CFr. *foi, cortois*).

2. *ei, ai* became identical (see preceding) as [ẹi] later [ai]; but before a consonant in AFr. this [ẹi] usually became *e* [ẹ̄]: *plesaunte* (CFr. *plaisant*); *plete* (CFr. *plait*); *refete* (CFr. *refait*) *dese* (CFr. *dais*).

The diphthong was usually only retained in AFr. finally or in hiatus (before a vowel): thus *restay, strayd* from AFr. *restaier, estraier*. But even in hiatus *ei* often became ẹ̄ with various later changes: either contraction, as in [lẹl] (*lelly* 305) from *leel, leial*, or introduction of a glide, as in *reiateȝ*; see p. 104.

Retention of the diphthong before a consonant is often seen in ME., possibly in many cases due to early borrowing before the AFr. change of *ei, ai* to ẹ̄. So usually *cortayse*, beside *corteȝ* 754; *wayted* 14; *raysoun* 268 beside the usual *resoun*.

3. *ga-* is found initially beside *ja-*, where CFr. has only *ja-*: hence *gardyn*, CFr. *jardin*. Similarly AFr. has initial *ca-* beside *cha-*. A probable example of the *ca-* type occurs in *cacchen, cach* in *Sir Gawain*, of which the past tense *caȝt(e)* is found in *Pearl*.

This is derived from an earlier borrowing from ONFr., as its assimilation in stem and conjugation to native *lacchen, laȝte* shows; *chace* 443 is a later borrowing from OFr. *chacier*.

4. AFr. has *w* beside *g, gu*, where CFr. has only *g(u)*: *wage, wayted, rewarde*; CFr. *gage, guaitier, regard*. But *Pearl* also has *gyle, gyse*.

5. During the twelfth century pretonic vowels coalesced with immediately following tonic vowels that were closely similar. On the Continent similar changes were a century or more later: *graunt* (noun), from the AFr. verb *gr(a)anter*; *rounde*, from AFr. *r(u)und*; *lelly*, from AFr. *l(e)el*. But *ẹẹ* was sometimes differentiated as *ie*; hence *ryal* in *Pearl* from AFr. *riel*, *rial, with *a* from Latin influence.

6. Pretonic *e* before a following tonic vowel was lost: *uesture* from *vesteure*, and similarly *lettrure*; *due*, from *deü*.

7. OFr. *ū* in most dialects when nasalized by a following *n* or *m* was lowered to nasal *ō*, but in Norman and Anglo-French the *ū* was preserved before nasal consonants and spelt as *u* until the middle of the thirteenth century, when the spelling *ou˙* was adopted for *ū* in all positions: *mount, founce, croune, contryssyoun, coumforde, resoun*, &c.

8. The form *vysayge* 178 perhaps represents ONFr. *visaige* with palatalization of *a* before *g*; but *ay* may simply express a weakened vowel in an unstressed syllable, as in *grauayl*; see below, p. 105.

Characteristics more probably developed independently in Anglo-French—though some are paralleled on the Continent—are:

(i) *ie* is simplified to *e* [ẹ]: *erbere, daunger*; cf. CFr. *herbier, dangier*. The *y* in *fyrce* is due to a ME. development (Phonology, 14). The change of *ie* to *e* in AFr. probably has no direct connexion with the parallel change in the south-west of France.

(ii) Nasalized *ã* before a nasal consonant appears as *au*. The exact significance of the spelling is uncertain, but eventually, if not originally, the *au* represented a rounded [ǭ], which in English adoptions at least was not nasalized: *daunce, launceȝ, braundysch, daunger, faunt, graunt*, &c. This vowel was sometimes unrounded to *ã* especially before *m*+labial: *chambre, flambe*. On *oun* where CFr. has *on* see 7, above.

(iii) The diphthong *ue* is often simplified as [ö], except after *k* and *g*, and this [ö] is unrounded to *e*. The unrounding took·

place partly in English use, but is also attested in AFr. texts. Hence *meue, preue*. After *k* or *g* the stress is shifted to the *e*, and the *u* becomes [w], as in *quaynt* (*Sir Gawain*); *quoynt* in *Pearl* is found in AFr. texts also, and is either a blend of the northern French type *cointe* with *cueinte*, or else *qu* is simply a graph for *k*. In *ceuer* 319 (*Sir Gawain, keuer*) *k* may be due to influence of forms without diphthong, as in inf. *re-covrer*.

(iv) AFr. [üi] and [ü] usually became [ü] spelt *u*. This [ü] shares in the late western unrounding to [i], seen in *Pearl* in *fryte, dystryed, rybé*: see Phonology 3. When not unrounded, AFr. *u* (= ü] became [iu], spelt in *Pearl w, ew*, or *u(e)*, &c. But in [cüi], before rounding, the stress had often shifted to the *i*, producing *qui* (cf. iii, above): so *aquyle* 690.

(v) *au* was simplified in late AFr. to *a* [ā] before labial consonants: *saf, saue*.

(vi) *eau* was reduced to *eu*: *bewté* 765, cf. *beau*, which retained the French spelling but was pronounced [biu]; *reme* 'realm' has *e* because OFr. *reaum* was from *reialm*.

(vii) In hiatus before or after front vowels the glide *i* was developed: *chayere, reiateȝ*.

(viii) Unstressed *e* between consonants was lost: *perré* (OFr. *perrerie*).

(ix) *v* was vocalized as *u* (*w*) before *r* or *l*: *pouer* (*pore*), *gyngure, renowleȝ*.

(x) Palatal *l* and *n* are resolved in AFr. as *il* and *in*: *aloynte, compayny, strayn*, &c. But in final position the resolution was often to *ly, ny*: *streny, repreny, atteny, fayly, bayly* 315 (?). With *bayly, fayly* the *-ly* may possibly be only a spelling variant since these words do not occur in decisive rhymes. See note to 313–15.

(xi) AFr. [sj], spelt *ss* or *s*, is identified with English *sch*: *braundysch* cf. *bornyste, obes* (cf. *obeched* in *Purity*).

(xii) Reduction and confusion of prefixes is characteristic of late AFr.: *affray, aloynte* (from *es*-); *acroche, encroche* (from *a*-); *endorde* (from *a*-). Often the prefix was dropped entirely, producing the so-called 'aphetic' forms: *baysment, faunt, serued, scale, spyt, sample, tached*, &c.

The words adopted from French often suffered further change in English use. The following changes may be noted:

(*a*) The principal accent was shifted to the root syllable. In ME. generally, words of French origin could be accented either in the English or the French way; in *Pearl* they are accented usually in the English way, and are given French stress only for the sake of rhyme. An exception is *reuer* 1055, and it is notable that in rhyme in 105 this word has, irregularly, open *ę* instead of close *ē*, see (i) above. Probably it was an unfamiliar word. The English shifting of accent caused final syllables to be weakened, and some confusion in the spelling resulted, as in *emerade, grauayl, synglure* (MS.) ; and similarly there has been a reduction under weak stress of the second syllable in *bonerté*.

(*b*) AFr. *ü* was unrounded to *i* in a small group of words (see Phonology 3).

(*c*) Intervocalic *v* in one early borrowing became preconsonantal by syncope of the following vowel, and was then vocalized as *u*: *paraunter*. This is a Northern and North Midland form.

French nouns and adjectives were generally adopted in the form of the accusative singular (without ending), but not *fyrce*, which has the *-s* of the nom. sg. masc. Of verbs it was the stem that was borrowed, and in *Pearl* French verbs are conjugated weak, except **fyne* which has the strong pa. t. *fon*.

The *Pearl* poet was evidently accustomed to read and speak French. He has several coinages of his own formed by adding French suffixes or prefixes to English words ; thus he turns the English adjectival ending *-y* into the French *-yf* in *gyltyf* and *mornyf*. He seems to have equated the English prefix *with-* with French *re-* in *withnay* (OFr. *reneier*), and he coins a new compound with French *re-*: *reparde*. Most of the French words in *Pearl* were probably of comparatively recent adoption, and some may well have been taken by the poet himself from his own knowledge of the language: words such as *bantels* and the names of the less known precious stones.

One aspect of French linguistic influence on *Pearl* is the use of *ʒe* pl. as the polite form of the singular 'you', and an understanding of this usage is of importance for a full appreciation of the poem.

ʒe (and *yow, your*) are used, in addressing one person, only to impart a tone of formality or humility. (The workmen were being insolent in using *þou* to the lord, 556). Thus the Pearl in her first greeting uses *ʒe*, 257–258, after which she uses *þou*, &c., throughout. The Dreamer uses *þou* throughout (and thus shows plainly that he is addressing no stranger, whether allegorical or not)—except notably after the severe rebuke ending at l. 360, when he uses *ȝe* 369–93, with intrusion of *þou* only in 375 (referring to the Pearl's childhood) and 385. He reverts to *þou* when he returns to the attack in 423 and 473 ff. In this latter passage we have *yow* only in 471 (under the influence of the *yow* pl. in 470, and a case where MS. alteration is possible). The Dreamer uses *ȝe* in a polite formula 914 (cf. *dyspleseȝ* pl. 422), and in 933. Only in the last instance is there no clear reason for the plural form, save that a pl. verb was required for rhyme. There are a few doubtful cases. The Pearl often uses *ȝe* with a general reference: 'all you people in the world.' So 858. This probably explains *ȝe* in 698, and similarly *your* 497, *yor* 761, *yow* 951. Also possibly *ȝe* 307, 308, *your* 305, 306. Similar is the colloquial use of *ȝe*, like modern *you* as 'anyone, one', seen in 1051; *at yow* 287 may be a case of pl. for sg., although it comes in the middle of a *þou* passage. If so, it has no reason other than alliteration. But it may be suspected that it is meant to be pl., and is due to the reference to *my Lorde* 285: the Dreamer already realizes that across the water is a different land; and his *yow* here refers to 'all you across the water'; cf. *yor worlde* used by the Pearl in 761.

For the use of *ȝe, þou* in *Sir Gawain* see Gollancz, edn. 1940, p. 111. Though the distinction between *þou, ȝe* (between equals) was beginning to be blurred, it cannot be neglected in the fourteenth century, especially in any work containing dialogue. *þou* was still in full colloquial use, and the substitution of *ȝe* was seldom without at least a change of tone; and the failure to use *ȝe* could in certain circumstances be either insolent or forward.

VI. ACCIDENCE

INFLEXIONAL -*e*

In a very large number of words in *Pearl* it is impossible to decide whether the -*e* of inflexional endings was pronounced or not. As in most ME. texts of the time, many words were probably used in double forms, one in which inflexional -*e* was sounded and one in which it had been dropped, according to varying conditions. For example, such factors as emphasis, occurrence at a pause in the sentence, and need for grammatical clarity seem to have favoured the use of the form with -*e* pronounced; lack of stress, occurrence in the middle of a phrase or other rhythmic group, or occurrence before a word beginning with a vowel or *h* seem to have favoured the dropping of the -*e*. Even when these conditions remain constant, however, the -*e* is retained more frequently in some grammatical endings than in others, e.g. when it is the reduction of the ending -*en* ; whereas the -*e* of the early ME. pa. t. suffix -*ede* has invariably been dropped in *Pearl*, and the -*e* of the dative sg. of nouns more often dropped than retained.

Inflexional -*e* appears to have been more stable at the end of the line than within the line. In the usage of some poets, as, for example, Chaucer and Gower, inflexional -*e* is normally sounded at the end of the line. And in *Pearl* when all the rhyme-words in a group have an -*e* that is organic (i.e. justified by etymological and grammatical history), it may be assumed with some probability that it was sounded. Thus -*e* was probably sounded in: pres. pl. *slepe* 115 ; pres. 1 sg. *dowyne* 326, *lede* 409 ; pa. t. pl. *bete* 93 ; infin. *forȝete* 86, *deuyse* 99, *swepe* 111, *wade* 143, *fare* 147, *schere* 165, &c. But in *Pearl* the variant usage is found even in rhyme. Thus -*e* has been dropped in: pres. 3 pl. *þay dyssentę* 627,[1] and the pa. t. pl. *þay wentę* 631, rhyming with *innocent*, *endentę* ; pres. 1 sg. *expoun* 37 : *seysoun, doun, gromylyoun* ; infin. *adaunt* 157 : *relusaunt, faunt, bleaunt* ; infin. *bytę* 640 : *parfyt* ; infin. *dryf* 777 : *styf* ; adj. pl. *schym* 1077 : *dym, grym* (both sg.).

Within the line final -*e* was probably dropped much more frequently. This at least is an assumption which agrees with the usual practice of ME. verse, and is supported by the MS. spelling. But the evidence of *Sir Gawain* is that the MS. is not careful in spelling and is unreliable in words with obscured *e*. And since in Pearl final -*e* has been added to many words in which it could never have been sounded (as in *arte* 707, *woste* 293, *I welke* 101, *rounde* 5, *fryte* 29, *corne* 40, *colde* 50, *bere* 67, &c.), it seems reasonable to suppose that in some cases where there is no final -*e* in the MS. its omission is scribal and not original. Clear cases of scribal omission of obscured *e* are *adubmente* 72 for *adubbement, counsayl* 319 rhyming with *bayly, fayle*. The difficulty is to decide just which of these omissions are scribal only. Metre does not provide a very clear guide to the pronunciation of final -*e* within the line, since the poet has considerable freedom in the placing of the dips and in the number

---

[1] *ę* is used in this section to denote an *e* that occurs in the MS. form, but is shown by etymology, rhyme, or other evidence to have been silent.

of syllables he includes in them. Thus line 17 is metrically plausible whether we keep the MS. spelling or assume that *prych* and *hert* should have final *e*. But it is noteworthy that the poet of *Pearl* usually avoids clashing the last two main stresses (though he likes the combination ´ ` ×, as in *wodshawez, godnesse*, &c.), and it is possible that in 17, 122, 286, 381, 486 the apparent clashing stresses are due to scribal omission of final *-e*; in all cases the *-e* is grammatically and etymologically justified. But the forms have not been altered in the text, because the evidence is not felt to be conclusive.

Elision, too, cannot be definitely proved, but it is probable. It is found elsewhere in ME. poetry. The *-e* of the definite article may also have been elided in such combinations as *The adubbemente* 85; this would accord with general ME. practice. It is unlikely, however, that the *-e* of the pronouns *me, þe, he* was ever elided.

It is probable that on occasion an unhistorical *-e* could be added and pronounced. Just as there were two forms of the pres. 1 sg. *dem* and *deme*, the endingless *wot* suggested a variant with final *-e*, and this occurs as *wate* in 502, rhyming with *date*. Similar forms are *owe* 543, and *schale* in *Sir Gawain* 1240. See also the note on *myne* 335. It is only in rhyme or when used with unusual emphasis that such forms are likely to occur.

There was an unstressed *e* pronounced in the endings *-ez, -es, -en, -ed* (*-et*): *justyfyet* 700, rhyming with *syz hit*; *veued* 976, rhyming with *heued*. Spelling provides evidence of syncope only after liquid and nasal consonants: *heuenz* beside *heuenez, vnstrayned* beside *straynd*. Probably there were alternative pronunciations.

As in Middle English generally, it is not uncommon in *Pearl* to find that an unetymological *e* has been inserted in compound and derivative words at the end of the first element, as in *arepede, holtewodez, stropemen, mysetente, loueloker, longeyng*, &c. This *e* was sometimes merely graphic, but in other words was at one time pronounced. In *Pearl* its significance is in most instances doubtful; but in the last three at least of those just cited, it appears to have been silent.

Nouns. The inflexional endings are:

Sg. nom. acc.	—, *-e*.	Pl. *-ez, -es, -esse*; *-z, -s*
gen.	*-ez*, —.	(after vowel or *n*).
dat.	*-e*, —.	

-e is often written in the nom. and dat. sg. when it is not pronounced; in both these cases the *-e* was more often dropped than maintained. Often the same noun has the final *-e* in one line and not in another: see *hert(e)*, &c., in the Glossary.

The endingless genitive, recorded also in the other poems of this group, but more frequently in Northern texts, occurs in *wommon* 236, *helle* 643, *Lombe* 1141, *Israel* 1040, and twice in the idiomatic phrase *quat kyn* (cf. *alle kynne3* 1028). The genitive in *-e3*, as *Lombe3* 872, is more frequent.

Two mutated plurals survive, *men* and *fete*; *schyldere3* (Vespasian Psalter *scyldru*) retains the mutation, but adds the usual plural ending. The old feminine plural survives in *honde* 49 (OE. *honda*), and an old neuter plural in *chylder* (OE. *cildru*); *hyne* is a ME. formation on the old gen. pl. *hīgna*. There is one noun with a weak pl.: *y3en*, *ene. After a numeral the sg. form is used in *3er* 483, unless this is the old neuter pl. form, and *forlonge* 1030, unless this is the old gen. pl. of measure. One anomalous plural *juele* occurs in rhyme in 929; this form may be an imitation of the French (nom.) pl., but is probably due to the exigences of rhyme. (Cf. the pl. *dame* (in rhyme) in *Sir Gawain* 1316.)

Adjectives

The plural ends in *-e*, and this is usually maintained in rhyme, but very often dropped in the middle of the line: *frech flauore3* 87, *smal* 6, &c. The weak form in *-e* is used in vocative expressions, after the definite article, a possessive adjective, or a demonstrative: *þou hy3e kyng* 596, *her fayre face* 169, *þe hy3e gate* 395. The *-e* of the weak adjective is one of the more stable final *-e*'s in the middle of the line, but it is also sometimes dropped, as in *þe fyrst day* 486, *þy hy3 hylle* 678. For the forms of the definite article and the demonstrative adjectives see the Glossary under ÞE, ÞAT, ÞO, ÞOSE, ÞIS.

Adjectives ending in *-ly(ch)* form their comparative in *-loker* and superlative in *-lokest*, which are descended from the late OE. development *-lucor*, *-lucost* of earlier *-licor*, *-licost*. The adjectives *old* and *colde* regularly have a comparative and superlative with a short vowel: *alder*, *aldest*, *calder*. Both these features are westerly in character.

Pronouns

The forms are recorded in the glossary. For the personal

pronouns see I, ᵽOU, HE, HO, SCHO, HIT ; WE, ȜE, ᵽAY, HEM. Specially noteworthy is the feminine *ho* 'she', which was characteristic of the West Midlands and especially of the North-West. This pronoun still survives in the North-West in a stressed form *oo* (implying a ME. *hō*), and an unstressed [ə], usually misspelt *her* in modern dialect writings. Notable also is the neuter gen. *hit* 'its', first recorded in this group of poems, and still known (in the form *it*) in modern dialects of Lancashire, Cheshire, and part of the West Riding. The genitive *hit* was not peculiar to the North-West, but was perhaps better established in general use there than elsewhere, since only in the North-West is there medieval evidence of it, and it now survives only in that region. In most dialects *hit* was apparently regarded as less dignified than *his*.

The emphatic pronouns made with *self*, *seluen* may be used alone, without a normal pronoun in apposition, as is usual in modern English except in reflexive use. Note that *hytself* 446 is probably genitive, 'its own'.

At this period the second person pl. was normally used in addressing a superior and in formal language between equals, and the singular for a greater degree of familiarity. On the use of *ȝe* and *þou* in *Pearl* see French Element, pp. 105–6.

Mon is used as the indefinite 'one', and the plural *men*[1] with much the same sense. Other indefinite pronouns are *who*, *quo* 'whoever', and *what*, *quatso* 'whatever'.

The usual relative pronoun is *þat*; *at* in 536 is only a phonetic reduction of *þat*. An oblique case of the relative was in ME. usually expressed by adding a personal pronoun in the relative clause, e.g. *þat . . . hys persoun* 'whose person' in *Sir Gawain* 912–13; this construction does not occur in *Pearl*. But by this period the oblique cases *whos*, *whom* were used as relatives, and *whom* (*wham*, *quom*) is so used in *Pearl* 131, 453.

Verbs

The endings of strong and weak verbs are almost identical and may therefore be described together.

Infinitive: *-en*, *-e*, —. The ending *-en* is found only in *leuen*

---

[1] The indefinite *men* is often sg. in ME., and is then a weakened form of *man*; but in these poems it never occurs with a verb that is certainly sg. In 331, however, where *men* is the antecedent of *he*, it is probably from earlier use of *men* sg.

69, *meten* 1032, *dyscreuen* 68, and, in reduced form after a vocalic stem, in *gon* 820. *-e* is maintained in rhyme more often than lost, but in the middle of the line it is frequently lost. The *-e* is apparently more readily dropped in verbs of French origin than in native verbs. Verbs with stems ending in an unaccented syllable regularly have no ending in the infinitive: *heuen* 16, *ceuer* 319, *fayly* 34, *wony* 284, &c.

As in most Northern and many Midland dialects the infinitive stems of verbs like OE. *bycgan, licgan, secgan* have been reformed from the present 2 and 3 sg: *byye, ly3, say(e)*.

In *to sene* 45 and *to done* 914 the OE. inflected infinitive with *to* survives, and is used as in OE. to express purpose. Another possible example of this form is *to dyscreuen* 68.

The use of *to* with the infinitive has already become almost as frequent as in modern English, and is once found even after the auxiliary *con* (1181). Notable, however, is the complementary infinitive without *to* in 15 and 226; *to* is 'split' from its infinitive in 2 (cf. *Sir Gawain* 88, 1540, 1863). The infinitive with *to* is several times used absolutely, either as the equivalent of a participle (the modern use), as in 22 and 474, or to express a condition, as in 580.

Indicative Present

Sg. 1 *-e*, —; *-e3*.   Pl. *-en, -e*, —; *-e3*,
  2 *-e3*; in monosyllabic forms *-3*,   *-t3*.
   -s, -t3.
  3 *-e3, -es*; in monosyllabic forms
   -3, -s, -t3.

The various endings of the plural and 1 sg. are all attested by rhymes; thus for the plural: *meuen* 64, *slepe* 115 and (endingless) *obes* 886, *pres* 957, *dyssentę* 627; *byde3* 75. 'Disjunctive' forms in *-e3*, used when a verb is separated from its subject by another verb, occur in the 1 sg. in *byswyke3* 568 (see note) and in the plural in *renowle3* 1080. Other plural forms in *-e3* or *-t3* are: *schyne3* 28, *wone3* 404, *got3* 510, *pyke3* 573. The peculiar shortened forms of the present of *saye, make, take* are noteworthy: see the Glossary and note to 532.

Indicative Past, strong verbs:
  Sg. no ending, though *-ę* is often written.
  Pl. *-en, -e*, —.

Sg. *wan* 107, *sprange* 13, *ros* 437; Pl. *weuen* 71, *trone* 1113, *bygonne* 549, *faʒt* 54, *þay nom* 587.

Weak verbs:

Sg. 1 and 3 -*e*, —.	Pl. -*en*, -*e*, —.
2 -*eʒ*, -*e*, —.	

-*eʒ* is the true historical ending of the 2 sg.; but the form of the 1 and 3 was also used for the second person. Pa. t. forms in -*ed* regularly had no ending in all persons of the sg. and pl., and -*e* might also be dropped in other types of weak pa. t., as in *caʒt* 50, *wroʒt* 555.

Subjunctive, Present and Past: Sg. and Pl. -*e* or —. Examples of the present: *þou leue* 865, *dryue* 1094, *marre* 359, *gef* 1211, *com* 598, *braundysch* 346; past: *sponne* 35, *syʒe* 308, *syʒ* 698.

Imperative: Sg. No ending (though -*e* sometimes written); -*eʒ*. Pl. -*eʒ*, and in monosyllabic forms -*tʒ*, -*s*.

Examples of sg.: *draʒ* 699, *tech* 936, *breue* 755; *kyþeʒ* 369; pl. *wyrkeʒ* 536, *gos* 521, *dotʒ* 521.

Present Participle: -*ande*, but probably the -*e* was not always sounded. One instance of -*yng*: *sykyng* 1175.

Past Participle: strong verbs in -*en*, -*n*, less frequently in -*e*, and in a few instances even the -*e* is lost: *coruen* 40, *schornę* 213, *bore* 239. There is one instance of the participial prefix: *ichose* 904, where *i*- is required metrically. To the p.p. of weak verbs a final -*e* is often added in writing.

THE STRONG CONJUGATIONS

Analogy has been the source of many changes in the strong conjugations, such as the levelling of the vowel *e* of the pa. t. pl. of the fourth and fifth conjugations into the pa. t. sg. (forming the so-called 'western preterite'), the transference of several verbs to other conjugations, and the development by many strong verbs of weak forms. These changes are seldom complete, and result in the use of alternative forms. New verbs, adopted from Norse or French, if they received strong conjugation, were assigned to conjugations suggested by their present stems, rhyming with well-known native words being a powerful influence. So [*trine*]¹ follows *schyne,* and [*flynge*] follows *sprynge,* *take* follows [*schake*], the French word *fyne* follows *schyne* making *fon* 1030 (cf. ME. and mod. E. *strove* from *strive,* OFr. *estriver,* after *drive*). Norse forms or alterations of native words follow the native conjugations (which are usually historically the same in both languages): so [*renne*] in conjugation 3, and *gyue, gete* in 5.

Infin.	Pa. t. sg.	Pa. t. pl.	P.p.
1. *dryue*	*drof*	[*drof*]	*dryuen*

The vowel of the pa. sg. has been levelled into the pl. Pa. pls. of this type occur in *glod* 1105, *trone* 1113; *schyne* has the weak pa. *schynde* beside *schon.*

2. [*chose*]	*chos*	[*chosen*]	*ichose*
	ches(e)		[*chosen*]
[*flete*]	**flet*	*fleten*	[*floten*]
	flot, [*flot(t)e, flette*]		
[*flyȝe*]	*fleȝe*	*flowen*	[*flowen*]
[*louke*]	*leke*		[*loken*]

[*schote*], originally like [*chose*,] has become weak, and shows shortening of the *o* before the double *tt* in the pa. t.; *schot* 58 is from earlier *schotte* (cf. *schotten* in *Sir Gawain* 1167). *Flete* similarly has a weak pa. with short *o*; but in its strong form the vowel of the pa. sg. has been levelled into the pl., as in *Sir Gawain* 1566 *flete*; *cleuen* 66 (see note) is probably a pa. pl. of the same type; *boȝe,* originally like [*louke*] has become weak.

3. *wynne*	*wan*	[*wonnen*]	*wonne*
fynde	*fandę*	[*founden*]	*founden, fonde, fonte*
spryng	*sprang(ę)*	[*sprange*]	
[*renne*]	*ran*	[*runnen*]	*runne*[*n*]
warpe	[*warp*]	[*warpen*]	

Like *wynne* are *blynne,* [*spynne*], *bygynne*; like *fynde* are [*bynde*] and *grynde*; like *spryng* are *flynge, stynge, swynge,* except that rounding of the *a* and unvoicing of the *g* may appear in the

---

¹ To make the account of the verbs clearer those parts of the conjugation not recorded in *Pearl* are cited from the other poems in the group when possible; such forms are enclosed in [ ].

pa. sg., as *stonge* 179, *flonc* 1165. The pa. pl. *faȝt* 54, [*warpen*]
and [*sprange*] have the vowel of the pa. sg.; but cf. *foȝt, Sir
Gawain* *874.

Infin.	Pa. t. sg.	Pa. t. pl.	P.p.
4. *bere*	*ber*(*e*)	[*bere*]	*bore, borne*
com	*come*	[*comen*]	[*comen*]
[*nyme*]	[*nom*]	*nom*	-*nome*
	nem	[*neme*]	[*numen*]
speke	*speke*	[*speken*]	*spoken*
	spakk		
heue	[*hef*]	[*heuen*]	[*houen*]

Like *bere* are *schere, stele*. The weak verb *were* has followed the
analogy of *bere, schere*, &c., and has the strong pa. *wer*. The
pa. *nem*, [*neme*] have *ē* from the analogy of the *bere*-type. *Speke*
has changed to this conjugation from class 5, as also [*steke*],
p.p. *stoken*, [*wreke*], p.p. *wroken* and [*weue*], p.p. [*wouen*]; *heue*
has been transferred to this class from 6.

5. *forȝete*	[*forȝete*]	[*forȝeten*]	[*forȝeten*]
	[*forȝate*]		
gyue	*gef*		[*geuen*]
	gaue		*gyuen*
lyȝ	*leghe*	[*leȝen*]	[*leyen*]
	[*lay*]		
se	*seȝ*(*e*), *syȝ*(*e*)	*seȝ*, [*syȝe*]	*sen*(*e*)
	saȝ		
[*sytte*]	*set*(*e*)	*sete*	[*seten*]

Like *forȝete* is *gete*; like *sytte* is *bydde*, except that the p.p. is
[*boden*] through confusion with [*bede*]. Pa. sg. forms with *e* from
the analogy of the pa. pl. are more frequent than the type *forȝate*,
saȝ, gaue, which preserves the historical vowel; *se* has as its p.p.
the adj. *sen*(*e*) from OE. *gesēne*.

6. *draȝe*	*droȝ*	*droȝ*, [*droȝen*]	*drawen*
stande,	*stod*(*e*)	[*stode*]	*standen*
stonde			
flyȝe			*flayn*
	[*slow*]	[*slowen*]	*slayn*

Like *draȝe* are *take* and *wade*, except that *take* has also shortened
forms, pres. 3 sg. [*tatȝ*], *totȝ*, p.p. *tan*, [*tone*]; *flyȝe* 'flay' is per-

haps formed from *flē* (so the vowel in the 2, 3 sg.) by addition of *ʒ* from the p.p., and the new *fleʒen* would give later *flyʒe*.

Infin.	Pa. t. sg.	Pa. t. pl.	P.p.
7. [*falle*]	*fel(le)*	*felle*	[*fallen*]
halde, [*holde*]	*helde*	[*helde*]	*halden*, [*holden*]
knaw	*knew*	*knewe*	*knawen*
let	*let, lette*		[*let*]
folde			*folde*
fonge, [*fange*]	[*feng*]		[*fonge*], [*fongeð*]
hete	*hyʒt(e)*, [*hette*] [*hat(te)*]		[*hyʒt*] [*hat(te)*]

Like *falle* are *walk*, *wasche*, and *wax*, except that pa. sg. *wax* occurs beside *wex* ; like *knaw* are *grow*, *prowe*. In *fonge, fange* the stem of the p.p., usually in this conjugation the same as the infin., has ousted the irregular OE. pres. *fon*. *Hete* has had a complex development. OE. had *hātan* ; *hĕht, hēt* ; *hāten* ; and a passive *hătte*. The pa. t. forms are due to blending in form and meaning of OE. pa. t. with the passive (taken as a weak pa. t.) ; *hete* is of obscure origin.

TYPES OF WEAK VERBS

The weak verbs are most conveniently classed as (i) those which have no -*e*- before the *d* or *t* of the suffix in the pa. t. and p.p., and (ii) those which have this -*e*-. Examples of (i) are : *lese*, pa. t. *leste* ; *make, made* ; *bye, boʒt* ; *drede, dred* ; *rere*, p.p. *rert*. Examples of (ii) are : *deme, demed* ; *leue, leued* ; *dyʒe, dyed*. These types are derived (i) from verbs of OE. Class I, in which the pa. t. suffix -*de*, -*te* was added direct to the apparent stem, and (ii) from verbs of other OE. classes, especially Class II, in which the pa. t. ended in -*ede*, -*ode*. But the OE. distribution was greatly disturbed in ME. and is no safe guide to the treatment of any given verb. One of the main causes of the disturbance was the fact that many verbs of Class I formed their p.p. in -*ed* (especially in Anglian), so *dēman, dēmed*, and this uncontracted form in ME. (where p.p. and pa. t. were closely associated or identified) was often used as pa. t., so *demed* 361 (OE. *dēmde*). Type (i) shortens a vowel which is long in the present stem before a consonant group in the pa. t. and p.p.: *lede*, p.p. *lad*; *schote*, pa. t. *schot*; *leue*, pa. t. *lafte*. An isolated pa. t. of this type is *yot*, from earlier *yodde* (*yode* with the usual weak suffix added), reduced to *yod* by loss of final -*e* and with final -*d* unvoiced. See note to line 10.

In type (i) the special group of OE. verbs with mutation only in the present stem still survives: see BRYNG, BYE, SOLDE, SECH, TELLE, ÞENKE, ÞYNK, WYRKE3 in the Glossary.

In type (ii) traces of the OE. infin. ending -*ian*, characteristic of Class II, are only found in a few forms: *wony* (beside *won*), pres. 3 sg. *wonys*, pres. p. *lyuyande*, p.p. *feryed*. The -*y* in the French verbs *fayly, repreny, streny*, &c., is of a different origin, arising from resolution of the palatal *l* or *n*: see French Element, p. 104.

Most verbs of French origin belong to type (ii); exceptions are (*a*) those assimilated by rhyme to native verbs: *cache* becomes *cacchen, ca3te* after *lacchen; estriver* becomes *striuen, strof* after *driuen*, and (*b*) verbs whose stem in OFr. ended in *ai, ei, oi, i*: *paien*.

Unvoicing of *d* to *t* was frequent in the pa. t. of both types, and was indeed regular in type (ii), where the -*d* of the suffix had invariably become final through early loss of the inflexional -*e*. This unvoicing is not always shown in spelling. In some instances the final dental was assimilated to a dental beginning a following word and was then omitted in spelling: see note to *hoped 142.

For the forms of the preterite-present verbs see the Glossary under CON, DAR, MAY, MOT, SCHAL, WOT; and for the anomalous and incomplete verbs see under AM, AR, ART, BE, DO, GON, WAT3, WYL.

GLOSSARY

In the Glossary completeness is aimed at. Intentional exceptions are: (i) references to frequently recurring forms and uses have been much curtailed; such curtailment is marked by *&c.*; (ii) the inflected forms of nouns, adjectives, and weak verbs have only exceptionally been recorded (for their normal forms see pp. 106–16). For abbreviations see p. vii.

Etymologies. These are given as an aid in interpreting spellings and differentiating words of diverse origin and similar appearance, and also as part of the evidence used to fix the meanings. They are necessarily extremely brief, and when discussion at length is called for, reference is made to *NED*. For the better explanation of the forms in the text, the Old French forms cited are largely Anglo-French (usually without specification), and the Old English forms are Anglian (especially Mercian). The marking of long vowels has not been attempted in Old French. In Old English the long vowels are marked as in *ān*; uncertain quantity or probable shortening in the Old English period is marked as in *cўmlic*; vowels lengthened in Old English (e.g. before *ld*) are marked as in *báld*, when the forms in the text point to, or allow of the possibility of this lengthening. On the forms cited from Old Norse see p. 100; long vowels are marked as in *ár*, except *æ* and *œ*, which were always long.

Arrangement. In the Glossary and Index of Names (i) ʒ in any function (see p. 91) has a separate alphabetical place immediately after **g**; (ii) þ has a separate place immediately after **t**; (iii) **u** and **v**, not differentiated in phonetic value in the MS., are treated as one letter following þ; (iv) **y** as a consonant has its usual place, but as a vowel it is interchangeable with **i** in the usage of the MS., and will be found in the Glossary in alphabetical place of **i**.

a, *indef. art.* a, a certain, some, 19, 23, 786, 1204, &c.; **an, on** (before vowels or *h*), 9, 530, 640, 869. [OE. *ān*.] See VCH.

abate, 617. See ABYDE.

abated, *pa. t.* put an end to, 123. [OFr. *abattre*.]

abyde, *v. trans.* endure, 348; **abiden,** *pp.* 1090; **abate,** *pa. t.*

intr. remained, endured, 617. [OE. *ābīdan*.]

able, *adj.* able, 599. [OFr. *able*.]

abof, *adv.* above, 1023; *prep.* 1017. [OE. *abufan*.]

aboute, abowte, *prep.* about, round about, 75, 149, 1077; concerning, 268; near, 513; *adv.* in the neighbourhood, 932. [OE. *abūtan*.]

abroched, *pp.* given vent, uttered, 1123. [OFr. *abroch(i)er.*]

acheue, *v.* achieve, 475. [OFr. *achever.*]

acorde, *n.* agreement, 509; *of care and me made acorde,* caused me to know sorrow, 371. [OFr. *acorde.*]

acorded, *pa. t.* accorded to, agreed with, 819. [OFr. *acorder.*]

acroche, *v.* acquire, 1069. [OFr. *acrocher.*]

adaunt, *v.* abash, daunt, 157. [OFr. *ada(u)nter.*]

adyte, *pres. subj.* accuse, arraign, 349. [OFr. *aditer.*]

adoun, *adv.* down, 988. [OE. *adūne.*]

adubbement(e), *n.* adornment, splendour, *72, 84, 85, 96, 108, 120. [OFr. *adubement.*]

affray, *n.* dismay, 1174. [OFr. *effrei.*]

after, *adv.* afterwards, then, 256; *prep.* along, 125; according to, 998. [OE. *æfter.*]

agayn, *prep.* against, 1199, 1200; facing, in (sun), 28; *adv.* again, 326. [ON. *i gegn*; OE. *ongegn.*]

agayn3, *prep.* against, upon, 79. [Prec.+adv. *-es.*]

age, *n.* age, 412. [OFr. *age.*]

agly3te, *pa. t.* slipped away, 245. [Uncertain.]

agrete, *adv.* all together, as a body, 560. [OE. *on+grēat.*]

a3t. See O3E.

a3tpe, *adj.* eighth, 1011. [OE. *æhtopa.*]

ay, aye, *adv.* ever, always, for ever, 33, 44, 56, *144, &c. [ON. *ei.*]

ayper, *adj.* each (of two), both, 831. [OE. *ǣgper.*]

al, alle, *adj.* all, 16, 73, 119, 285, 292, &c.; *pron.* all, everything, 360; everybody, 404, 447, 1124; *of al and sum,* in full, 584; *adv.* entirely, quite, everywhere, 97, 197, 258, 518 (see SAMEN), &c. [OE. *al(l).*]

alas, allas, *interj.* alas, 9, 1138. [OFr. *a las.*]

alder, aldest. See OLDE.

aldermen, *n. pl.* elders (rendering Vulgate *seniores*), 887, 1119. [OE. *aldormann.*]

alegge, *pres. subj.* plead, urge (a claim), 703 (note). [OFr. *aligier, alegier.*]

alyue, *adj.* living, 445. [OE. *on life.*]

almy3t, *adj.* Almighty, 498. [OE. *ælmiht.*]

Almy3ty, *adj.* Almighty, 1063. [OE. *ælmihtig.*]

aloynte, *pp.* far removed, 893. [OFr. *esloignier.*]

alone, *adv.* only, 933. [OE. *al āna.*]

alow, *v.* give credit for, 634. [OFr. *alouer.*]

also, als, *adv.* also, 685, 765, 872; moreover, 1071. [OE. *al swā.*]

alpa3, *conj.* although, 759, 857, 878. [OE. *al pěh.*]

am, *1 sg. pres.* am, 246, 335, &c. [OE. *eam, am.*]

amatyst, *n.* amethyst, 1016. [OFr. *amatiste.*]

among, *adv.* mingled, together, 905; *prep.* among, 470, 848, 1145, 1150. [OE. *on móng.*]

and (MS. & except in 1212), *conj.* and, 16, 18, 27, 29, 1076, &c.; *advers.* but, (and) yet, 273, 777, 906, 931, &c.; seeing that, 378, 560; if, 598; ande, 1212. [OE. *and.*]

anende, onende, *prep.* in respect of, concerning, 186, 697; against, close to, 1136. [OE. *on emn,* infl. by *ende.*]

anende3, *prep.* opposite, 975. [Prec.+adv. *-es.*]

angel-hauyng, *n.* angelic demeanour, 754. [OFr. *angele*+ME. *hauyng.*]

anger, *n.* sorrow, 343. [ON. *angr.*]

ani, any, *adj.* any (whatsoever), 345, 463, 617, 800, 1068, 1139. [OE. *ænig.*]

anioynt, *adj.* joined, united, 895. [OFr. *enjoint.*]

anon, *adv.* at once, straightway, 584, 629. [OE. *on ān.*]

anoþer, *adj.* a second, 297. [OE. *ān + ōþer.*]

answar, *n.* answer, 518. [OE. *andswaru.*]

an-vnder, on-vunder, *prep.* under, 775 (note), *1068, 1081, 1092, 1100; at the foot of, 166; *adv.* underneath, 991. [OE. *on under.*]

apassed, *pp.* as *prep.* past, 540. [OFr. *apasser.*]

apere, *v.* appear, 405. [OFr. *apareir, aper-.*]

apert, *adv.* plainly, 589. [OFr. *apert.*]

ap(p)ostel, *n.* apostle, 790, 836, 1008, 1053, &c. [OE. *apostol.*]

apparaylmente, *n.* adornment, array, 1052. [OFr. *apareille-ment.*]

apple, *n.* apple, 640. [OE. *æppel.*]

appose, *v.* confront with hard questions, interrogate, 902. [OFr. *aposer.*]

aproche, *v.* come to, 686; approach, 1119. [OFr. *aprochier.*]

aquyle, *v.* obtain, 690 (note); *pp.* aquylde, obtained (permission), 967. [OFr. *acuillir.*]

ar, arn(e), *pres. pl.* are, 384, 402, 628, 923, &c. [OE. *earon.*]

aray(e), *n.* arrangement; position, rank, 491; array, attire, 191; *in vche araye*, in every setting, 5. [OFr. *arei.*]

arayed, arayde, *pp.* prepared, 719; adorned, 791; *mad arayde*, in a state of frenzy, 1166. [OFr. *areier.*]

areþede, *n.* people of old times, 711. [ON. *ár + OE. þēod.*]

aryȝt, *adv.* straight on, 112. [OE. *on riht, ariht.*]

aryue, *v.* arrive, 447. [OFr. *ariver.*]

arme, *n.* arm, 459, 466. [OE. *earm.*]

aros, *pa. t.* arose, was raised, 181. [OE. *ārīsan.*]

art, arte, 2 *sg. pres.* art, are, 242, 276, 707, &c. [OE. *eart.*]

as, *conj.* as, like, in the way that, 20, 77, 787, 875, &c.; according to, 595; as if, 693; while, when, 980; because, since, 896, 915, 923. [Reduced from ALS.] See ÞERE.

as, *adv.* (just) as, correl. with AS, 76, 1024, &c.; *intensive*, as . . . as possible, 836, 1193 (note). [As prec.] See ASTYT.

asent(e), *n.* harmony, 94; concurrence, 391. [OFr. *asent(e).*]

asyse, *n.* fashion, 97. [OFr. *asise.*]

ask(e), *v.* ask (for), 316, 564, 580, 910. [OE. *āxian.*]

assemblé, *n.* union, 760. [OFr. *assemblee.*]

asspye, *v.* observe, descry, 704, 979, 1035. [OFr. *espier.*]

as(s)tate, *n.* condition, 393; rank, 490. [OFr. *estat.*]

astyt, *adv.* straightway, 645. [AS + TYT.]

astraye, *adv.* out of the right way, 1162. [OFr. *estraié.*]

at, *prep.* at, 161, 635, &c.; in, 321; beside, 287; according to, 199, 1164. [OE. *æt.*] See ON, ENE.

at, *rel. pron.* which, 536 (note).

atount, *pp.* astounded, 179. [OFr. *ato(u)ner.*]

atslykeȝ, *pres. 3 pl.* slip away, are spent, 575. [OE. *æt- + slīcan.*]

atteny, *v.* reach, 548. [OFr. *ateign-,* stem of *ateindre.*]

auenture, *n.* adventurous quest, 64. [OFr. *aventure.*]

aungeleȝ, *n. pl.* angels, 1121. [OFr. *a(u)ngele.*]

aunte, *n.* aunt, 233. [OFr. *a(u)nte.*]

avysyoun, *n.* vision, 1184. [OFr. *avisio(u)n.*]

away(e), *adv.* away, 655, 823; aside, 488; lost, 258. [OE. *on weg.*]

awayed, *pp.* instructed, taught, 710. [OFr. *aveier.*]

awhyle, *adv.* for a time, 692. [OE. *āne hwīle,* accus.]

bayle, *n.* outer wall of a castle, *1083. [OFr. *baile*, Med. Lat. *balium*.]

bayly, *n.* dominion, 442; domain, 315 (note). [OFr. *baillie*.]

bayn, *adj.* willing, 807. [ON. *beinn*.]

baysment, *n.* confusion due to surprise, 174. [AFr. *abaissement*.]

bale, *n.* torment, 478, 651; sorrow, 18, 123, 373, 807, 1139. [OE. *balu*.]

balke, *n.* mound (of grave), 62. [OE. *balca*.]

bantele3, bantels, *n.* bantels; projecting horizontal coursings, 992 (note), 1017. [OFr. **bantel*.]

baptem, babtem, *n.* baptism, 627, 653. [OFr. *bapteme*.]

baptysed, *pa. t.* baptized, 818. [OFr. *baptiser*.]

bare, *adj.* clear, 1025 (note); *adv.* **as bare**, as clearly as possible, 836. [OE. *bær*.]

barne, *n.* child, 426, 712, 1040. [OE. *bearn*.]

basse, *n.* base, 1000. [OFr. *base*, associated with *bas*, *adj.*]

basyng, *n.* foundation, 992. [Prec.+-*ing* of verbal noun.]

be, *v.* be, 29, 281, &c.; **ben(e)**, *pres. pl.* are, 572, 785; **bet3**, *future 3 sg.* 611; be, *subj. pres.* 379, 470, 523, 572, &c.; **be**, *imper. sg.* 344, 406; **ben**, *pp.* 252, 373. [OE. *béon*.]

be, 523. See BY.

beau, *adj.* fair, 197. [OFr. *beau*.]

beauté, bewté, *n.* beauty, 749, 765. [OFr. *beauté*.]

bede, 715. See BYDDE.

beyng, *n.* nature, 446. [From BE.]

bele, *v.* burn, 18. [ON. *bæla*.]

bem, *n.* beam, cross, 814. [OE. *béam*.]

bene, *adj.* pleasing, fair, 110; *adv.* beautifully, 198. [AFr. word of unknown origin.]

bent(e), *pp.* attached, 664; fixed, set, 1017 (note); bent, submitted, 1189. [OE. *béndan*.]

bere, *v.* bear, 466 (*subj.*); have, possess, 100, 756; have on, wear, 746, 854, 856, 1068; endure, 807; bear, produce, 1078; **ber(e)**, *pa. t. sg.* directed, 67; bore, 426; **bore, borne**, *pp.* born, 239, 626. [OE. *beran*.]

bereste. See BRESTE.

beryl, *n.* beryl, 110, 1011. [OFr. *beryl*.]

best(e), *adj. superl.* best, noblest, 863, 1131; *as sb.* noble one, 279. [OE. *betst*.]

beste3, *n. pl.* beasts, 886. [OFr. *beste*.]

bete, *v.* amend, 757. [OE. *bétan*.]

bete, *pa. t.* beat, *wynge3 bete*, flew, 93. [OE. *béatan*.]

better, *adv. compar.* rather, 341. [OE. *betera*, *adj.*]

bewté. See BEAUTÉ.

by, *prep.* by, by means of, 194, 468, 1019, &c.; beside, in, among, 141, 380, 751, 978, &c.; along, 107, 152, &c.; between, by the side of, 140 (note); according to, 580, 684, &c.; **be in** *be na3t*, by nightfall, 523. [OE. *bí*, *be*.]

bycalle, *v.* call upon, 913; **bycalt**, *pp.* summoned, 1163. [OE. *bí-*+CALLE.]

bycawse, *conj.* because, 296. [BY+ CAUSE.]

bycom, *pa. t.* became, 537. [OE. *becuman*.]

bydde, *v.* ask, bid, 520; **bede**, *pa. t. pl.* commanded, 715. [OE. *biddan*.]

byde, *v.* remain, stay, 399, 977; dwell, 907; endure, 664; **byde3**, *pres. 3 pl.* are set, 75; **bod**, *pa. t.* remained, 62. [OE. *bídan*.]

bydene, *adv.* straightway, 196. [Uncertain.]

bye, byye, *v.* buy, 478, 732; **bo3t**, *pa. t. and pp.* redeemed, 651, 893; bought, 733. [OE. *bycgan*.]

byfalle, *v.* happen, 186. [OE. *befallan*.]

byfore, bifore, *prep.* in front of,

ahead of, in presence of, 49, 294, 598, 885; *adv.* previously, 172; in front, 1110; *conj.* before, 530. [OE. *beforan*.]

byg, *adj.* big, 102; *compar.* greater, 374. [Uncertain.]

bygly, *adj.* inhabitable, pleasant, 963. [ON. *byggiligr*.]

bygyng, *n.* dwelling, 932; bygynge3 *pl.* *935. [ON. *bygging*, leasing; *dwelling-house (as in Icel.).]

bygynne, *v.* begin, 561, 581; bygyn, *imper.* 547; bygonne, *pa. t. pl.* 549; *pp.* in *is bygonne*, springs (from), 33. [OE. *beginnan*.]

bygynner, *n.* source, 436. [From prec.]

by3e, *n.* ring, 466. [OE. *bēg*.]

by3onde, *prep.* across, beyond, 141, 287, 981, &c. [OE. *begeóndan*.]

byhod. See BO3.

byholde, *v.* gaze, look, 810. [OE. *behóldan*.]

biys, *n.* fine linen, *197. [OFr. *bysse*, late Lat. *byssus*.]

bylde, *n.* dwelling, 727, 963. [Related to next.]

bylde, *pa. t.* edified, established, 123. [OE. *byldan, in pp. *gebyld*.]

byrþ-whate3, *n. pl.* fortunes of birth, 1041 (note). [OE. *gebyrd*, *gebyrð*- (in compounds) + *hwatu*.]

bysech, *v.* implore, 390. [OE. *besēcan*.]

byseme, *v.* befit, 310. [OE. *be-* + SEME.]

byswyke3, *pres. 1 sg.* cheat, 568 (note). [OE. *beswícan*.]

byta3te, *pa. t.* committed, 1207. [OE. *betǣcan*.]

bitalt, *pp.* shaken, 1161. [OE. *be-* + *taltian*.]

byte, *v.* bite; prick, move, 355; *b. vpon*, bite, taste, 640. [OE. *bítan*.]

bytyde, *v.* befall, 397. [OE. *be-* + *tídan*.]

bytwene, *prep.* between, 140, 658; *adv.* at intervals, 44. [OE. *betwēon(an)*.]

bytwyste, *prep.* between, 464. [OE. *betwyxt*.]

bla3t, *adj.* pure white, 212. [OE. *blǣht*, pp. of *blǣcan*.]

blayke, *adj.* yellow, 27. [ON. *bleikr*.]

blake, *adj.* black, 945. [OE. *blæc*.]

blame, *n.* rebuke, 715. [OFr. *bla(s)me*.]

blame, *v.* blame, 275, 303. [OFr. *bla(s)mer*.]

ble, *n.* colour, 76; colour of the face, complexion, 212. [OE. *blēo*.]

bleaunt, *n.* mantle of rich material, 163. [OFr. *bliaut*, AFr. *bliaunt*.]

blent(e), *pp.* blended, 1016; *b. in blysse*, set amidst joy, 385. [OE. *gebléndan*.]

blesse, *v.* bless, 850; *pp.* 436; *reflex.* cross oneself, 341; bless-yng, *n.* blessing, 1208. [OE. *blētsian*; *blētsung*.]

blynde, *adj.* dim, 83. [OE. *blind*.]

blynne, *v.* cease, 729. [OE. *blinnan*.]

blys(se), *n.* joy, happiness, 123, 372, &c. [OE. *bliss*.]

blysful, blysfol, *adj.* joyous, delightful, 279, 409, 907, 964, 1104; *as n.* blissful one, 421, 1100. [OE. *bliss* + *-ful*.]

blysned, *pa. t.* shone, 1048; blys-nande, *pres. p.* gleaming, 163, 197. [Cf. OE. *blysian*, blaze.]

blyþe, *n.* mercy, 354. [ON. *bliða*.]

blyþe, *adj.* glad, merry, serene, 352, 738; blyþest, *superl.* most serene, most gentle, 1131. [OE. *blíþe*.]

blyþely, *adv.* joyously, 385. [OE. *blíþelíce*.]

blo, *adj.* dark, dusky, 83, 875. [ON. *bldr*.]

blod(e), *n.* blood, 646, 650, 741, &c. [OE. *blód*.]

blody, *adv.* bloodily, 705. [OE. *blódig*, adj.]

blom, *n.* flower, 27; bloom, perfection, 578. [ON. *blóm*, *blómi*.]

blose, *n.* (?) rough uncouth person, 911 (note).

blot, *n.* stain, 782. [Uncertain.]

blunt, *adj.* stunned, 176. [Cf. ON. *blunda*, doze.]

blusched, *pa. t.* looked, gazed, 980, 1083. [OE. *blyscan*.]

blwe, *adj.* blue, 27, 76, 423. [OFr. *bleu*.]

bod. See BYDE.

body, *n.* body, 62, 460, 1070. [OE. *bodig*.]

bodyly, *adj.* of the body, 478; in the body, 1090. [From prec.]

boffete3, *n. pl.* buffets, 809. [OFr. *bufet*.]

bo3, *impers. pres.* it behoves; *bo3 vch man*, everyone must, 323; byhod, *pa. t.* 928. [OE. *behōfian*.]

bo3e, *v.* turn, go, 196; **bow**, *imper. sg.* 974; **bowed**, *pa. t. sg.* 126. [OE. *būgan*, str.]

bo3t. See BYE.

boye3, *n. pl.* ruffians, 806 (note). [Cf. AFr. *boie*.]

bok(e), *n.* book, 710, 837. [OE. *bōc*.]

bolde, *adj. pl.* bold, 806. [OE. *báld*.]

bolle3, *n. pl.* tree-trunks, 76. [ON. *bolr*.]

bolne, *v.* swell, 18. [ON. *bolgna*.]

bon, *n.* bone, 212. [OE. *bān*.]

bone, *n.* petition, prayer, 912, 916; boon, favour, 1090. [ON. *bón*.]

bonerté, *n.* beatitude, 762. [OFr. *boneurté*.]

bonk(e), bonc, *n.* shore, bank of stream, slope, 102, 106 (note), 196, 907, 931, 1169. [ON. *bakki*, older **banke*.]

bor, *n.* dwelling, 964. [OE. *būr*.]

borde, *v.* jest, 290. [OFr. *bourder*.]

bor3, burghe, *n.* city, 957, 980, 989, 1048. [OE. *burg*.]

borne, *n.* stream, 974. [OE. *burna*.]

bornyst(e), burnist, *pp.* polished, 77, 990; shining, 220. [OFr. *burnir*, *burniss-*.]

boro3t. See BRYNG.

bostwys, bustwys, *adj.* roughly massive, 814; rough, crude, 911. [AFr. *boisteus*, rough.]

bot, *adv.* only, but, 17, 18, 83, 269, &c.; *conj.* except, other than, 312, 336, 337, 496, 658, 952, &c.; unless, 308, 331, 428, &c.; but, however, yet, 66, 265, 413, &c. [OE. *būton*.]

bote, *n.* remedy, 275, 645. [OE. *bōt*.]

boþe, *pron.* both, 373, 950; *adv.* both (with *and*), 90, 329, &c. [ON. *báðir*.]

boun, *adj.* ready, 534; arranged, fixed, 992, 1103. [ON. *búinn*, *bún-*.]

bounden, *pp.* fastened (as adornment), 1103; trimmed, adorned, 198. [OE. *bindan*.]

bourne. See BURNE.

bowe, bowed. See BO3E.

brade. See BRODE.

bray, *v.* bray, cry out, 346. [OFr. *braire*.]

brayne3, *n. pl.* brains, 126. [OE. *bægen*.]

brayde, *pa. t.* brought in haste, 712; roused suddenly, startled, 1170. [OE. *bregdan*, str.]

brathþe, *n.* impetuosity, *1170; braþe3, *pl.* agonies, violent grief, 346. [ON. *bráðr*+OE. -*þu*, on analogy of WRATHÞE.]

braundysch, *v.* toss about, struggle (as in agony), 346. [OFr. *bra(u)ndir*, *bra(u)ndiss-*.]

bred, *n.* bread, 1209. [OE. *brēad*.]

brede, *n.* breadth, 1031. [OE. *brædu*.]

brede, *v. trans.* stretch, 814; *intr.* grow, flourish, 415. [OE. *brǣdan*.]

bredful, *adj.* brimful, 126. [ON. **breddfullr*; cf. OEN. *brædd* 'brim' and mod. Swed. *bräddfull*.]

bref, *adj.* quickly passing away, 268. [OFr. *bref*.]

breme, *adj.* intense, surpassing, 863; fierce, wild, 346. [OE. *brēme*.]

brende, *pp.* refined (by fire), bright (gold), 989 (cf. ON. *brent gull*). [ON. *brenna*.]

brent, *adj.* steep, 106. [Cf. OE. *brant*.]

breste, *n.* breast, 18, 222, &c.; **bereste,** 854. [OE. *brēost*.]

breue, *v.* tell, 755. [Med. Lat. *breviāre,* OE. *brēfan*.]

bryd, *n.* bride, 769. [OE. *brȳd*.]

brydde3, *n. pl.* birds, 93. [OE. *bridd,* young bird.]

bry3t, *adj. and adv.* bright, 75, 110, 769, 989, 1048; *as n.* fair (one), 755; **bry3ter,** *compar.* 1056. [OE. *berht, byrht*.]

brym(me), *n.* brink, 232, 1074. [OE. *brymme*.]

bryng, *v.* bring, 853, 963; **bro3te,** *pa. t.* 527; **bro3t, boro3t,** *pp.* *286, 628. [OE. *bringan*.]

brode, *adj.* broad, wide, 650, 1022, 1024; **brade,** 138. [OE. *brād*.]

bro3te, bro3t. See BRYNG.

brok(e), *n.* stream, 141, 146, 981, 1074. [OE. *brōc*.]

broun, *adj.* dark, 537; bright, shining, 990 (a sense found in verse, usually of allit. tradition, in OE. and ME). [OE. *brūn*.]

brunt, *n.* sharp blow, 174. [Obscure.]

burde, *pa. t. subj. impers.*; *þe burde,* you ought to, 316. [OE. *gebyrian*.]

burghe. See BOR3.

burne, bourne, *n.* man, 617, 712, 1090; *voc.* sir, 397. [OE. *béorn*.]

burnist. See BORNYST.

bur(re), *n.* blow, 176, 1158 (note). [ON. *byrr,* a following wind.]

busye3, *pres. 2 sg. refl.* trouble (yourself), 268. [OE. *bysigian*.]

bustwys. See BOSTWYS.

caggen, *pres. 3 pl.* tie up, 512. [Uncertain.]

ca3t(e), *pa. t.* caught; *c. to,* seized on, 50; *c. of,* took off, 237. [ONFr. *cach(i)er,* infl. by ME. *lacche,* LA3TE.]

cayre, *v.* traverse, 1031. [ON. *keyra,* drive.]

calder. See COLDE.

calle, *v. intr.* call, shout, 182, 542; *trans.* call, name, 273, 430; summon, 173, 572, 721, 762. [ON. *kalla*; OE. *ceallian*.]

calsydoyne, *n.* chalcedony, 1003. [OFr. *calcidoine*.]

cambe, *n.* comb; *comly onvunder c.,* fair lady, 775 (note). [OE. *cámb*.]

can. See CON, *v*[1].

care, *n.* sorrow, 50, 371, 808, 861. [OE. *cearu*.]

carp(e), *v.* speak, 381, 752, 949. [ON. *karpa,* brag.]

carpe, *n.* discourse, 883. [ON. *karp*.]

cas, *n.* matter, 673. [OFr. *cas*.]

caste, *n.* purpose, 1163. [ON. *kast*.]

castel-walle, *n.* castle-wall, 917. [Late OE. *castel* (from ONFr.) + OE. *wall*.]

cause, *n.* case (for judgement), 702. [OFr. *cause*.]

ceté. See CITÉ.

ceuer, *v.* attain, 319. [*c = k*; OE. *a-cofrian,* intr.; OFr. *(re)-couver, -keuvre,* trans.]

chace, *v.* chase; *chace of,* oust from, 443. [OFr. *chacier*.]

chayere, *n.* throne, 885. [OFr. *chaiere*.]

chambre, *n.* (bridal) chamber, 904. [OFr. *chambre*.]

chapel, *n.* chapel, 1062. [OFr. *chapel*.]

charde, *pa. t.* turned back, ceased to flow, 608. [OE. *cærran*.]

charyté, *n.* love of one's fellows, 470. [OFr. *charité*.]

chere, *n.* (expression of) face, 887, 1109; demeanour, 407. [OFr. *ch(i)ere*.]

ches(e), *pa. t.* chose, selected, 759, 954; **chos,** *pa. t.* beheld, 187; **ichose,** *pp.* chosen, 904. [OE. *cēosan,* pa. t. *cēas*.]

cheuentayn, *n.* ruler, Lord, 605. [OFr. *chevetaine*.]

chyche, *n.* niggard, 605. [OFr. *chiche,* adj.]

chyde, *v.* wrangle, 403. [OE. *cīdan.*]

chylde, *n.* child, 723; **chylder,** *pl.* 714, 718. [OE. *cīld,* pl. *cildru.*]

chos. See CHES.

cité, cyté, cyty, *n.* city, 792, 939, 1023, 1097; **ceté,** 927, 952. [OFr. *cité.*]

clad, *pp.* wrapped, 22. [OE. (rare) *clǣþan,* pp. **clǣdd.*]

clambe. See CLYM.

clanly, *adv.* fairly, radiantly, 2. [OE. *clǣnlīce, clānlīce.*]

clem, *v.* claim, 826. [OFr. *clamer (claime),* AFr. *clemer.*]

clene, *adj.* pure, 682, 767, 972; clear, bright, fair, 227, 289, 737, 969; *adv.* without flaw or error, 754, 949. [OE. *clǣne.*]

clente, *pp.* riveted (*or* fastened), 259 (note). [OE. **clencan,* cf. *be-clencan.*]

cler, *adj.* clear, bright, 74, 207, 227, 1011, 1050 (note), 1111; **clere,** 2, 620, 737; **cler,** *adv.* manifestly, 274; with clear voice, 882, 913. [OFr. *cler.*]

clerkeȝ, *n. pl.* clerks, priests, 1091. [OE. *cler(i)c;* OFr. *clerc.*]

cleuen, *pa. t. pl.* (?), clove the air, rose aloft, 66 (note). [OE. *clēofan.*]

clyffe, *n.* cliff, 159; **klyf(f)eȝ,** *pl.* 66, 74. [OE. *clif.*]

clym, klymbe, *v.* climb, 678, 1072; **clambe,** *pa. t.* 773. [OE. *climban.*]

clynge, *v.* waste away, 857. [OE. *clingan.*]

clypper, *n.* shearer, 802. [From ON. *klippa.*]

clyuen (*vpon*), *v.* adhere to, belong to, 1196. [OE. *clīfan,* str.; *clifian,* wk.]

cloystor, *n.* enclosure, 969. [OFr. *cloistre.*]

clos, *adj.* closed, 183; secure, 512. [OFr. *clos.*]

clos(e), *v.* close, enclose, 271, 803; set (a jewel), 2 (note). [From OFr. *clos,* n.]

clot, *n.* clod, clay, 22, 320; hill, 789; **clotteȝ,** *pl.* clods, earth, 857. [OE. *clott.*]

cnawyng, *n.* understanding, 859. [OE. *cnāwing.*]

cnoken, *pres. 3 pl.* knock, 727. [OE. *cnocian.*]

cofer, *n.* coffer, 259. [OFr. *cofre.*]

colde, *adj.* chilling, grievous, 50, 808; **calder,** *compar.* colder, 320. [OE. *cáld; caldra.*]

colo(u)r, *n.* (white) complexion, 22, 215 (note), 753. [OFr. *colour.*]

com, *v.* come, arrive, 676, 701; **cum,** *imper.,* 763; **commeȝ,** *pres. 3 sg.* arises, 848; **com(e),** *pa. t.* came, 155, 582, &c.; **com,** *pa. subj.* 574, 723, 724. [OE. *cuman.*]

come, *n.* coming, 1117. [From prec.]

comfort(e), coumforde, *n.* solace, consolation, 55, 357, 369. [OFr. *co(u)nfort.*]

comly, cumly, *adj.* fair, beautiful, 929; *as n.* 775 (note); *adv.* fairly 259. [OE. *cȳmlic, cȳmlīce,* infl. by ME. *becomen.*]

commune, *adj.* belonging equally, 739. [Lat. *commūnis;* OFr. *comun.*]

companyny, *n.* assemblage, 851. [OFr. *compai(g)nie.*]

compas, *n.* circuit, 1072. [OFr. *compas.*]

con, *v.*[1] *pres. 3 sg.* is able, can, 665, 729, 827; **con(ne),** *2 pl.* know how to, are able, 381, 521, 914; **cowþe, couþe,** *pa. t.* could, 95, 134, 855; **cowþeȝ,** *2 sg. in both senses,* could *and* knew, 484. [OE. *cann, conn; cūþe.*]

con, *v.*[2] *auxil.* used with infin. as equiv. of *pa. t.,* did, 78, 81, 149, 313, 1183, &c.; *through confusion with* CON, *v.*[1] *used also of the present (con bere = bere,* bear, 1078), 271, 294, 495, 509, 709, 769, 851, 931, 1093; **can,** 499; **coneȝ,** *2 sg.* 482 (note), 909, 925. [Prec. confused with ME. *gan,* did.]

conciens, *n.* conviction, 1089. [OFr. *conscience.*]

contryssyoun, *n.* contrition, 669. [OFr. *contricio(u)n.*]

corne, *n.* corn, 40. [OE. *corn.*]

coro(u)nde, *pa. t.* crowned, 415, 767; *pp.* 480, 1101. [OFr. *coro(u)ner.*]

coroun(e), *n.* crown, diadem, 205, 237, 451; croun(e), 427, 1100. [OFr. *coro(u)ne.*]

corse, *n.* body, 320, 857. [OFr. *cors.*]

cortayse, corteȝ, *adj.* gracious, 433, 754; cortaysly, *adv.* courteously, 381. [OFr. *corteis.*]

cortaysye, cortaysé, courtaysye, *n.* courtesy, nobility; divine grace (especially as manifested in Christian love and charity) 432 (note), 444, 456, 457, 468, 469; favour, generosity, 480, 481. [OFr. *co(u)rteisie.*]

corte, corteȝ. See COURT, COR- TAYSE.

cortel, *n.* kirtle, 203. [OE. *cyrtel.*]

coruen. See KERUEN.

couenaunt, couenaunde, *n.* agree- ment, 562, 563. [OFr. *cove- na(u)nt.*]

coumforde. See COMFORT.

counsayle, *n.* plan, course of action, *319. [OFr. *co(u)nseil.*]

counterfete, *v.* resemble, 556. [From OFr. *co(u)ntrefet,* pp.]

countes, *n.* countess, 489. [OFr. *co(u)ntesse.*]

countré, *n.* region, 297. [OFr. *co(u)ntrée.*]

court, corte, *n.* royal court, 445; judicial court, 701. [OFr. *cort, court.*]

couþe, cowþe. See CON, v.¹

crafteȝ, *n. pl.* powers, 356; arts, 890. [OE. *cræft.*]

craue, *v.* crave, beg for, 663. [OE. *crafian.*]

Crede, *n.* the Apostles' Creed, 485. [OE. *crēda.*]

cresse, *n.* cress; *not a c.,* not a jot, 343. [OE. *cresse.*]

creste, *n.* ornament worn on the head; crown, 856. [OFr. *creste.*]

crysolyt, *n.* chrysolite, 1009. [OFr. *crisolite.*]

crysopase, *n.* chrysoprase, 1013. [OFr. *crisopase.*]

crystal, *n.* crystal, 74, 159. [OFr. *cristal.*]

crokeȝ, *n. pl.* sickles, 40. [ON. *krókr.*]

croun(e). See COROUNE.

cum, cum-. See COM, COM-.

cure, *n.* care, 1091. [OFr. *cure.*]

day(e), *n.* day, daylight, 486, 517, 554, 1210, &c.; *boþe day and naȝte,* at all times, 1203; dayeȝ, *pl.* life-time, 416; daweȝ, in *don out of daweȝ,* put out of the world, dead, 282. [OE. *dæg.*]

day-glem, *n.* light of day, 1094. [DAY+GLEM.]

dayly, *v.* contend, dispute (?), 313 (note). [ON. *deila.*]

daleȝ, *n. pl.* valleys, 121. [OE. *dæl.*]

dam, *n.* body of water (in conduit or artificial pool), 324. [OE. *damm.*]

damysel(le), *n.* damsel, 361, 489 (note). [OFr. *damisele.*]

dampned, *pp.* damned, 641. [OFr. *dampner.*]

dar, *pres.* dare; *dar say,* venture to assert, 1089; dorst(e), *pa. t.* 143, 182. [OE. *dearr; dorste.*]

dare, *v.* cower with fear, 839; *pa. t.* in *dard to,* shrank in fear before? lay hidden, was inscrutable? 609 (note). [OE. *darian.*]

dased, *pp.* bewildered, dazed, 1085. [ON. *dasaðr.*]

date, *n.* point of time, hour, 529, 541; date of birth, 1040; season, 504, 505; limit, goal, 492 (note), 493; beginning, 517; end, 516, 528, 540. [OFr. *date.*]

daunce, *v.* leap (in agony), 345. [OFr. *da(u)ncer.*]

daunger, *n.* distress (of one who loves), 250. [OFr. *da(u)nger.*]

debate, *n.* dispute; *wythouten d.*, putting aside contention, 390. [OFr. *debat.*]

debonere, *adj.* gentle, gracious, 162. [OFr. *debonaire.*]

debonerté, *n.* meekness, 798. [OFr. *debonerté.*]

declyne, *v.* sink, fall from prosperity, 333 (note); *d. into acorde*, come to an agreement, 509. [OFr. *decliner.*]

dede, *adj.* dead, 31. [OE. *dēad.*]

dede, *n.* deed; *fre of dede*, lavish in action, 481; *in dede and po3te*, in performance and intention, truly, 524. [OE. *dēd.*]

degres, *n. pl.* steps, 1022. [OFr. *degre.*]

del, dele. See DOEL.

dele, *v.* mete out, 606. [OE. *dǣlan.*]

delfully, *adv.* grievously, 706. [From DOEL.]

delit, delyt, *n.* joy, pleasure, delight, 1105, 1116, 1117, 1129, &c.; *out of d.*, parted from joy, 642; *wyth d.*, joyously 1104; *la3t d.*, desired, 1128; *hade d. perto*, desired that, 1140. [OFr. *delit.*]

delyuered, *pa. t.* saved, 652. [OFr. *de(s)livrer.*]

dem(e), *v.* judge, consider, 313, 336; condemn, 325; censure, 349 (note); appoint, ordain, 348, 360; allow (to go), 324; judge of, 312; declare, speak of, 337, 1183; speak, 361. [OE. *dēman*, judge; (poet.) declare.]

demme, *v.* be dammed; be baffled, 223. [OE. *for-demman.*]

dene, *n.* valley, 295. [OE. *denu.*]

denned, *pa. t.* lurked, lay deep, 51. [From OE. *denn*, n.]

depaynt, *pp.* adorned, 1102. [OFr. *depeint*, pp.]

departed, *pa. t.* were parted, 378. [OFr. *de(s)partir.*]

depe, *adj.* deep, 143; intense, 215; *pl. as n.* depths, 109; dep, *adv.* 406. [OE. *dēop*; *dēope*, adv.]

depres, *v.* drive away, 778. [OFr. *depresser.*]

depryue, *v.* deprive, 449. [OFr. *depriver.*]

dere, *adj.* noble, glorious, 72, 85, 97, 108, 120, 121, 920; exalted, 492; prized, precious, 1183, 1208; good, 504; beloved, 368, 758, 795; pleasing, 400, 880; *as n.* worthy ones, 777; *adv.* for a great price, 733. [OE. *dēore.*]

dere, *v.* harm, 1157 (note). [OE. *derian.*]

dere3, *n. pl.* hindrances, 102. [From prec.]

derely, *adv.* splendidly, 995. [OE. *dēorlīce.*]

derk, *n.* darkness, 629. [OE. *deorc*, adj.]

derpe, *n.* splendour, 99. [ON. *dýrð*, infl. by DERE.]

derworth, *adj.* splendid, 109. [OE. *dēorwyrþe.*]

dese, *n.* raised platform on which the throne stood, 766. [OFr. *de(i)s.*]

desserte, *n.* merit, 595. [OFr. *desserte.*]

dessypele3, *n. pl.* disciples, 715. [OFr. *disciple.*]

destyné, *n.* destiny, Final End, 758. [OFr. *destinee.*]

determynable, *adj.* definite, determined, 594. [OFr. *determinable.*]

deth(e), *n.* death, 323, 630, 656, 860; *deth secounde*, perdition, 652. [OE. *dēaþ.*]

deuely, *adj.* desolating, dreary, 51 (note). [OE. **dēaflic*, after ON. *daufligr.*]

deuyse, *n.* dividing line, division, 139 (note); *at my d.*, as I could wish, (or) in my opinion, 199 (note). [OFr. *devise.*]

deuyse, deuise, *v.* gaze upon, 1129; describe in detail, 99, 984, 995, 1021. [OFr. *deviser.*]

deuysement, *n.* description, 1019. [OFr. *devisement.*]

deuoyde, *v.* cast out, get rid of, 15. [OFr. *de(s)void(i)er.*]

deuote, *adj.* devout, 406. [OFr. *devot.*]

dewyne, dowyne, *v.* languish, pine away, 11, 326. [OE. *dwīnan.*]

dyche, *n.* ditch, drain, 607. [OE. *dīc.*]

dy3e, *v.* die, 306, 642; dy(3)ed, *pa.t.* 705, 828. [ON. *deyja.*]

dy3t, *v.* dispose, ordain, 360; dy3t(e), *pp.* set, 920; adorned, 202, 987. [OE. *dihtan.*]

dylle, *adj.* slow, 680. [OE. **dylle.*]

dym, *adj.* dim, 1076. [OE. *dimm.*]

dyne, *n.* din, noise (of lamentation), 339. [OE. *dyne.*]

dyscreuen, *v.* descry, 68. [OFr. *descrivre.*]

dysplese3, *pres. t.* displeases, 455; *imper.* be displeased, 422. [OFr. *desplaisir.*]

dyssente, *pres. pl.* descend, 627. [OFr. *descendre.*]

dys(s)tresse, *n.* sorrow, 280; *for no d.,* through any constraint, 898. [OFr. *destresse.*]

dystryed, *pa. t.* put an end to, 124. [OFr. *destruire.*]

dyt. See DO, *v.*

do, *n.* doe, 345. [OE. *dā.*]

do, *v.* do, 496, &c.; done in *to done,* to be done, 914; do, *pres. 1 sg.* 366; dot3, *2 and 3 sg.* 17, 338, &c.; don, *pl.* 511; do, dot3, *imper. pl.* 521, 718; dyd, did, dyt, *pa. t. sg.* 102, 681, &c.; dyden, *pl.* 633; don(e), *pp.* 250, 1042, &c. Do, act, perform, 338, 496, 521, 681, 930; *don gret pyne,* toil hard, 511; put, place, 250, 366, 823, 1042; *don out of dawe3,* put out of the world, 282; *do way,* cease, 718; render, pay, 424; make, cause (to), 102, 306, 330, 556, 942; as periphrastic auxil., *dot3 mene,* means, 293, *dot3 to enclyne,* sinks towards (?), 630 (note). [OE. *dōn.*]

doc, *n.* duke, 211. [OFr. *duc.*]

doel, del(e), dol, *n.* grief, 51, 250, 326, 336, 642; lamentation, 339. [OFr. *doel, deol, dol.*]

doel-dystresse, *n.* stress of sorrow, 337. [DOEL+DYSTRESSE.]

doel-doungoun, *n.* dungeon of sorrow, 1187. [DOEL+AFr. *doungoun.*]

dol. See DOEL.

dole, *n.* part, 136. [OE. *dāl.*]

dom(e), *n.* judgement, trial, 699; decision, 667; award, 580; reason, 157, 223. [OE. *dōm.*]

dorst, dorste. See DAR.

dot3. See DO, *v.*

double, *adj.* in double rows, 202. [OFr. *double.*]

doun, *adv.* down, 30, 41, &c.; *prep.* 196, 230. [OE. *of dūne.*]

doun, down, *n.* hill, 73, 85, 121. [OE. *dūn.*]

dousour, *n.* sweetness, 429. [OFr. *dousur.*]

doute, *n.* doubt, 928. [OFr. *doute.*]

douth, *n.* company, host, 839. [OE. *duguþ.*]

dowyne. See DEWYNE.

dra3, *imper. sg.* bring, 699; dro3, *pa. t.* proceeded, 1116; drawen, *pp.* brought, 1193. [OE. *dragan.*]

dred, *pa. t.* was afraid, 186. [OE. *drēdan.*]

drede, *n.* fear, 181; *wythouten drede,* without doubt, in truth, 1047. [From prec.]

drem, *n.* dream, vision, 790, 1170. [Blend of ON. *draumr* 'dream' and OE. *drēam* 'music'.]

dresse, *v.* ordain, 495; *pp.* set up, drawn, 860. [OFr. *dresser.*]

dreue, *v.* make one's way, 323, 980. [OE. *drǣfan.*]

dry3e, *adj.* heavy, 823. [ON. *drjúgr,* older **drèug-.*]

dry3ly, *adv.* continually, 125; strongly, utterly, 223. [ON. *drjúgliga.*]

Dry3tyn, *n.* the Lord, 324, 349. [OE. *dryhten.*]

dryue, dryf, *v.* drive; *out dryf,* drive away, 777; *intr.* make one's way, *d. doun,* sink, 1094 (*pres. subj.*); drof, *pa. t.* came, entered, 1153; *d. doun,* sank

down, was buried, 30; **dryuen,**
pp. brought, 1194. [OE. *drīfan*.]

drof, dro3. See DRYUE, DRA3.

drounde, *pa. t.* immersed, drowned,
656. [ODan. *dro(v)ne*, **drugna;*
obscure, but probably from ON.
*drungna, **drunkna,* Icel.
drukna.]

drwry, *adj.* cruel, dire, 323. [OE.
drēorig.]

dubbed, dubbet, *pp.* arrayed, 73,
97; adorned, 202. [OFr. *aduber*.]

dubbement(e), *n.* adornment,
splendour, 109, 121. [OFr.
adubement.]

due, *adj.* belonging, 894. [OFr.
d(e)u.]

dunne, *adj.* dull brown, 30. [OE.
dunn.]

durande, *adj.* lasting, 336. [OFr.
durer.]

efte, *adv.* again, 328; afterwards,
332. [OE. *eft*.]

elle3, *adv.* else, on the other hand,
130, 567; else, if not, 491, 724;
else, by other means, 32. [OE.
elles.]

emerad(e), *n.* emerald, 118, 1005.
[OFr. *emeraude*.]

emperise, *n.* empress, 441. [OFr.
emperice.]

empyre, *n.* imperial rule, 454.
[OFr. *empire*.]

enchace, *v.* pursue, urge on, 173.
[OFr. *enchacier*.]

enclyin, *adj.* lying prostrate, 1206.
[OFr. *enclin*.]

enclyne, *v.* bow, 236; sink towards,
630 (note). [OFr. *encliner*.]

enclose, *v.* enclose; *cone3 e.,* are
endued with, 909. [From OFr.
enclos, pp.]

encres, *v.* increase, be intensified,
959. [AFr. *encres-,* stem of
encreistre.]

encroched, *pa. t.* brought, 1117.
[OFr. *encroch(i)er*.]

endele3, *adv.* infinitely, perfectly,
738. [OE. *endelēas*.]

endent(e), *pp.* inlaid (with fig.

reference to darkness), 629; laid
in, set, 1012. [OFr. *endenter*.]

endyte, *v.* utter in song, 1126.
[OFr. *enditer*.]

endorde, *pp.* as *n.* adored (one),
368. [OFr. *adorer,* with altered
prefix.]

endure, endeure, *v.* suffice, have
power (to), 225 (note); remain,
continue, 476 (note); endure,
support, 1082. [OFr. *endurer*.]

ene, *adv.* once; *at ene,* at one time,
at once, 291; *mad at ene,*
arranged, settled, 953. [OE.
ǣne.]

ene, 200. See Y3E.

enlé, *adv.* singly, 849. [OE.
ǣnlīce.]

enleuenþe, *adj.* eleventh, 1014.
[OE. *endleofon*+ordinal suffix
-þa.]

enpryse, *n.* glory, renown. 1097.
[OFr. *enprise*.]

ensens, *n.* incense, 1122. [OFr.
encens.]

entent, *n.* will, purpose, 1191.
[OFr. *entent*.]

enter, *v.* enter, 38, 966, 1067.
[OFr. *entrer*.]

enurned, *pp.* adorned, 1027. [OFr.
aorner, with altered prefix.]

er(e), *adv.* before, 164, 372; first,
319; *prep.* before, 517; **er, er
þenne,** *conj.* before, 188, 224,
631, 1094, &c. [OE. *ǣr; ǣr
(þǣm, þon),* conj.]

erber(e), *n.* grassy place in a garden, often among trees, 9, 38,
1171. [OFr. *herb(i)er*.]

erde, *n.* land, 248. [OE. *éard*.]

ere, *n.* ear, 1153. [OE. *ēare*.]

erytage. See HERYTAGE.

erle, *n.* earl, 211. [OE. *éorl*.]

erly, *adv.* early, 506; *erly and late,*
all the time, 392. [OE. *ǣrlīce*.]

errour, *n.* error; *speke e.,* say what
is mistaken, 422. [OFr. *errour*.]

erþe. See VRþE.

eschaped, *pa. t.* eluded, slipped
away from, 187. [OFr. *eschaper*.]

eþe, *adj.* easy, 1202. [OE. *ē(a)þe*.]

euel, *adv.* ill, 310, 930. [OE. *yfele*.]

euen, *adv.* exactly, 740. [OE. *efen*.]

euen, *v.* compare, vie, 1073. [From *euen* 'equal' infl., by ON. *jafnask*.]

euensonge, *n.* evensong, 529. [OE. *ēfensóng*.]

euentyde, *n.* evening, 582. [OE. *ēfentīd*.]

euer, *adv.* forever, 416, 959; always, continually, 144, 153, 349, 618; *with compar.* constantly, 180, 600; at any time, 200, 609, 617, &c.; *strengthening* ER, *conj.*, 328, 1030; *for euer*, 261. [OE. *ǣfre*.]

euermore, *adv.* at all times, 591, 666, 1066. [OE. *ǣfre+māre*, neut.]

excused, *pp.* excused, 281. [OFr. *excuser*.]

expoun, *v.* describe, 37. [OFr. *expo(u)n*-, stem of *expo(u)ndre*.]

expresse, *adv.* plainly, 910. [OFr. *expres*.]

fable, *n.* fable, 592. [OFr. *fable*.]

face, *n.* face, 169, 434, *675, 809; *bere þe face towarde*, proceeded in the direction of, 67. [OFr. *face*.]

fader, *n.* father, 639; Father (Creator), 736; **Fadereȝ**, *gen.*, 872. [OE. *fæder*.]

faȝt, *pa. t.* fought, contended, 54. [OE. *fehtan*.]

fay(e), *n.* faith; *in faye*, truly, 263; *þar ma fay*, by my troth, 489. [OFr. *fei*.]

fayly, fayle, *v.* fail to be productive, 34; wither, 270; *fayle of*, fail to obtain, 317. [OFr. *faillir*.]

fayn, *adj.* glad, 393, 450. [OE. *fægen*.]

fayr(e), *adj.* fair, comely, beautiful, 147, 169, 177, 747, 810, 946; pleasing, 46; desirable, 490; **feier**, *compar.* 103 (note). [OE. *fæger*.]

fayr(e), *adv.* courteously, 714;

pleasantly, 88; rightly, becomingly, 884; evenly, accurately, 1024. [OE. *fægre*.]

fande. See **FYNDE**.

farande, *adj.* fitting, seemly, 865. [ON. *farandi*, fitting.]

fare, *n.* demeanour, 832. [OE. *faru*.]

fare, *v.* go, proceed, 147; act, behave, 129 (note); *fare to*, behave towards, 467. [OE. *faran*.]

fasor, *n.* Creator, 431. [OFr. *faiseor, faisour*.]

fasoun, *n.* fashion, manner, 983; *of þe same fasoun*, in the same fashion, 1101. [OFr. *faso(u)n*.]

faste, *adv.* obstinately, 54; diligently, 150. [OE. *fæste*.]

fasure, *n.* fashion, form, 1084. [OFr. *faisure*.]

fateȝ, *pres. t.* fades, 1038 (note). [OFr. *fader*.]

faunt, *n.* child, 161. [OFr. *enfa(u)nt*.]

fauo(u)r, *n.* grace, beauty, 428; *þurȝ gret fauor*, out of His great kindness, 968. [OFr. *favour*.]

fax, *n.* hair, 213. [OE. *fæx*.]

fech, *v.* fetch, strike (a blow), 1158 (note); **feche**, *subj.* bring in, 847. [OE. *fetian, feccan*.]

fede, *pp.* faded, 29 (note). [Cf. OFr. *fade*.]

feier. See **FAYR(E)**.

fel, felle, *pa. t.* sank down, 57; *felle to*, prostrated themselves before, 1120; *fel in gret affray*, became greatly agitated, 1174. [OE. *fallan*; *fēoll* pa. t., and *fēolan*.]

felde, *pa. t.* felt, 1087. [OE. *fēlan*.]

fele, *adj.* many, 21, 874, 1114; *as n.* many (people), 439, 716. [OE. *fela*.]

felle, *adj.* deadly, cruel, 367, 655. [OFr. *fel*.]

felonye, *n.* crime, 800 (note). [OFr. *felonie*.]

Fenyx, *n.* phoenix, 430 (note). [OE. and OFr. *fenix*.]

4464　　　　K

fer, *adv.* far, 334; (by) far, 1076; fyrre, *compar.* farther, further, 103, 127, 152, 347; moreover, 544; *fyrre þen,* beyond, 563; *adj.* on the farther side, 148. [OE. *feorr*; compar. *firra, firr.*]

fere, *n.*[1] fortune, rank, dignity, *616 (note). [OFr. *afeire*?]

fere, *n.*[2] company; *in fere,* together, 89, 884, 1105. [OE. *gefére,* but *in fere* altered from earlier ME. *i-feren,* (as) companions.]

fere3, *n. pl.* companions, 1150. [OE. *geféra.*]

fere3, *pres. t.* conveys, 98; feryed, *pp.* 946. [OE. *ferian.*]

ferly, *adj.* marvellous, 1084; *as n.* amazement, 1086. [OE. **feorlic* remote, strange; prob. modelled on ON. *ferligr.* See d'Ardenne, *Iuliene,* p. 91.]

feste, *n.* rejoicing; *ma feste* (= OFr. *faire feste*), rejoice, 283. [OFr. *feste.*]

fete. See FOTE.

fewe, *adj.* few, 572. [OE. *féawe.*]

fyf, fyue, *n.* five, 451, 849. [OE. *fíf(e).*]

fyfþe, *adj.* fifth, 1006. [Prec.+ ordinal suffix *-þa.* OE. *fífta.*]

fygure, *n.* form, 170, 747; apparition, 1086. [OFr. *figure.*]

fyldor, *n.* gold thread, 106. [OFr. *fil d'or.*]

fylþe, *n.* impurity, 1060. [OE. *fýlþ.*]

fyn, fyin, *adj.* excellent, of the noblest, 1204; pure, refined (of gold), 106; exquisitely fashioned, 170. [OFr. *fin.*]

fynde, *v.* find, discover, 150, 508, 514; fande, *pa. t.* perceived, 871; fonde, fonte, founden, *pp.* found (again), 283, 327; found (by experience), 1203; perceived, 170. [OE. *findan.*]

fyne, *adv.* completely, 635 (note). [OFr. *fin.*]

fyne, *v.* cease, 353; end one's life, 328; fon, *pa. t.* came to an end, 1030. [OFr. *finer.*]

fynger, *n.* finger, 466. [OE. *finger.*]

fyrce, *adj.* vehement, *54. [OFr. *fier-s,* nom. sg.]

fyrre. See FER.

fyrst(e), *adj. and n.* first, 486, 548, 549, 570, 571, 999, 1000; *adv.* 316, 583, 1042; in the beginning, 638; *at þe fyrst* first, at once, 635 (note). [OE. *fyr(e)st.*]

fla3t, *n.* stretch of turf, 57. [ON. **flaht-*; cf. Icel. *fláttr* 'flaying'.]

flayn. See FLY3E.

flake, *n.* spot, blemish, 947. [? ON. *flaki*; see Falk and Torp, s.v. Flage II.]

flambe, *v.* shine, 769; flaumbande, *pres. p.* glowing, 90. [OFr. *fla(u)mber.*]

flauore3, *n. pl.* odours, 87. [OFr. *flaur.*]

fle, *v.* flee, 294. [OE. *fléon.*]

fle3e, *pa. t. sg.* flew, 431 (note); flowen, *pl.* 89. [OE. *fléogan.*]

fleme, *v.* drive, 334; *of f.,* banish, *358 (note). [OE. *fléman.*]

flesch, *n.* flesh, body, 306, *958. [OE. *flæsc.*]

fleschly, *adj.* bodily, 1082. [OE. *flæsclic.*]

flet, *n.* floor; ground (of city), 1058. [OE. *flett.*]

fleten, *pa. t. pl.* flowed, floated, 21; flot, *pa. t. sg.* 46. [OE. *fléotan, flotian.*]

fly3e, *v.* flay, tear (skin); scourge, 813; flayn, *pp.* 809. [OE. *fléan.*]

flyte, *v.* chide, 353. [OE. *flítan.*]

flode, *n.* river, 1058; water, 736; flode3, *gen. pl.* 874. [OE. *flód.*]

flok, *n.* flock, company, 947. [OE. *flocc.*]

flonc, *pa. t.* rushed, 1165. [ON. **flinga* str.; cf. *flengja,* wk.]

flot(e), *n.* company, 786, 946. [OFr. *flote.*]

floty, *adj.* well supplied with streams, 127. [Stem of OE. *flotian*+adjectival *-ig.*]

flour, flor, *n.* flower, 29, 962 (*fig.*); *vyrgyn flour,* virginity, 426; flowre3, *pl.* 208. [OFr. *flour.*]

flour-de-lys, flor-de-lys, *n.* fleur-de-lis, a kind of iris, 195, 753. [OFr. *flour de lis.*]

floury, *adj.* flowery, 57. [From FLOUR.]

flowen. See FLE3E.

flowred, *pa. t.* bloomed, 270. [From FLOUR.]

flurted, *pp.* figured (with flowers), 208. [OFr. *floreter.*]

fode, *n.* food, 88. [OE. *fōda.*]

foysoun, *n.* plenty; *as adj.* copious, 1058. [OFr. *foiso(u)n.*]

folde, *n.* land, 334, 736. [OE. *fólde.*]

folde, *v. trans.* bend, bow down (under the weight of the cross), 813; *pp.* in *folde vp hyr face,* with her face upturned, 434. [OE. *fáldan.*]

fol3ed, *pa. t.* followed, 127, 654; **folewande,** *pres. p.* following the order of, 1040. [OE. *folgian.*]

fon. See FYNE, *v.*

fonde, *v.* try, attempt, 150; seek, visit, 939. [OE. *fóndian.*]

fonde (283), **fonte.** See FYNDE.

fonge, *v.* take, receive, 439, 479, 884. [OE. *fōn,* pp. *gefongen.*]

for, *conj.* for, 31, 71, 269, *700, &c.; because, 568. [OE. *for þām* (*þe*).]

for, *prep.* for (sake of), on behalf of, 263, 940, &c.; for (purpose of), to be, as, 211, 713, 830, &c.; because of, through, 50, 154, 811, &c.; in spite of, 890; during, 586 (and see EUER); **fore,** in exchange for, 734; *for to,* in order to, to, 99, 333, 403, &c. [OE. *for.*]

forbede, *v.* forbid, 379. [OE. *forbēodan.*]

forbrent, *pp. intr.* burned up, 1139. [OE. *forbeornan,* ON. *brinna.*]

fordidden, *pa. t. pl.* abolished, removed, 124. [OE. *fordōn.*]

fordolked, *pp.* grievously wounded, 11 (note)]. [From MDu. *dolch, dolk,* 'wound'; cf. OE. *dolg.*]

foreste, *n.* forest, 67. [OFr. *forest.*]

forfete, *v.* forfeit, lose right to, 619, 639. [From OFr. *forfet,* n.]

forgarte, *pp.* ruined, made corruptible, 321. [OWN. *fyrgøra,* OEN. *forgøra.*]

forgo, *v.* miss, lose, 328, 340. [OE. *forgān.*]

for3ete, *v.* forget, 86. [OE. *forgetan.*]

forhede3, *n. pl.* foreheads, 871. [OE. *forhĕafod.*]

forlete, *pa. t.* lost, 327. [OE. *forlētan.*]

forloyne, *pres. subj.* go astray, 368. [OFr. *for(s)loignier.*]

forlonge, *n.* furlong, 1030. [OE. *furlong.*]

forme, *n.* form, 1209. [OFr. *forme.*]

forme, *adj.* first; *forme fader,* first father (Adam), 639. [OE. *forma.*]

formed, *pa. t.* fashioned, 747. [OFr. *former.*]

forpayned, *pp.* greatly afflicted, 246. [OE. *for-*+OFr. *peiner.*]

forsake, *v.* renounce, 743. [OE. *forsacan.*]

forser, *n.* casket, 263. [OFr. *forcer.*]

forth, *adv.* forth, forward, onward, 98, 101, 510, 980, 1116. [OE. *forþ.*]

forty, *num.* forty, 786, 870. [OE. *feowertig.*]

fortune, fortwne, *n.* fortune, fate, 98, 129, 306. [OFr. *fortune.*]

forþe, *n.* ford, 150. [OE. **forþ, ford.*]

forþy, *adv.* for this reason, and so, 137, 234, 701, 845. [OE. *for þȳ.*]

fote, *n.* foot; *of measure,* 350, 970; **fete,** *pl.* feet, 1120. [OE. *fōt.*]

foundemente3. See FUNDAMENT.

founden. See FYNDE.

fowle3, *n. pl.* birds, 89. [OE. *fugol.*]

fowre, *num.* four, *786, 870, 886. [OE. *fēower.*]

frayne3, *pres. 3 sg.* makes trial, 129 (note). [OE. *fregnan*.]

frayste, *pa. t.* examined, 169. [ON. *freista*.]

fraunchyse, *n.* liberation, privilege, 609 (note). [OFr. *fra(u)nchise*.]

fre, *adj.* noble, 299; fair, 796; liberal, lavish, 481. [OE. *frēo*.]

frech, *adj.* refreshing, 87; *as n.* blooming, gay (one), 195. [OFr. *freis*, fem. *fresche*; OE. *fersc*.]

freles, *adj.* flawless, 431. [ON. *frýja*, older *frǣja+OE. *-lēas*; cf. ON. *frýjulaust*.]

frelich, *adj.* noble, *1086; **frely**, *as n.* fair (one), 1155. [OE. *frēolic*.]

frende, *n.* friend, 558, 1204. [OE. *frēond*.]

frym, *adj.* of rich growth, 1079 (note). [Obscure.]

fryt(e), *n.* fruit, 29, 87, 1078; *newe fryt*, first-fruits, 894 (Vulgate *primitiae*). [OFr. *fruit*.]

fryth, *n.* woodland, 89, 98, 103. [OE. *gefyrhþe*, n., *fyrhþ*, f.]

fro, *prep.* away from, from, 10, 13, 46, &c.; *fro me warde*, from me, 981; *adv.* away, 347. [ON. *frá*.]

fro, **fro þat**, *conj.* after, since, 251, 375, 958. [Prec.+ÞAT, *conj.*]

frount, *n.* forehead, 177. [OFr. *fro(u)nt*.]

ful, *adj.* full, 1098. [OE. *full*.]

ful, *adv.* very, quite, full, 28, 42, 50, &c. [OE. *ful*.]

fundament, *n.* foundation, 1010; **foundemente3**, layers of the foundation, 993. [OFr. *fo(u)nde-ment*, Lat. *fundamentum*.]

furþe, *adj.* fourth, 1005. [OE. *fēorþa*.]

gay(e), *adj.* gay, bright, fair, 7, 260, 1124, 1186; *as n.* fair damsel, 189, 433. [OFr. *gai*.]

gayn, *prep.* opposite, 138. [ON. *gegn*.]

gayne3, *pres. sg.* profits, 343. [ON. *gegna*.]

galle, *n.* spot of impurity, 189, 915; filth, impurity, 1060. [OE. *galla*, unsound spot.]

gardyn, *n.* garden, 260. [ONFr. *gardin*.]

gare3, *pres. sg.* causes, 331; **gart**, *pa. t. sg.* 1151; **garten**, *pl.* 86. [ON. *gøra*, pp. *gǫrr*, runic pa. t. *karþi*.]

garlande, *n.* garland, (fig.) circle of the blessed, 1186 (note). [OFr. *garlande*.]

gate, *n.* road, street, 1106; way, manner, 619; *hy3e gate*, highway, 395 (fig.); *3ede his gate*, went his way, 526. [ON. *gata*.]

gaue. See GYUE.

gawle, *n.* bitterness, rancour, 463 (note). [OE. *galla*, gall.]

gef. See GYUE.

gele, *v.* linger, stroll, 931. [OE. *gǣlan*.]

gemme, *n.* gem, 7, 118, 219, 253, &c. [OFr. *gemme*.]

generacyoun, *n.* generation, ancestry, 827. [OFr. *genera-cio(u)n*.]

gent(e), *adj.* courteous, gracious, 265, 1134; fair, elegant, noble, 118, 253, 1014. [OFr. *gent*.]

gentyl(e), *adj.* of gentle birth, noble, 264, 605, 632, 895; courteous, excellent, 278, 883, 991; **gentyleste**, *superl.* 1015; *as n.* **gentyl**, gentle damsel, 602. [OFr. *gentil*.]

gesse, *v.* conceive, form an idea, 499. [Cf. MDu. *gessen*.]

geste, *n.* guest; person that has newly arrived, 277. [ON. *gestr*.]

gete, *v.* procure, 95. [ON. *geta*.]

gyfte, *n.* giving, act of giving, 565 (note); gifts (of spiritual powers = *gratiae* in 1 Cor. xii. 4 f.), 607. [ON. *gift*.]

gyle, *n.* guile, treachery, 671, 688. [OFr. *guile*.]

gilofre, *n.* gillyflower, clove-scented pink, 43. [OFr. *gilofre*.]

gylte3. See GULTE.

gyltyf, *adj. as n.* guilty, 669. [OE.

gyltig, infl. by OFr. adj. suffix
-*if*.]

gyltle3, *adj. as n.* innocent, guiltless (one), 668, *799. [OE.
gyltleas.]

gyng, *n.* company, 455. [ON.
gengi.]

gyngure, *n.* ginger, 43. [OFr.
gingivre.]

gyrle, *n.* girl, 205. [OE. *gyrl-* in
gyrlgyden, virgin goddess.]

gyse, *n.* garb, 1099. [OFr. *guise*.]

gyternere, *n.* player of the cithern
(instrument of the guitar type),
91. [OFr. *guiternier*.]

gyue, gef, *pres. subj.* give, grant,
allow, 707, 1211; gyf, *imper.* 543,
546; gef, gaue, *pa. t.* 270, 734,
765; dealt (a blow), 174; pre-
scribed, 667; gyuen, *pp.* granted,
*1190. [OWN. *gefa*.]

glace, *v.* glide, 171. [OFr. *glacer*.]

glade, *adj.* joyful, glad, 136, 1144;
gladder, *compar.* 231; gladdest,
superl. 1109. [OE. *glæd*.]

glade3, *pres. sg.* gladdens, 861;
gladande, *pres. p.* gladdening,
171. [OE. *gladian*.]

gladne3, *n. pl.* joys, 136. [OE.
glædnes.]

glayre, *n.* white of egg, as used in
the illumination of MSS. &c.,
1026. [OFr. *glaire*.]

glayue, *n.* lance, spear, 654. [OFr.
glaive.]

glas(se), *n.* glass, 114, 990, 1018,
1025, 1106. [OE. *glæs*.]

glauere3, *pres. sg.* deceives, 688.
[See *NED*.]

gle, *n.* joy, 95, 1123. [OE. *glēo*.]

glem, *n.* gleam, 79. [OE. *glǣm*.]

glemande, *pres. p.* gleaming, 70,
990. [From prec.]

glene, *v.* glean, 955. [OFr. *glener*.]

glent(e), *pa. t.* deviated, 671;
glinted, shone, 70, 1001, 1026,
1106. [ON. *glenta*; cf. Norw.
glenta, slip to the side, glance
off; and see *NED*.]

glente, *n.* beam of light, 114; *pl.*
looks, 1144. [From prec.]

glet, *n.* slime, filth, 1060. [OFr.
glette.]

glyde3, *pres. 3 sg.* glides, falls, 79;
glod, *pa. t.* proceeded, 1105.
[OE. *glīdan*.]

gly3t, *pa. t.* glinted, 114. [Uncer-
tain; but for senses compare
GLENT(E), AGLY3TE.]

glymme, *n.* radiance, 1088. [OE.
gleomu, *glimu*; cf. Norw. *glim*.]

glysnande, *pres. p.* shining, 165,
1018. [OE. *glisnian*.]

glod. See GLYDE3.

glode3, *n. pl.* clear patches of sky,
79. [Obscure; rel. to GLADE in
original sense 'bright'?]

glory, *n.* glory, splendour, resplendent beauty, 70, 171, 934, 959;
praise, 1123. [OFr. *glorie*.]

gloryous, *adj.* glorious, 799; splendid in beauty, 915; *adv.* gloriously, 1144. [OFr. *glorious*.]

glowed, *pa. t.* shone like fire, 114.
[OE. *glōwan*.]

God, *n.* God, 314, 342, &c.;
God(d)e3, *gen.* 63, 591, 601, 1193,
&c. [OE. *god*.]

god, goude, *adj.* good, righteous,
generous, 310, 568, 674, 818,
1202. [OE. *gōd*.]

god, goud(e), *n.* good thing, 33
(2nd); that which is good, 33
(1st); goods, wealth, 731, 734.
[OE. *gōd*, n.]

godhede, *n.* divinity, 413. [OE.
god + ME. -*hede*.]

godnesse, *n.* generosity, 493. [OE.
gōdnes.]

golde, *n.* gold, 2, 165, 213, 989,
1025, *1111. [OE. *góld*.]

golden, *adj.* of gold, 1106. [OE.
gylden, infl. by GOLDE.]

golf, *n.* a space underground (as
source of a stream), 608 (note).
[ON. *golf*, if identical with
modern dial. *goave*; cf. OFr.
golfe, gulf.]

gome, *n.* man, 231, 697. [OE.
guma.]

gon, *v.* go, 820; got3, *pres. 3 sg.*
365; 3 *pl.* 510; go, *subj. sg.* in

go doun, sink, set, 530; *imper. sg.* depart, 559; *gos, got3, imper. pl.* go, 521, 535; *gon, pp.* gone, departed, 63, 376. [OE. *gān.*] See 3EDE.

gospel, *n.* gospel, 498. [OE. *gōdspell.*]

goste, *n.* spirit, 63, 86. [OE. *gāst.*]

gostly, *adj.* ghostly, supernatural, 185; spiritual, 790. [OE. *gāstlic.*]

gote, *n.* stream, 608, 934. [Cf. *got* in OE. *gegot*, shedding.]

got3. See GON.

goud(e). See GOD.

grace, *n.* grace, mercy of God in salvation, 436, 612, 623, 624, 636, 648, 660; (as personified in Christ), 425; grace of regeneration in man, 625, 661, 670; *in Gode3 grace*, in God's mercy, 63; *by grace*, by good fortune, 194. [OFr. *grace.*]

gracio(u)s, *adj.* fair, pleasing, charming, *95, 189, *934; *as adv.*, 260. [OFr. *gracious.*]

graye, *adj.* gray; gray-blue (?), 254 (note). [OE. *grēg.*]

grayne3, *n. pl.* grains, 31. [OFr. *grain.*]

graypely, *adv.* aptly, 499. [ON. *greiðliga.*]

grauayl, *n.* gravel, 81. [OFr. *gravele.*]

graunt, *n.* permission, 317. [From OFr. *gra(u)nter, v.*]

greffe, *n.* grief, 86. [OFr. *gref.*]

greme, *n.* resentment, 465. [ON. *gremi.*]

grene, *adj.* green, 38, 1001, 1005. [OE. *grēne.*]

gresse, *n.* grass, 10, 245; plant of grass or corn, 31. [OE. *gærs, græs.*]

gret(e), *adj.* large, big, 90; great in number, 851, 926; noble, 637; great in degree or extent, 250, 612, *1104, &c. [OE. *grēat.* See AGRETE.]

grete, *v.* weep, 331. [OE. *grētan.*]

greue, *n.* grove; *Paradys greue*, the garden of Eden, 321. [OE. *græfa.*]

greue, *pres. subj.* give offence, 471. [OFr. *grever.*]

grewe. See GROW.

grym, *adj.* grim, ugly, 1070. [OE. *grimm.*]

grymly, *adv.* cruelly, 654. [OE. *grimlīce.*]

grynde, *v.* grind, crunch, 81; **grounde**, *pp.* sharpened, 654. [OE. *grindan.*]

gryste, *n.* anger, spite, 465. [OE. *grist.*]

gromylyoun, *n.* gromwell, 43. [OFr. *grumillon* (not recorded till 1545); cf. *gremillon, gromil.*]

grouelyng, *adv.* prostrate, 1120. [ON. *á grúfu*, on one's face + ME. adverbial *-ling.*]

grounde, 654. See GRYNDE.

grounde, *n.* ground, earth, 10, 81, 434, 1173; foundation, 372, 384, 396 (note), 420. [OE. *grúnd.*]

grow, *v.* grow, come into being, 31; **grewe**, *pa. t.* 425. [OE. *grōwan*]

gulte, *n.* sin; *þe olde gulte*, the sin of Adam and Eve, 942; **gylte3**, *pl.* 655. [OE. *gylt.*]

3are, *adv.* clearly, 834. [OE. *gear(w)e.*]

3ate, *n.* gate, 728, 1034, 1037, 1065. [OE. *gæt.*]

3e, *pron.* you, 290, 515, 917, &c.; *of one person*, 257, 371, &c.; (any) one, 1051; **yow**, *accus. and dat.* (to) you, 470, 524, 928; *of one person*, 471; **your, yor**, *poss. adj.* your, 761, 924; *of one person*, 257, 258, 369, &c. [OE. *gē, ēow, ēower.*] See Appendix V, p. 105.

3ede, *pa. t.* went, passed, 526, 713, 1049. [OE. *ēode.*]

3emen, *n. pl.* hired labourers, 535. [OE. *geongman.*]

3er(e), *n.* year, 503, 505; *on 3er* (OE. *on gēr*), each year, 1079; **3er**, *pl.* (?), 483. [OE. *gēr.*]

3erned, *pa. t.* desired, 1190. [OE. *géornan.*]

3et, *adv.* yet, up to the present,

200, 1065; also, further, 46, 205, 215, 697, 1021; *with compar.* still, 145, 1033; (and) yet, nevertheless, 19, 374, 585, &c.; ȝete, 1061. [OE. *gēt, gēta.*]

ȝete, *v.* grant; *no waning ȝete,* propose to make no curtailment (of what is due), 558. [Late OE. *gē(a)tan,* after ON. *jǻta.*]

ȝif, ȝyf, *conj.* if, 45, 482, 662; if, 147, 264, &c.; though, 363; whether, 313. [OE. *gif.*]

ȝys, *adv.* yes, 635. [OE. *gēse.*]

ȝon, *adj.* that, yon, 693. [OE. *geon.*]

ȝong(e), *adj.* young, 412, 474, 535. [OE. *geong.*]

ȝore, *adv.* in time past; *for long ȝore,* for a long time, 586. [OE. *geǻra, iǻra.*]

ȝorefader, *n.* father of old (Adam), 322. [Prec.+FADER.]

had, hade, haf. See HAUE.

hafyng, *n.* possession, 450. [From HAUE; cf. OE. *hæfen.*]

haylsed, *pa. t.* greeted, 238. [ON. *heilsa.*]

halde, *v.* hold, possess, 454, 490; consider, account, 301; helde, *pa. t.* occupied, 1002; contained, 1029; halden, *pp.* restrained, 1191. [OE. *hǻldan.*]

haleȝ, *pres. t.* flows, 125. [OFr. *haler.*]

half, *n.* side, 230. [OE. *half.*]

half, *adv.* half, 72. [OE. *half.*]

halle, *n.* hall, 184. [OE. *hall.*]

halte, *adj.* lame; *take me halte,* stop my advance, 1158 (note). [OE. *halt.*]

han. See HAUE.

hande. See HONDE.

happe, *n.* good fortune, happiness, 16, 713, 1195. [ON. *happ.*]

harde, *adj. as n.* what is hard, 606. [OE. *heard.*]

hardyly, *adv.* boldly; firmly, 3, 695. [OFr. *hardi*+ME. adverbial *-ly.*]

harme, *n.* evil, hurt, 681; grief, 388. [OE. *hearm.*]

harmleȝ, *adj.* innocent, 676, 725. [From prec.]

harpe, *n.* harp, 881. [OE. *heǻrpe.*]

harpen, *pres. pl.* harp, play, 881. [OE. *hearpian.*]

harporeȝ, *n. pl.* harpers, 881. [OE. *heǻrpere.*]

hate, *adj.* hot; grievous, 388. [OE. *hǻt.*]

hate, *n.* hatred, 463. [Stem of next.]

hated, *pp.* hated, 402. [OE. *hatian.*]

hatȝ. See HAUE.

haþel, *n.* man, 676. [OE. *hæleþ,* infl. by *æþele.*]

haue, haf(e), *v.* have, possess, *and auxil.,* 132, 194, 661, &c.; *1 sg.* 14, 242, 244, &c.; hatȝ, *2 and 3 sg.* 291, 441, 770, &c.; haf, hauen, han, *pl.* 373, 554, 776, 859, 917, &c.; had(e), *pa. t.* 164, 170, 209, &c.; *pa. subj.* would have, 1194, if ... had, 1090, 1189. [OE. *habban, haf-.*]

hawk, *n.* hawk, 184. [OE. *hafoc.*]

he, *pron.* he, 302, *479, 705, &c.; hym, *acc. and dat.* (to, for) him, 324, 360, 662, &c.; *reflex.* (for) himself, 478, 732, 813; *pleonastic,* 711, 1033; hymself, himself, 680, 808, 811, 812; his, hys, *poss. adj.* his, 285, 307, 819, 1133, &c.; hysse, *absol.* his (possession), 418. [OE. *hē; him,* dat.; *his,* gen.]

hed, hede. See HEUED.

hede, *v.* observe, 1051. [OE. *hēdan.*]

heȝt. See HYȜT.

helde, *adv.* readily, likely, 1193 (note). [ON. *heldr.*]

helde. See HALDE.

hele, *n.* well-being, 16; healing, 713. [OE. *hǽlu.*]

helle, *n.* hell, 442, 643 (*gen.*), 651, 840, 1125. [OE. *hell.*]

hem, *pron. dat. and acc. pl.* (to, for) them, 69, *532, *635, *715, &c.;

reflex. 551; **her,** *poss. adj.* their, 92, 451, 714, &c.; his, 687 (note), 688. [OE. *heom, heora.*]

hemme, *n.* hem, 217; projecting edge (forming step), 1001. [OE. *hemm.*]

hende, *adj.* quiet, still, 184; **hynde,** *as n.* gracious one, 909. [OE. *gehende,* convenient.]

hente, *v.* take, seize, 1195; get, chance to have, find, 388, 669. [OE. *hentan.*]

her. See HO, HEM.

her(e), *adv.* here, 263, 298, &c.; **hereinne,** in this place, 261; in this arrangement, 577. [OE. *hēr, hēr inne.*]

herde. See HERE, *v.*

here, *n.* hair, *210. [OE. *hēr.*]

here, *v.* hear, 96; **herde,** *pa. t.* 873, 879, 1132. [OE. *hēran.*]

herytage, erytage, *n.* heritage, 417 (note), 443. [OFr. *heritage.*]

herneʒ, *n. pl.* brains, 58. [ON. *hjarni,* older **hearne.*]

hert(e), *n.* heart, mind, secret thoughts and feelings, 17, 51, 128, 682, 1136, &c. [OE. *heorte.*]

heste, *n.* commandment, 633. [Extended from OE. *hǣs.*]

hete, *n.* heat, 554, 643. [OE. *hǣtu.*]

hete, *v.* assure, 402; **hyʒt(e),** *pa. t.* promised, 305; was named, 999. [OE. *hātan;* pa. t. *hēt, hēht.*] See Appendix VI.

heterly, *adv.* bitterly, 402. [OE. *hetellice* infl. by *biter;* cf. MLG. *hetter.*]

heþen, *adv.* from here, 231. [ON. *hēðan.*]

heue, *v.* raise; address (words), 314; exalt, 473. [OE. *hebban, hef-.*]

heued, hed(e), *n.* head, 209, 459, 465, 1172; source, 974. [OE. *hēafod.*]

heuen, *n.* heaven, 473, 490, 500, 873, 988, 1126; **heuen(e)ʒ, heuenesse,** *pl.* heaven, 423, 441, 620, 735 (note) (*pl.* from Biblical idiom). [OE. *heofon.*]

heuen, *v.* exalt, increase, 16 (note). [OE. *hafenian,* infl. by HEUE.]

heuenryche, *n.* the kingdom of heaven, 719. [OE. *heofonrīce.*]

heuy, *adj.* grievous, 1180. [OE. *hefig.*]

hyde, *n.* skin, 1136. [OE. *hȳd.*]

hider, hyder, *adv.* hither, here, 249, 517, 763. [OE. *hider.*]

hyʒ(e), *adj.* high, lofty, 678, 1024; high (of special dignity), exalted, 596, 1051, 1054; chief, 395 (see GATE); overbearing, 401; *hyʒ seysoun,* festival, 39; **hyʒ(e), hiʒe,** *adv.* high, aloft, 207; to an exalted position, 473, 773; *ful hyʒe,* supremely, 454. [OE. *hēh.*]

hyʒt, heʒt, *n.* height, 1031; *on hyʒt,* on high, 501. [OE. *hēhþu.*]

hyʒt(e). See HETE, *v.*

hil, hyl(le), *n.* hill, *678, 789, 976, 979. [OE. *hyll.*]

hylle, 1172. See HUYLE.

hyl-coppe, *n.* hill-top, 791. [OE. *hyll + copp.*]

hynde. See HENDE.

hyne, *n. pl.* labourers, 505, 632; servants, 1211. [OE. *hīga,* nom. pl. *hīgan,* gen. *hīgna.*]

hir, hyr. See HO.

hyre, *n.* hire, pay, reward, 523, 534, 539, 543, 583, 587. [OE. *hȳr.*]

hyre, *v.* hire, 507, 560. [OE. *hȳrian.*]

hit, hyt, *pron.* it, 10, 46, 283, &c.; *impers.* 147, 512, 569, 914, &c.; *hit arn,* they are, 895, 1199; *pleonastic,* 41; **hit,** *poss. adj.* its, 108, 120, 224; **hytself,** *gen.* its own, 446. [OE. *hit.*]

hytteʒ, *pres. 3 sg.* chances, attains as a result, 132. [ON. *hitta.*]

hyul. See HUYLE.

ho, *pron.* she, 129, 177, 1149, &c.; hir, hyr, *acc. and dat.* (to) her, 8, 9, 188, &c.; her, hir, hyr, *poss. adj.* her, 4 (note), 6, 22, &c. [OE. *hēo, hēo; hire, heore.*]

hol, *adj.* complete, 406. [OE. *hāl.*]

holy, *adj.* holy, 592, 618, 679. [OE. *hālig.*]

holy, *adv.* completely, 418. [From HOL.]

holteȝ, *n. pl.* woods, 921. [OE. *holt.*]

holtewodeȝ, *n. pl.* woods, 75. [OE. *holtwudu.*]

homly, *adj.* belonging to the household, 1211. [OE. *hām+lic.*]

honde, hande, *n.* hand; *com on honde,* became evident, 155; *in hande nem,* seized, 802; **honde,** *pl.* hands, 49, 218; **hondeȝ,** 706. [OE. *hánd, hónd.*]

hondelyngeȝ, *adv.* with the hands, 681. [OE. *hondlinga*+adverbial *-es.*]

hondred. See HUNDRETH.

hone, *v.* remain; be situated, 921. [Unknown.]

honour, *n.* honour, worship, 424, 475, 852, 864; **onoure,* 690 (note). [OFr. *honour.*]

hope, *n.* hope, trust, 860 (note). [OE. *hopa.*]

hope, *v.* suppose, believe, 139, 142, 185, 225. [OE. *hopian.*]

horneȝ, *n. pl.* horns, 1111. [OE. *horn.*]

houreȝ. See OURE, *n.*

how, *adv.* how, in what way, 334, 690, 711, 1146. [OE. *hū.*]

hue, *n.* shout, 873. [OFr. *hu.*]

huee. See HWE.

huyle, *n.* mound (overgrown with plants), 41 (note); **hyul,** 1205; **hylle,** 1172. [Cf. mod. Lancs. *hile.*]

hundreth, hundreþe, hondred, *n.* hundred, 786, 869, 1107. [ON. *hundrað,* OE. *hundred.*]

hurt, *pp.* wounded, 1142. [OFr. *hurter.*]

hwe, huee, *n.* colour, 90, 842, 896. [OE. *hīw.*]

I, *pron.* I, 3, *363, *977, &c.; **me,** *acc. and dat.* (to, for) me, 10, 19, 98, &c.; *reflex.* myself, 66; **my,** *poss. adj.* my, 15, &c.; **myn,** *before*

h or vowel, 128, 174, &c.; **myn(e),** *following its noun,* 335, 1208; **myn,** *absol.* my own (property), 566; **myseluen, myself,** myself, 52, 1175; me (in person), 414. [OE. *ic, mē, mīn.*]

ydel, *adj.* idle, unemployed, 514, 515, 531, 533. [OE. *īdel.*]

ichose. See CHES(E).

if. See 3IF.

yȝe, *n.* eye, 302, 567, 1153; **yȝen, ene,** *pl.* 183, *200, 254, 296. [OE. *ēge.*]

yle, *n.* domain, 693. [OFr. *ile.*]

ilk(e), *adj.* same, 704, 995. [OE. *ilca.*]

ille, *adv.* wrongfully, 681; ill, 1177. [ON. *illa.*]

in, *prep.* in, on, at, 2, 133, 1103, &c. (**inne,** 656, after *wyth,* by confusion with *wythinne*); in regard to, 5, 428, &c.; into, 38, 366, &c.; *of time,* in, during, 116 (2nd), 416, 659, &c. [OE. *in.*]

ynde, *n.* indigo blue, 1016. [OFr. *inde.*] See YNDE in Index of Names.

inlyche, *adv.* alike, 546, 603. [Alteration of *ilyche,* OE. *gelīce,* owing to *i = in,* and obsolescence of *i-* prefix.]

inmyd(d)eȝ, *prep.* in the middle of, 222, 740, 835 (after Apoc. v. 6 *in medio throni*). [From OE. *in middan,* prep.; cf. *tō middes,* adv.]

inne, *adv.* in, 940. [OE. *inne.*]

innogh(e), *adj.* sufficient, 649, 661; *absol.* 625; **innogh(e), inoghe, in(n)oȝe,** *adv.* enough, 612, 624, 636, 648, 660; well enough, 637. [OE. *genōh, genōg-, genōge,* adv.]

innocens, *n.* innocence, 708. [OFr. *innocence.*]

innocent, innos(s)ent, inoscente, *adj.* innocent, 672; *as n.* 625, 666, 684, 696, 720. [OFr. *innocent.*]

innome, *pp.* trapped, refuted in argument, 703 (note). [OE. *genumen.*]

into, *prep.* into, 245, 509, 521, &c.; to, 231. [OE. *inn tō.*]

inwyth, *adv.* from within, 970. [OE. *in+wiþ.*]

is, *pres. 3 sg.* is, 26, 33, *309, &c. [OE. *is.*]

yuore, *n.* ivory, 178. [OFr. *yvore.*]

iwys(s)e, *adv.* indeed, certainly, 151, 279, 394, 1128. [OE. *mid* (or *tō*) *gewisse.*]

jacynght, *n.* jacinth, *1014. [Late Lat. *jacinctus.*]

jasper, *n.* jasper, 999, 1026; **jasporye,** 1018. [OFr. *jaspre.*]

joy(e), ioy(e), *n.* joy, 128, 234, 266, 577, &c. [OFr. *joie.*]

ioyful, ioyfol, *adj.* joyful, 288, 300. [Prec.+OE. *-full.*]

joyleȝ, *adj.* joyless, 252. [OFr. *joie*+OE. *-lēas.*]

joyned, *pa. t.* added, 1009. [OFr. *joindre.*]

joly, jolyf, *adj.* fair, bright, 842, 929. [OFr. *joli, jolif.*]

joparde, *n.* uncertainty, 602 (note). [Alteration of OFr. *jo part.*]

juel(e), iuel(e), juelle, *n.* jewel, 23, 249, 253, 277, 278, 795, 929, 1124. [OFr. *j(o)uel.*]

jueler(e), iueler, joueler, *n.* jeweller, 252, 264, 301, 734, &c. [OFr. *jouelier, jueler.*]

jugged, iugged, *pa. t.* appraised, 7; tried, 804. [OFr. *jug(i)er.*]

justyfyet, *pp.* justified, 700. [OFr. *justifier.*]

kaste. See KESTEN.

kene, *adj.* keen, sharp, 40. [OE. *cēne.*]

kenned, *pa. t.* taught; imparted, 55. [OE. *cennan.*]

keruen, *pres. pl.* cut, 512; **coruen,** *pp.* 40. [OE. *ceorfan.*]

kesten, *pa. t. pl.* scattered, 1122; **kest(e), kaste,** *pp.* set down, 66; cast out, 1198; removed, 861. [ON. *kasta.*]

keue, *v.* sink (down), 320, 981. [ON. *kefja,* impers.; *kefjask.*]

kyn, *n.* kind; *orig. gen.* in *quat* (*what*) *kyn,* of what kind, what kind of, 755, 771, 794; *alle kynneȝ,* all kinds of, 1028. [OE. *cynn.*]

kynde, *n.* nature, 55, 74, 270, 271, 752. [OE. *gecýnd.*]

kynde, *adj.* gentle, courteous, 276. [OE. *gecýnde,* natural.]

kyndely, *adv.* kindly, 369. [OE. *gecyndelīce,* naturally.]

kyndom, *n.* kingdom, 445. [OE. *cynedōm.*]

kyng, *n.* king, 448, 468, 480; *hyȝe kyng,* God, 596. [OE. *cyning, cyng.*]

kyntly (MS.), 690. See KOYNTISE.

kyrk, *n.* church, 1061. [ON. *kirkja.*]

kyste, *n.* chest, 271. [ON. *kista.*]

kytheȝ, *n. pl.* regions, 1198. [OE. *cýþþu.*]

kyþe, *v.* show, 356, 369. [OE. *cýþan.*]

klyfeȝ, klyffeȝ. See CLYFFE.

klymbe. See CLYM.

knaw, *v.* know, recognize, 410, 505, 516, &c.; **knew,** *pa. t. sg.* 66, 164, &c.; **knewe,** *pl.* 890; **knawen,** *pp.* 637. [OE. *cnāwan.*]

knelande, *pres. p.* kneeling, 434. [OE. *cnēowlian.*]

knot, *n.* throng, 788. [OE. *cnotta.*]

Koyntise, *n.* Wisdom, *690 (note). [OFr. *cointise.*]

Krysten, *adj.* Christian, 461. [OE. *cristen.*]

Krystyin, *adj. as n.* Christian, 1202. [OFr. *christiien.*]

labor, *v.* labour upon, cultivate, 504. [OFr. *labo(u)rer.*]

labour, *n.* labour, 634. [OFr. *labour.*]

lad. See LEDE.

lade, *pp.* laden; filled to overflowing, 1146. [OE. *hladan.*]

laden, ledden, *n.* voice, 874, 878. [OE. *lǣden.*]

lady, *n.* lady (of rank), 453, 491. [OE. *hlǣfdige.*]

ladyly, *adj.* queenly, exalted, 774. [From prec.]

ladyschyp, *n.* queenly state, exalted rank, 578. [LADY+OE. *-scipe.*]

laften, *pa. t. pl.* forsook, 622. [OE. *lǣfan.*]

laȝt(e), *pa. t.* received, 1205; took, 1128. [OE. *lǣccan,* pa. t. *lǣhte.*]

layd(e), *pp.* laid, 1172; laid in the grave, 958. [OE. *lecgan,* pp. *gelegd.*]

layned, *pp.* concealed, 244. [ON. *leyna.*]

lambe. See LOMBE.

langour, *n.* sorrow, 357. [OFr. *langour.*]

lantyrne, *n.* lantern, 1047. [OFr. *lanterne.*]

lappeȝ, *n. pl.* hanging sleeves, 201. [OE. *læppa.*]

large, *adj.* generous, abundant, 609; large, 201. [OFr. *large.*]

lasse, lesse, les, *adj. compar.* less (in quantity or number), 852, 864, 901; (in volume), 876; (in importance), 339; lower (in rank), 491; *þe lasse in werke,* those who have done less work, 599, 600; *as n.* 601; diminution, 853; **les,** *adv. compar.* 865 (note), 901 (note); less (in volume of sound), 888. [OE. *lǣssa.*]

laste, *adj. superl.* last, 547, 570, 571. [OE. *lætest.*]

laste, *v.* endure, last, 956, 1198. [OE. *lǣstan.*]

laste, *pp.* loaded, charged, 1146. [OE. *hlæstan.*]

late, *adj.* late, 538; *adv.* 392, 574, 615. [OE. *læt; late,* adv.]

laueȝ, *pres. 3 sg.* pours, 607. [OE. *lafian.*]

launceȝ, *n. pl.* boughs, 978. [OFr. *la(u)nce.*]

laweȝ, *n. pl.* laws, 285. [OE. *lagu,* from ON. **lagu, lǫg,* pl.]

ledden. See LADEN.

lede, *n.* man; *voc.* my good man, 542. [OE. (verse) *lēod.*]

lede, *v.* lead (life), 392, 409, 774; **lad,** *pp.* led, 801. [OE. *lǣdan.*]

lef, *n. collect.* leaves, foliage, 77; **leueȝ,** *pl.* leaves (of book), 837. [OE. *lēaf.*]

lef, *adj.* dear, beloved, 266; *as n.* 418. [OE. *lēof.*]

legg, *n.* leg, 459. [ON. *leggr.*]

leghe. See LYȜ.

legyounes, *n. pl.* multitudes, 1121 (this use from Matt. xxvi. 53). [OFr. *legio(u)n.*]

leke, *pa. t.* enclosed, 210 (note). [OE. *lūcan,* pa. t. *lēc.*]

lelly, *adv.* faithfully, 305. [AFr. *leël*+OE. *-līce.*]

leme (MS.), 358. See note.

lemed, *pa. t.* gleamed, 119, 1043. [OE. *lēoman,* WS. *lȳman.*]

lemman, *n.* beloved one, 763, 796, 805, 829. [OE. **lēofman.*]

lenge, *v.* stay, 261, 933. [OE. *lengan.*]

lenger. See LONGE, *adv.*

lenghe, *n.* extent, duration, 416; *on lenghe,* for a long time, 167. [OE. *lengu.*]

lenþe, *n.* length, 1031. [OE. *lengþu.*]

lere, *n.* face, 398. [OE. *hlēor.*]

lere (MS.), 616. See note.

les, lesse, *adj. compar. and adv. compar.* See LASSE.

lesande, *pres. p.* loosening, opening, 837. [OE. *lēsan.*]

lesyng, *n.* lie, 897. [OE. *lēasing.*]

lest, *conj.* lest, 187, 865. [OE. *þe lǣs þe.*]

leste, *pa. t.* lost, 9, 269. [OE. *lēosan,* str.] Cf. LOSE.

let, *v.* let, allow, 718, 901, 912, 964; *let be,* let be, cease, 715; **let(te),** *pa. t.* let, allowed, 20, 813. [OE. *lētan.*]

lette, *pa. t.* obstructed, prevented, 1050. [OE. *lettan.*]

lettrure, *n.* learning, science, 751. [OFr. *lettreüre.*]

leþeȝ, *pres. 3 sg.* softens, is assuaged, 377. [OE. *geleoþian.*]

leue, *n.* permission, 316. [OE. *lēaf.*]

leue(n), *v.* believe, 304, 311, 469,

876; *trans.* believe (in), 69, *302, *308, 865; *leven on*, believe in, 425. [OE. *gelēfan*.]

leued, *pp.* having leaves, 978. [From LEF.]

lyf, *n.* life, 247, 305, &c.; lyue3, *gen.* 477, 578, 908. [OE. *līf.*]

lyfed, *pa. t.* lived, 483; lyuyande, *pres. p.* 700; lyued, *pp.* 477, 776. [OE. *lifian*.]

lyfte, *pp.* raised, 567. [ON. *lyfta*.]

lygynge3 (MS.), 935. See note.

ly3, *v.* lie; *ly3 þeroute*, sleep out of doors, 930; lys, *pres. sg.* exists, is admissible, 602; *lys in hym*, is in his power, 360; leghe, *pa. t.* lay, 214. [OE. *licgan*.]

ly3e, *n.* lie, 304. [OE. *lyge*.]

ly3t, *n.* light, 69, 119, 1043, 1050, 1073. [OE. *lēht, līht*.]

ly3t, *pa. t.* descended, 943; ly3t(e), *pp.* 988; set down, settled, 247. [OE. *līhtan*.]

ly3t(e), *adj.* bright, 500; pure, 682. [OE. *lēht*, adj.¹]

ly3te, *adj.* glad, joyful, 238. [OE. *lēht*, adj.²]

ly3te, *adv.* lightly, 214. [OE. *lēhte*.]

ly3tly, *adv.* easily, quickly, 358. [OE. *lēhtlīce*.]

lyk(e), *adj.* like, 735, 874; *lyk to*, like, 432, 501, 896. [OE. *gelīc*.]

lyke3, *pres. impers.* pleases; in *me lyke3*, I please, 566. [OE. *līcian*.]

lykyng, *n.* delight, pleasure, 247. [OE. *līcung*.]

lykne3, *pres. sg.* compares, 500. [From LYK.]

lym, *n.* limb, member, 462; lymme3, *pl.* 464. [OE. *lim*.]

lyne, *n.* line; *by lyne*, in regular succession, 626. [OE. *līne*, OFr. *ligne*.]

lynne, *adj.* linen, 731. [OE. *linnen*.]

lys. See LY3.

lyste, *n.* desire, 173; joy, 467, 908. [ON. *lyst*.]

lyste, *pa. t. impers.* desired, 1141; *me lyste*, I desired, 146, 181. [OE. *lystan*.]

lysten, *v.* listen to, 880. [OE. *hlysnan*.]

lyth, *n.* limb, 398. [OE. *liþ*.]

lyttel, *adj.* little, small, 387, 604, 1147; unimportant, 574; *wyth lyttel*, with small result, 575; *adv.* but little, 172 (note), 301. [OE. *lytel; lȳtle*, adv.]

lyþe, *v.* assuage, 357. [OE. *līþian*.]

lyþer, *n.* evil; *to lyþer is lyfte*, is turned to evil, 567. [OE. *lȳþre*.]

lyued, lyuyande. See LYFED.

liuré3, *n. pl.* garments, 1108. [OFr. *liveré*.]

lo, *interj.* lo! behold, 693, 740, 822. [OE. *lā*.]

lo3e, *n.* pool, 119. [OE. *luh*.]

loke, *v.* see, observe, 1145; *loke what*, consider what, 463; *loke on*, gaze upon, look at, 710, 934; *loke to*, gaze at, 167. [OE. *lōcian*.]

loke3, *n. pl.* expression of face, 1134. [From prec.]

lokyng, *n.* gaze, 1049. [OE. *lōcung*.]

lombe, lomp, *n.* lamb, 802, 815, 830; þe Lombe, the Lamb, Christ, 413, 741, *861, 1110, &c.; þe Loumbe, 867; þe Lompe, 945; þe Lamb(e), 407, 757, 771, 785; the Lombe, *gen.* 1141. [OE. *lámb, lómb*.]

lombe-ly3t, *n.* lamplight, 1046. [OFr. *la(u)mpe* + OE. *lēht*.]

londe, *n.* land, 148, 937. [OE. *lónd*.]

lone, *n.* roadway, 1066. [OE. *lone*.]

longande, *pres. p.* that belongs, 462. [From OE. *gelóng*, adj.]

long(e), *adj.* long, 1024; *þe long day*, all day long, 597. [OE. *lóng*.]

long(e), *adv.* long; *for long 3ore*, for a long time, 586; *hys lyue3 (þise daye3) longe*, all his life, all this day, 477, 533; lenger, *compar.* longer, 168, 180, 977; *þe lenger þe lasse*, continually the less, 600 (note). [OE. *lónge*, adv.; *lengra*, compar. adj.]

longed, *pa. t. impers.* in *me longed*, I had a desire, 144. [OE. *lóngian*].

longeyng, *n.* sorrow, 244, 1180. [OE. *lóngung*.]

lorde, *n.* owner, master, 502, 506, 557, &c.; Lord (God or Christ), 285, 304, 1199, &c.; *as interj.* 108, 1149. [OE. *hláford*.]

lore, *n.* rule of behaviour, manner, 236. [OE. *lár*.]

lose, *v.* be lost, fade, 908; lose, 265; loste, *pp.* lost, 1092. [OE. *losian*, infl. by *léosan*]. See LESTE.

lote, *n.*¹ sound, 876; word, speech, 238, 896. [ON. *lát*.]

lote, *n.*² fortune, 1205. [OE. *hlot*.]

loþe, *n.* grief, 377. [OE. *láþ*, n.]

loude, *adj.* loud, 878. [OE. *hlúd*.]

loue, *v.* praise, 285, 342, 1124, 1127. [OE. *lofian*.]

loueloker, louely. See LUFLY.

loueȝ, *pres. sg.* likes, 403, 407. [OE. *lufian*.]

louyly, *adj.* lawful, 565 (note). [OE. *lagu*+*-lic*; cf. OE. *lahlic*.]

loute, *v.* make one's way, go, 933. [OE. *lútan*, str.]

lowe, *adv.* low, 236, 547. [ON. *lágr*, adj.]

lowest, *adj. superl.* lowest, 1001. [ON. *lágr*.]

luf, *n.* love, 467, 851. [OE. *lufu*.]

luf-daungere, *n.* power of love, 11. [Prec.+DAUNGER.]

lufly, louely, *adj.* fair, beautiful, 693, 962; loueloker, *compar.* 148; lufly, *adv.* fairly, delightfully, 880, 978. [OE. *luflic*; *luflíce*.]

luf-longyng, *n.* longing of love, 1152. [LUF+LONGYNG.]

lufsoum, *adj. as n.* lovely (one), 398. [OE. *lufsum*.]

lureȝ, *n. pl.* sorrows, 339, 358. [OE. *lyre*.]

lurked, *pa. t.* made one's way (under cover), 978. [Cf. Norw. *lurka*, sneak off.]

ma, in *par ma fay*, by my faith, 489. [OFr. *par ma fei*.]

ma, mad, made. See MAKE.

mad, *adj.* mad, 267, 1199; madde, *pl.* 290; mad, *adv.* madly, 1166. [OE. *gemǽdd*.]

madde, *pres. subj.* behave madly, rave, 359 (note). [From prec.]

maddyng, *n.* madness, 1154. [From prec.]

may, *n.* maiden, 435, 780, 961. [ON. *mær*, *meyj-*; OE. (verse) *mǽg*. See note on 435.]

may, *pres. sg.* can, may, 296, 300, 310 (will), 487, 703, &c.; *pl.* 29, 918; *no fyrre may*, can go no farther, 347; moun, *pl.* 536 (OE. *mugon*); myȝt, *pa. t. sg.* could, might, 69, 135, &c.; *pl.* 579; myȝteȝ, *2 sg.* 317; moȝt(e), *sg.* 34, 475, *1196; moȝt, *pl.* 92, 1051. [OE. *mæg*, pa. t. *mihte*; *muhte*, *mohte*, corresponding to the occasional pres. pl. *mugon*, is not recorded in OE.]

mayden(n), *n.* maiden, 162, 1115; virgin, 869 (note). [OE. *mægden*.]

maynful, *adj.* powerful, 1093. [OE. *mægen*+*ful*.]

mayster, *n.* lord, 462, 900. [OFr. *maistre*.]

maysterful, *adj.* arrogant, 401. [From prec.]

make, *n.* spouse, 759. [OE. *gemaca*.]

make, *v.* make, cause to be, 176, 474; ma, 283; be guilty of, 304; make, *pres. 1 sg.* make, 281; matȝ, *3 sg.* 610; man, *pl.* 512; mad(e), *pa. t.* 371, 522, 539, 1149; mad(e), *pp.* made, 486, 953; fashioned, 140, 274. [OE. *macian*.]

makeleȝ, *adj.* matchless, peerless, 435, 757, 780, 784; makelleȝ, 733 (note). [OE. *gemaca*+*-léas*.]

malte, *v.* melt; *malte in*, enter into, comprehend, 224; *to maddyng malte*, gave way in frenzy, 1154. [OE. *mæltan*.]

man, 512. See MAKE, *v.*

man, man(n)eȝ. See MON.

maner, manayre, *n.* mansion, abode, 918; lordly establishment, 1029. [AFr. *maneir, maner* (e.g. in Grosseteste's *Rules*).]

manereȝ, *n. pl.* manners, courtesy, 382. [OFr. *man(i)ere.*]

mankyn, *n.* mankind, 637. [OE. *mancynn.*]

mare. See MORE.

margyrye, *n.* pearl, 1037; **margarys, mariorys,** *pl.* 199, 206. [OFr. *margerie.*]

maryag(e), *n.* marriage, 778; *to hys maryage,* to be his spouse, 414. [OFr. *mariage.*]

marked, *n.* market, 513. [Cf. late OE. *gearmarket.* For derivation from one of the other Germ. langs. see *MLR.* xlvii, 152 ff.; ult. from Lat. *mercatus.*]

marre, *pres. subj.* lament, 359 (note). [OFr. *marrir.*]

marreȝ, *pres. 2 sg.* are destroying, 23. [OE. *mærran.*]

mas, mes(se), *n.* mass, 497, 862, 1115. [OE. *messe, mæsse.*]

maskel(l)eȝ, maskelleȝ, mascelleȝ, *adj.* spotless, 732, 744, 745, 756, 768, 769, 780, 781, 900, 923. [From next.]

masklle, mascle, *n.* spot, 726, 843. [AFr. *mascle.*]

mate, *adj.* dejected, 386. [OFr. *mat.*]

mate, *v.* abash, shame, 613. [OFr. *mater.*]

matȝ. See MAKE, *v.*

me. See I.

mede, *n.* reward, 620. [OE. *mēd.*]

meyny, *n.* servants of the estate, 542; retinue, company, 892, 899, 925, 960, 1127, 1145. [OFr. *mai(s)nee.*]

meke, *adj.* gentle, submissive, 404, 815, 832, 961. [ON. *mjúkr,* older **méuk-.*]

mekenesse, *n.* meekness, 406. [From prec.]

mele, *v.* speak, tell, 497, 589, 925. [ON. *mæla,* OE. (verse) *mǣlan.*] See Appendix IV, pp. 100–1.

melle, in *in melle, prep.* among, as one of, 1127. [ODan. *i melle.*]

melle, *v.* speak, tell, 797, 1118. [OE. *meþlan,* with variant form due to contact with OFr. *medler, meller,* 'meddle'.]

membreȝ, *n. pl.* limbs, members, 458. [OFr. *membre.*]

men. See MON.

mendeȝ, *n. pl.* recompense, 351. [OFr. *amendes.*]

mendyng, *n.* improvement, 452. [From OFr. *amender.*]

mene, *v.* signify, mean, 293, 951; refer to, 937. [OE. *mǣnan.*]

mensk(e), *n.* courtesy, 162, 783. [ON. *menska.*]

menteene, *v.* maintain; affirm, 783. [OFr. *maintenir.*]

mercy, merci, mersy, *n.* mercy, 356, 383, 576, 623, 670. [OFr. *merci.*]

mere, *n.* pool, body of water, 140, 158, 1166. [OE. *mere.*]

merked, *pp.* situated, 142. [OE. *me(a)rcian,* ON. *merkja.*]

meruayle, merwayle, *n.* amazement, wonder, 1130; what is marvellous, 157; marvel, portent, 64, 1081. [OFr. *merveille.*]

meruelous, *adj.* marvellous, 1166. [OFr. *merveillous.*]

mes(se). See MAS.

meschef, *n.* misfortune, distress, 275. [OFr. *meschef.*]

mesure, *n.* measure; value, significance, 224. [OFr. *mesure.*]

mete, *adj.* fitting, 833; noble, excellent, 1063. [OE. *gemēte,* ON. *mætr,* excellent.]

mete, *n.* food, 641. [OE. *mete.*]

mete, *v. intr.* meet, 380; be together, 918; *trans.* find, 329. [OE. *mētan.*]

meten, *v.* measure, 1032. [OE. *metan.*]

meuen, *pres. pl.* move; take place, exist, 64; stir, 156. [OFr. *moveir,* stressed stem *meuv-.*]

m̄y, myn(e). See I.

myȝt, myȝteȝ. See MAY.

myȝt(e), *n.* power, 765, 1069. [OE. *miht.*]

mykeȝ, *n. pl.* friends; the elect, 572 (note). [OFr. *amike,* Lat. *amīcus.*]

mylde, *adj.* gentle, 961, 1115; *as n.* gentle ones (Christ's disciples), 721. [OE. *milde.*]

mynde, *n.* mind, 156, 224, 1130, 1154. [OE. *gemýnd.*]

mynge, *v.* turn one's mind to, think (of), 855. [OE. *myndgian.*]

mynne, *v.* remember, 583. [ON. *minna.*]

mynster, *n.* church, cathedral, *1063 (note). [OE. *mynster.*]

myry, *adj.* fair, 23, 158, 781, 936; myryer, *compar.* more joyful, 850; myryest(e), *superl.* fairest, 199, 435. [OE. *myrige.*]

mirþe, myrþe, *n.* delight, joy, 140 (note); song, music, 92; *made mirþe,* rejoiced, 1149. [OE. *myrgþ.*]

myrþeȝ, *pres. sg.* causes to rejoice, 862. [From prec.]

myserecorde, *n.* mercy, 366. [OFr. *misericorde.*]

mysetente, *pp.* not given proper attention to, told wrongly, 257. [OE. *mis-* +OFr. *attendre.*]

mysse, mys, *n.* sense of loss, sorrow, 262, 364. [OE. *miss.*]

mysse, *v.* lose, 329; lack, 382. [OE. *missan.*]

mysseȝeme, *v.* abuse, 322. [OE. *misgēman.*]

myste, *n.* spiritual mysteries, 462 (? rendering *spiritalibus,* 1 Cor. xii. 1). [OE. *mist,* infl. by next.]

mysterys, *n.* mysteries, 1194. [Lat. *mysterium.*]

myte, *n.* mite (coin); *not a myte,* not a jot, 351. [OFr. *mite.*]

myþe, *pres. subj.* conceal (one's feelings), 359 (note). [OE. *mīþan.*]

mo, *adj.* more (in number), 151, 870; *n.* a greater (additional) number, more, 1194; *þe mo,* the greater part, the better portion, 340; *þe mo þe myryer,* the greater

the number, the more joy, 850 (earliest record of the phrase). [OE. *mā,* adv. and n.]

mod(e), *n.* mood, temper, 401, 832; (*fig.*) quality, character, 738. [OE. *mōd.*]

moder, *n.* mother, 435. [OE. *mōdor.*]

modeȝ, *n. pl.* strains of music, 884 (note). [OFr. *mode.*]

moȝte, moȝt. See MAY.

mokke, *n.* filth, 905. [OE. *moc,* recorded in *hlōs-moc* KCD. 1002; cf. ON. *myki.*]

mol. See MUL.

moldeȝ, *n. pl.* clods, earth, 30. [OE. *mólde.*]

mone, *n.* moon, 1044, 1093, &c.; month, 1080; (*an*)*vnder mone,* on this earth, 1081; in existence, altogether, at all, 923, 1092. [OE. *mōna.*]

mon, man, *n.*[1] man, 310, 386, 661, 685, &c.; *as pron.* one, 165, 194, 334, 799; *vch* (*no, mony*) *m.,* everybody, nobody, many, 69, *323, 340, 603, &c.; man(n)eȝ, *gen. sg.* human (being's), 223, 1154; mankind's, 940; men, *pl.* 290, 514, &c.; *indef.* (*possibly sg.*), they, one, 331, 336, 728. [OE. *mon, man.*]

mon, *n.*[2] grief, 374. [OE. **mān.*]

mony, *adj.* many, 572; *mony a* (*with sg.*), many (a), 775; (without *a*), 160, 340. [OE. *monig.*]

moote. See MOT(E).

more, *adj. compar.* greater, larger, 128, 234, 576, &c.; *absol.* more, further, 132, 133, 552, &c.; *adv.* more, 144, 588, &c.; *forming compar.* 565; mare, *adv.* 145; moste, *superl.* 1131. [OE. *māra,* adj.; *mǣst,* late North. *māst.*]

morne, *pres. subj.* grieve, mourn, 359. [OE. *murnan.*]

mornyf, *adj.* sorrowful, 386. [From prec.+OFr. *-if;* cf. OFr. *morni.*]

mornyng, *n.* mourning, grief, 262. [OE. *murnung* (once).]

mot, *pres. t.* may; expressing a wish, 397; must, *25, 31, 320, 663; moste, *2 sg.* 319, 348; moste, *pa. t. pl.* must, 623. [OE. *mōt*, pa. t. *mōste*.]

mot(e), moote, *n.* spot, stain, 726, 764, 843, 972; *wythouten mote*, of unstained purity, 924, 948, 960. [OE. *mot*.]

mote, *n.*¹ walled city, 142, 936, 937, 948, 949, 973. [OFr. *mote*.]

mote, *n.*² dispute, 855. [OE. *mōt*.]

moteles, moteleȝ, *adj.* spotless, 899, 925, 961. [From MOT(E).]

moteȝ, *pres. 2 sg.* argue, 613. [OE. *mōtian*.]

moul, *n.* earth, the earth of the grave, 23. [Obscure variant of MUL.]

moun. See MAY.

mount, *n.* mount, hill, 868. [OFr. *mo(u)nt*.]

mounteȝ, *pres. pl.* are increased, 351. [OFr. *mo(u)nter*.]

mouth, *n.* mouth, 183, 803. [OE. *mūþ*.]

much, *adj.* much, great, 244, 604, 776, 1118, 1130; *absol.* 1149; *adv.* much, greatly, 234, 303, 374, 576. [OE. *mycel*.]

mul, mol, *n.* dust, 382, 905. [Cf. OE. *myl*, MDu. *mul, mol*.]

munt, *n.* intention, 1161. [OE. *gemynt*.]

naȝt, naȝte. See NYȜT(E).

name. See NOME.

nature, *n.* nature, 749. [OFr. *nature*.]

naule, *n.* navel, 459. [OE. *nafela*.]

nauþeles, nawþeles, nowþelese, *adv.* nevertheless, 877, 889, 950. [OE. *nōhte þy lǣs*.]

nauþer, nawþer, *nouþer, conj.* neither; *nauþer . . . ne*, neither . . . nor, 465, 484, 485, *848, 1044, 1087; *adv.* in *ne . . . nawþer*, nor . . . either, 751. [OE. *nāwþer*.]

nawhere, *adv.* nowhere, 534, 932. [OE. *nāhwēr*.]

ne, nee (262), *adv.* not, 35, 65, &c.; *with another negative*, 4, 362, 825, &c.; *conj.* nor, (*after neg.*) or, and, 262, 334, 485, 688, &c. [OE. *ne*.]

nece, *n.* niece, 233. [OFr. *n(i)ece*.]

nedde, *pa. t. impers.* in *hem nedde*, they needed, 1044. [OE. *nēodian*, blended with *nēdan*, compel.]

nede, *n.* need, 1045. [OE. *nēd*.]

nedeȝ, *adv.* of necessity, 25, 344. [OE. *nēdes*.]

***nem**, *pa. t. sg.* took, laid hold of, 802; nom, *pl.* received, 587. [OE. *niman*.]

nemme, *v.* name, 997. [OE. *nemnan*.]

nente, *adj.* ninth, 1012. [OE. *nigon*+ME. *-t* in *fift, sixt*, &c.]

ner(e), *adv.* near, *262; *as prep.* near to, 286, 404. [ON. *nǣr*.]

nerre, *adj. compar.* nearer; of nearer kin, 233. [OE. *nērra*.]

nesch, *adj. as n.* (what is) soft, pleasant, 606. [OE. *hnesce*.]

neuer, *adv.* never, 4, 19, 71, 1071, &c.; not at all, in no way, 333, 376, 825, &c.; *neuer oneȝ*, of no one, 864; *neuer þe les(se)*, in no way the less (for the consideration stated or implied), 852, 888, no less (than that), 876; *after neg.* any the less, 864; notwithstanding, 900 (note). [OE. *nǣfre*.]

neuerþelese, *adv.* none the less, notwithstanding, 912, 913. [See prec.]

new, newe. See NWE.

nieȝbor, *n.* neighbour, 688. [OE. *nēhgebūr*.]

nyȝt(e), *n.* night, 116, 243, 1071; niyȝt, 630; naȝt(e), 523, 1203. [OE. *niht, nǣht*.]

nis, nys, 100, 951 (= NE+IS.) [OE. *nis*.]

no, *adj.* no, 32, 69, 225, &c.; non(e), 206, 209, &c.; *foll. noun*, 440, 764, 1061. [OE. *nān*.]

no, *adv.* no, 347, 951, 977, 1190. [OE. *nā*.]

noble, *adj.* glorious, stately, 922, 1097. [OFr. *noble.*]

noȝt, *adv.* not (at all), by no means, 563, 588; **not,** 29, 34, 92, &c. [OE. *nāht, nōht.*]

noȝt, *n.* nothing, 274, 1050; *after neg.* anything, 520; *noȝt bot,* nothing but, only, 337, 657, 955. [OE. *nāht, nōht.*]

nome, name, *n.* name, 872, 998 (note), 1039. [OE. *nama, noma.*]

non, *pron.* none, not any, no one, 443, 455, 544, 700, &c.; *after neg.* any, 812, 825; nothing (of), 215 (note). [OE. *nān.*]

not. See NOȝT.

note, *n.*[1] matter, 155; piece of work, structure, 922. [OE. *notu.*]

note, *n.*[1] (musical) note, song, 879, 883. [OFr. *note.*]

noþynk, noþyng, *n.* nothing, 308, 496, 587, 1157. [OE. *nān þing.*]

nouþer. See NAUþER.

now, *adv.* now, 271, 379, 613, &c.; *conj.* now (that), 283, 377, 389. [OE. *nū.*]

nowþelesē. See NAUþELES.

nw(e), newe, *adj.* new, fresh, novel, 155, 527, 792, 879, 882, 943, 987; *newe fryt,* first fruits, 894; **new, nwe,** *adv.* anew, 662, 1080, 1123. [OE. *nēowe.*]

O, *interj.* O, 23, 241, 745, 1182.

o, *prep.* See OF.

obes, *pres. pl.* do obeisance to, 886. [OFr. *obeiss-,* stem of *obeir.*]

odour, *n.* fragrance, 58. [OFr. *odo(u)r.*]

of, *adv.* off, 237, 358; of, about, 925, 1118; *prep.* of; from, out of, 31, 33, 425, &c.; (consisting, made) of, 110, 206, 929, &c.; by, with, 11, 25, 119, 248, &c.; having, with, 76 (1st), 207, &c.; *as equivalent of gen.,* 55, 612, &c.; *partitive,* of, 309, 577, &c.; in, 1101; in, as regards, 74, 398, 682, &c.; o, 309, 429, 792, 1018. [OE. *of.*] See OUT.

offys, *n.* office, position, *755 (note). [OFr. *office.*]

ofte, *adv.* often, 14, 340, 388; **ofter,** *compar.* 621. [OE. *oft.*]

oȝe, owe, *pres. sg.* ought, 552 (*impers.*); owe, 543; **aȝt, oȝte,** *pa. t.* ought, 341 (*impers.*), 1139. [OE. *āgan.*]

oȝt, *n.* something, 274; anything, 1200. [OE. *ā(wi)ht, ō(wi)ht.*]

olde, *adj. wk.* old, ancient, 941, 942; **alder,** *compar.* 621; **aldest,** *superl.* 1042. [OE. *dld; aldra,* compar.]

on, *adj. and pron.* one, a single (one), 293, 551, 557, *860, 864; one (as opposed to 'other'), 953; *at on,* at one, in harmony, 378. [OE. *ān.*]

on, *prep.* (up)on, 60, 78, 214, 826, &c.; *in postposition (orig. adv.)* 45, 843; in, 97, 425, 1095, &c.; *distributively,* each, a, 1079; *on a day,* a day, 510; *of time,* on, at, 243, 486; *adv.* on, 77 (note), 255. [OE. *on.*]

one, *adv.* only, alone; *hys one,* his alone, 312; *as n.* in *by myn one,* by myself alone, 243. [OE. *āna,* adv.]

onende. See ANENDE.

only, *adv.* excepted, alone, 779. [OE. *ānlic,* adj.]

onoure. See HONOUR.

onsware, *v.* answer, 680. [OE. *on(d)swarian.*]

on-vunder. See AN-VNDER.

open, vpen, vpon, *adj.* open, 183, 198, 1066. [OE. *open.*]

or. See OþER, *conj.*

oryent(e), orient, *n. and adj.* the orient, 3 (note); *perle of oryente, perle orient,* resplendent pearl (from the orient), 82, 255. [OFr. *orient.*]

oþer, *adj. and pron.* (an)other, of another kind, 206, 319, 842, &c.; *pl.* others, 585, 773, 778; *þat oþer,* the other, 955; *vchon . . . opereȝ,* each . . . the other's, 450. [OE. *ōþer.*]

oþer, *conj.* or, 118, 491, &c.; or

else, 592; *correl. with* W(H)EÞER, 130, 567, &c.; or, 233. [OE. *ā(w)þer, ō(w)þer.*]

ouer, *adv.* across, on the other side, *138; too, 473; *prep.* above, over, 454, 773; (stretched out) upon, 1205; across, 318, 324, 1166. [OE. *ofer.*]

ouerte, *adj.* open, plain to see, 593. [OFr. *overt.*]

ouerture, *n.* opening (at the neck of garment), 218. [OFr. *overture.*]

oure, *n.* hour, 530, 551; houreȝ, *pl.* 555. [OFr. *(h)oure.*]

oure. See WE.

out(e), *adv.* out, away, 777; *out(e) of,* out of, from, 3, 1163. &c.; *out of delyt,* not in, deprived of, delight, 642. [OE. *ūt.*]

outfleme, *adj.* driven out, 1177. [OE. *ūt+flēme,* adj.]

outryȝte, *adv.* (directly) out, 1055. [OUT+RYȝTE.]

outsprent, *pa. t.* gushed forth, 1137. [OE. *ut+ON. *sprenta.*]

owe. See OȝE.

owne, *adj.* own, 559. [OE. *āgen.*]

pace, *n.* passage, 677. [OFr. *pas.*]

pay, *v.* please, 1201; *impers.* 1165, 1177; pay, 524 (*fut.*), 542, 584, 603, 632, 635. [OFr. *paier.*]

pay(e), *n.* pleasure, 1200; *at paye,* (*vn)to paye,* as (one) likes, so as to please, 1, 1164, 1176, 1188, 1189, 1212. [OFr. *paie.*]

payment, *n.* payment, 598. [OFr. *paiement.*]

payne, *n.* pain, 954; penalty, 664; *pl.* sorrows, 124. [OFr. *peine.*]

paynted, *pa. t.* painted, 750. [OFr. *peindre,* pp. *peint.*]

payred, *pp.* worn, broken, 246. [OFr. *apeirer.*]

pakke, *n.* company, 929. [MLG. *pak.*]

pale, *v.* appear pale (by comparison), 1004. [OFr. *palir.*]

pane, *n.* side (of a walled enclosure), 1034. [OFr. *pan.*]

par, in *par ma fay,* by my faith, 489. [OFr. *par.*]

parage, *n.* high lineage, 419. [OFr. *parage.*]

paraunter, *adv.* perhaps, 588. [OFr. *par aventure.*]

parfyt, perfet, *adj.* exquisite, perfect, 208, 638, 1038. [OFr. *parfit, parfet, per-.*]

part, *n.* share, 573. [OFr. *part.*]

partleȝ, *adj.* deprived, 335. [Prec. +OE. *-lēas.*]

passe, *v.* proceed, go, 1110; go free, go unsentenced, 707; pass over, cross, 299; pass (by), 528; surpass, 428, 753. [OFr. *passer.*]

Pater, *n.* the Lord's Prayer, 485. [Lat. *pater noster.*]

pechche, *n.* fault, impurity, 841. [OFr. *peché.*]

penaunce, *n.* penance, 477. [OFr. *peneance,* AFr. *penaunce.*]

peny, pené, *n.* penny (silver coin), 510, 546, 560, 562, 614. [OE. *peni(n)g.*]

pensyf, *adj.* sorrowful, 246. [OFr. *pensif.*]

pere, *n.* equal, 4. [OFr. *per.*]

pereȝ, *n. pl.* pear-trees, 104. [OE. *pere.*]

perfet. See PARFYT.

perle, *n.* pearl, 1, 12, 82, &c. [OFr. *perle.*]

peryle, *n.* risk, jeopardy, 695. [OFr. *peril.*]

perré, *n.* precious stones, 1028; *perré pres* (cf. OFr. *perrerie de pris*), jewels of price, 730. [OFr. *perr(er)ie.*]

pes, *n.* peace, concord, 742, 952, 953, 955. [OFr. *pais, pes.*]

pyece, *n.* person, being, 192, *229. [OFr. *p(i)ece.*]

pyȝt, *pa. t.* set, fixed, 742; adorned, 768; pyȝt(e), *pp.* set, placed, fixed, 117, 193, 216, 228, 991; adorned (with gems), 192, 205, 217, 229, 240, 241. [OE. *piccan,* pa. t. *pihte.*]

pykeȝ, *pres. pl.* pick; gather, get, 573; *pyked of,* adorned with,

1036. [OE. *pīcan; cf. *pīcung*, pricking.]

pyle, *n.* castle, stronghold, 686. [Not known.]

pynakled, *pp.* with pinnacles, 207. [From OFr. *pinacle*.]

pyne, *n.* grief, 330; toil, 511. [Early ME. *pine*; forms point to weak OE. *pīne*, f.]

pyonys, *n. pl.* peonies, 44. [OFr. *pioné*.]

pyty, pyté, *n.* compassion, 355; *pyty of*, sorrow for, 1206. [OFr. *pité*.]

pytosly, pitously, *adv.* compassionately, 370, 798. [From OFr. *pito(u)s*.]

place, *n.* place, 175, 440; abode, city, 405, 679, 1034. [OFr. *place*.]

play, *v.* rejoice (traditional of the bliss of heaven), 261. [OE. *plegan*.]

playn, *n.* meadow, 104, 122. [OFr. *plain*, n.]

playn, *adj.* polished, 178 (note); *adv.* plainly, 689. [OFr. *plain*, adj.]

playnt, *n.* complaint, 815. [OFr. *plaint*.]

planete3, *n. pl.* planets, 1075. [OFr. *planete*.]

plate3, *n. pl.* sheets of metal, plates, 1036. [OFr. *plate*.]

pleny, *v.* complain, 549; **playned**, *pa. t.* lamented, mourned, 53; *pp.* 242. [OFr. *plaign*-, stem of *plaindre*.]

plesaunte, *adj.* pleasing, 1. [OFr. *plaisant*, AFr. *plesaunt*.]

plese, *v.* please, 484. [OFr. *plaisir*, AFr. *plesir*.]

plete, *v.* sue for, claim, 563. [OFr. *plaitier*, AFr. *pleter*.]

plye, *v.* form, express, 1039. [OFr. *plier*.]

ply3t, *n.* state, condition, 1075. [OE. *pliht*, danger, infl. by next.]

plyt, *n.* evil condition, hard plight, 647, 1015; *in plyt*, in (their) array, 1114. [AFr. *plit*.]

plontte3, *n. pl.* shrubs, young trees, 104. [OE. *plonte*.]

pobbel, *n.* pebble, 117. [Cf. OE. *papolstān*.]

poyned, *n.* wristband, 217. [OFr. *poignet*.]

poynt, *n.* instance, 309; phrase, strain (of music), 891; pronouncement, established proposition, 594. [OFr. *point*.]

pole, *n.* pool, 117. [OE. *pōl*.]

porchase, porchace, *v.* seek, strive for, 439; acquire, 744. [OFr. *porchacier*.]

porfyl, *n.* embroidered border, 216. [OFr. *porfil*.]

porpos(e), *n.* purpose, 267, 508; significance, 185. [OFr. *porpos*.]

portale3, *n. pl.* gateways, 1036. [OFr. *portal*.]

possyble, *adj.* possible, 452. [OFr. *possible*.]

pouer, pore, *adj.* poor, 573; deficient, wretched, 1075. [OFr. *povre, poure*.]

poursent, *n.* compass; enclosing wall, 1035 (note). [OFr. *po(u)rceint*.]

powdered, *pp.* scattered, 44. [OFr. *poudrer*.]

pray, *n.* what is won in contest, prize, 439 (note). [OFr. *preie*.]

pray, *v.* pray, 484; beseech, ask, 714, 1192. [OFr. *preier*.]

prayer(e), *n.* prayer, 355, 618. [OFr. *preiere*.]

prayse, *v.* praise, 301; *pp.* precious, 1112. [OFr. *preis(i)er*.]

precio(u)s, *adj.* 4, 48, *60, *192, &c. [OFr. *precio(u)s*.]

pref, *n.* test by experience; *is put in pref to*, has proved in fact to be, 272. [OFr. *prueve, preve*.]

pres, *n.* crowding, 1114. [OFr. *presse*.]

pres, *v.* press forward, hasten, 957. [OFr. *presser*.]

pres(e), *n.* great worth, 419; *adj.* precious, 730. [OFr. *pris*, infl. by AFr. *preser*, to value.]

present(e), *n*. presence; *in your p.*, with you, 389; *to Godeʒ p.*, into God's presence, 1193. [OFr. *present*; *en present*.]

preste, *n*. priest, 1210. [OE. *prēost*.]

pretermynable, *adj*. who pre-or-dains (?), *596. [See note.]

preued. See PROUED.

pryde, *n*. pride, 401. [OE. *prȳdo*.]

prince, prynce, prynse, *n*. sovereign, king, 1, 1164, 1176, 1188, 1189, 1201. [OFr. *prince*.]

prys, *n*. excellence, nobility, 419; *of prys*, exquisite, precious, 193, 272, 746. [OFr. *pris*.]

pryse, *v*. esteem, 1131. [OFr. *priser*.]

priuy, pryuy, *adj*. one's own, of special intimacy or favour, 12, 24. [OFr. *privé*.]

proferen, *pres. pl*. propose, profer, 1200; *pa. t*. addressed, 235. [OFr. *proferer*.]

professye, *n*. prophecy, 821. [OFr. *profecie*.]

profete, prophete, *n*. prophet, 797, 831. [OFr. *prophete*.]

proper, *adj*. fair, 686. [OFr. *propre*.]

property, *n*. property, special vir-tue, 446; **properteʒ**, *pl*. 752. [OFr. *proprieté*.]

prosessyoun, *n*. procession (as at a religious ceremony), 1096. [OFr. *processio(u)n*.]

proudly, *adv*. with dignity, 1110. [OE. *prūdlīce, prūtlīce*.]

proued, *pa. t*. found (by proof), 4; **preued**, *pp*. established, shown, 983 (note).[OFr. *prover*, accented stem *proev-, preuv-*.]

pure, *adj*. clear, unsullied, 227, 745, 1088. [OFr. *pur*.]

purly, *adv*. clearly; *purly pale*, show pale and clear, 1004. [From prec.]

purpre, *adj*. purple, 1016. [OE. *purpure*.]

put, *v*. put, set, 267, 272. [OE. *pūtian*.]

qu-. See WH-.

quayle, *n*. quail, 1085. [OFr. *quaille*.]

quelle, *v*. put to death, 799. [OE. *cwellan*.]

queme, *adj*. pleasant, 1179. [OE. *cwēme*.]

quen(e), *n*. queen, 415, 448, 492, &c.; referring to the Virgin Mary, 432, 433, 444, 456. [OE. *cwēn*.]

quere-so-euer. See WHERE.

query, *n*. complaint, 803. [Lat. *quert*, complain.]

quyke, *adj*. lifelike, vivid, 1179. [OE. *cwic*.]

quyt(e), qwyte. See WHYT.

quyteʒ, *pres. 2 sg*. repay, reward, 595. [OFr. *quiter*.]

quod (MS.), *pa. t*. said, 241, 569, &c. [OE. *cwepan*.]

quoynt, *adj*. skilful, 889. [OFr. *cointe*.]

raas, *n*. headlong course, 1167. [ON. *ras*.]

ray, *n*. beam of light, 160. [OFr. *rai*.]

raykande, *pres. p*. flowing, rolling on, 112. [ON. *reika*.]

rayse, *v*. raise from death, 305. [ON. *reisa*.]

raysoun. See RESOUN.

ran, *pa. t*. flowed, 646, 1055; **runne(n)**, *pp*. run, in *r. on resse*, gathered in a rushing torrent, 874; *r. to rot*, fallen into decay, *26; *be r.*, may have mounted up, 523. [ON. *renna* replacing OE. *(ge-)eornan*, which in this MS. gives *ʒerne*.]

randeʒ, *n. pl*. strips of land by the border of a stream, 105. [OE. *rand*.]

rapely, *adv*. quickly, 1168; rashly, 363. [ON. *hrapalliga*.]

rasch, *adj*. eager, active, 1167. [Cf. MDu. *rasch*.]

raue, *v*.[1] go astray, 665. [Cf. Icel. *ráfa*.]

raue, *v.*² rave, talk foolishly, 363. [OFr. *raver*.]

rauyste, *pp.* enraptured, 1088. [OFr. *raviss-*, stem of *ravir*.]

raupe, *n.* grief, 858. [OE. *hrēow* + *pu*; cf. ON. *hrygg∂*.]

rawe, *n.* row, 545; hedge-row, 105. [OE. *rāw*.]

raxled, *pa. t.* stretched (myself), 1174. [Cf. OE. *raxan*.]

rebuke, *v.* rebuke, 367. [ONFr. *rebuk(i)er*.]

recen, *v.* recount, tell, 827. [OE. *gerecenian*.]

rech, *pres. sg.* care; *rech neuer* (*to*), count it no matter (to), 333. [OE. *reccan*.]

recorde, *n.* testimony, recorded words, 831. [OFr. *record*.]

red(e), *adj.* red, 27, 1111. [OE. *rēad*.]

rede, *v.* counsel, 743; read, 709. [OE. *rēdan*.]

redy, *adj.* ready (to act), 591. [From OE. *gerǣde*.]

refete, *v.* refresh, 88; **refet**, *1064 (note). [OFr. *refet*, pp. of *refaire*.]

reflayr, *n.* fragrance, 46 (note). [OFr. *reflair*.]

reget (MS.), 1064. See note.

regioun, *n.* country, 1178. [OFr. *regio(u)n*.]

regne, rengne, *n.* kingdom, 501, 692. [OFr. *regne*.]

regretted, *pp.* grieved for, 243. [OFr. *regretter*.]

reiate3, *n. pl.* royal dignities, 770. [OFr. *reiauté*.]

reken, *adj.* ready; fresh, gay, 5, 92, 906. [OE. *recen*.]

reles, *n.* remission; *wythouten reles*, (cf. OFr. *sans reles*), without ceasing, 956. [OFr. *reles*.]

relusaunt, *adj.* gleaming, 159. [OFr. *reluisant*.]

reme, *n.* kingdom, 448, 735. [OFr. *re(a)ume*.]

reme, *v.* cry out, lament, 858, 1181. [OE. *hrēman*.]

remnaunt, *n.* remainder, 1160. [OFr. *remena(u)nt*.]

remorde, *pp.* afflicted, 364. [OFr. *remordre*.]

remwe, *v.* take away, 427; depart, 899. [OFr. *remuer*.]

rengne. See REGNE.

renoun, *n.* glory, 986, 1182. [OFr. *reno(u)n*.]

renowle3, *pres. t.* renews, 1080. [OFr. *renoveler*.]

rent, *pp.* rent, 806. [OE. *rendan*.]

repayre, *v.* come together, be present, 1028. [OFr. *repairer*.]

reparde, *pp.* barred, withheld, 611. [OFr. *re-* + ME. *parre*, enclose.]

repente, *v. impers.* cause to feel regret; *3if hym repente*, if he repent, 662. [OFr. *repentir*.]

reprené, *v.* find fault with, 544. [OFr. *repreign-*, stem of *reprendre*.]

requeste, *n.* request; *make requeste*, beg, 281. [OFr. *requeste*.]

rere, *v.* rise up, 160; **rert**, *pp.* upraised, supreme, 591. [OE. *rǣran*.]

rescoghe, *n.* rescue, 610 (note). [From OFr. *rescou-*, stem of *rescoure*, v.]

reset, *n.* refuge, 1067. [OFr. *recet*.]

resonabele, *adj.* reasonable, 523. [OFr. *resonable*.]

resoun, raysoun, *n.* reason, 52, 665 (note); speech, words, 716; ground, cause, 268. [OFr. *raison, resoun*.]

respecte, *n.* relatioh; *in respecte of*, by comparison with, 84. [Lat. *respectus*.]

respyt, *n.* respite, 644. [OFr. *respit*.]

resse, *n*, rush, torrent, 874. [OE. *rǣs*.]

rest, *v.* rest, 679. [OE. *restan*.]

restay, *v.* restrain, prevent, 716, 1168; pause, 437. [OFr. *resteir*.]

reste, *n.* rest, 1087 (note); *withouten reste*, without intermission, 858. [OE. *rest*.]

restored, *pp.* restored, 659. [OFr. *restorer*.]

retrete, *v.* reproduce, 92. [OFr. *retraitier*, *retreter*.]

reue, *n.* steward, overseer, 542. [OE. *gerĕfa.*]

reuer, *n.* river, river-bank, 105 (note), 1055. [OFr. *riv(i)ere.*]

rewarde, *n.* estimation, due recognition of merit, 604 (note). [ONFr. *reward.*]

rewfully, *adv.* sorrowfully, 1181. [From OE. *hrĕow.*]

ryal, ryalle, *adj.* royal, befitting a king, 191, 193; splendid, 160; royal, magnificent, 919; ryally, *adv.* royally, magnificently, 987. [AFr. *real, rial.*]

rybé, *n.* ruby, 1007 (note). [OFr. *rubi.*]

ryche, *n.* kingdom, 601, 722, 919. [OE. *rīce.*]

riche, rych(e), *adj.* splendid, costly, rich, 68, 993, 1036; fair, exquisite, 105, 906; high, noble, glorious, 770, 1097, 1182; precious, 646. [OE. *rīce*, OFr. *riche.*]

ryche3, *n.* wealth, 26. [OFr. *richece.*]

ryf, *adj.* abundant, 770, 844. [Late OE. *rȳfe*, **rīfe.*]

ry3t, *adv.* right, just, even, 298, 461, 673, 885, 1093, 1169; *ry3t no3t*, *(after neg.)* anything at all, 520. [OE. *rihte.*]

ry3t(e), *n.* what is right, 622; what is just, justice, 496, 591, 665; justifiable title, one's right, 580, 703, 708; *by ry3t(e)*, through justification (by grace), 684, 696, 720; justly, 1196. [OE. *riht.*]

ry3te, *adj.* justified, sanctified by divine grace, 672 (note). [OE. *riht.*]

ry3twys, *adj.* righteous, 675, 685, 689, 697, 739. [OE. *rihtwīs.*]

ry3twysly, *adv.* rightly, 709. [OE. *rihtwīslīce.*]

rys(e), *v.* rise, 519, 1093; get up (from bed), 506; grow, 103; *r. vp*, stand up, 191, 437; ros, *pa. t.* 437, 506, 519. [OE. *arīsan.*]

rode, *n.* cross, 646, 705, 806. [OE. *rōd.*]

roghe, *adj.* ungentle, cruel, 646. [OE. *rūh, rūg-.*]

rokke3, *n. pl.* rocks, 68. [OFr. *ro(c)que*; cf. OE. *stān-rocc.*]

ronk, *adj.* abundant, 844; impetuous, 1167. [OE. *ronc.*]

ros. See RYS(E).

rose, *n.* rose, 269, 906. [OE. *rose.*]

rot, *n.* decay, 26. [ON. *rot.*]

rote, *n.* root, 420. [ON. *rót.*]

rote, *v.* decay, 958. [OE. *rotian.*]

rounde, *adj.* round, 5, 657, 738. [OFr. *roônd*, AFr. *round.*]

rourde, *n.* noise, murmur, 112. [OE. *rĕord.*]

route, *n.* company, 926. [OFr. *route.*]

rownande, *pres. p.* whispering, 112. [OE. *rūnian.*]

ruful, *adj.* piteous, 916. [OE. *hrĕow+ful.*]

runne, runnen. See RAN.

sad(d)e, *adj.* grave, dignified, 211, 887. [OE. *sæd.*]

sade. See SAY(E).

saf, saue, *adj.* safe; redeemed, 672, 684, 696, 720. [OFr. *sauf.*]

saffer, *n.* sapphire, 118, 1002. [OFr. *safir.*]

saghe, *n.* utterance, speech, 226; sawe3, *pl.* words, 278. [OE. *sagu.*]

sa3. See SE and (689) SAY(E).

sa3t(e), at peace; *set(t)e s.*, (cf. ON. *setja sátta*), reconcile, propitiate, 52, 1201. [Late OE. *sæht*, from ON. *sáttr*, **saht-.*]

say(e), *v.* say, tell, declare, 226, 391, 482, 1089, &c.; saye, *pres. I sg.* 3; says, say(t)3, *2 sg.* 295, 315, 615, &c.; says, sayt3, *3 sg.* 457, 501, 693, &c.; sa3, 689 (note); sat3, 677; sayd(e), *pa. t. sg.* 289, *433, &c.; sade, 532 (note), 784; sayden, *pl.* 534, 550; sayd, *pp.* 593. [OE. *secgan.*]

saynt, *n.* saint, 457, 818; sant, 788; saynte3, *pl.* the elders in the New Jerusalem (Rev. v. 6), 835. [OFr. *saint.*]

sake, *n.*[1] (criminal) charge, 800.
[OE. *sacu.*]

sake, *n.*[2] in *for mane3 sake*, on
behalf of mankind, 940. [ON.
fyrir sakir.]

sakerfyse, *n.* sacrifice, host, 1064.
[OFr. *sacrifice.*]

same, *adj.* same, 1099, 1101. [ON.
sami.]

samen, *adj.* together, *al samen*, with
one accord, 518. [ON. *saman,
allir saman*; OE. *æt samne.*]

sample, *n.* illustration, parable,
499. [OFr. *ensample.*]

sange. See SONGE.

sant. See SAYNT.

sardonyse, *n.* sardonyx, 1006.
[OFr. *sardonyx.*]

sat3. See SAY(E).

saue, *v.* save from perdition, admit
to eternal bliss, 666, 674. [OFr.
sauver.]

saue, 696. See SAF.

Sauter, *n.* Psalter, 593, 677, 698.
[OFr. *saut(i)er.*]

sauerly, *adj.* sweet, to one's liking,
adequate, 226. [From OFr.
savour.]

sawe3. See SAGHE.

sawle, saule, *n.* soul, *461, 845.
[OE. *sāwol.*]

scale, *n.* surface, 1005. [OFr.
escale.]

schadowed, *pa. t.* cast a shadow,
42. [OE. *scadwian.*]

schafte3, *n.* beams of light, 982.
[OE. *scæft.*]

schal, *pres. 1 sg.* shall, will, must,
328, 569, &c.; *2 sg.* 265, 298, &c.;
3 sg. 332, 348, &c.; schalte, *2 sg.*
564; schulde, *pa. t.* should,
would, ought to, 153, 186, 314,
903, &c.; was about to, 1162.
[OE. *scal*, pa. t. *scolde.*]

scharpe, *adv.* powerfully, 877.
[OE. *scearpe.*]

schede, *v.* sever; fall, be lost, 411;
pa. t. shed, 741. [OE. *scēadan.*]

schene, *adj.* bright, fair, 42, 80,
203, 1145; *as n.* fair (maiden),
166, 965. [OE. *scēne.*]

schente, *pp.* discomfited, 668. [OE.
scéndan.]

schep, *n.* sheep, 801. [OE. *scēp.*]

schere, *v.* cut, 165 (note); schere3,
pres. 3 sg. meanders along, 107
(note); schorne, *pp.* 213. [OE.
sceran. In 107 possibly a different verb; see *NED. sheer*, v.[2],
not there recorded before 1600.]

schewe3, *pres. 3 sg.* shows, 1210;
scheued, *pa. t.* 692. [OE.
scēawian.]

schylde, *v.* prevent, 965. [OE.
scīldan.]

schyldere3, *n. pl.* shoulders, 214.
[OE. (V. P.) *scyldru.*]

schym, *adj.* bright, 1077. [Cf. OE.
scima, n.]

schymeryng, *n.* gleaming, 80.
[From OE. *scimerian.*]

schyne3, *pres. sg.* shines, 1074; *pl.*
28; schon, *pa. t.* 166, 213, 982,
1018, 1057; schynde, *pa. t.* 80.
[OE. *scīnan.*]

schyr(e), *adj.* bright, 28, 42, 213,
284; schyrrer, *compar.* 982.
[OE. *scīr.*]

scho, *n.* she, 758. [OE. *sēo.*]

schon. See SCHYNE3.

schore, *n.* shore, bank, 107, 230;
cliff, 166 (cf. *Sir Gawain* 2161).
[OE. *scora* (Birch CS 381).]

schorne. See SCHERE.

schot, *pa. t.* sprang, rose, 58. [OE.
scēotan, str., *scotian*, wk.]

schowted, *pa. t.* (*impers.*) raised a
loud cry, 877. [Unknown; earliest
known occurrence of *shout.*]

schrylle, *adv.* dazzlingly, 80. [OE.
scrill, variant of *scyl*; cf.
scralletten, to sound shrill.]

schulde. See SCHAL.

sclade. See SLADE.

scrypture, *n.* inscribed letters,
1039. [Lat. *scrīptūra.*]

se, *v.* see, perceive, 96, 296, &c.;
sene in *on to sene* (OE. *tō sēonne*),
to look upon, 45; se, *pres. 1 sg.*
377, &c.; se3, *3 sg.* 302; sa3, *pa.
t. sg.* 836, 1021, 1147; segh(e),
790, 867; se3, 158, 175, 200, 531,

1155; sy3(e), 788, 985, 986, 1032, 1033; sy3(e), *subj. pa. pl.* 308, *698; sen(e), *adj. as pp.* seen, visible, 164, 194, 787, 1143. [OE. *sêon*; *gesêne*, adj.]

sech, *v.* seek, 354; so3te, *pa. t.* 730; so3t, *pp.* found, given, 518. [OE. *sêcan*, pa. t. *sôhte.*]

secounde, *adj.* second, 652, 1002. [OFr. *seco(u)nd.*]

sede, *n.* seed, 34. [OE. *sêd.*]

segh(e), se3. See SE.

seysoun, *n.* time of year, 39. [OFr. *seison.*]

selden, *adv.* seldom, 380. [OE. *seldan.*]

self, *adj.* the same, 203; very, 1076; *þe self God*, God himself, 1046; *as n.* self; *þe hy3e Gode3 self*, high God himself, 1054. [OE. *self.*]

sely, *adj.* blessed, 659. [OE. *sêlig.*]

semb(e)launt, *n.* demeanour, 1143; face, 211. [OFr. *sembla(u)nt.*]

seme, *n.* seam, border; *sette in seme*, attached to the border, 838. [OE. *sêam.*]

seme, *adj.* of seemly demeanour, 1115; *adv.* becomingly, fairly, 190. [ON. *sœmr.*]

semed, *pa. t.* befitted, 760 (note). [ON. *sóma*, infl. by prec.]

semly, *adj.* fair, 34, 45, 789. [ON. *sœmiligr.*]

sen, sene. See SE.

sende, *pres. subj.* send, 130. [OE. *sêndan.*]

sengeley, *adv.* apart, 8. [From OFr. *sengle.*]

serlype3, *adv. as adj.* single, individual, 994. [ON. *sér*, for oneself, separately + OE. *(ān)-lêpes.*]

sermoun, *n.* speech; account, 1185. [OFr. *sermo(u)n.*]

sertayn, *adv.* assuredly, 685. [OFr. *certain.*]

seruaunt, *n.* servant, 699. [OFr. *serva(u)nt.*]

serued, *pp.* deserved, 553. [OFr. *deserver.*]

serue3, *pres. t.* avails, profits, 331. [OFr. *servir.*]

sesed, *pp.* in *s. in*, made possessor of, 417. [OFr. *seisir.*]

set(e), *pa. t.* sat, 161, 835, 1054. [OE. *sittan.*]

sete, *v.* set; cause to be, 1201; setten, *pres. pl.* 307; set, *imper. sg.* place, arrange, 545; set(te), *pa. t.* esteemed, valued, 8, 811 (see VAYN); caused to be, 52 (see SA3TE); set(te), *pp.* set, fixed, 222, 838; built, 1062. [OE. *settan.*]

seuen, *num.* seven, 838, 1111. [OE. *seofan.*]

seuenþe, *adj.* seventh, 1010. [OE. *seofoþa*, infl. by prec.]

sexte, *adj.* sixth, 1007. [OE. *sexta.*]

syde, *n.* side, 6, 1137; slope, 73; bank (of river), 975; *at syde3*, at the (slashed) sides (of garment), 198, 218. [OE. *stde.*]

sy3, sy3e. See SE.

sy3t, *n.* (marvellous) sight, 226, 839, 1151, 1179; glimpse, view, 968; vision, 952; *sy3 wyth sy3t*, beheld, 985. [OE. *sihþ, gesiht.*]

sykyng, *pres. p.* sighing, 1175. [OE. *stcan.*]

syluer, *n.* silver, 77. [OE. *silfor.*]

sympelnesse, *n.* simplicity, 909 (note). [Next + OE. *-nes.*]

symple, *adj.* free from pride, meek, 1134. [OFr. *simple.*]

syn. See SYþEN.

synge, *v.* sing, 891; songe(n), *pa. t. pl.* 94, 882, 888, 1124. [OE. *singan.*]

synglere, *adj.* unique; *in s.*, as unique, *8. [OFr. *sengler.*]

synglerty, *n.* uniqueness, 429. [OFr. *sengl(i)erté.*]

syngnette3, *n. pl.* seals, 838. [OFr. *signet.*]

synne, *n.* sin, 610, 726, 811, 823. [OE. *synn.*]

synne3, *pres. sg.* sins, 662. [From prec.]

sir, *n.* sir, 257, 439. [OFr. *sire.*]

syt, *n.* grief, 663. [ON. **sȳt.*]

sytole-stryng, *n.* string of the citole, 91. [OFr. *citole*+OE. *streng.*]

syþeȝ, *n. pl.* times, 1079. [OE. *sīþ.*]

syþen, *adv.* afterwards, 643, 1207; *conj.* since, 13, 245; syn, 519. [OE. *siþþan.*]

skyfte, *v.* apportion, arrange, 569. [ON. *skifta.*]

skyl(le), *n.* reason, judgement, 312, 674; reasoning, argument, 54. [ON. *skil.*]

slade, sclade, *n.* valley, 141, 1148. [OE. *slæd.*]

slaȝt, *n.* slaughter, 801. [OE. *slæht.*]

slayn, *pp.* put to death, 805. [OE. *slēan*, pp. *slægen.*]

slake, *v.* abate, cease; *don to slake,* brought to an end, 942. [OE. *slacian.*]

slente, *n.* slope, 141. [ON. **slent.*]

slepe, *v.* sleep, 115. [OE. *slēpan.*]

slepyng-slaȝte, *n.* a sudden onset of sleep, 59 (note). [From prec. +OE. *slæht.*]

slyde, *v.* glide; *on slydeȝ,* slides on (the trees), 77 (note); slode, *pa. t.* slipped, fell, 59. [OE. *slīdan.*]

slyȝt, *adj.* slender, 190. [ON. *slḗttr,* older **sleht-.*]

slode. See SLYDE.

smal(e), *adj.* slender, fine, 6 (note), 190; small, 90. [OE. *smæl.*]

smelle, *n.* smell, scent, 1122. [See NED.]

smoþe, *adj.* smooth, 6, (of skin), 190. [OE. *smōþ.*]

so, *adv.* so, thus, in this way, 22, 97, 338, 1186, &c.; then, 1187; to such an extent, so, 5, 6, 1144, &c.; such a, 72, 95, 1081; even so, so too, (following *as*), 166, 803, 948; *intens.* 2, 74, 190, 1183, &c.; *so ... þat,* 102, 618; (without *þat*), 5, 6, 97; *so ... as,* so (such) *. . . as,* 19, 95, 1081; *with indef. pron.* 566. [OE. *swā.*]

sobre, *adj.* serious, earnest, 391, 532; soberly, *adv.* gravely, 256. [OFr. *sobre.*]

sodanly, sodenly, *adv.* suddenly, 1095, 1098, 1178. [From OFr. *sodain.*]

soffer. See SUFFER.

soȝt, soȝte. See SECH.

solace, *n.* pleasure, 130. [OFr. *solas.*]

solde, *pa. t.* sold, 731. [OE. *sellan.*]

sommoun. See SUMOUN.

sonde, *n.* sending, 943. [OE. *sónd.*]

sone, *adv.* straightway, quickly, 537, 1078, 1197; *as sone as,* as soon as, 626. [OE. *sōna.*]

songe, sange, *n.* song, 19, 882, 888, 891. [OE. *sáng, sóng.*]

sonne. See SUNNE.

sor(e), *n.* pain, sorrow, 130, 940. [OE. *sār.*]

sore, *adv.* toilsomely, hard, 550. [OE. *sáre.*]

sorȝ(e), *n.* grief, 352; contrition, 663. [OE. *sorg.*]

sorquydryȝe, *n.* pride, 309. [OFr. *surcuiderie.*]

soth, *adj.* true, 482, 1185; soþe, *n.* truth, 653; *for soþe* (OE. *for sōþ*), indeed, 21, 292. [OE. *sōþ.*]

sothfol, *adj.* truthful, 498. [OE. *sōþ*+*-full.*]

sotyle, *adj.* of fine texture, transparent, 1050. [OFr. *sotil.*]

soun, *n.* voice, 532. [OFr. *so(u)n.*]

sounande, *pres. p.* sonorous, 883. [OFr. *so(u)ner.*]

space, *n.* extent, 1030; *in space,* after a time, 61 (note); *in þat space,* at that time, then, 438. [OFr. *(e)space.*]

spakk. See SPEKE.

sparred, *pa. t.* rushed, 1169.

spece. See SPYCE.

spech(e), *n.* discourse, words, 400, 471, 793, 1132; pronouncement, 704; *in s. expoun,* describe, 37; *profered me s.,* addressed words to me, 235. [OE. *sp(r)ēc.*]

special, specyal, *adj.* excellent, precious, 235, 938. [OFr. *special.*]

spede, *v.* bless, prosper, 487. [OE. *spēdan.*]

speke, *v.* speak, say, declare, 422, 594; *pa. t.* 438, **spakk**, 938; spoken, *pp.* 291. [OE. *sp(r)ecan.*]

spelle, *n.* discourse, what is said, 363. [OE. *spell.*]

spelle, *v.* discourse, tell, 793. [OE. *spellian.*]

spenned, *pa. t.* clasped, *49; imprisoned, 53. [ON. *spenna.*]

spent, *pp.* expended; *of speche spent*, words spoken of, described, 1132. [OE. *spendan.*]

spyce, spyse, spece, *n.* creature, person, *235, 938; spice-bearing plant, 25, 35, 104. [OFr. (*e*)*spice*, (*e*)*spece.*]

spyryt, *n.* spirit, 61. [OFr. (*e*)*spirit.*]

spyt, *n.* evil deed, outrage, 1138. [Shortened from OFr. *despit.*]

sponne, *pa. subj. pl.* would spring up, 35. [OE. *spinnan.*]

spornande, *pres. p.* stumbling, 363. [OE. *spórnan.*]

spot(e), spotte, *n.* spot, blemish (physical or moral), 12, 24, 36, 48, 60, 764, 945, 1068; place, 13, 25, 37, 49; *fro spot*, from that place, 61. [Cf. MDu. *spot(te).*]

spotleȝ, *adj.* spotless; pure in colour, 856. [Cf. WFlem. *spottelos.*]

spotty, *adj.* spotty, 1070. [From SPOT.]

sprang(e). See SPRYNG.

sprede, *v.* be overspread (with growth), 25. [OE. *sprǣdan.*]

spryng, *v.* be born, 453; grow, flourish, *35; **sprang(e)**, *pa. t.* slipped, fell, 13; ascended, 61. [OE. *springan.*]

stable, *adj.* steadfast, 597. [OFr. (*e*)*stable.*]

stable, *v.* come to a stand, remain, 683. [OFr. *establir.*]

stage, *n.* degree of advancement, 410. [OFr. (*e*)*stage.*]

stayre, *adj.* steep, 1022. [OE. *stǣger.*]

stale, *n.* place in a series, 1002. [OE. *stalu*, or OFr. *estal*; see *NED. stale*, sb.[3] and sb.[4]]

stalked, *pa. t.* walked fearfully, 152. [OE. *stalcian.*]

stalle, *v.* bring to a stand, stop, 188. [OFr. *estaller*; cf. OE. *forþstallian.*]

stande, stonde, *v.* stand, 113, 514, 515, 533, 547, 867 (*reflex.*); **stod(e)**, *pa. t.* 182, 184, 740, 1023, 1085; remained, 597; **standen**, *pp.* 519, 1148. [OE. *stándan, stóndan.*]

stare, *v.* stare, 149; shine, 116 (note). [OE. *starian.*]

start, *v.* rush, plunge, 1159, 1162. [OE. *stertan (WS. *styrtan*).]

stele, *v.* steal, come softly, 20. [OE. *stelan.*]

step, *n.* footstep, 683. [OE. *stepe.*]

stepe, *adj.* bright, 113 (note). [OE. *stēap.*]

stere, *v.* govern, rule (one's fate), 623; restrain from, 1159 (note). [OE. *stēoran.*]

sterneȝ, *n. pl.* stars, 115. [ON. *stjarna.*]

steuen, *n.*[1] sound (of singing), 1125. [OE. *stefn*, f.]

steuen, *n.*[2] meeting; *at steuen*, for a meeting, 188. [OE. *stefn*, m.; ON. *stefna.*]

styf, *adj.* bold, 779. [OE. *stif.*]

stykeȝ, *pres. 2 sg.* are set, 1186. [OE. *stician.*]

stylle, *adj. and adv.* quiet, 20; still, motionless and silent, 182, 1085; at rest, 683. [OE. *stille.*]

stynt, *imper.* in *stynt of*, cease, *353. [OE. *styntan.*]

stok, *n.* tree-trunk, tree; *by stok oþer ston*, in any place, ever, 380. [OE. *stocc.*]

stoken, *pp.* shut, 1065. [OE. **stecan.*]

ston, *n.* stone, 380, 822; precious stone, gem, 113, 206, 994, 997, 1006. [OE. *stān.*]

stonde. See STANDE.

stonge, *pa. t. sg.* affected (with emotion) 179 (note). [OE. *stingan.*]

store, *n.* supply; body of persons, 847. [OFr. *(e)store.*]

stote, *v.* halt, stop, 149. [Uncertain.]

stounde, *n.* hour, time, 20, 659. [OE. *stúnd.*]

stout(e), *adj.* valiant, 779; stately, splendid, 935. [OFr. *(e)stout.*]

stray, *adv.* in bewilderment, 179. [Shortened from ASTRAYE.]

strayd, *pa. t.* slipped away, was lost, 1173. [OFr. *(e)straier.*]

strayn, streny, *v.* strain, stir, 128; make go, 691; *reflex.* exert oneself, 551. [OFr. *estreign-,* stem of *estreindre.*]

strange, *adj.* surprising, 175. [OFr. *(e)strange.*]

strateȝ. See STRETE.

strech(e), *v.* make one's way, 971; *on streche,* rest upon, 843. [OE. *streccan.*]

streȝt, *adj.* straight, 691. [*pp.* of prec.]

strem, *n.* stream, 125, 1159, 1162. [OE. *stréam.*]

stremande, *pres. p.* streaming (with light), 115. [From prec.]

strenghþe, *n.* power, intensity, 128. [OE. *strengþu.*]

stresse, *n.* affliction, sorrow, 124. [OFr. *destresse.*]

strete, *n.* street, 971, 1059; **streteȝ,** *pl.* 1025; **strateȝ,** 1043 (note). [OE. *strēt.*]

stryf, *n.* strife, contention, 248, 776, 848. [OFr. *(e)strif.*]

stryke, *v.* strike; *intrans.* pass, 1125; *þat strykeȝ,* who comes (for reward), 570; *trans.* **strok,** *pa. t.* struck, 1180. [OE. *strícan.*]

stryuen, *pres. pl.* strive; *s. agayn,* oppose, 1199. [OFr. *(e)striver.*]

strok. See STRYKE.

stronde, *n.* shore, 152. [OE. *strónd.*]

stronge, *adj.* strong, 531; steadfast, 476. [OE. *stróng.*]

strot, *n.* wrangling, 353, 848. [Cf. Norw. *strutt,* obstinate resistance.]

stroþe-men, *n. pl.* ? men of this earth, 115 (note).

such(e), *adj. and pron.* such, so great, 26, 58, 407, 719, 727; *suche . . . as,* such . . . as, 171; *such . . . þat,* such . . . as, 1099; (with *þat* omitted) so great a . . . (that), 1043. [OE. *swylc.*]

sve, swe, *v.* follow, 892, 976. [OFr. *suir,* AFr. *siwer.*]

suffer, soffer, *v.* endure, suffer, 554, 940, 954 (*intr.*). [OFr. *soffrir, suffrir.*]

suffyse, *v.* suffice; *s. to,* be adequate for, 135. [OFr. *suffire, suffis-.*]

sulpande, *pres. p.* polluting, 726. [Cf. North. dialect *sowp* 'drench'; Norw. dial. *sulpa,* splash; German dial. *sölpern,* soil.]

sum, summe, *adj. and pron.* some, 428, 508; *of al and sum,* in general and particular, in full, 584. [OE. *sum.*]

sumkyn, *adj.* some kind of, some, 619. [OE. *sumes cynnes.*]

sumoun, sommoun, *n.* summons, 1098; *mad sumoun,* gave summons, 539. [From OFr. *somo(u)n-,* stem of *somondre,* v.]

sumtyme, *adv.* at some time, 620; at one time, 760. [OE. **sume tíman;* cf. *sum tíma* in B.T. Supp.]

sunne, sonne, *n.* sun, 28, 519, 530, 982, &c. [OE. *sunne.*]

sunnebemeȝ, *n. pl.* sunbeams, 83. [OE. *sunnebéam.*]

supplantoreȝ, *n. pl.* usurpers, 440. [OFr. *supplant(e)or.*]

sure, *adj.* firm, certain, 1089; *adv.* securely, 222. [OFr. *s(e)ur.*]

sute, *n.* suit; *of self s., in s.,* of the same colour (and material), to match, 203, 1108. [OFr. *s(e)ute.*]

swalt, *pa. t.* died, 816; **swalte,** *pa. subj.* 1160. [OE. *sweltan.*]

swange, *pa. t.* rushed, 1059. [OE. *swingan.*]

swange, *pa. t.* toiled, 586. [OE. *swingan* or *swincan.*]

swangeande, *pres. p.* swirling, 111.

[Cf. OE. *swangettung*, swirling, tossing.]

sware, *n.* square, 1029 (note); *adj.* square, 837, 1023. [OFr. *(e)square*, n.; *(e)squarré*, adj.]

sware, *v.* answer, 240. [ON. *svara*.]

swat, *pa. t.* sweated, laboured, 586. [OE. *swǣtan*.]

swe. See SVE.

swefte. See SWYFT.

sweng, *n.* labour, 575. [OE. *sweng*.]

swepe, *v. intr.* sweep by, 111. [Obscurely rel. to *swoop* (OE. *swāpan*), or lost OE. *swēpan, rel. to ON. *sópa*.]

swete, *adj.* pleasing, lovely, 19; fragrant, 1122; harmonious, 94; beloved, 763, 829; *as n.* fair maiden, 240, 325; *adv.* pleasantly, 111, 1057. [OE. *swēte*.]

swetely, *adv.* graciously, 717. [OE. *swētlice*.]

sweuen, *n.* sleep (*or* dream), 62. [OE. *swefen*.]

swyft, *adj.* swift, 571; **swefte,** *adv.* quickly, 354. [OE. *swift*.]

swymme, *v.* swim, 1160. [OE. *swimman*.]

swyþe, *adv.* swiftly, 354, 1059. [OE. *swīþe*.]

swone, *n.* in *in swone*, into a swoon, 1180. [Mistaken analysis of ME. *iswowen*, OE. *geswōgen*, pp.]

tabelment, *n.* tier of foundation structure, 994. [OFr. *tablement*.]

table, *n.* tier of foundation structure, 1004. [OFr. *table*.]

tached, *pp.* attached; *fig.* implanted, 464. [OFr. *atach(i)er*.]

take, *v.* take, 559, 1067; adopt, 944; receive, 539, 552, 599; take (notice), 387; *take in vayne*, use foolishly, spend in folly, 687 (note); *take me halte*, stop my advance, 1158 (note); **tot3,** *pres. 3 sg.* goes, 513 (note); **toke,** *pa. t.* received, took, 414, 585; *toke on hymself*, took the burden of,

808; **taken, tan,** *pp.* received, 614; *taken for*, recognized as, 830. [ON. *taka*.]

tale, *n.* account, statement, words, 257, 311, 590, 865, 897; enumeration, 998. [OE. *talu*.]

tan. See TAKE.

tech, *v.* direct, 936. [OE. *tǣcan*.]

teche, *n.* stain, guilt, 845. [OFr. *teche*.]

telle, *v.* tell, speak, 653; tell of, express, 134; *t. of*, speak of, 919; **tolde,** *pa. t.* uttered, 815. [OE. *tellan*.]

temen, *pres. pl.* are joined (to), belong, 460. [OE. *tēman*, appeal.]

temple, *n.* temple, 1062. [OFr. *temple*.]

tempte, *v.* test presumptuously, 903. [OFr. *tempter*.]

tender, *adj.* tender, 412. [OFr. *tendre*.]

tene3, *n. pl.* pain, bitterness, 332. [OE. *tēona*.]

tenoun, *n.* tenon, joining; *of riche tenoun*, admirably joined (? *or* having elaborately adorned tenons), 993. [OFr. *teno(u)n*.]

tente, *n.* notice; *tente on*, notice of, 387. [OFr. *atente*.]

tenþe, *adj.* tenth, 136, 1013. [OE. *tēn*+ordinal *-þa*.]

terme, *n.* appointed period, 503; *in terme3*, in express words, plainly, 1053. [OFr. *terme*.]

that, the. See ÞAT, ÞE.

theme, *n.* subject; *take in t.*, give an account of, 944. [OFr. *tesme* (*es = ē*), theme.]

then(ne), this, thow. See Þ-.

throne. See TRONE.

ty3ed, *pp.* fastened, fixed, set, 464; **ty3t,** 1013 (note). [OE. *tēgan*.]

ty3t, *v.* come, 718; **ty3te,** *pa. t.* set forth, 1053; **ty3t,** *pp.* come, arrived, 503. [OE. *tyhtan*, infl. by *dihtan*.]

tyl(le), *prep.* to, 676; *tyl ... þat*, until, 548, 979; (without *þat*), 976. [ON. *til*; OE. (rare North.) *til*.]

tyme, *n.* time, period, 503; occasion, 833. [OE. *tíma*.]

tynde, *n.* branch, 78. [OE. *tind*.]

tyne, *v.* lose, 332. [ON. *týna*.]

tyt, *adv.* quickly, 728. [ON. *titt*.] See AS-TYT.

to, *prep.* to, 107, 319, &c.; (in)to, 10, 26, 32, &c.; to, towards, 468, 630; for, 507, 508, 638, 719, &c.; as, to be, 272, 759; *with infin.* 22, 45, &c.; *for to*, 99, 333, &c.; *in 'split' infin.* 2; *adv.* in *to ne fro*, in any direction, 347; *þat . . . to*, to which, 957. [OE. *tō*.]

to, *adv.* too, 481, 492, 615, 1070, 1075, 1076, 1118. [OE. *tō*, orig. same as prec.]

todraweȝ, *pres. 2 sg.* dispel, 280. [OE. *tō-+dragan*.]

togeder, *adv.* together, 1121. [OE. *tē gædere*.]

to-ȝere, *adv.* this year; for a long time, 588. [OE. *tō gēre*.]

toȝt, *adj.* firm; *made hit toȝt*, made a compact of it, 522. [OE. **toht* 'drawn tight', related to *tēon*.]

toke. See TAKE.

token, *n.* sign; *in token of*, as a symbol of, 742. [OE. *tācn*.]

tom, *n.* leisure, 134; *toke more tom*, spent a longer time, 585. [ON. *tóm*.]

tong(e), *n.* tongue, 100, 225, 898. [OE. *túnge*.]

topasye, *n.* topaz, 1012. [OFr. *topase*, infl. by late Lat. *topazius*.]

tor, *adj.* difficult, 1109. [ON. *tor-*.]

tor, *n.* tower; stronghold, castle, 966. [OE. *tūr*, OFr. *tur*.]

torente, *pp.* cruelly torn, 1136. [OE. *torendan*.]

toriuen, *pp.* torn asunder; shattered, 1197. [OE. *to-+ON. rífa*.]

torreȝ, *n. pl.* hills, 875 (note). [OE. *torr*, from Celtic.]

totȝ. See TAKE.

touch, *v.* lay hand on, 714; towched, *pa. t.* came near to, 898. [OFr. *toucher*.]

toun, *n.* walled city, 995. [OE. *tūn*.]

towarde, *prep.* towards, 67, 974, 1113; *me towarde*, to me, 438; *to hym warde*, to him, 820. [OE. *tōweard*, *tō him weard*.]

towen, *pp.* drawn; *towen in twynne*, severed, sundered, 251. [OE. *tēon*, pp. *togen*.]

tras, *n.* course, way; *trone a tras*, made (their) way, proceeded, 1113. [OFr. *trace*.]

trauayle, *n.* toil, 1087 (note). [OFr. *travail*.]

trauayled, *pa. t.* toiled, 550. [OFr. *travailler*.]

traw, *v.* believe, think, 282, 295, 487; trowe, 933. [OE. *trēowian*, *trūwian*.]

trawþe, *n.* justice, 495. [OE. *trēowþ*.]

trendeled, *pa. t.* rolled, 41. [OE. in *a-trendlian*.]

tres, *n. pl.* trees, 1077. [OE. *trēo*.]

tresor(e), *n.* treasure, 331; *of grete tresor*, of great price, 237. [OFr. *tresor*.]

tryȝe, *v.* test; *to tryȝe*, when put to the proof, 311; tryed, *pp.* brought to trial, 702, 707. [OFr. *trier*.]

trylle, *v.* quiver, 78. [Cf. MDu. *trillen*, vibrate.]

tryste, *adj.* trusty; *as adv.* faithfully, *460. [Cf. ON. *treystr*, pp. and see *NED.*, s.v. *Trist*, adj.[1]]

trone, *n.* throne, 835, 920, 1051, 1055; throne, 1113. [OFr. *trone*, Lat. *thrōnus*.]

trone, *pa. t.* went, marched, 1113. [OEN. **trína*; cf. OSwed. *trína*, ODan. *trene*.]

trw(e), true, *adj.* faithful, 725; trusty, steadfast, 822, 1191; true, accurate, 311, 421, 831; trwe, *adv.* steadfastly, 460. [OE. *trēowe*.]

twayned, *pp.* parted, 251. [From OE. *twēgen*, two.]

twelfþe, *adj.* twelfth, 1015. [OE. *twelfta* with altered suffix.]

twelue, *adj.* twelve, 992, 1022, 1078, &c. [OE. *twelfe*.]

twyeȝ, *adv.* twice, 830. [OE. *twiga* +adverbial *-es.*]

twynne, *adj.* in *in twynne*, asunder, apart, 251. [OE. *twinn.*]

twynne-hew, *adj.* of two colours, *1012. [OE. *twinn*+*-hēowe*; cf. OE. *twihēowe.*]

two, *adj.* two, 483, 555, 674, 949. [OE. *twā.*]

þaȝ, *conj. with subj.* though, if, even if, 52, 134, 368, &c. [OE. *þē(a)h*, unaccented *þah*, *þæh.*]

þay, *pron. pl.* they, 80, 94, 509, &c. [ON. *þeir.*]

þare, þore, *adv.* there, 562, *830, 1021. [OE. *þǎra.*]

þat, *conj.* that, 185, 393, 1188, &c.; so that (*effect*), 119, 356; (after *so*), 35, 102, 619; in order that, 544; *pleonastic with other conjs. or interrogs.* (q.v.), 334, 548, 958, 979. [OE. *þæt, þætte.*]

þat, *adj.* that, the, 12, 195, 253, &c.; *as def. art.* 953, 955; *pron.* that, 17, 536, 783, 965, &c. [OE. *þæt*, neut.]

þat, *rel. pron.* that, which, who, 15, 37, 631, *856, *892, &c.; that which, what, 327, 521, 559, 658. [OE. *þæt, þætte.*]

þe, the, *def. art.* the, 28, 69, 85, 109, &c.; *with a part of the body*, 67. [Late OE. *þe* (for *se*).]

þe, the, *adv. with compar.* the, so much (the), 152, 169, &c.; for that, any, 852, 864; *correl.* in *þe ... þe*, the ... the, 127–8, 600, 850, &c. [OE. *þȳ, þē.*]

þe. See þou.

þede, *n.* land, 483. [OE. *þēod.*]

þef, *n.* thief, 273. [OE. *þēof.*]

þen, þenne, then(ne), *adv.* then, next, in that case, 155, 277, 326, 361, 589, 599, &c. [OE. *þænne.*]

þen(n), *adv.* than, 134, 555, &c. [OE. *þanne, þon.*]

þenne, in *er þenne*. See ER.

þenk(e), *v.* think of, be mindful of, 22; intend to, resolve to, 1151;

þenkande vpon, mindful of, 370; þoȝt, *pa. t.* thought, believed, 137, 1138, 1157. [OE. *þencan.*]

þer(e), *adv.* there, in that place, 21 (*or indef.*), 28, 167, &c.; *indef.* (when subject follows verb), 113, 161, &c.; *rel.* where, 26, 30, 835, &c.; *þer as*, where, 818, 1173; wherever, 129; *combined with advs.*, þerate, there, 514; þerfore, because of that, 1197; þerinne, þere-ine, in(to) that place, 447, 633, 724, &c.; in that action, 1168; þerof, of it, 99, &c.; from it, 1069; þeron, on it, 1042; after that, 645; of it, 387; þeroute, out of doors, 930; þerto, to it, for that, 664, 833, 1140; thither, 172 (note). [OE. *þēr, þær.*]

þese. See þys.

þike, *adv.* thickly, 78. [OE. *þicce*, adj.]

þynk, *pres. impers.* seem; *me* (or *vus*) *þynk*, I (we) think, 267, 316, 552, 553, 590; þoȝt, *pa. t.* in *þoȝt me*, I thought, 19; *me þoȝt*, 153. [OE. *þyncan*, pa. t. *þūhte*.]

þyder, *adv.* thither, 723, 946. [OE. *þider.*]

þyng(e), *n.* thing, matter, 771, 910. [OE. *þing.*]

þis, þys, þise, this, thys, *adj.* this, 65, 250, 533, 733, 841, &c.; *pron.* 421; þysse, *dat sg. stressed*, 370; þis(e), þys(e), þese, *pl.* these, the, 42, 287, 505 (note); *pron.* 384, 551, 555. [OE. *þis*, neut.]

þo, *adj. pl.* the, those, 73, 109, &c.; *pron.* in *on of þo*, one of them, 557; *þo fyue*, five of them, 451. [OE. *þā.*]

þoȝ, *conj.* though, 345. [ON. *þóh.*]

þoȝt. See þENKE, þYNK.

þoȝte, *n.* intention, 524. [OE. *þōht.*]

þole, *v.* endure, 344. [OE. *þolian.*]

þonc, *n.* thanks, 901. [OE. *þonc.*]

þoo, *adv.* then, 873. [OE. *þā.*]

þore. See þARE.

Glossary

þose, adj. pl. those, 93, 127; þos, pron. dat. them, 515. [OE. þās.]

þou, þow, thow, pron. thou, 23, 337, 411, &c.; þe, accus. and dat. 244, &c.; þy(n), poss. adj. thy, 266, 559; þyself, nom. 298, 313, 779; reflex. 473; þyseluen, reflex. 341. [OE. þū, þē, þīn.]

þowsande, þousande, n. thousand; sg. after num. (orig. pl.), 786, 869, 870; pl. 926, 1107. [OE. þūsend, pl. -u.]

þrange, adj. as adv. oppressively, grievously, 17. [ON. þrǫngr.]

þre, adj. three, 291, 292, 1034. [OE. þrēo.]

þrete, v. wrangle, 561. [ON. þræta.]

þrych, v. thrust; oppress, afflict, 17; þryȝt, pp. in a throng, 926; pierced, 706; brought, 670. [OE. þryccan.]

þryd(e), þrydde, adj. third, 299, 833, 1004. [OE. þridda.]

þryf, v. thrive, 851. [ON. þrífask.]

þryȝt. See þRYCH.

þryuen, adj. fair, 868, 1192. [ON. þrífinn, pp.]

þro, adj.¹ stubborn, 344. [ON. þrár.]

þro, adj.² in phrase þryuen and þro, fair and noble, 868. [? Prec. infl. by ON. þróask, thrive.]

þroweȝ, pres. sg. rolls, 875. [OE. þrāwan.]

þunder, n. thunder, 875. [OE. þunor.]

þurȝ, prep. through, 10, 323, 706, 1049, &c.; by means of, by, in, 413, 640, 670, 730, &c. [OE. þurh.]

þurȝoutly, adv. completely, 859. [OE. þurhūt+-līce.]

þus, adv. thus, 526, 829, &c. [OE. þus.]

vayl, v. prevail, 912. [OFr. valeir.]

vayn(e), adj. in in vayn(e), to no purpose, foolishly, 687 (see TAKE); at nought, 811 (see SETE). [OFr. vein; en vein, Lat. in vanum, in vano.]

vayned. See WAYNE.

valeȝ, n. pl. vales, 127. [OFr. val.]

vch(e), adj. each, every, 5, 31, 603, &c.; vch(e) a, every, 78, 117, &c.; vchon, pron. each one, every one, 450, 863, &c. [OE. ylc.]

veray, ueray, adj. true, 1184, 1185. [OFr. verai.]

verce, n. verse, 593. [OFr. vers.]

vere, v. turn; v. vp, raise, 177, 254. [OFr. ver-, stem of pres. sg. of vertir.]

vergyn, vyrgyn, n. virgin, 1099; as adj. 426. [OFr. virgine, v(i)ergine.]

vergynté, n. virginity, 767. [OFr. virginité.]

Vertues, n. pl. Virtues, 1126. [OFr. vertu.]

uesture, n. raiment, 220. [OFr. vesture.]

veued. See WEUE.

vyf, vyueȝ. See WYF.

vygour, n. power, 971. [OFr. vigour.]

vyne, uyne, n. vineyard, 502, 504, 521, 582, 628, &c. [OFr. vigne.]

vyrgyn. See VERGYN.

vys(e), n. face, 254, 750. [OFr. vis.]

vysayge, n. countenance, 178. [OFr. visage.]

vmbegon, pp. lying around, encompassing, 210. [ME. umbe (see NED.)+GON; cf. OE. ymbegān.]

vmbepyȝte, pp. arrayed round about, adorned, 1052. [ME. umbe+pp. of PYȜT.]

vnavysed, adj. thoughtless, rash, 292. [OE. un-+OFr. avisé.]

vnblemyst, adj. unstained, 782. [OE. un-+OFr. blemir, blemiss-.]

vncortayse, adj. discourteous, *303. [OE. un-+CORTAYSE.]

vndefylde, adj. undefiled, 725. [OE. un-+a blend of OFr. defouler with OE. fȳlan.]

vnder, n. the third hour (about 9 o'clock), 513. [OE. undern.]

vnder, *prep.* under, 923. [OE. *under.*]

vnderstonde, *v.* understand; in *to v.*, that is to say, to wit, 941. [OE. *understondan.*]

vnhyde, *v.* reveal, 973. [OE. *on-+hȳdan.*]

vnlapped, *adj.* unbound, 214. [OE. *on-+-læpped.*]

vnmete, *adj.* unfit, unworthy, 759. [OE. *unmēte,* immoderate.]

vnpynne, *v.* unbolt, open, 728. [From OE. *pinn,* n.; cf. *onpennian,* open.]

vnresounable, *adj.* unreasonable. 590. [OE. *un-+*AFr. *resonable.*]

vnstrayned, *adj.* untroubled, 248. [OE. *un-+*pp. of STRAYN.]

vnto, *prep.* to, 362, 712, 718, 1169; for, 1212; as, 772. [OE. **untō;* cf. OSax. *untō.*]

vntrwe, *adj.* false, untrue, 897. [OE. *untrēowe.*]

uoched, *pp.* summoned, 1121. [OFr. *voch(i)er.*]

vp, *adv.* up, 35, 177, &c. [OE. *up(p).*]

vpon(e), *prep.* (*equivalent of* ON), on, upon, 57, 370, 824 (see WORCHEN), 1054, &c.; in, 545; into, 59; to, 1196; *adv.* on it, 208. [OE. *upp on.*]

vpen, vpon (198). See OPEN.

vrþe, *n.* earth, 442, 893, 1125; **erþe,** 840. [OE. *eorþe.*]

vrþely, *adj.* earthly, 135. [OE. *eorþlic.*]

vtwyth, *adv.* from outside, 969. [OE. *ūt+wiþ.*]

vus. See WE.

wace. See WATȜ.

wade, *v.* wade, 143, 1151. [OE. *wadan.*]

wage, *v.* guarantee; pay (hire); *intr. or absol.* continue securely *or* bring reward, 416. [ONFr. *wager.*]

way, *n.* path, course, 350, 691; *by þe way of,* in accordance with, 580. [OE. *weg.*]

way, *adv.* away, 718. (See DO). [From AWAY.]

wayneȝ, *pres. sg.* sends, 131; **vayned,** *pp.* 249. [OE. *(be)wægnan.*]

wayted, *pa. t.* watched, looked for, 14. [ONFr. *wait(i)er.*]

wakned, *pa. t.* woke up, 1171. [OE. *wæcn(i)an.*]

wal, *n.* wall, 1017, 1026. [OE. *wall.*]

wale, *v.* choose; pick out, perceive, 1000, 1007. [ON. *velja,* pa. t. *valði.*]

walk, *v.* walk, wander, 399; **welke,** *pa. t.,* 101, 711 (*reflex.*). [OE. *walcan.*]

wallande, *pres. p.* welling, gushing, 365. [OE. *wallan.*]

walte, *pp.* cast, set, 1156. [OE. *wæltan.*]

wan. See WYNNE, *v.*

waning, *n.* curtailment, 558 (see ȜETE, *v.*). [OE. *wanung.*]

war, *adj.* aware; *watȝ war of,* perceived, 1096. [OE. *wær.*]

ware. See WATȜ.

warde, *adv.* in *to hym warde,* towards him, 820; *fro me warde,* from me, 981. [OE. *weard.*]

warpe, *v.* cast; utter, 879. [WMid. development of OE. *weorpan,* pp. *worpen.*]

wascheȝ, *pres. sg.* washes (away), 655; **wesch,** *pa. t.* 766. [OE. *wascan.*]

wasse, wate. See WATȜ, WOT.

water, *n.* water, 111, 653, &c.; stream, 107, 230 (*dat.*), 299, &c. [OE. *wæter.*]

watȝ, *pa. t. sg.* was, 45, 372, 1088, &c.; **wace,** 65; **wer(n), were, ware, wore,** *pl.* were, 68, 71, 151, 154, 1027, 1107, &c.; **wasse,** 1108, 1112 (both in rhyme); **wer(e), wore,** *pa. subj. sg.* would (should) be, 142, 288, 972, &c.; was, 232, 1167, &c.; *were I,* if I were, 287; **wore, wern,** *pa. subj. pl.* were, 451, 574. [OE. *wæs;* pl. *wēron, wæron, wāron.*]

wawe3, *n. pl.* waves, 287. [ON. *vág-r*.]

wax. See WEX.

we, *pron.* we, 251, 378, &c.; **oure,** *poss. adj.* our, 304, &c.; **vus,** *acc. and dat.* (to) **us,** 552, 651, &c. [OE. *wē, ūre, ūs*.]

webbe3, *n. pl.* (woven) fabrics, 71. [OE. *webb*.]

wedde, *v.* wed, 772. [OE. *weddian*.]

weddyng, *n.* marriage, 791. [OE. *weddung*.]

wede, *n.* clothing; raiment, 748, 766; *pl.* garments, raiment, 1102, 1112, 1133. [OE. *wēd, gewēde*.]

weete. See WETE.

wel, *adv.* well, fully, without doubt, clearly, 164, 302, 411, 505, 673; very, quite, 537; much, still, 145, 148; *predic.* in *wel wat3 me,* fortunate was I, 239; *wel is me,* I am happy, 1187. [OE. *wel*.]

welcum, *adj.* welcome, 399. [OE. *wilcum,* n.; ON. *velkominn*.]

wele, *n.* precious thing, 14; joy, delight, 133, 154; prosperity, happiness, 394; *in wele and wo,* in prosperity and in adversity, always, 342. [OE. *wela*.]

wely, *adj.* blissful, 101. [OE. *welig*.]

welke. See WALK.

welkyn, *n.* the heavens, 116. [OE. *wolcen, welcn,* cloud.]

welle, *n.* spring, fount, 365, 649. [OE. *well(a)*.]

welnygh, welne3, *adv.* almost, 528; *welnygh now,* but a little time ago, 581. [OE. *wel-nēh*.]

wemle3, *adj.* spotless, 737. [From next.]

wemme, *n.* stain; *wythouten w.,* flawless, unblemished, 221, 1003. [OE. *wamm, womm,* infl. by *wemman,* v.]

wende, *v.* go, depart, 643; **went(e),** *pa. t.* 525, 631, 761; *in mynde went,* filled the mind, 1130. [OE. *wendan*.]

wene, *v.* think, suppose; doubt, 1141; *I wot and (I) wene,* I know

full well, in truth, 47, 201; **wende,** *pa. t.* supposed, 1148. [OE. *wēnan*.]

wer, *pa. t.* wore, 205. [OE. *werian,* wk.]

wer(e), wern. See WAT3.

werke, *n.* work, 599. [OE. *werc*.]

werkmen, *n. pl.* labourers, 507. [OE. *wercmann*.]

werle, *n.* ? circlet, circular ornament, 209 (note). [OE. *hwyrfel;* cf. ON. *hvirfill,* MDu. *wervel*.]

wesch. See WASCHE3.

westernays, *adj.* reversed, awry, 307 (note). [OFr. *bestorneis,* infl. by ME. *west*.]

wete, weete, *adj.* wet; rainy, damp, 761; wet (with blood), 1135. [OE. *wēt*.]

weþer. See WHEÞER.

weue, *v.* go, pass, 318; **veued,** *pp.* brought, 976. [OE. *wǣfan,* infl. by ON. *veifa*.]

weuen, *pa. t. pl.* wove, 71. [OE. *wefan*.]

wex, *pa. t.* grew, became, 538, 648; **wax,** came forth, flowed, 649. [OE. *wæxan,* pa. t. *wēox*.]

whal, *n.* whale; *whalle3 bon,* ivory (from walrus), 212. [OE. *hwæl*.]

what, quat, *interrog. adj. and pron.* what, 186, 249, 293, &c.; why, 1072; *indef.* whatever, 523; **quat-so,** what(ever), 566. [OE. *hwæt; swā-hwæt-swā*.]

when, quen, *interrog. and rel. adv.* when, 40, 79, 332, 1162, &c. [OE. *hwænne*.]

where, quere, *interrog. and rel. adv.* where, 65, 68, 376, 617; **quere-so-euer,** wherever, 7. [OE. *hwǣr, hwēr; swā hwēr swā*.]

whete, *n.* wheat, 32. [OE. *hwǣte*.]

wheþer, *adv.* (and) yet, 581, 826. [OE. *hwæþere*.]

wheþer, weþer, *interrog. adv.* (introd. direct question), 565; introd. alternative conditions, *wheþer . . . oþer,* whether . . . or, 130, 604; **queþer-so-euer,** whether, 606. [OE. *hwæþer*.]

4464   M

why, wy, quy, *interrog. adv.* why, 290; 329, 561, &c.; *interj.* why! (incredulous), 769. [OE. *hwɪ̄*]

whyle, *adv.* formerly, 15. [OE. *hwīle.*]

whyt(e), quyt(e), qwyte, *adj.* white, 163, 219, 844, 1011, 1102, &c.; *n.* 842. [OE. *hwīt.*]

who, quo, *interrog. pron.* who, 427, 678, 747, 827, 1138; *indef.* whoever, 709; one who, 693; you who, 344; **wham, quom,** *rel. dat.* ʷvhom, 131, 453. [OE. *hwā.*]

wy. See WHY.

wyde, *adj.* wide, 1135. [OE. *wīd.*]

wyf, vyf, *n.* wife, 772, 846; **vyueȝ,** *pl.* 785. [OE. *wīf.*]

wyȝ, *n.* man, person, 100, 131, 722; **wyȝeȝ,** *pl.* 71, 579. [OE. *wiga.*]

wyȝt(e), *n.* person; maiden, 338, 494. [OE. *wiht.*]

wyȝte, *adj.* valiant, 694. [ON. *vigt,* neut. adj.]

wyl, *conj.* until, 528. [From OE. *hwīl,* in *þā hwīle þe.*]

wyl, *pres. 1 and 3 sg.* will, wish (to), 443; intend to, 558; *merging into auxil. of future,* 350, 965; *2 sg. subj.* wish, 794; **wolde,** *pa. t.* wished (to), would (wish), 304, 390, 391, 977, 1155, &c. [OE. *wil(l)e;* pa. t. *wōlde.*]

wylle, *n.* will, desire, 131 (note); will, self-will, 56. [OE. *willa.*]

wylneȝ, *pres. 2 sg.* wish, 318. [OE. *wilnian.*]

wyn, *n.* wine, 1209. [OE. *wīn.*]

wyngeȝ, *n. pl.* wings, 93. [OEN. *vinge.*]

wynne, *adj.* delightful, 154; precious, 647. [OE. *wynn-* in compounds.]

wynne, *v.* win, attain, 579, 694, 722; **wan,** *pa. t.* came, 107; **wonne,** *pp.* brought, 32; come, 517. [OE. *(ge)winnan.*]

wynter, *n.* winter, 116. [OE. *winter.*]

wyrde, *n.* fate, 249, 273. [OE. *wyrd.*]

wyrkeȝ. See WORCHEN.

wys, *adj.* skilful, 748. [OE. *wīs.*]

wyschande, *pres. p.* longing for, 14. [OE. *wȳscan.*]

wyse, *n.* guise, array, 133; manner, fashion, 1095; state, 101. [OE. *wīse.*]

wyse, *v.* show, be visible, 1135. [OE. *wīsian.*]

wyste. See WOT.

with, wyth, *prep.* with; (i) (= OE. *mid*), with, having, 183, 201, 332, 1111, &c.; (together) with, 284, 298; by (means of), 40, 200, 688, 806, &c.; (ii) (= OE. *wiþ*), 575 (see LYTTEL). [OE. *mid, wiþ;* ON. *við.*]

wythdroȝ, *pa. t.* withdrew, removed, 658. [OE. *wiþ-+dragan.*]

wyt(te), *n.* understanding, wisdom, 294, 903. [OE. *witt.*]

wyþer, *adj.* opposite, 230. [OE. *wiþer.*]

wythinne, *adv.* within, inside, 1027; *prep.* 440, 679, 966. [OE. *wiþinnan.*]

withnay, *v.* refuse, reject, 916. [OFr. *reneier,* with OE. *wiþ*-substituted for *re*-.]

wythoute(n), withouten, *prep.* without, 12, 36, 644, &c. [OE. *wiþūtan.*]

wlonk, wlonc, *adj.* noble, 903; lovely, splendid, 122, 1171. [OE. *wlonc.*]

wo, *n.* sorrow, grief, 56, 154 (note); adversity, 342 (see WELE.) [OE. *wā.*]

wod, *n.* forest, 122. [OE. *wudu.*]

wode, *adj.* senseless, wild, 743. [OE. *wōd.*]

wod-schaweȝ, *n. pl.* groves, 284. [OE. *wudu+scaga.*]

woghe, *n.* evil, misery, 622. [OE. *wōh.*]

woȝe, *n.* wall, 1049. [OE. *wāg.*]

wolde, *v.* possess, be responsible for, 812. [OE. *wāldan.*]

wolde. See WYL.

wolen, *adj.* woollen, 731. [Late OE. *wullen.*]

wolle, *n.* fleece, 844. [OE. *wull.*]

wommon, *n.* woman, 236 (*gen.*). [OE. *wífmonn, wimmon.*]

won, *n.* dwelling-place, dwelling, 1049; **woneȝ,** *pl.* 32, 917, 924, 1027. [ON. *ván.*]

won, *v.* dwell, 298, 315, 644, 918; **wony,** 284; **wonys,** *pres. 3 sg.* 47; **woneȝ,** *pl.* 404. [OE. *wunian.*]

wonde, *v.* hesitate, shrink, 153. [OE. *wóndian.*]

wonder, *adj.* marvellous, 221, 1095. [OE. *wundor-* in compounds.]

wonne. See WYNNE.

wont(e), *adj.* accustomed (to), 15, 172. [OE. *gewunod,* pp.]

wonted, *pa. t.* lacked, 215. [ON. *vanta.*]

worchen, *pres. pl.* work, labour, 511; **wyrkeȝ,** *imper. pl.* 536; **wroȝt,** *pa. t. sg.* fashioned, 748; committed (sin), 825; **wroȝt(e), wroȝten,** *pl.* laboured, 525, 555; wrought (evil or wrong), 622, 631; **wroȝt,** *pp.* created, 638; *wroȝt vpon,* practised, been active in committing, 824 (note). [OE. *wyrcan,* pa. t. *worhte.*]

worde, *n.* word, talk, 294; *pl.* words, statement(s), 291, 307, 314, 367, 819. [OE. *wórd.*]

wore. See WATȝ.

worlde, *n.* world, earth, 537, 761; worldly life, 743; *al(le) þys w.,* all mankind, 424, 824; *in (þis) w.,* at all, 65 (note), 293; in this world, on earth, 476; *in þe w.,* 579, 657. [OE. *woruld.*]

worschyp, *n.* honour, 394, 479. [OE. *weorþ-, worþscipe.*]

worteȝ, *n. pl.* plants, 42. [OE. *wyrt.*]

worþe, *adj.* worth, 451. [OE. *weorþe.*]

worþe, *pres. subj.* let there be, 362 (note); **worþen,** *pp.* in *is w. to,* has turned to, is become (one of), 394. [OE. *weorþan, wurþan.*]

worþy, worþé, *adj.* worthy, 100, 616; noble, 494. [OE. *wyrþig, *weorþig.*]

worþly, worthyly, *adj.* glorious, 1073; honoured, 846; **worþyly,** *as n.* precious one, 47. [OE. *weorþlíc,* infl. by prec.]

worþly, *adv.* becomingly, gloriously, 1133. [OE. *weorþlíce.*]

wot, *pres. 1 sg.* am assured, 47, 201, 1107; **wate,** believe, 502; **wost(e),** *2 sg.* know, 293, 411; **wyste,** *pa. t. 1 sg.* knew, 65, 376; **wysteȝ,** *2 sg.* 617. [OE. *wát,* pres. 1 sg.; pa. t. *wiste.*]

woþe, *n.* peril, 151, 375. [ON. *váði.*]

wounde, *n.* wound, 650, 1135, 1142. [OE. *wúnd.*]

wraȝte, *pa. t.* was pained, 56. [OE. *wǽrcan,* pa. t. *wǽrhte.*]

wrang(e), *n.* harm, evil, 631; hurt, sorrow, 15. [Late OE. *wrang,* from ON. **wrangr.*]

wrang(e), *adv.* unjustly, wrongly, 488, 614. [From ON. **wrangr.*]

wrathþe, *n.* offence, 362. [OE. *wrǽþþu.*]

wreched, *adj.* unhappy, 56. [From OE. *wrecca,* n.]

wryt, writ, *n.* gospel, 997; *Holy Wryt,* the holy Scriptures, 592. [OE. *writ.*]

wryteȝ, *pres. 3 sg.* writes, 1033 (*reflex.*); **wryten,** *pp.* 834, 866, 871. [OE. *wrítan.*]

wryþe, *v.* twist; exert oneself, toil, 511; turn aside, 350; *wryþe so wrange away,* turn so unjustly from the true path, 488. [OE. *wríþan.*]

wro, *n.* nook; corner, passage, 866. [ON. *rá,* older **wrá.*]

wroȝt, wroȝten. See WORCHEN.

wroken, *pp.* banished, removed, 375. [OE. *wrecan.*]

wroþe, *adj.* angry; at variance, 379. [OE. *wráþ.*]

y- before a consonant. See I-.

yot, *pa. t.* went, fell, 10 (note). [Variant of ȜEDE.]

yow. See ȜE.

INDEX OF NAMES

BIBLICAL QUOTATIONS AND ALLUSIONS

References specifically to the Vulgate are in brackets.

Lines

31–32	1 Cor. xv. 36–38; John xii. 24.
107	Cf. Rev. xxii. 1–2.
163	Rev. xix. 8.
197	Rev. xix. 8.
205	Cf. Ps. (xx. 4).
285	? Cf. Ps. cxix. (cxviii) 70, 97, 163–5, 174–5; or Ps. i. 2.
301–12	Perhaps suggested by John xx. 29.
349	Ps. (l. 6).
365	Cf. Ps. xxii. (xxi) 14 (15).
413–14	Rev. xix. 7.
416	? Ps. xxiii. (xxii) 6.
417	Gal. iv. 7; Rom. viii. 17.
439	1 Cor. ix. 24–25.
458–66	1 Cor. xii. 12–17, 21–27.
501–72	Matt. xx. 1–16.
595–6	Ps. lxii. 11–12 (lxi. 12–13); cf. Rom. viii. 29–30.
652	Rev. xx. 14, xxi. 8.
650, 654	John xix. 34.
656–9	1 Cor. xv. 22.
675	Ps. xxiv. (xxiii) 5–6; cf. Rev. xxii. 4, 1 Cor. xiii. 12, Matt. v. 8.
678–9	Ps. xxiv. (xxiii) 3; cf. Ps. xv. (xiv) 1.
681–2	Ps. xxiv. (xxiii) 4; cf. Ps. xv. (xiv) 2.
683	Ps. xv. (xiv) 5; cf. Ps. xxvi. (xxv) 12, cxxi. (cxx) 3.
685–8	Ps. xxiv. (xxiii) 4.
689–92	Wisd. x. 9–10.
693–4	Gen. xxviii. 13–15; cf. xiii. 14–15.
699–700	Ps. cxliii. (cxlii) 2.
711–24	Luke xviii. 15–17; cf. Matt. xix. 13–15, Mark x. 13–16.
727–8	Luke xi. 9–10.
730–5	Matt. xiii. 45–46.
763–4	Song of Songs iv. 7–8.
766	Rev. vii. 13–14.
786–9	Rev. xiv. 1, 3–4.
785, 791–2	Rev. xix. 7–8, xxi. 2.
799–803	Isa. liii. 4–9 (esp. 7).
807–9	Isa. liii. 4–5.
809–10	Luke xxii. 64; Matt. xxvi. 67; Mark xiv. 65.
811–15	Isa. liii. 4–7.
817–18	Luke iii. 3; cf. John i. 28, Matt. iii. 13, Mark i. 4, 5, 9.
819	John i. 23; Matt. iii. 3; Luke iii. 4.
821–4	John i. 29; Isa. liii. 4–6, 8.

Lines
825	Isa. liii. 9.
826	Isa. liii. 11.
827–8	Isa. liii. 8.
835–7	Rev. v. 6–7.
837–8	Rev. v. 1.
839–40	Cf. Rev. v. 13 and v. 3, 8.
841–4	I Peter i. 19; Rev. i. 14; cf. Dan. vii. 9.
845–6	Rev. xiv. 4–5, xix. 7–8.
859	Cf. I Cor. xiii. 11–12.
860	Heb. x. 10, 12, 14.
867–72	Rev. xiv. 1.
869–70	Rev. xiv. 3–4.
873–81	Rev. xiv. 2.
881–93	Rev. xiv. 3.
894–900	Rev. xiv. 4–5.
943	Rev. xxi. 2.
948	Rev. xxi. 27.
952	Heb. xii. 22; Rev. iii. 12; cf. Ezek. xiii. 16.
966, 970–2	Rev. xxi. 27, xxii. 14.
976	Rev. xxi. 10.
979–80	Rev. xxi. 10.
982	Rev. xxi. 11.
986–8	Rev. xxi. 10.
989–90	Rev. xxi. 18.
991–4	Rev. xxi. 14, 19.
999–1016	Rev. xxi. 19–20.
1007	Rev. xxi. 20; Exod. xxviii. 17.
1017–18	Rev. xxi. 11, 18.
1023–4	Rev. xxi. 16.
1025	Rev. xxi. 21.
1026	Rev. xxi. 18.
1029–32	Rev. xxi. 15–16.
1034–5	Rev. xxi. 12–13.
1036–8	Rev. xxi. 21.
1039–42	Exod. xxviii. 9–11; Rev. xxi. 12; Ezek. xlviii. 31–34.
1043–8	Rev. xxi. 23, xxii. 5.
1049	Rev. xxi. 11.
1051–4	Rev. iv. 2–11.
1055–60	Rev. xxii. 1.
1061–3	Rev. xxi. 22.
1064	Cf. Rev. v. 6, 12.
1065–6	Rev. xxi. 25.
1067–8	Rev. xxi. 27.
1069	Rev. xxi. 23.
1071	Rev. xxi. 25.
1072–6	Rev. xxi. 23.
1077–80	Rev. xxii. 2.
1099	Rev. xiv. 4.
1102, 1107–8	Rev. v. 11, vii. 9, 14.
1106	Rev. xxi. 21.

PRINTED IN GREAT BRITAIN
AT THE UNIVERSITY PRESS, OXFORD
BY VIVIAN RIDLER
PRINTER TO THE UNIVERSITY

DATE DUE